The Courtesan's Daughter

Claudia Dain

BERKLEY SENSATION, NEW YORK

THE BERKLEY PUBLISHING GROUP
Published by the Penguin Group
Penguin Group (USA) Inc.
375 Hudson Street, New York, New York 10014, USA
Penguin Group (Canada), 90 Eglinton Avenue East, Suite 700, Toronto, Ontario M4P 2Y3, Canada
(a division of Pearson Penguin Canada Inc.)
Penguin Books Ltd., 80 Strand, London WC2R 0RL, England
Penguin Group Ireland, 25 St. Stephen's Green, Dublin 2, Ireland (a division of Penguin Books Ltd.)
Penguin Group (Australia), 250 Camberwell Road, Camberwell, Victoria 3124, Australia
(a division of Pearson Australia Group Pty. Ltd.)
Penguin Books India Pvt. Ltd., 11 Community Centre, Panchsheel Park, New Delhi—110 017, India
Penguin Group (NZ), 67 Apollo Drive, Rosedale, North Shore 0632, New Zealand
(a division of Pearson New Zealand Ltd.)
Penguin Books (South Africa) (Pty.) Ltd., 24 Sturdee Avenue, Rosebank, Johannesburg 2196, South Africa

Penguin Books Ltd., Registered Offices: 80 Strand, London WC2R 0RL, England

This is a work of fiction. Names, characters, places, and incidents either are the product of the author's imagination or are used fictitiously, and any resemblance to actual persons, living or dead, business establishments, events, or locales is entirely coincidental. The publisher does not have any control over and does not assume any responsibility for author or third-party websites or their content.

THE COURTESAN'S DAUGHTER

A Berkley Sensation Book / published by arrangement with the author

PRINTING HISTORY
Berkley Sensation trade paperback edition / October 2007
Berkley Sensation mass-market edition / October 2008

Copyright © 2007 by Claudia Welch.
Excerpt from *The Courtesan's Secret* copyright © 2008 by Claudia Welch.
Cover art by Richard Jones.
Cover design by George Long.
Hand lettering by Ron Zinn.
Interior text design by Tiffany Estreicher.

ISBN: 978-0-425-22422-9

BERKLEY® SENSATION
Berkley Sensation Books are published by The Berkley Publishing Group,
a division of Penguin Group (USA) Inc.,
375 Hudson Street, New York, New York 10014.
BERKLEY SENSATION and the "B" design are trademarks of Penguin Group (USA) Inc.

PRINTED IN THE UNITED STATES OF AMERICA

10 9 8 7 6 5 4 3 2 1

Praise for

The Courtesan's Daughter

"This cleverly orchestrated, unconventional romp through the glittering world of the Regency elite—both admirable and reprehensible—is filled with secrets, graced with intriguing characters, laced with humor, and plotted with Machiavellian flair. A joy to read." —*Library Journal*

"You must read this book! Claudia Dain's historical is wildly inventive, deeply romantic, and exactly the sort of novel to place on your keeper shelf. *The Courtesan's Daughter* has everything there is to love about a historical with sinfully delicious new twists and turns. If that isn't enough to tempt you, the scenes between her characters surely will. I'm very excited to give Claudia Dain's *The Courtesan's Daughter* the highest rating of five blue ribbons. Add Claudia Dain to your must-read authors." —*Romance Junkies*

Praise for Claudia Dain's Previous Novels

"Claudia Dain's emotionally charged writing and riveting characters will take your breath away."
—*New York Times* bestselling author Sabrina Jeffries

"Claudia Dain writes with intelligence, sensuality, and heart, and the results are extraordinary!"
—*New York Times* bestselling author Connie Brockway

"Claudia Dain never fails to write a challenging and complex romance." —*A Romance Review*

"Dain is a talented writer who knows her craft."
—*Romantic Times*

"[Claudia Dain writes] a red-hot romance."
—*Publishers Weekly*

Thanks to the Biaggi Bunch; without you,
it would have been a lot less fun.

One

London 1802

"I am not certain it has ever been said before, but I believe you play too hard, too long, and too often," Caroline Trevelyan said to her mother, the Countess of Dalby.

It was an hour past dawn and not at all unusual for Sophia Dalby to return home from an evening's entertainment at that time of morning, which certainly did not help the situation, the situation being that Caroline was in need of a proper husband. Her mother's entertainment choices, and the hour in which she ended them, were not helping. Then again, it was perhaps wishful thinking that anything her mother did or did not do would help at this late stage of things.

"Darling, that sounds positively wicked and is, I am quite certain, completely untrue," Sophia said, pressing the cold compress over her eyes as she reclined on her velvet-draped bed. "It certainly is unlikely that anyone could be said to play *too* hard, though I was hardly at play last night. I was working as ever on your behalf, Caro, so I would appreciate a bit more appreciation. It's exhausting work, scouring London for a suitable husband. Man's work, really. Your father died most inopportunely."

"Mother, Father died seven years ago."

"Death is always inopportune, is it not?" Sophia answered on a sigh. "He could have managed this husband hunt so much more efficiently than I."

"Somehow, I doubt that," Caro said wryly, lifting the cold cloth over her mother's eyes to replace it with another, fresher compress. "Just where are you hunting?"

"Oh, the usual places."

"Usual to whom?" Caro said sarcastically.

"Darling, my head. I really am most exhausted."

"You do know that I would prefer not to marry a man given to excessive gaming."

"Even if he wins?" Sophia said, the barest smile revealed beneath the cloth.

Caroline took the compress away from her mother with a grunt of annoyance and said, "It is statistically impossible to always win."

"I know nothing of statistics, darling, but fortune can swing most regularly in a predetermined direction. Some people, the fortunate few, are regularly favored by fortune. Why should they be the subject of scorn simply because of an accident of birth?"

"Nevertheless, I would not choose to live that sort of life," Caro pronounced regally.

Sophia kept her eyes closed and took a deep breath; her dressing gown gaped open to reveal the curved shape of smooth white breasts. Impossible on a woman in her thirties, but that was Sophia Dalby, the epitome of impossibility. No wonder she favored a reliance on fortune; fortune had served her so very well.

"Let us review," Sophia said, her arms folded in repose across her waist. "You will not marry a man past fifty. You will not marry a man you do not know. You will not marry a man toward whom you feel no ardent longings, which I completely agree with, by the way. I felt *most* ardently for your father."

"Yes, thank you, Mother. That's sufficient."

"Speaking of sufficiency," Sophia said, her eyes still closed against the morning light dappling the parquet floors of her bedroom, "though you have yet to mention it, I assume that you would prefer a man of sufficient wealth to sustain you. I can assure you that, while other qualities might distract or titillate, a healthy fortune is the most lasting of a man's good qualities. In sufficient quantities, even a man of fifty who is a complete stranger can become sufficiently attractive to merit consideration."

"Mother," Caro said, standing up and walking to the

open window, which she closed with a snap, "love cannot be bought."

"Caro," Sophia said, opening her eyes to stare in amusement at her daughter, "don't be absurd. *Everything* can be bought. It is merely a matter of price."

"Then let me rephrase. *I* cannot be bought."

Sophia only smiled and closed her eyes again.

"You don't believe me," Caro said.

"I believe you are very young and very naïve," Sophia said, "for which I am usually very thankful. Yet in this case"—Sophia shrugged—"let me do the bargaining, darling. I'm more attuned to it."

"Bargaining? It shall require bargaining to snare a husband for me?" Caro said.

At that, Sophia opened her eyes and sat up, her back resting against the burled walnut headboard. "Snare? Such an unpleasant word. You are a perfectly lovely seventeen-year-old girl who has had the benefit of a careful education and a sheltered upbringing, which was not by accident, I assure you. You are possessed of physical beauty, good health, and a more than sufficient dowry; few other qualities are considered when making a successful matrimonial match."

"And as to bargaining?"

"Caro, life is composed of one bargain after another. Trust me to arrange the best match possible."

Caro smiled and nodded, willing the conversation to an end, forcing her mind to ignore what had not been said and what could never be said.

There was one other quality that any man of merit and position would want in a wife, and that quality was pedigree. A good, respectable, honorable family name coupled with an unimpeachable family history was what was lacking. And it was lacking because of Sophia.

Sophia, the Countess of Dalby, had been the most infamous courtesan in London almost twenty years ago, until she had snared, by popular report, the devilishly wild Stuart Trevelyan, Earl of Dalby, and seduced him into marrying her. Caroline was the fruit of that scandalous union; John Markham, her older brother by one year, the first fruit.

Twenty years had not dimmed the rumors about Sophia, most probably because twenty years had not dimmed Sophia's charms.

Twenty years, and Caro did not have a hope of making any kind of respectable marriage, no matter how perfect her deportment, her beauty, or her fortune.

It was most disheartening, especially since she could hardly confide the reason for her lack of hope to her mother.

"You do trust me, don't you, Caro?" Sophia asked, holding out her slim, white hand for her daughter to grasp. "You do know that I will arrange an acceptable match for you?"

Caro held her mother's hand lightly and smiled down at her. She *did* look exhausted.

"I know you will do whatever you must."

"And that I will succeed," Sophia added with a smile.

"And that you will succeed," Caro said with an answering smile as she told the most gracious of lies to her mother. It was hardly likely that her mother would succeed in this most delicate of tasks.

Most disheartening.

Two

"SHE still believes she will manage it," Caro said softly, gazing out the window.

The sun, such as it was, was full up and the pigeons cooing noisily. Caro found it a singularly depressing sound.

"She just might," Anne said as she poured out the morning chocolate from her perch by the fireplace.

Caro turned and considered her friend, who, though widowed at the ridiculous age of eighteen, after having been married to her husband for only eight months, was still of a rosy frame of mind about the world in general and Sophia in particular.

"You don't think so. Not truly," Caro said.

Caroline Trevelyan was not of a rosy frame of mind about the world, her mother, or her situation. She chose to think of herself as a woman of a sensible aspect, not given to idle thoughts or romanticism. Her mother would have been forced to agree, if she could be forced to anything, which was doubtful.

"I do think so," Anne said. "She is of a most determined nature, and she has the weight of experience on her side."

"It is her weight of experience that is the problem."

Anne smiled and handed Caro her cup. "And yet it did not stop her from making a good match. Your father was besotted."

"It was an intemperate match," Caro said.

"And your father was besotted," Anne said with a grin.

"And my father was besotted," Caro reluctantly agreed.

"The same could happen to you and for you. You are your mother's daughter."

Yes and no, and that was the problem. She was Sophia's daughter, the daughter of a former courtesan, and therefore her pedigree was a disaster. And yet, though she was Sophia's daughter, she had none of her fire, certainly none of her mystique, and most definitely none of her experience. Fully intentional on her part, on both their parts to be honest, yet it left her in the strange situation of being chillingly proper and completely unacceptable in the same instant.

To say she was disheartened was to say it politely. She was, hopelessly and irretrievably, on the shelf. There was not an eligible man of her station and her situation who would even dare to speak with her beyond the most cursory exchange of pleasantries. An invitation to Almack's was beyond hope.

It was not as if she were overdramatizing the situation. She had been considering her prospects since the age of fourteen, when she had realized that her dancing instructor had beautiful eyes and her riding instructor had quite a spectacular seat. Men, she had discovered, were fascinating. Unfortunately, it had become simultaneously obvious that men were not fascinated by her.

Of course, the daughter of an earl did not go about marrying dancing masters or riding instructors, and she had logically tested the waters in a more proper pond.

The pond was frigid. One might even say frozen.

Her mother, too well connected and too well married to ignore, was fully in Society, which meant that Caro was as equally in, but that did not mean that the proper sort of man, one who would chat her up at a sedate dinner, considered her the proper sort of wife.

She had received no offers. In point of fact, she had received not the barest glimmer of interest. Logically, there was but one conclusion to draw: she was unmarriageable.

Marriage, no matter how she longed for it, was out of reach.

"You may have hope," she said to Anne. "I do not."

"Learn to find hope or you will perish of despair, Caro. Find your hope where you may, but find it."

Caro looked at Anne, at her ginger-haired beauty and her

solemn gray green eyes, and said, "You know where I thought to find hope. You argued against it."

"And I still do," Anne said. "You should talk to Sophia about your . . . plans."

"Plans," Caro said with a crooked grin. "You mean to say folly, but you are too polite to be that openly brutal in your assessment."

"Since you said it first," Anne said with an answering grin, "then let us call it folly, for folly it most certainly is. Ask your mother and see if she does not call it the same or worse."

"She won't discuss such things with me," Caro said. "For a former courtesan, she is most prudish."

"She is trying to protect you."

"From what? From the only avenue open to me? I am a woman. I want to live as a woman. I may be my mother's daughter, after all. It is said that blood will tell," Caro said softly, running a hand down her thigh. "Did you not just say it? I am my mother's daughter, am I not?"

"Oh, Lord, what are you planning now?" Anne said.

Caro looked up and pierced Anne with her gaze. "I know that I have no future as a wife. But perhaps I can, like my mother before me, have a future as a courtesan. Certainly I should have some experience before I plunge into the courtesan's life."

"You don't even understand what it is you're saying, that's the frightening part," Anne said, standing up and beginning to pace the bedroom. "You have no idea what it is to be a courtesan."

"Yes, yes, you've said that before. Well, if I don't understand, there's only one thing to do," Caro said. "I must get myself some experience at these sorts of things, mustn't I?"

"These sorts of things? I presume you mean men?"

"Of course. What else?" Caro said with as much sophistication as she could manage; not much, she was afraid.

And she was afraid, that was the whole problem as well as the entire point. She was Sophia's daughter and Sophia was infamous. Unfortunately for her, she was not at all infamous, not for any reason. She was not infamously beautiful nor infamously reckless nor infamously desireable. She was Sophia Dalby's very invisible daughter, a well-brought-up daughter of a peer with nothing at all remarkable to distinguish her, unless it be her remarkable mother.

Being the unremarkable daughter of an infamously remarkable mother had effectively closed the door to respectable and profitable matrimony. Of course, she could marry unprofitably, to some minor baron or, worse, a man of industry, but she was enough her mother's daughter to find an unprofitable marriage completely unacceptable. Better profit than respectability.

Yes, she was fully Sophia's child in that regard. And so, her decision. She would be a courtesan, just like her mother before her. Men would bankrupt themselves for a single kiss from her virgin lips. Of course, her lips, as well as other parts of her, would not remain virgin for long, so it was absolutely imperative that she bankrupt as many men as possible before all her virginal qualities were spent. And then she would move on to bankrupting men for her distinctly *un*virginal qualities. It was a plan that pleased her as it had the air of being so very sophisticated and so very luridly debauched; exactly the sort of plan a practiced courtesan might hatch.

Of course, the fact that she knew little or nothing about the details of being a proper courtesan was just the tiniest fly in the ointment. But she could fix that with almost no effort at all. There was a very convenient man waiting downstairs for her mother even now and he would do nicely; she could practice her seductive skills on him. The fact that he was, she strongly suspected, her mother's current lover was just the least bit inconvenient. Still, one had to work with whatever, or whomever, was available.

Viscount Richborough was just available enough.

≈

LORD Richborough was pacing the yellow salon as Caroline softly entered the room. Softly, because she didn't intend to startle him. Softly, because she had just managed to shush Anne and leave her in the foyer, where she suspected Anne was listening avidly at the door. Caroline did not enter softly because she was afraid. Far from it. She was going to find out if she had any skill at seduction at all before commencing a life of profitable seduction. A perfectly logical plan, as anyone would attest. Anyone except Anne. Anne was ridiculously conservative about things of this nature, which Caro considered quite odd since Anne *had* been married and certainly had a working knowledge of such things, such things being those acts that occurred between men and women.

Richborough was a man and she was a woman. Things ought to proceed nicely from there, oughten they?

As men went, Richborough was above average in appearance; quite above average. Her mother wouldn't have tolerated him otherwise. He was tall, slim without being fragile, possessed of remarkably even features capped by a luxuriant cap of tousled dark brown hair that was a complete match to his dark brown eyes. Naturally, as he had been coming round to see her mother, she'd had a fair chance to study him. If he wore his jackets a bit snug across the shoulder and if his wit was a bit thin, she didn't suppose anyone would notice those small deficiencies. But she did.

She knew her mother did as well. Nothing escaped Sophia's notice, though perhaps quite a lot escaped her comment. There was likely some proverb about age and the wisdom of discretion, but as Caro was seventeen, she didn't suppose she should be expected to know it. Or practice it.

Attempting to seduce her mother's lover was hardly discreet, but she did need to know if a man could find her appealing, and this man would just have to do. It was almost a scientific experiment. In fact, if her mother found out about her attempted seduction of Lord Richborough, she would claim exactly that. A scientific experiment, nothing at all personal about it.

She didn't suppose Lord Richborough needed to be told that, however. What she knew of men indicated that they were rather humorless about things of that sort. Dour things, really, but strangely compelling in spite of it.

Lord Richborough stopped pacing and turned upon hearing the door close, and her heart did a little flutter. He was such a tall man and not a little imposing in that particular way men had of imposing themselves upon absolutely everyone, no matter the occasion. All in all, she rather liked that about men.

"Lady Caroline," he said, bowing gracefully. "How good to see you again."

"Thank you, Lord Richborough," she said, curtseying quickly. "You're calling early today. My mother is not yet receiving. I'm afraid you must make do with me."

That had not come out *at all* as she had hoped. She hardly wanted to be thought of in terms of yesterday's toast. She was almost certain that successful courtesans did not go about announcing that they must be made do with.

"Delighted," Richborough said with a somewhat stiff smile.

He looked disappointed. Not at all the response she'd been hoping for. Caro sat down upon the silk damask sofa and arranged herself as beautifully as possible. Richborough sat as well, though not beautifully. He did not appear to care if she thought him nicely arranged or not.

It was difficult not to begin to think that Richborough might be a bit stupid. Without being vulgarly obvious, how far did he expect her to go in her invitation for his attentions? Apparently farther still.

"And how have you been entertaining yourself lately, Lord Richborough?" she asked, running a finger across her collarbone. "Have you done anything particularly amusing?"

"Not particularly, no," he answered. "What of you, Lady Caroline? Have you seen the new play at the Theatre Royal?"

"I'm afraid not," she said. "Have you?"

"Yes," he said, sounding altogether bored and distracted. "It was tolerably good."

"I suppose it was very wicked," she said. "I so long to be exposed to something wicked."

There. That got his attention.

Lord Richborough stopped his rather poorly concealed fidgeting and stared at her. In actual point of fact, he stared *hard* at her, as if he were unsure of what he had clearly heard her say. Since he was having so much trouble with it, it would only do that she repeat it, or perhaps some even more scandalous version of it.

"Are you wicked, Lord Richborough? I do hope so," she said. It seemed to her exactly the sort of remark a courtesan would make.

Oddly enough, Richborough got a very distracted look again and shifted his weight on his chair. It was a most disappointing response to the clearest invitation she could imagine a woman giving a man. She couldn't be as unappealing as all that, could she?

"I am here to call upon Lady Dalby," he said, still squirming slightly in his seat. "You are aware of that, I presume, Lady Caroline?"

"Of course," she said. "However, you may not have noticed it, but I live here as well. I only thought that we could . . . entertain ourselves until my mother has completed her toilette."

"Entertain ourselves," he said softly, staring at her rather more intimately than she was accostumed to. "In precisely what manner?"

Oh, bother, he *was* stupid. Well, what was left but for her to spell it out for him?

"In the usual manner," she said. She was quite certain she sounded as experienced as the most accomplished courtesan, even if she did only have the foggiest sense of what she was implying. Certainly Richborough must be counted upon to carry *some* of the weight of this exchange.

He responded by coughing into his fist. Most peculiar and not at all what she had hoped for.

Worse, she was almost completely certain that the footsteps she heard in the foyer were Anne's, running to fetch Sophia. Now she would have to seduce Richborough all the faster so that going to be a bit tricky as Richborough was most decidedly slow at reading the proper signals. No wonder her mother was so often exhausted; seducing Richborough was turning into one of those impossible tasks constantly referred to in all those boring Greek myths.

"I am not certain I understand what you mean by 'usual,'" Richborough said, standing up to fuss with his waistcoat.

"I mean, Lord Richborough," she said in some annoyance, "that some men might enjoy a few minutes alone with me, but as you are clearly not one of them, I shall leave you to your solitude."

She stood up so abruptly that she was not altogether certain she had not ripped a seam in her hem, which seemed to suit the occasion precisely.

"Excuse me, Lady Caroline," he said, blocking her in the most subtle manner possible from the closest doorway to the foyer. But he was blocking her, which she considered very nice of him. "I have insulted you in some fashion, which I would never do. I do not prefer solitude to your engaging company. It is only that you are young and I would not see your reputation damaged by a misspoken word, or deed, on my part."

Deed? Perhaps he was not so stupid as he first appeared. Certainly he must have some redeeming qualities or her mother would never tolerate him, though, to be honest, her mother did not mind stupid men as long as they were not stupid in showing her the proper appreciation, a position Caro found altogether logical.

"I am not so innocent, nor so diabolical, Lord Richborough, that I would allow my reputation to be ruined on something so whimsical as a *word*," she said. There, she had laid it all out for him. Let him now show her just how desirable he found her. She would prefer *in deed*, but she would tolerate *in word*. She was not unreasonable, after all.

"A lady of rare virtue," he said. It did not sound at all complimentary. "However, I would consider it a failure to my manhood if I did not endeavor to protect you from any possible harm."

He bowed as he said it. As if that excused him from the insult he had dealt her. Caro might be innocent but she was not stupid; she knew very well that men in the throes of blazing desire did not give a fig for anything beyond satisfying that desire upon any likely female.

It was patently obvious that she was not even remotely a likely female.

Her mother, the most likely female that the men of London had apparently ever seen, chose that exact moment to enter the yellow salon. It was the most perfectly dreadful cap to a most hideously embarrassing situation.

"Lord Richborough," Sophia said smoothly, "how early you are today. I had not thought to see you until this afternoon. I trust Caroline has kept you entertained?"

Hardly. At least not in any way that mattered. Things had not gone *at all* the way she had hoped, but when did they ever?

"Perfectly," Lord Richborough said, kissing Sophia's outstretched hand. It seemed to Caro that her mother's hand was always outstretched for one reason or another and that she *always* managed to achieve whatever it was she was reaching for. Caro was not at all certain how she did it. "She is your daughter in every delightful detail."

Sarcasm, if she'd ever heard it, and she had.

"But of course she is," Sophia said with a smile. "Now, how may I entertain you, Lord Richborough? In much the manner my daughter has already done? Or are you ready for a change of pace?"

From that moment on, neither Richborough nor her mother had eyes for any but each other. Caro made her excuses and then her exit, all her questions about her desirability answered in the most demoralizing manner conceivable. This courtesan business was getting more complicated by the moment.

Three

Lord Ashdon arrived promptly at the Countess Dalby's Upper Brook Street house for his eleven o'clock appointment. The time was just past eleven. He considered that arriving just past eleven was as prompt as he was willing to deliver; the Countess of Dalby, Sophia to her many intimates, was not going to have him walking the street in front of her immaculately maintained London home, begging entrance early. He had some pride left to him. Not much, but enough.

Arriving late was a small insult, but deserving, nonetheless. What the Countess of Dalby was attempting deserved at least some responding insult.

He knocked, was admitted with a cordial nod by Fredericks, famously loyal to Sophia from her courtesan days to this, and was led to the yellow salon. Where he was made to wait until almost noon.

"Unfailingly prompt," Sophia said, entering in a rustle of soft muslin. "Thank you for that, Lord Ashdon. One finds manners so appallingly on the down these days."

Which meant, of course, that she knew exactly when he had arrived and was repaying insult for insult. She was rather famous for doing that.

He watched her as she arranged herself on a yellow silk damask sofa, toying with the folds of her ivory-colored muslin skirt. She was the beauty she had always been. Tall and slim, her breasts high and white, her throat smooth, her complexion creamy. Her black hair was still dark and glossy, no trace of silver to mark her years. Her almond-shaped eyes were black pools set under a straight and narrow brow. Her lips were full and red, her nose slim and aristocratic, her face a perfect oval of feminine beauty. She exuded serene poise, aristocratic condescension, and simmering sensuality.

No wonder she had been the talk of her time.

No wonder Dalby had married her.

No wonder she had him by the purse now.

"Be seated, if it please you," she said, waving a slim arm in the general direction of the chair opposite her.

He sat, though he was not the least bit pleased to do so.

"Refreshments, or do you have other appointments you must keep?" she asked.

He had no other appointments. "I'm afraid that my visit must be brief, Lady Dalby."

"Of course," she said with a smile. She knew he lied. "You are a man of the world, Lord Ashdon, and as such, I know you have considered your position and my offer most carefully. You have been well educated in your duty to your family and your estate. As you may recall, I know your father well and I know that he would not neglect to instruct you in the responsibilities of your station."

Knew his father well; that was exactly to the point. She had "known" his father, and been kept by him until Dalby had snatched her from under his father's hand. Westlin, his father, and Dalby were old rivals, well before the onset of Sophia's arrival in the streets of London, yet Sophia had used that rivalry to increase her own purse. He did not blame her for it, though neither did he applaud her.

She was a businesswoman to the last, no matter her title now.

That his father still lusted after her made the whole subject decidedly galling.

That Sophia clearly understood his father still hated her was what brought him to her salon now.

"I know my responsibilities, madam," he said, crossing his legs.

"How fortunate for us both," she said, running a lace handkerchief between her fingers in a gentle rhythm. He found himself staring at her hands, at her long fingers and the bundle of lace that passed again and again through them. White against cream, stroke by stroke.

She was both crass and obvious, and he had expected nothing less from her.

"And I can manage my own life," he said, lifting his gaze away from her hands and that damned bit of lace.

"I do not doubt it, sir. In point of fact, I am quite relying on it. But the question is, can you manage your debts?"

"Given time."

"And good fortune," she added. "Unfortunately, time does not wait." She tucked her bit of lace into a fold of her muslin skirt and considered him with her dark and unfathomable eyes. He met her stare and stilled the urge to squirm. "I have purchased your debts by paying them, Lord Ashdon. You now are in debt to me. The sum is thirty-eight thousand pounds. Can you pay it?"

This was *not* as this scene was to have been played. He had grossly miscalculated her, in spite of all his father's instruction.

"Not at present," he said stiffly, keeping his legs crossed and his posture relaxed.

"The present is all we have, Lord Ashdon," she said. "The future, as ever, is uncertain. At present, you have a debt that you cannot pay. At present, I have a daughter who must be married. Surely you see the solution to our present problems."

"You think to buy me? I am not a stallion, madam. I cannot be bought for your daughter's pleasure."

Sophia smiled and said, "You cannot be bought? Have I not just done so? As to my daughter's pleasure, I am not certain she even wants you. You were . . . available, and I gambled in buying up your debt. Whether she finds you to her pleasure is completely up to her. And to you, I suppose," she said in afterthought.

"You take much pleasure in this, Lady Dalby," he gritted out. "A revenge of sorts against Westlin."

"Lord Ashdon, I have not thought of Westlin in years. I live in the present, as should you. But, if it makes you feel better, your father paid much less for me. Thirty-eight thousand pounds is quite a sum. I would feel flattered, were I you."

"You are not me."

"No, I am not, but I know what it is to be purchased for a sum. How nice that we have something in common, besides our enjoyment of the gaming tables and the thrill of a wager."

He flinched inwardly. She was as cruel as his father had said, and as merciless. "You cannot buy me. I cannot, I *will not* be bought," he gritted out through clenched teeth.

"Darling Ashdon," she said softly, her smile sweet and kind. What an actress she was. "Let us not be crass. You must pay your wagers. Your good name depends upon it. If one chooses to play, one must honor one's losses."

"Give me time. I will borrow the funds. I will pay off this debt."

"By borrowing? Is that not incurring yet more debt? Have you learned nothing at all?" Sophia ran a finger over the swells of her creamy breasts, considering him solemnly. "I do not know that I want my daughter to marry a man of such profligate ways. She is much opposed to risk and would prefer a more stable, mature man at her side. I cannot say I disagree with her."

Now he was not good enough for the daughter of a courtesan? Insult upon insult.

"Westlin will never allow it," he said. "My father has his own plans for me, and they do not include your daughter."

"I would wager that Westlin's plans do not include the payment of a thirty-eight-thousand-pound debt, sir. Will you ask him to pay it? And before you answer, let me ask you another question. Do you think he can pay it, should he be so inclined?"

The look in her eyes, the shock of her question throughout his bones—the combination of the two sent realization thrumming through him.

"Yes," she said, nodding, like a tutor pleased with a pupil. "He cannot pay your debt, Lord Ashdon, because he cannot pay his own. Serve me in this, in this one small deed, and your debt is cancelled. You will be free to gamble yourself into penury again, if that is your inclination."

"And your daughter? You would see her so served?" he said softly.

"My daughter will be protected from intemperate men,

never doubt it. I will have the papers drawn and you will sign them. Gamble as freely as you wish with your money, but hers will be set aside for herself and her children. You and your father shall not touch it. Are we agreed?"

He had no choice as things now stood. By every device laid before him, his future was gambled upon the seed of a courtesan.

"We are agreed," he said, rising to his feet. "Her name?"

He meant to insult her. He knew her daughter's name from years past when his father had found the scent of Dalby's widow and pursued her again through the salons of London. Had Westlin succeeded? Ashdon did not know. Given Westlin's feelings about the woman, it did not seem likely.

"Caroline," she said, smiling up at him, her very posture smug. "You may begin courting her this very day."

"A courtship? After this bargaining?"

"Of course a courtship. A courtship always follows on the heels of a bargaining and is, by the bounds of civility, required," she said, coming to her feet with languid grace. "What else did you think a marriage was, Ashdon?"

He wanted to kill her.

"Come round later this afternoon, will you? You may begin then," she said. "And change your shirt. The one you are wearing has the tiniest spot on the cuff, just there." And she touched his hand above the wrist to show him, a fleeting touch, a spark of female warmth that burned his pride. On the tide of that touch, she laughed her way out of the room.

Four

"WELL, that's settled," Sophia said as she entered the white salon. "Such a fuss over a simple marriage settlement. He played the outraged child to perfection. One wonders if he practices such theatrics at home."

"You don't blame him," Viscount Richborough said from his leonine lounge on her milk blue damask sofa.

"Don't I?" she said, sitting politely on the twin sofa facing him. "Why don't I?"

"Because, my dear Sophia, he has obligations to his family and his name."

"As do I, Richborough."

"And your obligation is to see your child well married. That is Westlin's charge as well. You seek the same ends."

"Along different paths, is that your point?" she said softly. "Caro shall be married well, at least as well as I have done."

"A high mark to set for her. She hasn't your . . . natural advantages."

"Careful, Richborough," Sophia said with a smile. "I am still annoyed with you for whatever happened between you and Caro this morning. To judge by the look on her face, I should probably throw you out. Should I throw you out, Richborough? Did you abuse my daughter shamelessly and did she bruise your considerable pride? Why else for you to insult her now?"

"Insult her?"

"Caroline has every advantage a girl needs in this world. How very odd that you cannot see that. She must have rejected you quite firmly," she said, watching him as he held her gaze with all the innocence of a puppy. And all puppies had the unfortunate habit of relieving themselves upon the smallest whim and upon the very best carpets.

"Nothing happened beyond the normal meaningless conversation that one reserves for virgins," he said, leaning forward to take her hand in his. She allowed him that, suspecting where it would lead. As long as he left off his speculation about Caro, she would allow him to lead the conversation elsewhere. "I understand that you are ambitious for your child, as any mother would be. I understand," he said, kissing her fingertips, "that you would see Westlin turn upon the point of your knife for failing to offer marriage to you when he offered everything else."

"You speculate," she said, watching him take her index finger into his mouth and suckle it. "You were a boy at school when I first met Westlin. All you know is the gossip you have heard in the clubs of St. James."

"Is anything truer than the rumors that swirl in the air of the clubs? He has never forgotten you, madam, why else for his son to resent you as he does?"

"Because I hold the paper on his debts?" she said as she watched him seduce her by way of her hand.

"You have bought Ashdon's will, for a time. Do not think you have bought the man."

"What a fine point you put on it, Richborough," she said, removing her hand from his. "Ashdon will do what I want him to do because he must. He has no skill for poverty, I think, nor does he wish to develop such skills. Let him think what he wants of being bought or free, his thoughts are his own. I only require that he do what I need of him, and that is to court and marry my daughter. She will be the Countess of Westlin and the Countess of Ashdon. She deserves as much."

"Are you certain this is about what she deserves or what Westlin deserves, having your daughter spewing out the future Earls of Westlin?"

"You mention nothing of what I deserve," Sophia said, looking at Richborough's dark brown eyes and fashionably windblown dark brown hair. He was a handsome man, knew it, and played upon it, which she thought very wise of him.

"I thought I was giving you what you deserve," he said,

reaching across the space between the matched sofas to cup her face in his hands.

"Given that I have a high opinion of my worth, I have always enjoyed getting what I deserve," she said with a sly smile as Richborough's mouth came down upon hers.

Five

CARO sat at her mirror and stared at her face in brutal self-analysis.

She had a good face. She had her mother's complexion, creamy and smooth, her father's dark blue eyes, and her mother's black, softly curled hair.

All in all, she thought she could have a moderately successful run as a courtesan.

Her figure was good, a nice full bust, her hands slender and her fingers well shaped. Beyond that, she did not know how to compare herself to the rest of the female population. She did not know, beyond a clear complexion and a firm bust, what a man found attractive.

But there was clearly something more. Richborough had been insultingly tepid in his response to her completely blatant invitation to debauch her in some small fashion. If the fault was not with her, and she certainly hoped it wasn't, then the fault must lie with Richborough. He was either profoundly stupid or, and this was not beyond reason, he was afraid of stepping wrong with her mother. *That* was entirely possible. It might have nothing at all to do with her. She might be the most fatally desirable woman since Helen and all those ships.

It might not be a bad idea to ask her brother, John Markham Stuart Grey Trevelyan, the ninth Earl of Dalby, when he got home.

On second thought, it might be a very bad idea.

Judging by Anne's reaction to her decision, she didn't suppose Markham would respond any better. It was a good thing that he was out of town or he might try to do something foolish, like talk her out of it. What her mother would do when she found out she did not dare to think, though it was not in Sophia's style to go about talking people out of things. No, it was much more her style to talk them *into* things. Like marriage.

All the talking in the world was not going to change the fact that no worthy man would take her to wife. The world was reasonable and predictable and logical, and there was nothing reasonable about Caro's situation. She was the perfectly respectable daughter of a famously unrespectable mother.

No, there was nothing for it. She was going to follow fully in her mother's footsteps and make her way in the world as a courtesan.

She only hoped she had what it took to be famously unrespectable. Judging by Richborough's reaction to her, she was not off to a very promising start. The only thing to do was to stop thinking about Richborough and his disappointing performance.

"I thought he'd never leave," Sophia said, coming into Caro's bedroom with an exaggerated sigh of exasperation.

"Who?"

"Richborough. He gives a fair imitation of the most debauched man in London. I think he'd die of shame if I told him that he *is* only an imitation and nothing approaching the real thing."

"I think he's besotted, Mother." And if he were, then that might explain why he had behaved so dismally in not even giving the appearance of wanting to seduce her. Why, he hadn't even tried to kiss her hand, the dullard.

"Do you really think so?" Sophia said, insinuating herself onto a chaise longue covered in blush-colored silk damask. Sophia ran a hand over the back of her hair and smiled like a cat.

"We both think so," Caro said with a grin, putting off thoughts of the excessively dull Lord Richborough. "How do you do it, Mother?"

"Do what, darling?"

"How do you make a man besotted? How do you, especially at your age, make a man . . . want you?"

"I was enjoying this conversation until you said 'at your age' in that dumbfounded fashion. Really, Caro, I'm only thirty-four. You make me sound eighty."

"Which reminds me, you had two children by the age of eighteen. I can scarcely match you in that as I am fully seventeen now."

"I was precocious."

"I am on the shelf," Caro rejoined.

"On the shelf? Don't be ridiculous, Caro. You are at the peak of your beauty and desirability. Let your mirror guide you in that truth if my words do not."

"Yes," Caro said, squirming a bit on her silk-covered cushion. "I've been thinking about that, actually, and I've come to a decision. I won't be talked out of it, Mother, I'm telling you that now. I am quite firm, quite decided."

"Really?" Sophia said, sitting up, eyes alight. "What have you decided? I'm breathless in anticipation."

"I'm," she began, but the words suddenly stuck in her throat. Thinking about being a courtesan and talking about it with her mother were entirely different propositions, but Caro was nothing if not forthright and determined, or at least she wanted to believe so. "I've decided that, since a worthwhile marriage is out of the question, I've decided that . . ."

"Yes, darling, you've decided what?"

"That I want to be . . . I intend to become . . . a courtesan."

The words, far from shining with promise and excitement in the air between them, fell like lead shot to plunge into the parquet floors beneath their feet.

"A courtesan," Sophia repeated solemnly, blinking.

"Yes. Like you."

What was intended as a compliment of sorts came out rather more like an indictment.

"Like me? Your declaration has something to do with me?" Sophia said, her voice rising.

"Well, actually, what I meant to say was that, well, it seems a likely start for someone like me."

"You mean someone of your upbringing, education, and privilege?" Sophia said, her voice crisp with sarcasm.

"Someone of my limited prospects," Caro said.

"You have the prospect of a life of ease before you, married or not, that is certainly true."

"But I don't want to live an aimless life, Mother. I want to *do* something, be someone in my own right."

"In your own right? You clearly have no understanding of what it is to be a courtesan, Caro," Sophia said stiffly.

"Then tell me. Teach me," Caro said, rising from her stool and walking to her mother across the luxurious bedroom so that she could sink onto her knees at her mother's feet. "I want to succeed at something, Mother. I would wish to be a wife to a worthy man, but if I cannot, then let me at least be the object of a worthy man's attention. Teach me how to make a man want me. Teach me how to make a man besotted."

Sophia sat back upon the chaise, rubbing her ring finger over her lower lip, deep in thought, her dark eyes upon Caro. Caro could never read her when she assumed that look, that contemplative, lost-in-speculation look. Her father had claimed to have feared that soulful introspection, but she didn't believe that. Her father had feared nothing, not even the scandal of marrying Sophia Grey, courtesan.

"Does Richborough have anything to do with this?" Sophia asked.

"Nothing at all," Caro answered honestly.

"And your conversation in the yellow salon with him this morning?"

"Dull beyond description," Caro said in brutal honesty.

"You want me to believe you're serious."

"I am serious," Caro answered.

"Then you're a fool," Sophia said dismissively.

"Not a fool, Mother, just desperate," Caro said, meeting her mother's darkly penetrating gaze. "I want a man to want me. I want to be desired and pursued."

"And caught," Sophia said. "To be a courtesan is to be pursued and caught, and caught, and caught."

"But at least pursued, and caught only when I decide. Isn't that so?"

"It is usually your empty stomach that decides for you."

"I just want to be like you, Mother."

"Don't be ridiculous, darling. There is no one like me. I arranged that most deliberately," Sophia said softly, her dark eyes looking quite mysterious all of a sudden.

Caro actually didn't care what her mother's eyes did in that precise moment; she was not going to be distracted or discouraged. She *was* going to become a courtesan, and she was going to become famously wonderful at it.

"Mother, I am going to do this. I am going to be a courtesan."

Sophia smiled and patted her on the head. It was meant to be insulting, and it most definitely was. "You have everything now, at your fingertips, that a courtesan works for. You have money, a lovely home, jewels, protection. What do you think this is, Caro? A game? Women become courtesans because of what they lack. You lack for nothing."

"I lack purpose."

"A courtesan's purpose is to find a protector and to keep him happy."

"I can do that," Caro said, hoping she wasn't blushing.

Sophia shrugged and walked across the room. "You shall have no opportunity to find out. I've lived the life you seem determined to pursue. I know what it is. I will not throw my daughter into it. Besides," she said, turning, her fingers toying with the strand of pearls at her throat, "I have done what you have deemed impossible. I have arranged a marriage for you."

"You have? When? With whom?"

"I have, just now, with Lord Ashdon, heir to the Earl of Westlin. A tidy match, wouldn't you agree?"

Caro walked toward her mother, the pearled light of London casting gentle light upon them both. "He offered for me?"

"We have reached a marriage arrangement."

That was rather too carefully worded for comfort.

"He did not approach you?"

Sophia shrugged and turned from Caro to walk over to the fireplace where she fussed with the arrangement of tulips there. As a very strict rule, Sophia did not fuss.

"How was this arrangement proposed?" Caro asked.

"If you must know, he had some outstanding debts, which I covered, and now, well, darling, I hoped you'd be happy. I paid his debts and now he is going to marry you. Isn't that lovely? You could hardly wish for a better match, and he is both young and handsome enough to credit you."

"You *bought* me a husband?" Caro sputtered.

"Yes. Isn't it delicious?" Sophia said smoothly, smiling in delight. "And he's all yours. Now, I was thinking that the wedding could be six weeks from Tuesday. Wouldn't Denmark be lovely for your honeymoon?"

"Mother, I am *not* going to marry a man you had to *buy* for me!"

"Why ever not?" Sophia said. "How else do you think marriages are made if not on a solid financial foundation?"

"Not everything is about money!"

Sophia laughed. "And you thought to be a courtesan? Darling, you obviously don't have the necessary commercial interests that drive such an enterprise. Best you marry and see to producing lots of lovely grandchildren for me."

"I am not going to marry him," Caro said stiffly, staring her mother down.

Sophia was not in the habit of being stared down and she gave every appearance of being disinclined to learn.

"But I've already paid for him," Sophia said. "He's yours, darling, all you need to do is simply collect him."

"Then you'll have to return him, or whatever it is one does with unwanted . . . merchandise!" Caro snapped.

"Well," Sophia said, a mild scowl forming between her brows, "I certainly never anticipated this. I suppose I shall have to tell him, or would you rather?"

"No, I think you should do it. I should die of shame to look at him."

"Now, Caro, are you completely certain this is what you want, because I don't think I can possibly arrange to buy another husband for you. This took quite a bit of effort and planning and just plain good fortune on my part."

"Mother, *please*. Just do it. Make him go away. I'd like us both to pretend that this never happened."

"If that's what you want," Sophia said, shaking her head

ruefully and walking toward the bedroom door. "But I will not tolerate any more of your ridiculousness about becoming a courtesan. I forbid you mention it again, do you understand?"

"Yes, Mother," Caro said serenely. "I promise to never mention it again."

Which, of course, wasn't at all to the point.

Six

"I'M sorry, Lord Ashdon, but she just won't have you," Sophia said.

The daughter of a courtesan would not have *him*? Was this the world as it was meant to run? It was most definitely not.

"Pardon me, madam?" he said crisply, standing almost at attention in her famed white salon. As the story went, Sophia had once been gifted with a rare and priceless porcelain cup, fully two hundred years old, out of the depths of mysterious China. The blanc de Chine cup was worth a tidy fortune and the room had been designed to showcase it. Only those few who had danced their way into the next level of intimacy were allowed into the white salon. The parquet floors were waxed to a dark sheen, like a lake at midnight, while her furnishings were all of milk blue damask and ice white velvet, ice floes on a winter lake, pristine and coldly beautiful, much like the famed lady herself.

She turned to face him, a smile of delicate chagrin on her fine-boned face, her dark eyes sympathetic. Did the daughter look like the mother?

He had seen her once or twice, at the opera, on Bond Street, but that was all. He knew her name: Caroline. He knew her lineage: questionable. He knew her dowry: substantial.

And he knew her mother. Or of her, be it better said.

Who lived within Society who did not know Sophia in one manner or another?

She had arrived in London in 1781, from the American colonies it was rumored, though he had trouble believing that.

Sophia Grey had charmed and beguiled the most sophisticated, the most debauched men of her day, and a girl from a colonial backwater could hardly have done that. Others said that she was Parisian, the daughter of an old aristocrat fallen into bad ways and hard times. That he could more readily believe because her French was flawless and her manner continental. There was about her that inbred arrogance of the aristocrat, a bone-deep belief in her own superiority and her own sublime worth. It was that arrogance, coupled with her aristocratic beauty, which had resulted in her fabled price.

His father had sent her a sapphire bracelet for the privilege of an introduction. Westlin had been allowed fifteen minutes in her salon before being ushered to the door by Fredericks. She had kept the bracelet.

That had been just the beginning.

Her daughter now was playing the same game, using the same tricks? *He* was not good enough for *her*? That was not how this game would play. He would make certain of it.

"She says she won't have you, Lord Ashdon," Sophia repeated softly. "I cannot explain it for it defies explanation, does it not?" Sophia sat down on the small white sofa and bid him do the same with a graceful gesture of her hand. He remained standing. "You are released from your obligation."

"What do you mean, she won't have me?" Ashdon asked.

Sophia raised one silken eyebrow slightly. "She refuses the match, sir. I do not know how to put it more plainly. Indeed, it is quite plain enough. I would avoid the vulgarity of plain speaking if I could, but I would not have you exist on false hope. A diet of false hope inevitably turns bitter on the tongue."

"Other things also taste bitter on the tongue, madam. Rancor. Revenge."

"You think I have set my table for revenge? You are wrong, sir. I seek only my daughter's security and happiness."

"Security and then happiness. In that order?"

"What other order is there? How to find happiness without security?"

"And your daughter, your Caroline, does not seek either happiness or security?"

"On the contrary, sir, she seeks them both. Though not, I fear, in you."

He could indeed feel the gall of bitterness roiling in his mouth, but he kept his tongue tamed and commanded himself to swallow his outrage whole. That he did not gag on it was a minor miracle.

"What did you tell her?" he calmly asked.

"Tell her?" Sophia poured out the tea into delicate black Wedgwood cups. She poured for him, though he had not been invited to stay to tea. "I simply told her that a marriage had been arranged for her. I told her your situation and your name, that is all. What happened next is hardly to be credited."

"If you don't mind, madam, just what did you tell her of my situation?"

"Only the truth, Lord Ashdon, which certainly should never cause harm, yet in this case . . ." She shrugged and handed him his cup. He sat stiffly opposite her and took it. "She did not react with either maturity or sophistication, I'm forced to admit. A negligence in her upbringing, I don't doubt. She has no desire to marry a man who, according to her words, I had *purchased* for her use."

That Ashdon managed to keep his cup from clanking against his saucer he considered remarkable. High points for poise were surely his.

"In point of fact," Sophia continued, stirring her tea with silent swirls of her tiny spoon, "she has decided upon another course entirely. I have been very negligent as a parent, I fear, for my daughter to have reached such a state."

Ashdon looked for tears to glisten in her dark eyes. He saw none.

"Of course, none of that is your concern," Sophia said softly, smiling wistfully at him. He didn't believe she had one wistful bone in her treacherous body. "Since the default was on my end, and because you have behaved with such honor throughout, no surprise to me since I know your father so well, you may rest assured that your debt to the Dalby name is cancelled. You have done your part. The fault lies entirely with Caro. I would be less than a lady if I held you accountable for her deplorable behavior."

Less than a lady? There was the certain truth.

His tea was growing cold in the cup. He let it.

"Deplorable behavior? Perhaps you are being harsh," he said. "She is young, obviously willful. A strong and equally determined husband could set her to rights. Not an unusual situation, from what I hear."

"I suppose that's true," Sophia said slowly, taking a sip of her tea, her eyes lowered against his scrutiny.

"If you will allow, I could meet with her, talk to her, try to assure her that—"

"That you have not been purchased for her pleasure?" Sophia said sweetly. "But how could you convince her of that when she is convinced it is the truth? Oh, I am sorry. I see I have offended you. Please forgive me. I am distraught. If you only knew, if you only suspected what her plan is, you would forgive me readily."

Ashdon carefully relaxed his jaw. His back teeth squeaked in thankfulness.

"She has plans for security and happiness, did you not say?" he asked. "What plans are those that they do not include a reputable husband?"

"The most disreputable of plans," Sophia said, putting down her cup with a shaking hand and folding her hands tightly in her lap. He could almost believe her truly distraught. But he did not believe her; he would not. She was a dissembler, a deceiver, a player upon men's emotions with no tender emotions of her own.

"Madam," he said, leaning forward in falsely earnest concern, "I would see our arrangement through. My honor demands no less of me. The debt is paid. I must uphold my end, no matter the difficulties. Tell me, what is it that disrupts this tidy arrangement? If it be nothing more than a daughter's sharp willfulness against the wisdom wrought of experience, then let me enter the battle for your daughter's future at your side. Let me convince her."

"I am not certain she can be convinced," Sophia said, her voice colored by the faintest shade of hope.

"Then let me only talk to her," Ashdon said. "I can perhaps speak in ways that a mother cannot." Of that he was most certain, most decidedly certain.

Sophia tilted her dark head, the late afternoon sunlight illuminating her skin so that it glowed like pearl. Oh, let the daughter be like the mother; that would make this task that much sweeter.

"That is true, isn't it?" she said. "As a man, you could explain to her the folly of her plan. You might have an authority with her, the voice of male perspective, which I do not possess."

"Yes," he said. "Let me only help you. Let us together manage what is best for your daughter."

"You are too good," she said, smiling. Did he imagine it? Was there some cold, sharkish rapacity to her smile? In the next instant, she melted, softened. He had imagined it.

"Tell me, what is her plan? How does she thwart your best intentions for her future happiness?" he asked.

"Lord Ashdon," she said, her smile disappearing slowly. "I must ask. Just this morning you were less than enthusiastic about an alliance with my daughter. What has changed in these few hours?"

Changed? Nothing, of course, except that the plans formed over the course of his lifetime spilled out if he made a single misstep. It was too late for missteps now and Sophia herself had seen to that.

"It is only the welcome bonds of honor, madam, nothing less. We have an arrangement, no matter its beginnings. I must hold to them, by all good faith and fair dealing. I have no other course open to me."

No other course, how very true that was.

"How noble of you," she said in a gentle undertone, considering him. He met her gaze, looking as innocent and guileless as he could manage. "And to be so good-humored in your pursuit of honor. A rare blending of virtues, I assure you."

"Thank you, madam," he said, bowing slightly from the neck.

"I had supposed, you know"—and here she laughed slightly but without embarrassment—"that you might have managed to accrue a few more lost wagers in the few hours since we first met. Debt can be a sharp motivator. I am so glad that is not the case."

"Hardly," he bit out.

"Then, what is the time? Coming up on five? And you are still solvent?"

"Completely," he said, not bothering to smile.

"A man of honor, then. I do so hope you can convince my daughter to agree to this marriage. As I'm sure you are aware, honor is so rarely found in these modern times. One scarcely knows whom to trust."

"Madam," he said, "you may put your trust in me."

"Thank you, Lord Ashdon. That is such a relief to know. A woman alone must be so very careful, must she not?"

"Most assuredly." A woman alone. If there was ever a woman who was not alone it was Sophia Dalby. "Now, as to the problem?"

"Yes," she sighed. "I don't know quite how to tell you this, Lord Ashdon, and I don't quite know how you will manage it, but Caro has come up with the most ridiculous plan for her future, a plan she is completely certain will result in her complete happiness."

"Don't most women make plans for their complete happiness?"

"How wise you are," she said, rising to her feet and walking away from him. Her walk invited erotic contemplation. He refused the invitation. "Yes, that is true. But what is not as often true is the decision Caro has made."

"Which is?" he said, rising to his feet and walking to stand with her at the large window that gave a slanted view of Hyde Park. It was a spectacular view.

"Which is this, sir," she said, giving him her profile to study. "Caro has declined a suit of marriage from you to pursue the life of a courtesan."

Ashdon felt his lungs freeze in his chest, felt his ribs curl in to jab his heart, felt his eyes glaze over with red fog fury. The daughter of a whore had refused to marry him so that she could pursue a whore's life?

It only took a moment, a long moment, for the red to fade and for his lungs to expand. She wanted to be a whore?

Very well, then. That made everything so very much clearer.

"Lord Ashdon? Do you still believe you can convince her?" Sophia's voice came to him from out of a pink-tinged haze. Destiny, what else to think?

"Yes," he said. "I'm quite sure I can."

Sophia smiled, a slow curve of her lips, her dark eyes sparkling. "I so enjoy it when things are well managed. To a successful endeavor, Lord Ashdon," she said, taking a delicate sip from her cup.

Ashdon felt only the faintest tingle pass over his skin, a warning of . . . something.

Well managed? Indeed.

Seven

THERE was a rout being given at Devonshire House, to which Sophia and her marriageable daughter were naturally not invited, but the Countess Dalby was hosting an intimate dinner for twenty-four, to which Ashdon had not been invited. Things being what they were, Sophia sweetly begged Richborough to give up his seat at table in the cause of Caroline's matrimony to Ashdon. Richborough complied, sullenly. Ashdon arrived, promptly.

It was a fine start to the evening's events.

Caro was wearing white; white blond over white crepe, a white pearl-encrusted cross at her throat and a diamond pin in her dark upswept hair. She looked spectacular.

Anne Warren, at her side for comfort, support, and true friendship, was wearing a bodice of tucked ivory poplin with matching skirt covered in ecru lace, the colors a perfect compliment to her dark red hair and ivory skin. Anne's fair skin shone and her greenish eyes glistened. She looked wonderful, but Caro, a mother's prejudice notwithstanding, looked spectacular. Sophia only hoped Ashdon had the wit to see what it was she had tossed into his lap.

At times, she doubted it.

In that, he might, unfortunately, take after his father. Westlin had been rather a dolt in regard to her, a point that still rankled. She'd told Ashdon that she never thought of Westlin. A small, inconsequential lie. She thought of Westlin often, especially since Dalby's death in 1795. That Westlin was still alive, well, that just gave her more time to get her due revenge upon him, didn't it?

Ashdon was dressed smartly and looked every inch the

pampered aristocrat. He was, she was pleased to say, a very well-featured man. He had good height and was broad through the shoulder; his coat fit him to perfection, his cravat and cuffs sparkling. He had that rumpled hair that was so popular now and that it was dark and softly wavy seemed to favor the look. His eyes were the clear and vivid blue of his deceased mother's. His nose, long and a bit wide, was his father's. Pity, that. His mouth was good, perhaps a shade too wide, but his bones were fine and chiseled and his teeth were good.

If she thought of him as something like a stallion she had purchased to stud, she supposed she should be forgiven for that.

All in all, he was a likely looking man of approximately thirty years, and aside from a gambling habit, which was hardly unusual, Caro could do a lot worse. But in point of fact, she hardly intended for Caro to do any worse at all.

Ashdon should be just the thing.

Sophia smiled as she greeted her guests, making it a point not to encourage a meeting between Ashdon and Caro. Things of that nature proceeded best when a bit ignored.

On the other hand, there was nothing like a good, solid dam to make the waters surge and the pressure build.

"Caro, darling," she said, taking both her daughter and Anne by the arm and casually but very purposefully leading them to a quiet corner of the yellow salon, the bigger of the two salons. "I'm so sorry. Naturally, I felt I *had* to invite him, what with the marriage arrangement and all. Even if it did fall out today, I didn't feel it quite right to refuse him admittance. Are you terribly put out? Shall I send him off or can you bear up under the strain of seeing the man who might have been yours?"

Caro looked across the room to where Lord Ashdon stood talking to Viscount Staverton, an old acquaintance of her mother's. How old and in what way they were acquaintances Caro had never had the cheek to ask. Though now that she was supposed to be launching a life as a courtesan, a very well-paid courtesan, she should probably ask those exact sort of questions.

She didn't. It didn't seem the time, what with Lord Ashdon, her almost husband, standing just across the room.

He certainly dominated a room.

He was very tall and very handsome and very romantic looking. His hair was tossed forward so that it brushed in dark curls against his brows. With his dark hair and black jacket, his eyes appeared that much more blue. He hadn't looked at her yet, they hadn't even been introduced, but she could just imagine how those blue eyes would pierce her.

If she were to become a courtesan, it was clear that *something* would pierce her, and very soon.

Oh dear, where had *that* thought come from?

"Caro?" her mother said, taking her hand and rubbing it. "Are you quite all right? You look jumbled all of a sudden. A broken engagement can do that, I suppose, though I hardly speak from firsthand experience since no man ever broke an engagement with *me*, of any sort."

Anne blushed and ducked her head.

Caro glared at her mother and felt herself becoming less . . . jumbled. "I'm fine, Mother. I'm not the least bit jumbled."

"I don't suppose I should introduce you," Sophia said, looking across the room at Ashdon, who was not looking in their direction. He hadn't looked at Caro since entering the salon.

Was he intentionally snubbing her? It wasn't as if he could be upset that she was rejecting his pursuit of her since he hadn't *pursued* her at all. He'd been bought and paid for, like a bit of lace or a saddle or a bonnet. *She* hadn't gambled herself into penury. *She* hadn't agreed to a marriage just to keep the creditors off her doorstep. *She* was the one who should be snubbing *him*. Though, watching how thoroughly he ignored her, and she the daughter of the hostess no less, she thought that perhaps snubbing him might be exactly what he would want.

If there was anything she'd decided in the last few moments of furious introspection it was that Lord Ashdon did not deserve to get what he wanted and certainly not from her.

"Oh, I think we ought to be introduced," Caro said, slipping her arm through her mother's and catching Anne's hand in hers. "After all, we have something of a connection now. I think it only proper that I meet the man you bought for me."

"Really, darling," Sophia breathed, "there's no need to be coarse."

"I'm only being honest," Caro said in an undertone as she made her way across the room, practically pulling Anne and her mother behind her.

"If being honest results in being coarse," Sophia said, "it is far better to dissemble gracefully than to be vulgarly truthful."

She might have been able to think up some clever rejoinder if Lord Ashdon hadn't suddenly become alarmingly close, turning from his conversation with Viscount Staverton to impale her with his piercing blue eyes.

She'd been right about those eyes.

He was wearing a black coat, a lapis blue silk waistcoat, and white knee breeches and cravat. He looked . . . delicious, if one discounted the bored and superior look on his face.

She decided not to discount it since he probably thought she *should* discount it.

Was there anything worse than a man who could be purchased? Definitely not. He had nothing to feel superior about. Why, with the snap of her fingers, she could have had him delivered to her doorstep like a barrel of oysters.

Wouldn't it be lovely if she threatened him with just that?

She didn't bother to wonder where *that* thought had come from because she knew exactly where it had come from: wounded pride. First Richborough and now Ashdon; was there a man alive who found her desireable? It was becoming perfectly obvious that not only would a man not choose to marry her, he would not, unless pressed past all endurance, choose to debauch her. The situation, at this precise moment, looked hopeless. One could hardly be a well-paid courtesan if well-heeled men refused to pay for the promised delights. And as to marriage, if she didn't have a hope of marrying well without having her mother buy her a husband, the least Lord Ashdon could have done was refuse to be bought.

"Lord Ashdon, I do not believe you have met my daughter, Lady Caroline Trevelyan?"

"A pleasure, Lady Caroline," Lord Ashdon said, bowing slightly.

Caro dipped her head and curseyed just as slightly.

What was it about this man that drove needles into her joints and pokers into her heart? She disliked him on principle . . . and she couldn't stop staring at him.

Which was just one more reason to dislike him.

"You remember Lord Staverton, of course," her mother said, smiling at Lord Staverton. Lord Staverton, looking the height of fashion, was ruddy cheeked and fifty if he was a day.

He had known her mother from her first days in London and, according to a passing comment her father had once made, seemed to have been one of her mother's first friends. She had never quite warmed to Lord Staverton. It might have been because he still looked at her mother as if she were a treat he wanted to partake of at any moment. It might have been because one of his eyes was crossed. It might have been because she didn't like to think of her mother having had . . . *friends*.

But that was all going to change now, now that she was going to have friends of her own.

"Delighted, Lady Caroline," Lord Staverton said warmly.

Whatever one could say about Lord Staverton, he did have lovely manners. Lord Ashdon had barely said one word in greeting. Lord Ashdon was eyeing her like an unruly carthorse. Lord Ashdon could go to the devil.

"And you must remember Mrs. Warren," Sophia said, whereupon Anne curtseyed gracefully, a curl of her shining red hair tumbling forward to land in her flawless cleavage. Both men's eyes went to Anne's cleavage, and stayed there for approximately four seconds too long.

"Of course, and how are you this evening, Mrs. Warren?" Lord Staverton gushed, his good eye twitching back and forth between Anne's face and her cleavage.

The unsubstantiated rumors of Lord Staverton's interest in Anne as a possible wife seemed slightly more substantiated.

Was everyone in the world going to be married while she was busy being a courtesan?

"Very well, thank you, Lord Staverton," Anne said mildly.

This conversation was boring beyond words and was taking her nowhere in her inexplicable desire to make Lord Ashdon wretched.

"I'm so glad we've had the opportunity to meet, Lord Ashdon," she said. "I daresay we have our mutual curiosity to satisfy."

There. In with both feet and not a moment's regret.

A startled silence spread out from their small group to touch the others in the room so that conversation stalled and stilled until only the most hesitant whispers could be heard in the far corners. Oh, dear. And those blue eyes were so chilling and so still, as if she were the only person in the room and still of no interest to him. Horrid man. She'd had quite enough of being undesirable for one day, and she was in no frame of mind to tolerate it from *this* man.

She half expected her mother to say something to smooth the moment; her mother excelled at that sort of thing. But her mother said nothing.

"As to curiosity," Lord Ashdon said, his voice low and controlled, "yes, that itch is scratched. As to satisfaction," he almost purred, "no, Lady Caroline. Not at all. I am far, far from being satisfied."

"To your misfortune," she said, caught in his cold blue gaze and fighting back with her tongue. "I find myself most satisfied, all my questions answered."

Somehow, with some hurried breath of words, her mother and Staverton left them. Anne probably wished to escape, but could think of no excuse that would carry her off. Caro reached back and grabbed Anne by the arm, linking them. Anne turned away and looked at a vase of early roses on the sideboard as if she had never seen pink roses before. Caro felt more alone with Lord Ashdon than if she had been locked in a cupboard with him, though being locked in a cupboard brought to mind all sorts of delicious sensations and dangers, not that Lord Ashdon looked at all as if he would participate.

She gripped Anne's arm tighter.

"You'll pardon me," Lord Ashdon said, staring into her eyes, "but you do not look satisfied. Far from it."

"Your eyes deceive you," she declared.

"Something is endeavoring to deceive me," he said. Was that a smile? No, he was too surly for smiles.

"Surely you are not implying that I practice deceit."

"I would certainly never imply that you have perfected deceit."

Anne tried to pull off. Caro held on.

"Lord Ashdon, this conversation is entirely too familiar," Caro said, raising her chin.

"Lady Caroline," he said—he *was* smiling—"perhaps more than our conversation could be entirely too familiar, then we might both be well satisfied."

Caro, in spite of all logic, felt a thrill tumble down her spine. If she was not mistaken, Lord Ashdon had made a comment with a decidedly debauched tone to it. She could hardly keep herself from grinning, which would have been a completely inappropriate response. No, she should be insulted, and she was. She was just very, very delighted that he had clearly felt the irresistible urge to insult her. Anne wrenched her arm free and was halfway across the room before Caro could stop her.

"Look what you've done," she snapped under her breath, truly irritated. It was far easier to be delighted by a debauched sentiment and a wicked blue gaze when one did not have to face wickedness and debauchery alone.

"Managed to get you all to myself? I'd say I've done well," he said.

"Lord Ashdon," she said, throwing her shoulders back and thrusting her chin out, "I was under the assumption that we both understood our current standing. You and my mother"—she paused, embarrassed—"well, the agreement that you reached between you is not to my, that is, I don't plan to marry."

"Yes, Lady Dalby said as much," he said, taking one step closer to her, pushing all the air out of the room. He was very tall and very broad and his eyes were very, very blue. "You don't want to be my wife. You would rather be a courtesan."

He was furious. She could feel it in the air all around him. She hadn't thought he would be furious about her refusal; after all, they didn't even know each other. But to be refused so that a courtesan's life could be pursued . . . yes, that might make a man angry.

Where was her mother when she needed her? The entire room seemed to have emptied out, leaving her alone to face a furious man. He would likely strangle her, letting her inert body fall to the floor before anyone dared to gaze in his direction.

"Come, come, Lord Ashdon," she said, taking a step back. If he were planning on strangling her, he'd have to catch her first. "Let us not color it too prettily. You had debts to pay and I was the means to pay them. I would not be any man's purse. Strangely, I would like to liked for myself."

"And you shall have ample opportunity to be liked for yourself, and to measure your likeability on the strings of any man's purse. Any man who can pay your price."

"How very crude you are," she said, taking another step backward.

Unfortunately, he was very tall, his steps were rather larger than hers, and he was still following her.

"Perhaps," he said softly. "But is that not the life to which you impetuously aspire?"

"I am not impetuous. I am practical."

"If you were truly practical, you would have accepted the husband arranged for you."

"Don't you mean to say 'bought for me'?" she snapped as she tripped over the train of her skirts and heard a small rip. *Horrid*, horrid man.

"As you say," he snarled softly, the muscles in his jaw rippling. "But do you pretend to be my superior? Are you not prepared to go to any man who can afford your price? Are you not, Lady Caroline, arranging a future for yourself where you will be bought and traded? You refuse me as husband. Can you afford to refuse me as patron?"

It was then that she backed into the sideboard, knocking the vase of early pink roses to the floor and flooding the back of her white dress with water.

Eight

THINGS were going beautifully.

It wasn't that Ashdon had planned to engage in a snarling salon battle with Caroline Trevelyan, but that, having done so, he was enjoying himself immensely.

Yes, she was beautiful. He had expected as much of her, knowing her mother. Even Stuart Trevelyan, the eighth Earl of Dalby and Caroline's father, had been fashionably attractive in his day. Lady Caroline ran true to her bloodlines; that was clear in her ivory skin, dark blue eyes, and black hair. What was not as clear was her temperament.

Was Sophia as fiery? Certainly not in public.

Had Dalby been as stubborn? Perhaps, though rather more elegantly.

Caroline, all proclamations to the contrary, certainly had a lot to learn about being a courtesan if tonight's example was to be her calling card. Courtesans did not provoke, unless the provocation be erotic. Courtesans did not argue. Courtesans did not insult. Courtesans did not back into furniture. Courtesans did not knock over vases. Courtesans did not repair upstairs for a change of clothes without inviting a man along to help loosen water-drenched stays. An extra pair of strong hands would surely be needed to pry her out of her gown.

Ashdon shifted his weight against the growing bulge in his breeches. The salon of Sophia Dalby was no place to lose control.

"I thought I was good, but I hadn't heard even the first rumor of a marriage arrangement between you and Lady Caroline," Calbourne said.

"But you've heard now," Ashdon said, turning to face the fourth Duke of Calbourne.

He and Cal had met at Eton on their first day, at a fight actually in which they'd both found themselves, along with five other boys. What the fight had been about was inconsequential now. What they had found was that the field had cleared and they'd been back to back, fists raised. They were still in that position, and Ashdon got great pleasure from it. If there were anyone to have at one's back, it was the Duke of Calbourne. Cal stood a full head taller than any man he'd yet to meet, raised his fist, but not his voice, at a moment's notice, and was the most cheerfully irritating person in the whole of England.

"Only enough to whet my appetite," Cal said, staring across the room at Sophia Dalby. Half the men in the room were staring at Sophia Dalby. It appeared to be some sort of rule. "Care to expound?"

"I do not, but that won't end it, will it?" Ashdon said.

"Of course not. You can either relinquish all the details gracefully or be hounded until you bleed from a thousand cuts. I would choose the graceful option, were I you," Cal said, grinning.

"I agreed to marry the girl, she declined, that's the short of it," Ashdon said.

"No, it won't do," Cal said crisply. "Lady Caroline must be of fresh dress before dinner is served. You have at least fifteen minutes to tell me the long of it. Proceed."

Ashdon scowled and motioned for Cal to walk with him to a relatively secluded alcove at the least populated end of the room. Given what had occurred with the vase and his stalking of Lady Caroline, the other guests seemed well content to have him move off.

"I have had some debts pile up and the Countess Dalby made good use of them. She sought to buy a husband for her girl."

"You?"

Ashdon bowed in acknowledgment.

"What sort of debts?" Calbourne asked.

"The usual sort. Gaming debts."

Cal raised his eyebrows and made a rolling motion with his hand. Ashdon continued.

"Thin on options, I agreed to marry Lady Caroline. The lady refused. It seems she would prefer another sort of life entirely than that of being the Countess of Westlin."

"She would prefer to be a duchess?"

"She would prefer to be a whore," Ashdon said grittily.

"Well, there's a step in an odd direction," Cal said softly.

"Blood tells. Here's the proof of it," Ashdon said.

Calbourne looked at him carefully. "How much of your father is in this, Ash? This has the feel of him, from start to end."

Ashdon met Calbourne's pale hazel gaze. "You know the bonds of family, Cal, you have a son and heir of your own. What more is there to life than honoring those bonds?"

"Honor has limits, Ash," Cal said. "If Westlin has not taught you that, let life be your teacher."

"This? From you?" Ashdon smiled and shook his head. "You, who have ever been constant, even vigilant, in honoring your duty to your family name and legacy? Why else did you marry at twenty a girl of your father's choosing, begetting an heir within the year? How is Alston, by the way?"

"Thriving," Cal said. "But do not seek to drive me off my point. I married, yes; I did my duty and produced an heir. Was I happy? Is there happiness to be found in responsibility? Yes, of a sort. But did I love the girl chosen for me? No. You know yourself I said a prayer of thanks the day Sarah died. Another year together and we would have drawn blood."

"Yet you did your duty. Your father was content."

"Yes, and in the ground himself a scant month before Sarah. It does no good to please the dead. Please yourself. That is what life teaches."

Ashdon was shaking his head before Cal had even finished. "I cannot. His hurts, his wounds, are mine."

"His wounds are imagined," Calbourne urged. "Let this die with him, Ash. What can be gained from a marriage with Sophia's brat?"

"Revenge," Ashdon said softly, looking at Sophia.

"Revenge is overrated. By refusing you, Lady Caroline has

denied you a path to your own destruction. I may kiss her in thanks," Cal said, trying to jest when the mood between them was leaden.

Ashdon smiled and looked down at his feet.

"What?" Cal said. "This is the end of it. She has refused you. You will move on."

Ashdon shrugged and kept smiling.

"Tell me," Cal commanded, sounding very ducal.

"She has refused to be my wife, that is true. She has made her choice," Ashdon said, looking at his friend with glittering eyes. "What's left now but for her to be my whore?"

Nine

"OAF," Caro said as she was being laced into fresh, dry stays.

"You did it yourself," Anne said, holding Caro's new gown, a cream white silk with tiny florets of icy white embroidery on the sleeves, while the maid laced the stays.

"Did it myself? When he was practically chasing me around the room? What else was I to do? Stand in place and let him throttle me?"

"You exaggerate," Anne said calmly.

"I most certainly do not. *You* did not see his eyes. They were positively lethal. And I always thought blue eyes were so pleasant, so cheerful, before now. That oaf has *ruined* blue eyes for me forever."

"Better to have blue eyes ruined than be ruined yourself," Anne said in an undertone.

"What was that?" Caro said stiffly as the maid tied off her stays.

"Just talking to myself," Anne said.

"You were not," Caro said, dismissing the maid, "but I hate to call you a liar to your face."

"Isn't that what you just did?" Anne said, grinning.

"Not exactly, no," Caro said with an answering grin.

"Well, I suppose I can't exactly take offense then, can I? How fortunate for me that I don't offend easily."

"No, how fortunate for *me*."

"You are fortunate in all things, Caro," Anne said more seriously. "Don't toss fortune into the wind, especially not in the name of revenge."

"Revenge?" Caro said, staring at herself in the mirror

and toying with a curl next to her left ear. "I don't have a vengeful bone in my body."

"Then vengeance must reside elsewhere," Anne said dryly. "Perhaps in your liver?"

"Don't be ridiculous, Anne."

Anne grinned and stood behind Caro to gently fuss with her hair. "You sound just like your mother."

"That's to the good, I think," Caro said, her hands falling to her sides.

"In most ways, yes, I think so as well," Anne said softly, staring at Caro in the mirror. "I admire Sophia. She lifted me out of a life that . . . well, that was beyond bearing, really. Almost beyond comprehension. I'm quite certain that I'd be dead by now, if not for her generosity."

"You'd be fine. You'd have survived."

"As what?"

"I don't know, perhaps as a—"

"Courtesan?" Anne finished for her.

"There are worse things," Caro said defiantly.

"How would you know?" Anne countered.

Caro lifted her chin and stood up from the padded stool in front of the mirror. "My mother managed. She was a courtesan and she managed to find a man, a man who wanted her enough to marry her, no matter what Society said."

But, of course, he had done so for Sophia, and there was truly but one of her. She was unique. For all that Caro was Sophia's daughter, she was not Sophia.

"And of course you want the same," Anne said, taking Caro's hands in hers. Caro did not return her grasp. "But there are other roads to the same end."

"Buying a husband for me is hardly one of those roads."

"How do you know? It could be," Anne said urgently. "What you do know is that becoming a courtesan will end your life in so many ways. You have everything a woman could want: security, a home, family. Become a courtesan and you throw all that away."

"My family would not throw me away."

"But you would throw away every chance for a life in Society, Caro. Think what an outcast you'd make of yourself."

"I'm an outcast now."

"No, no, you're not. At least, not in the way a courtesan is. Even your mother is not an outcast like that anymore. She has a title, children, a legitimacy that a courtesan—"

"But she was a courtesan first!" Caro snapped, pulling her hands away from Anne's.

Anne stared at Caro, so young, so sheltered, and so very foolish, and said, "Do you think you're honoring her by emulating her, Caro? Do you think to love her more by living her life, by righting old wrongs?"

Caro turned abruptly and walked to the bedroom door. "I don't know what you mean."

"Why did you really refuse Lord Ashdon?" Anne said from across the room, her voice ringing like an unwelcome bell. "At least tell me that."

Caro froze at the door, her hand on the knob. "Because my mother bought him for me."

"Which is how marriages are made, as you well know."

"Because," Caro said, staring down at her hand clasped on the knob, thinking how strange a thing it was that she had her hand on the means of escape and yet she was still trapped. A metaphor for her life, really. She simply had to turn the knob in her hand and she would be free. "Because . . . the Earl of Westlin insulted her . . . and so I insult his son. Fairly mild in the 'an eye for an eye' family code of honor, but the best I can do, I'm afraid."

"Did you never think that by marrying him, your mother would have been repaid for every insult of Lord Westlin's?" Anne said.

Caro turned sharply and said in astonishment, "No, I never did."

Caroline Trevelyan *was* very young and very sheltered, most especially in the ways of vengeance.

～

As far as revenge went, it was fairly mild.

Sophia had arranged the seating at dinner to put Caroline and Ashdon directly opposite each other. The table was slightly too wide to hold a conversation across its width, but the candlesticks provided just the right degree of glowing yellow light to accentuate Caro's very pretty cleavage and shining blue eyes.

A mild revenge to enact upon Ashdon, but enjoyable nonetheless.

She did note that Ashdon spent more time staring grimly at Caro than he did in talking to his dinner partners. Lovely what a little revenge could to do to spice an evening to perfection. The hours spent at the table passed far too quickly, but then the dining table was cleared for a few hours of gaming, which was fun as well.

It was impossible not to enjoy watching Lord Ashdon lose his money so energetically. The man had an amazing aptitude for bad luck, bad timing, and bad decisions. The only thing she could say in his credit was that he *was* devilishly good-looking and that he had quite nice friends. The fourth Duke of Calbourne being the perfect example of this good taste.

She had always enjoyed the man, though the third Duke of Calbourne had been a bit of a sot; it was nice to know that blood did not always tell. Charles, the fourth Duke of Calbourne, was so high in the ton that he could do whatever he wished, a situation that could hardly be more convenient or more pleasant, and so, sweetly, he occasionally attended her dinners. It had helped with the few monsters of protocol who still shunned her. Calbourne was without wife and highly eligible; not many hostesses or guests would ignore those two facts in conjunction.

Ashdon was playing whist at the moment, Calbourne standing just off and watching him. Sophia glided over to Calbourne and said, "He does lose rather brilliantly, doesn't he?"

Calbourne smiled crookedly and said, "Everyone must do something brilliantly."

"Then how fortunate that he has found his brilliance so early in life."

Calbourne looked down at her from his remarkable height. "Now, Lady Dalby, we both know that you and Lord Ashdon are almost of an age."

Sophia fluttered her fan and smiled. "You are a brilliant liar, your grace. It is what, I believe, makes you so charming as a dinner companion."

"Have I charmed you, then?" He grinned softly. "To charm Sophia . . . you must know that sonnets are written instructing us how."

"But not every man can follow instruction, your grace," she said, her eyes shining at him from above the rim of her fan.

"I think, sometimes, the teacher must take the fault of that."

"Said the disgruntled student," she said, laughing lightly.

"I am an able student, Lady Dalby," he said, his golden hazel eyes burning with sudden heat.

"And I an able tutor," she countered. "But, alas, all that is past. I am past my prime, according to my daughter."

"Children are ruthless, pushing us into old age before our inclination."

"But not before our time?" she joked. "But you are too young, your grace, to think these thoughts. Your son is how old now?"

"Seven, and he makes me feel one hundred."

"The trick, your grace, is to not look as old as you sometimes feel. You are doing brilliantly. You look . . . remarkable."

Calbourne bowed crisply. "Is that my talent, then? To look remarkable? Looks to be remarked upon? I daresay, that calls forth all sorts of images."

"When a man of your age and situation must hunt and peck for compliments," Sophia said, laughing, "can England long survive?"

"I believed we were discussing how long Calbourne was to survive," he said, laughing with her.

Ashdon looked up from the table and grumbled something. Sophia, unfortunately, couldn't hear what.

Calbourne took her by the elbow and led her to a small sofa angled into a corner of the room. Sophia sank to the sofa like a peacock feather. His grace sat beside her, his long legs almost dwarfing the sofa.

"Shall we continue to flirt, your grace, or would you rather talk plainly?" Sophia asked. "I find immeasurable pleasure in either form of conversation."

"Which is why a man finds so much enjoyment in conversing with you, madam. You are accommodating, and entertaining, in the extreme."

"And still he flatters," she said, looking across the room to where Viscount Staverton had apparently trapped Anne Warren into stilted conversation. She would have to attend to Anne soon; enough time had been given to the Duke of Calbourne for one evening, as much as she enjoyed him.

"I am losing you, lady. Your gaze wanders."

"As does my interest, your grace," she said softly, looking at him with the lightest of glances.

"Speak of what you will. I am held prisoner."

"Then I will speak of Lord Ashdon," she said, letting her eyes wander the room. "How well do you know him?"

"Better than any man," he said softly. "Better than you, I should think."

Sophia chuckled. "I should hope so. I am hardly Eton material." She paused to close her fan and lay it on her lap. "You know of his debts?"

"Yes."

"You know of my remedy to relieve him of them?"

"Yes."

She cast him a sideways glance of inquiry. He matched it with an easy smile.

"You know of the refusal?" she said.

"Yes."

"Then, your grace, in this small list of knowable things, we are of equal understanding."

"As you say, it is a small list. Hardly enough to comprise a man," Calbourne said calmly.

"But, your grace, this small list is all that matters to me. I do not care to know more."

"Now, Lady Dalby, that I cannot believe, for it is well known that you are a woman of rare energy and imagination," he said, his voice slipping down seductively. "Surely, in knowing more, you would increase your odds of winning."

"You want me to win?"

"I want him to win," he said.

"Even if it goes against his own schemes?" she said, turning to face him slightly.

"Even so," he said, taking her hand in his and raising it to his mouth. He brushed the lightest of kisses upon her gloved hand, his breath warming her skin. Sophia smiled. "Are you not working against your daughter's schemes for her own good?"

"Your grace, I like you better and better, and I liked you well enough from the start."

Calbourne grinned and kissed the tips of her fingers before releasing her hand.

"Then, Countess Dalby, we all win."

Ten

"Now, Anne, throw off every polite and practical instinct you possess and tell me the truth. Do you have any interest at all in a proposal of marriage from Lord Staverton?"

Anne looked into Sophia's black eyes and felt every shred of common sense tumble off her and land on the carpeted floor.

"No. I don't. I'm a fool."

"A fool is someone who doesn't know her own mind. You are hardly a fool," Sophia said. "Now Caro, she might be a fool yet. All this courtesan idiocy. Only a fool, a fool with a good roof over her and healthy food in her, would talk so ridiculously."

"Thank you, Mother," Caro said sarcastically.

The evening had waned into morning and still the party roared with energy. True, Lord Dutton was drunk and snoring by the fire, but if one discounted snoring drunks at a party, it could hardly be counted as a party at all, at least according to Lady Dalby. Anne had learned to pay attention to what Lady Dalby said about things and events and people. Lady Dalby saw things that other people didn't. Lady Dalby was shrewd, and that was the least of it.

"You are certain?" Sophia asked her. "It would be a good match. He's ridiculously wealthy and sweetly generous, and he would make you a viscountess."

"Mother, he's ancient and has that . . . eye," Caro said. "Anne is a beautiful young woman in her prime. It's a ridiculous match."

Sophia cast a dark look in her daughter's direction. "For a woman who's announced her intention to be a courtesan, you are remarkably ill-informed. And spoilt. I'd begun to wonder if it might do you some good," she said softly. "This latest remark quite decides it."

"If you think I should marry the viscount, of course I will," Anne said. She couldn't stay with Caro forever, especially if Caro actually pursued a courtesan's life. Unless she pursued it at her side. The thought niggled into her heart and settled there, coldly and heavily.

"I would never presume to tell you what to do, Anne," Sophia said, giving her hand a squeeze. "I only feel it is my duty to point out a good match when I see one. It is your choice to make, as it is your life to live. You have a home with me for as long as you wish it, even after Caro moves out to pursue her life's goal."

"Excuse me?" Caro said. "Move out?"

"Well, I can hardly have a known courtesan living under my roof, can I?" Sophia said. "Think what it would do to my reputation."

"Mother, you can't mean to say that you would . . . throw me out to make my way on, on the streets, do you? Would you?" Caro said, her elegant features wreathed in shock and disbelief.

"Darling, just where do you think a courtesan begins, if not on the streets?" Sophia said sweetly. But there was iron beneath that sugary coating; Anne could feel it. Could Caro?

"When I said I wanted to be a courtesan—"

"Darling, what you said was that you were *going* to be a courtesan," Sophia interrupted.

"Yes, well," Caro stuttered, "it was in the hope of finding a man who would want me for myself and to do that, to achieve that goal, it's going to take time to find the right man. I am not going to rush. I am not going to allow just any man to . . . to, well, to . . ."

"If you can't say it, Caro, how on earth are you going to do it?" Sophia said with a sarcastic smile.

"Whatever I allow him to do," Caro rallied, "it will be because *I* have chosen him, not because I am *desperate* or any such low thing."

"Yes, darling," Sophia said. "I quite understand your

thinking. Your plans are quite clear. Unfortunately, they have little if anything to do with the way things truly are."

"I understand how things truly are!" Caro flared.

As much as Anne adored Caro, she had to side with Sophia. Caro was very protected and very pampered. She had no idea what the world was like outside of the shelter erected by money and position.

"Caro, being a wife is much preferable to being a courtesan," Anne said solemnly.

"I'm less than certain of that," Caro said stiffly.

"You should listen to your mother," Anne said. "She's been both, you've been neither. Perhaps it's not too late to accept the arrangement with Lord Ashdon. He certainly seemed . . . interested in you earlier."

"Interested? He wanted to break my neck," Caro said. "Besides which, any interest he had in human companionship fled his mind the minute the gaming tables were set up. The man's a remorseless gambler. I will not—"

"Yes, darling, I think we are all well aware of the many things that you *will not*. Let us not discuss it now. I must go and tell Staverton the bad news regarding Anne, you *are* certain, Anne, that a match with him is not to be?"

Anne was less certain of everything the longer she listened to Sophia and Caro argue, but she nodded, letting the die be cast as she cursed herself for a sentimental idiot.

"Very well," Sophia said. "No woman should be forced to marry a man not to her tastes and inclinations."

"*Exactly*," Caro snapped, her eyes gleaming in righteous fervor.

"But what a woman who is a courtesan is forced to do," Sophia snapped in reply, her own dark eyes gleaming ruthlessly, "is an entirely different matter. You, my darling daughter, have set a course for yourself. As of tomorrow, you must be prepared to make your way in it."

"What? Wait a minute, Mother—"

"A clever woman would use every hour and every man available to her, beginning now, when the hour is late and the men are well into their cups, to find herself a protector. A silly woman would argue and whine until the hour of noon tomorrow until she found herself deposited on James Street considering the loveliness of Green Park. I leave it to you, Caro. Use that famous intellect of yours. Now, on to Staverton."

And with that, she left them in a quiet corner of the yellow salon, where both young women stared at each other in complete shock.

"She can't mean it," Caro said.

Anne didn't reply since it was blatantly obvious that she did mean it, every word of it. Sophia, always smiling and pleasant, had a will of steel and was not shy in inflicting her steel on others.

"Can you not find it in you to make amends with Lord Ashdon?" Anne asked. "It would be a good match for you."

"Only until he killed me," Caro said wryly. "And you speak to me of good, wise matches? Run, and tell my mother you have changed your mind about Staverton and I will do the same about Ashdon."

"You would?" Anne said softly.

Anne knew the answer, of course.

Caro leaned her shoulders against the wall and sighed. "Absolutely not. I hate him. He is a vile man, horrible, ill-mannered, and ungovernable."

"Ungovernable?"

"Did he not gamble his way onto the marriage block? Did my mother not buy him for me?"

"What is it you hate, Caro, that your mother bought him or that he allowed himself to be bought?"

"What is the difference between the two? He was for sale and the sale was made. Or almost made. He disgusts me."

"And he ruined your gown," Anne said wryly.

"Add clumsy brute to his list of faults. I should make him pay for it, just to add to his financial burdens. He should be made to, you know. A gentleman would offer, would make some effort at gracious apology. He really should be made to pay."

Caro's gaze slipped to the fine turned leg of the small sofa nearest them. They were almost alone in the room, except for the soft snores that marked the location of Lord Dutton.

"Caro?" Anne said.

Caro looked at her with the light of inspiration, devilish inspiration, surely, in her eyes. "He really *should* be made to pay, shouldn't he?"

Oh, Lord.

"Caro, what are you thinking?" Anne said, just a bit desperately.

Caro looked up at her, her dark eyes gleaming with just a hint of malice. "I'm thinking that a little revenge would be in order. And so well deserved, too."

"Revenge? Because he made an offer of marriage for you?"

"Was that what it was? I thought I was merely the means to cancel his debts."

"Caro, marriages are made on just such a foundation every day. Why are you so very insulted?"

"Because," Caro said softly, her voice coming out in a hiss of anger, "I have spent my whole life learning to be the perfect woman, and for what? So that some man who's never even *seen* me before should make an offer for me, merely to clear himself of debt? I want to be wanted, and I will be. Being a courtesan, being wanted by absolutely hoards of men, sounds completely wonderful. I won't have a husband who must be bribed and bought for me. I want to be wanted, for myself, no matter who my mother is."

"Caro," Anne said in frustration, "that is all beside the point at the moment. You are about to be tossed out onto the streets by your mother. You must find a haven. Is there anywhere you can go, anyone who will take you in?"

"Markham will never allow it," Caro said.

"I am sure that is true, but Markham is not in Town and hardly able to help you by tomorrow noon. Is there anyone to help you? Have you no friends? No relatives in Town?"

Caro lifted her chin and said, "You are my friend, Anne. I . . . well, I am not very well liked, I'm afraid. I don't have many friends, and my father's relatives are all deceased. My mother's family, aside from our guardian, has little to do with us. I am quite alone. Except for you. I quite understand," she said, voice quivering just slightly, "that my mother bought you for me as she tried to do with Lord Ashdon. I know that, unless destitute, you would never have lowered yourself by coming into my mother's house to befriend me. I have chosen to believe that you have come to actually like me, in spite of everything."

Caro's dark eyes, so large and expressive, were filled with unshed tears, yet she looked anything but cowed. In spite of admitting herself friendless and without hope of succor, she had the look of a warrior set to face his final battle, unafraid and clothed in honor. It was one of the most endearing aspects of Caro and one of which she was entirely unaware, this stalwart warrior in silk and pearls, dark blue eyes unblinking.

"You *are* a complete idiot," Anne said, taking her by the hand and leading her past the still snoring Lord Dutton and to the doorway of the salon that opened onto the dining room at the rear of the house. "You know I adore you, for one. And for another, there are things you don't know about me, things which your mother kept from you out of kindness on my behalf."

"What don't I know about you?" Caro said as Lord Dutton's snores slipped into drunken mumbling.

"Dear Caro," Anne said. "You know nothing of the life I lived before coming to live with you."

"You're a widow. Your husband died at sea."

"Yes, true, but how did your mother find me? I'll tell you how. She and my mother were friends of a sort. They were both courtesans, though my mother did not fare as well as yours."

"What? I don't believe it!"

"Believe it," Anne said crisply. "Also believe me when I say that the courtesan's life is not what you imagine. Not at all."

"I don't believe a word of it. You're just saying this to try and change my mind."

"I am trying to change your mind, that's certainly true, but all the rest is true as well. You think being a courtesan is easy? Try your hand at it now, while they are gaming. Try and find a man who will pay a month's income for the promise of your kiss. If you cannot, beg on your knees to your mother that she will forgive you your willfulness. Marry the next man she buys for you. Do anything to avoid that life. I beg you, Caro. 'Tis no fit way to live."

"You don't think I can, do you?" Caro said. "You don't think any man *would* want me that much." And with that dire pronouncement, Caro sailed into the dining room.

Anne followed nervously behind her, murmuring, "That is not at all what I meant!"

When the yellow salon was empty and all hope of further conversation dashed, Lord Dutton stopped snoring, sat up, and said to the sparkling crystal chandelier above him, "Sophia really does provide the most delightful entertainments." And with that, he straightened his cravat and sauntered into the dining room.

Eleven

CARO surveyed the dining room like a seasoned general, which spoke more to her determination than experience. Unfortunately, she had no idea how to seduce a man, but it couldn't be that difficult, could it? Richborough *had* to have been some sort of horrid abberation, mustn't he?

She really didn't want an answer to that question. She didn't even want to think about that question. She just wanted to prove to herself and to, as long as she was being honest, the whole of London, that she was desirable, even on the most base of levels.

That's where men dwelt as a matter of preference, wasn't it, on the most base of levels?

Another question she didn't want an answer to.

Caro considerd possible targets, mentally classifying the occupants of the room as either friend or foe. Ashdon was sulking, frowning down into his cards: foe. Anne was right behind her, breathing warnings and pleadings into her ear: in this instance, foe. Her mother was talking softly to Lord Staverton, her hand on his arm in gentle comfort: most definitely foe. Lord Dutton, having ceased his snoring, was leaning against the drapes and studying her with an interested gleam: a possible friend. More than friend? Dutton was a very attractive man, though rather a wastrel. At least he was a solvent wastrel. Such could not be said of the insolvent Ashdon.

Her gaze went back to Ashdon, for what reason she could not imagine since he had already been itemized. The cards were being shuffled, and Ashdon was straightening his waistcoat over what appeared, based on her very casual observation, to be an extremely taut belly. The churning in her own belly to that most casual and disinterested of observations clearly placed him, unreservedly, in the foe-to-the-death classification. She need waste no more time on Lord Ashdon. She would ignore him like the insect he was and make her move on some other gentleman currently taking up space in the Dalby town house. She would never waste another thought for the indolent and insulting Lord Ashdon.

Caro walked straight over to where Lord Ashdon sat, indolently, and stood behind his chair.

Lord Ashdon ignored her.

"How much have you lost?" she said to the top of his head. His hair was very glossy and very thick, which was only proper as he was a complete wolf.

"Not as much as you're about to lose," he said lazily.

"I have no idea what you're talking about."

"Would you like me to explain it to you?" he said, looking askance at her in sullen and sulky boredom.

"What? And break up the game?" Viscount Tannington said. Caro had never much liked Lord Tannington; he was entirely too savage looking, added to which he displayed the most obvious manner with her mother.

"It's broken," the Duke of Calbourne said, standing up and discreetly stretching. The Duke of Calbourne was endlessly and reliably discreet, at least according to gossip. Actually, Calbourne might make a lovely candidate for her favor, and with the way he was looking at her, she could confidently place him in the "friend" category. "I'm out as well. Switch to piquet, if you've a mind. I'm off for home."

"Cannot I not tempt you to stay, your grace?" she said before caution could hobble her. In for a penny, in for a pound, and with nowhere to stay as of noon, she was most definitely in for a pound.

Calbourne, his hazel eyes smiling, said softly, "Lady Caroline, I believe you could tempt me to anything."

She was quite beyond proud that she did not blush at these words, particularly since they were practically the first words Calbourne had ever said to her. There was definitely something to this courtesan business, something she enjoyed quite a lot.

"You make me feel quite decadent, your grace," she said with a coy dip of her head.

"One of the duke's most well-versed skills, Lady Caroline," Ashdon said, rising to his feet, nearly knocking over the small chair he had been using, "that of enticing to decadence. You'd do well to be on guard against his particular brand of enticement."

"I've never been enticed before, Lord Ashdon," she said, looking at the Duke of Calbourne with a soft smile. "Not to decadence, nor even to folly. Tell me, *is* there a particular brand of enticement, your grace, and are you practicing it on me?"

"I am merely responding to the temptation of you, Lady Caroline," Calbourne said. "If it leads to decadence or folly or even damnation, I find I cannot stop myself. Your eyes beguile me."

Beguiled. How far was it from beguiled to besotted? And could she get there by noon?

"Go home to your son, Calbourne," Ashdon growled. "The night is done. There is nothing for you here, I promise you."

The Duke of Calbourne smiled, bowed to her, kissed her hand, and made his way over to her mother to make his departure of the hostess, all before Caro could say a word past the rage in her throat at Ashdon's high-handedness.

"'Nothing for you here,' was that insult directed at me, Lord Ashdon?" she said finally, almost sputtering.

Ashdon took her by the elbow and led her to one of the rear windows in the dining room. The predawn sky was pale black and empty of stars, the last moments of night empty of sound. Her heart pounded loudly against her lungs, filling the universe with its beat. All because of the heated look in Lord Ashdon's intense blue eyes and the feel of his hand hard on her arm. It was with extreme disgust that Caro realized that if anyone could lead her into folly, it was Ashdon. He apparently could do it by merely touching her arm above the glove.

She wanted to strike him, a lovely, vicious blow right in the eye. The only thing that held her back was the look in Ashdon's eyes that proclaimed that he'd like to do the same to her. Beastly man.

"You really are nothing like your mother," he said.

He could not possibly have hit upon a more violent insult. Her entire dilemma was that she was nothing like her mother in appeal and too much like her mother in Society.

"And you really are speaking out of turn," she countered, pulling her arm free of his grasp. "You are not well acquainted with my mother and you know me not at all. By every action you declare yourself an impulsive and explosive man of questionable character. That you are of limited means only adds to your list of flaws."

Ashdon took a step nearer to her, his shoes slipping under the hem of her gown. It was most improper. She couldn't make herself move to thwart him. Hideous beast of a man.

"And you are ill-mannered and of marginal intelligence," he snarled softly, looking at the occupants of the dining room over the top of her head. How unspeakably rude, not to even give her the consideration of his gaze, but what could one expect of a wolfish beast?

"Again, Lord Ashdon," she snipped, "I repeat, casting serious doubt upon your own intelligence, that you do not know me at all and can know nothing of my intelligence. As to my manner, how to answer but that it seems particularly appropriate when directed at you?"

"Hardly the manner of an eager courtesan."

"Perfectly the manner when the courtesan has no eagerness, no, nor desire, to spend one minute more in your questionable company."

"No desire?" he murmured, still watching the room. "Must you force me to add deceit to your list of character traits? Is not being ill-mannered enough for you, Lady Caroline? Must you reach ever higher, or would that be ever lower?"

"Standing this close to you must certainly rank as being ever lower," she said, fighting for a full, deep, purging breath. There was something about this odious man that robbed her of every thought beyond punishing him. What she was punishing him for she did not dare scrutinize, her own superior intelligence notwithstanding.

"Come, come, Lady Caroline," he mocked, finally looking directly into her eyes, "a courtesan must in all ways be pleasing. You are off to a troubled start. Dare I say, I think you would have found the role of wife more in line with your abilities."

"My abilities? But that is exactly the point, Lord Ashdon," she said, matching his stare and forcing herself to keep breathing. "I found I possessed no talent at all for being a wife if you were to be the husband."

❧

"ARE you certain that the marriage contract between them has been broken? They are behaving rather oddly for a couple with no history between them," Lord Dutton said softly. "I would swear under oath that he is snarling at her exactly like a husband."

Anne moved a step away from the whispering Lord Dutton. Lord Dutton followed her. Though she avoided gazing directly at his face, she could *feel* his grin.

"We thought you were sleeping, Lord Dutton," Anne murmured, trying to catch Sophia's eye, but Sophia was busily engaged with Lord Staverton. She really ought to rethink her decision not to marry Lord Staverton. There were worse things than being a viscountess, much worse. "Your snores were so very convincing."

"Thank you," he said, bowing crisply, still grinning that ridiculous grin. He was a devilishly good-looking man with blue eyes that were so direct and so inherently good-natured that one sometimes forgot that he was a complete rogue. He would hardly have frequented Lady Dalby's salon otherwise. "I perfected the technique while still in the nursery. It allowed me to hear so very many interesting discussions between my nurse and the second-best footman."

"I'm sure," Anne said, refusing to return his smile, though she was tempted.

That was the trouble with Lord Dutton—he was a temptation. What was worse was that he was well aware of it.

What was the absolute worst of all was that she was almost certain that he knew what a temptation he was to her. His blue-eyed gaze and disarming grin were a good part of the reason why she had refused even the prospect of an offer from Lord Staverton.

She was a complete and utter fool.

"Why didn't she accept his offer?" he said.

"This is none of our concern, Lord Dutton," she said crisply, moving away from him. He moved with her. She should have been more upset about it; as it was, she was just slightly charmed by it. Just slightly, as if degrees in foolishness had any meaning.

"Which is why it is so intriguing," he said, his breath fanning the hair at her nape. "If it were my concern I'm quite certain I'd find it unrelentingly boring. Other people's trials are so much more interesting, are they not, Mrs. Warren? For instance, I found the revelation that your mother had been a courtesan to be absolutely riveting. I'd love to hear the full story."

"With illustrations, no doubt," she said, seriously moving off now. He seriously followed her. In this instance, she was not charmed by it. Of all the things she most ardently did not wish to discuss it was her past, and her past most decidedly included her mother's occupation.

"Oh, pantomime would suffice for me. No need to get out the pencils and parchment."

"I think I preferred you snoring, Lord Dutton."

"Do you know, my nurse once told me the very same thing," he said, and then he did the most appalling thing. Lord Dutton took her by the arm and made to guide her to the dining room doorway that led to the private white salon. And what was worse, she did nothing to stop him. "I simply must convince you that I have other skills besides snoring, and then you must in turn convince me that you have other skills besides a keen friendship with Lady Caroline. Fair?"

They were in the white salon, the door closed behind them with a definite click, his back leaning against the door and his smile, as ever, in place. Fair? There was nothing fair about it.

❧

"I don't think I've been given a fair run at this, Sophia," Lord Staverton said as he and Sophia sat across the table from each other, pretending to play a quiet game of vingt-un. "Mrs. Warren would be far better off as my wife than as companion to your daughter."

"You don't have to convince me, Stavey," Sophia said. "I put forth your case with as much enthusiasm as was seemly. For the moment," she said, watching as Lord Dutton practically shoved Anne through the doorway into the white salon, equally noting Anne's lack of resistance, "I believe her interest is engaged elsewhere. If you can be a bit patient, I believe she will consider your suit again."

"Patience at my age is a high-stakes gamble, Sophia, as you well know. I could topple into my tea tomorrow."

"Then you certainly don't need a wife tonight," she said, smiling.

"On the contrary," he said with an annoyed sniff. "It makes the urge for a wife all the more urgent. One must jump whilst he still has the legs for it."

"You are a randy goat, Stavey. 'Tis no wonder Anne is skittish around you."

"If I am a randy goat it's because whenever Anne is around, you are there as well. It's possible I could be persuaded to forget Anne if you would let me just once come into your bed."

"A lovely effort, but Anne is the woman who makes your eyes dance," Sophia said, grinning, "and you were randy long before I came on the scene. As much as I would wish, I cannot take the credit for what nature has endowed. As to taking to your bed, why tarnish a lovely, lasting friendship with the coils of the flesh? I treasure you too much, Stavey. You are quite my oldest and dearest friend in London."

Staverton actually blushed and cast his gaze down at his cards, sniffing loudly.

"I always secretly presumed that Fredericks was your oldest friend. He has been at your side from the start, hasn't he?" Staverton said.

"From the start? Most definitely," she said softly, "yet Freddy is more family than friend."

"You could cause a riot saying things like that, Sophia," Staverton blustered, regaining his composure. "Declaring one's butler is like family, it's not done."

"I do so many things that aren't done, Stavey. What's one more?" she said.

"You jest, as usual," he said, "but we both know that you have family and that, with the right approach, they would likely take you in and forgive all."

"How charming you are, darling Stavey," she said softly, "but not only do I not require forgiveness, I have not at all decided if I shall ever forgive them."

Staverton shook his head slowly and fingered the cards on the table, not looking at her. "It was all long ago, Sophia."

"That all depends upon how one measures time, Stavey," she said, smiling gently as she changed the subject. "Will you wait for Anne to realize what a fine man you are and what a stellar husband you'd be to her? Will you wait just a little while, and take care in the waiting that you do not topple into your tea?"

Lord Staverton coughed and said, "I'll drink nothing but brandy for the next fortnight."

Sophia grinned and toasted him with her wineglass. "To the next fortnight, and an unstinting supply of brandy. We shall make you a husband yet, Stavey, never fear."

❧

"But I am not going to be a husband, and most particularly not your husband, am I, Lady Caroline?" Ashdon said in a soft growl. "Rumor has it that you have chosen a different course for yourself entirely."

"By rumor I suppose you mean my mother," Caro snapped, determined to open the space between them and unable to. Ashdon had her backed up against the window ledge. It was either face him down or go tumbling out of the window. She almost preferred tumbling to staring into his relentless blue eyes.

"Does it matter?" he said, running his hand down her gloved arm in a manner that could have been a caress if it hadn't been so rough. The man was intemperate in all things, obviously. "A woman in your position, with your ambitions, certainly could only benefit by some careful advertising."

"I'm afraid you've misunderstood the entire thing, Lord Ashdon, and you've certainly misunderstood me."

"Have I?" he breathed. He smelled of clean wool, fresh linen, and brandy. The scent of him was an unwelcome assault upon her senses. Far better for her if he smelled of sweat and dirty feet. "Explain it to me, will you? I want to get the details exactly right when I mention your name at White's."

"I would prefer it if you did not bandy my name about in the clubs of St. James Street," she hissed softly, looking over her shoulder at her mother.

Sophia was engaged in conversation with Lord Staverton. They'd been talking for close to an hour now; what could they possibly have to discuss? Not Anne, certainly. That subject had been closed. Would that she could close the current subject with Lord Ashdon. There was something decidedly coarse about discussing her future plans as a courtesan with the man who might have been her husband.

"I suppose then that you'd not be pleased if wagers were placed as to how soon and with whom you tumble into your chosen . . . well, what to call it?" He frowned and looked up at the ceiling. She tried to pull her arm free while he was distracted. He didn't release her a fraction. Obviously, he was difficult to distract.

"You needn't call it anything," she said, still pulling against his grasp. "And there will certainly be no wagers placed with my name attached to them."

"On the contrary, Lady Caroline," he said, pulling her toward him fractionally, his eyes boring into hers with all the finesse of a hot poker. "I intend to place the first wager myself."

"You have ill luck at wagering, Lord Ashdon. I would

refrain, were I you," she snapped, yanking her arm free, no matter how rude she appeared. Maintaining appearances was beyond her when dealing with the profligate Lord Ashdon.

"Not this wager," he murmured intently. "I intend to wager that Lady Caroline will become the *fille de joie* of Lord Ashdon by noon this day. It's a good wager, Lady Caroline. I'd be more than happy to place a bet on your behalf."

It was then that she slapped him.

        ❦

"WELL, that was worth waiting for," Lady Louisa Kirkland, the unmarried and slightly scandalous daughter of the Marquis of Melverley, said from her perch on a small carved chair. Lady Louisa didn't particularly care for gambling or for Lady Dalby or for Lady Caroline, but she did care particularly for Lord Dutton. Lord Dutton was a frequent guest at Lady Dalby's, and so Louisa developed a taste for Lady Dalby's particular brand of amusements.

Her father was not pleased with her tastes. Her father could go to the devil.

"Let's call it a matter of opinion, shall we?" remarked Lord Henry Blakesley, fourth son of the Duke of Hyde. Blakesley was lounged in apparent discomfort, his long legs stretched out before him, his fragile chair tipped back to rest against the dining room wall. His longish blond hair was tangled and his blue eyes were rimmed red. As ever, his expression was one of boredom and cynicism. Louisa enjoyed his company thoroughly.

"Don't tell me you saw that coming?"

"A pigeon on the spires of Westminster saw it coming three hours ago," he said, closing his eyes and leaning his head against the wall.

Blakesley was a lean, muscular sort and, conversely, it was never so apparent as when he was completely relaxed. Not that she had ever seen him completely relaxed. Lord Henry Blakesley was a bit like a faulty gun in that one never quite knew when he would go off. Nor, it seems, did he.

Consequently, being around him was a bit like frolicking with a venomous and irritated snake.

Her father absolutely distrusted Lord Henry. She liked that about him as well.

"What do you think he said to make her slap him?" Louisa asked softly.

"A guess?" Lord Henry lazily replied, his eyes still closed. "He told her what everyone has been saying about her all night."

"That she'd refused him to be a courtesan? Why slap him for telling the truth?"

Lord Henry cocked an eye open to look at her. "You like the truth paraded out directly in front of you, do you? I shall have to remember that."

Louisa shifted her weight, straightened her skirts, cleared her throat, and fussed with her fan. Lord Henry had closed his eyes again, ignoring her. He really did do too much of that of late. He was entirely too easy in her company. It simply wouldn't do for Lord Henry to be easy in her company, not to the point of snoring, which he was close to approaching now.

"Well, we've seen the explosion," she said. "I suppose we might as well leave now."

"Oh, I wouldn't leave now, not without being asked," he said softly.

"Why not?"

"Because, my dear, that slap, if I don't miss my guess, is going to bring Ashdon to life in a way you have not yet seen."

"Really?" Louisa said, leaning forward avidly.

"Besides, I can't imagine that you want to leave Dutton and Mrs. Warren alone in the white salon without knowing what they're engaged in. Misses the point, doesn't it? Why else do you hunt him throughout London if not to encourage him to catch you?"

Lord Henry Blakesley could be rather insulting and entirely too direct. She did not particularly like that about him, but as he made a very willing and very commendable escort, she held her tongue on the matter. But she did *not* like it.

❧

"I don't particularly like being forced into a room, Lord Dutton," Anne said firmly.

"I'm so sorry, Mrs. Warren. I had no intention of forcing you. I merely wanted to be alone with you and assumed you wanted the same."

"You have no basis for such an assumption."

Lord Dutton smiled and cocked his head, looking at her skeptically. "I stand corrected. The last thing I want to do with you, at this particular moment, is to argue with you."

"At this particular moment?"

"Or at any moment."

Calm reason itself, on its face, but she didn't trust him. She wasn't even going to bother feeling guilty about it. Some instincts were just too urgent to be ignored.

"Now, what were we discussing, besides your abduction into the famed white salon of the famed Lady Dalby? Oh yes, we were discussing you, Mrs. Warren, and your mother."

"I was discussing no such thing," she said, walking to the doorway that led into the entrance hall.

"I don't mind, you know," he said softly, and the words stopped her cold. "It doesn't bother me that your mother was a courtesan, just as it doesn't bother me that Lady Dalby started life on that foot."

"No one starts life on that foot, Lord Dutton," Anne said, turning to face him.

"Of course not. Excuse my poor choice of words," he said, bowing crisply.

He looked very contrite and very sweet and, of course, very handsome. She found that the voice of instinct became an annoying whisper when faced with the sweet expression in the Marquis of Dutton's vivid blue eyes.

"I ask your pardon, Lord Dutton," she said with a curtsey. "It is late and I am of an uncertain temper."

"I must disagree, Mrs. Warren," he said softly, "for I have found your temper to be ever certain, ever agreeable. In point of fact, you prove the exception to the tale that women with flaming ginger hair must in fact also be of flaming temper."

Just as she was opening her mouth to thank him in some socially respectable way, some way that preserved the emotional distance they must maintain between them, he added, "Unless your passionate temper is revealed at other, more intimate moments? Shall we put it to the test, Mrs. Warren? Shall we test the veracity of your glorious red hair?"

In just a few steps, he was upon her. In those few moments, she thought nothing, she only felt the rising of her heart into her throat and the trembling of her hands. He was a smooth predator, like a mongoose, silkily silent, swift, remorseless.

The Marquis of Dutton laid his large hand upon the side of her throat, pressed his long legs against her fragile skirts, and kissed her. Softly, relentlessly, and thoroughly.

It was everything she had ever hoped for. It was nothing at all that she wanted.

She waited in her response, waited long enough for him to know that she was unmoved and unmoving, and when she was certain he knew that, when his kiss stumbled, she pushed against his very fine ruby damask waistcoat until she broke the kiss.

She broke the kiss. Let him remember that, if he remembered her at all.

"That will quite enough, Lord Dutton," she said crisply. "Have I passed the test or failed? In all, I find I do not much care."

Anne had the singular pleasure of knowing that she had rendered the charming and affable Lord Dutton speechless, at least for the moment. On that happy thought, she left the white salon and made her way up the stairs to bed.

∽

IF she could have found herself in bed, with the covers pulled up over her head for good measure, Caro would have been far happier than she found herself now, facing the very frightening aspect of Lord Ashdon's intense regard. It was not that he looked ready to bellow, or break the porcelain, or throw his fist against a wall. No, it was that he looked completely and chillingly civil. If one discounted the quiet and icy rage in his riveting blue eyes, that is.

She was rather too close to him to discount it.

Their breaths, rapidly expelled, mingled.

Their clothes were entangled.

Their gazes were locked.

And as she watched, a rosy red imprint, just the exact shape and size of her hand, appeared on his left cheek. She had marked him. She was not exactly displeased that she had because, in point of fact, Lord Ashdon seemed determined to be unmarked by her. And that, of course, was flatly unacceptable.

She didn't know quite how she'd come to this pass. She was a logical, practical sort of girl and she lived her life by solidly practical rules and expectations. The trouble was that Lord Ashdon brought out none of those qualities. Lord Ashdon, who hadn't wanted her but merely his debts settled, who hadn't had the courtesy to conduct a proper courtship no matter the reality of his debts, who looked at her as though she had insulted him beyond measure for choosing a courtesan's life over a life with him, brought out the very worst tendencies in her. Tendencies of a violent and, she suspected, passionate nature.

She might, in fact, be more her mother's daughter than she had at first assumed.

"Not a good beginning to our bargaining, Caro," Ashdon breathed, shocking her anew by using the intimacy of her given name. "How shall you negotiate a high price when you go about assaulting the man who would pay for you?"

Lord, but she hated him.

"You have no money, Lord Ashdon," she said coldly. "You cannot afford me."

"What is your price?" he countered. "See if I can meet it."

"You cannot."

"Try me."

Caro cast a quick glance about the room. Her mother was coming over, no doubt as a result of that slap; the guests were leaving; dawn was pushing against the night sky. She had only seconds to answer Ashdon.

Things were moving too quickly. She was not entirely certain anymore that she wanted to be a courtesan. It seemed a vastly complicated business all of a sudden and she was less than certain she would be successful at it. But Lord Ashdon was staring down at her, his blue eyes just as piercing and challenging as they had been when first she met him, and her mother was going to cast her out of the house in just a few hours unless she did something to prevent it . . . and there was something decidedly delicious about sparring with the devilish Lord Ashdon.

"I believe pearl earrings would suit me very well, Lord Ashdon," she said softly.

"And what would I get in return for a pair of fine pearl earrings?" he whispered.

"Come by at eleven o'clock and I shall tell you."

Lady Dalby, still looking fresh and perfectly composed as the dawn broke the sky into yellow shards of light, said, "Caroline, I am quite dismayed by your behavior. Must I apologize for her again, Lord Ashdon? I am quite prepared to do so."

Lord Ashdon bowed serenely and said, "Completely unnecessary, Lady Dalby. Lady Caroline and I have worked things out nicely."

With just a few more words of parting, he was gone. And Caro was left to face her mother.

Twelve

"WORKED things out nicely?" Sophia said once they were alone and in her bedroom. The servants were cleaning up, the grate was being brushed, the silver polished, the crystal washed, and the tables cleared. Anne was in her bed, asleep. Fredericks was supervising the servants. In short, there was no one and nothing to divert her mother's attention, to Caro's great misfortune. "Does that mean you have chosen him, the man you refused as husband, to be your first . . . well, to be your first?"

Oh, my. To be her first. She hadn't quite thought that far ahead.

"I'm . . . not quite certain," Caro said as her mother stretched out her long legs atop the elegantly proportioned recamier positioned by the front bedroom windows. Not that anyone interesting would be out at this hour, but her mother liked to keep an eye on things.

"You'd best become certain, Caro," Sophia said calmly.

"I know, Mother. I know. Everything is just so confused. I don't quite know how I got to this moment."

"You decided not to marry and to become a courtesan," Sophia said softly and not unkindly.

"Yes, I remember deciding that. It seemed so sensible a decision at the time."

"You mean in the safety of your home, surrounded by your loved ones?"

Caro looked at her mother and felt her eyes fill with tears. "Yes. Exactly."

"Darling?" Sophia said. "Tell me honestly, do you like Lord Ashdon?"

"Like him?" Caro said, her tears drying instantly. "I think he's a horrible man. He's intemperate and without manners and . . . just . . . horrible."

"Yes, I quite agree with you, but that doesn't quite answer, does it? Do you like him? Or let me ask instead, do you want him?"

It was miserable, what her mother was asking of her, to look inside her tumbled heart and try to see what lay hidden in its depths. She was seventeen, too young to be looking into something as darkly treacherous and unpredictable as a human heart.

But as she was looking, the face of Lord Ashdon, that handsome, sardonic, impossible face, looked back at her. Her heart turned on itself and she caught her breath.

"I do," she said before she had quite got her breath back. "It's shameful. He's not the proper sort of man at all. But I do."

Sophia smiled and said, "I have yet to meet a man who is the proper sort, darling. I think that man must be the invention of poets and playwrights."

Yes, trust her mother to talk of poets and playwrights when her life was tumbled into the gutter. She had no husband, and no prospect of one, and the very man who had been purchased for her was now on an errand set to purchase her for himself and his debauched tendencies. Her heart did the impossible and dropped into her hips.

"Caro? Are you listening?"

"Oh, yes, Mother," she said. She had not been listening. She had been listening to her heart, treacherous thing.

"Will you follow my instruction? Do everything exactly as I say?" Sophia asked.

Do everything her mother said? This was some parental trick, a lesson in obedience. What did Ashdon have to do with obeying her mother?

"I . . . I don't see how you can help, Mother. Things have proceeded too far, too much has been said."

"And let us not forget that slap," Sophia said languidly.

Oh, Lord.

But he had earned that slap. Why did she want him, anyway?

To make him suffer? That was a good answer, and at least it had the benefit of being founded in pride. Better pride than wretched longing for a man who couldn't say a civil word to her if ten thousand pounds depended on it.

"I don't think it very wise of me to want him," Caro gritted out as she paced the room.

"Wanting is seldom wise, but that doesn't mean it has to be wrong," Sophia said.

"That doesn't make any sense, Mother."

"Doesn't it?" Sophia said with a gentle smile. "You slapped him, insulted him, and rejected him. Is he coming back?"

Caro stopped pacing and stared at her mother. "He said he would."

"And is he bringing gifts? Something rare and costly?" Sophia asked, still smiling.

Caro found that she was smiling as well. "A pair of pearl earrings. I don't see how he can get them."

"But he will try, won't he? You're certain of that."

That was the strange part; she was certain. She was almost certain that Lord Ashdon would stop just short of murder to present her with a pair of pearl earrings.

"I am," Caro said in wonder. "I am certain of that."

"As am I."

"But why, Mother? I mostly hate him and he just might have cause to hate me in return. Why would he beggar himself to bring me a gift?"

Sophia stretched her arms over her head in a sinuous stretch. "Because he wants you, Caro, even if it is not very wise of him to do so. Now, will you do as I say, no arguments?"

"Why?"

"So that you may have what you want, darling; Lord Ashdon for a husband."

❧

ANNE awoke at ten and knew whom she would marry. She had taken Lord Dutton's measure, put him up against what she knew of Lord Staverton, and made her decision. It was obvious, really. She was appalled that she'd been blind to it for so long.

Lord Dutton was a rogue.

There, she'd admitted it. She felt immeasurably better.

She was no schoolgirl, far from it. She did not have Caroline's excuse of innocent trust coupled with a strong habit of invulnerability. No, she had seen the world, too much of the world, at an uncomfortably close proximity. She understood men and she understood what they usually wanted; more, she understood their methods for achieving what they wanted.

Lord Dutton had treated her like very pretty wallpaper, seen once, admired, and then ignored. Until he had heard her confess to Caroline about her mother. Then, he had been all interest, all attention, all charm. So it always was at the start. It was at the finish that a woman had to be sharp and vigilant. Her mother had never learned that, but Anne had.

Anne was not her mother.

Anne, if she tried very, very diligently, might model herself after Sophia.

Sophia would not allow Lord Dutton to distract her. Sophia would see the future, and the future was Lord Staverton and a life as a viscountess. That was a future worth aiming for. Lord Dutton offered nothing, nothing beyond a smile and a torrid kiss.

It *had* been a torrid kiss.

As long as she was being honest, she should admit, at least to herself, that her husband had not been very accomplished as a kisser. He had had other qualities to be sure, but kissing had not been one of them. That was it exactly. He had not been a quality kisser.

She was *not* going to plan her future on the basis of a torrid and quite effective kiss.

She was not even going to speculate as to what kind of kisser Lord Staverton was going to prove. A woman could live without kisses, but what she could not live without was a solid roof over her head and a table full of food. Her mother had never learned that, either.

A scratch at the door that connected Caro's room to hers interrupted her thoughts, and then Caro's dark head poked around the corner.

"Oh, good. You're awake. I have so much to tell you."

"Yes," Anne said, checking the mantel clock as she sat up fully in bed, "and you had best hurry since it's just a bit more than an hour before you find yourself thrown upon the streets."

"Oh, that," Caro said, coming over to sit upon the foot of the bed. "My mother and I have come to terms. I am not to be thrown out. I am to marry instead."

"I'm much relieved to hear it," Anne said, though she felt a bit guilty for thinking of her own marital dilemma while Caro had faced being cast from her home. She was a selfish, self-serving woman and she must think more of others. And now that she had the problem of the tempting Lord Dutton settled, she would. "Are you to marry anyone I know?"

"Of course you know him," Caro said. "I will marry Lord Ashdon. Who else?"

"Who else? Why, I would have thought *anyone* else. You refused him."

"I changed my mind," Caro said brightly.

"Why did you change your mind?"

"Well, as to that, I'm not quite certain," Caro said, her smile faltering. "It might have been the cut of his blue waist-coat, or the way his hair sort of tumbles about his eyes. He has rather nice eyes, don't you think?"

"They're blue, aren't they?"

"Definitely blue," Caro said, staring up at the ceiling with a vacuous look on her face. "The most incredible shade of blue that I ever saw."

Men with blue eyes ought to be outlawed. What color were Lord Staverton's eyes? She was ashamed to admit that she had no idea; she tried very hard not to look at his wobbly eyes.

"I thought you told me that he had put you off blue eyes forever," Anne said.

"Oh, Anne, try to keep up. That was *yesterday*," Caro said artlessly.

Oh, Lord, Caro was going to marry a man she despised because she was taken by a pair of lovely blue eyes. Anne, unfortunately, knew exactly how that felt, only she was too experienced to fall completely. No, she had the wits and determination to pull herself out of the trap a pair of beguiling blue eyes could set.

"Caro, what has changed between yesterday and today?" Anne said.

"Well, for one, I slapped Lord Ashdon."

"You what?"

"I slapped him," Caro said somewhat proudly. "And he well deserved it, too."

"Then why do you want to marry him?"

"Because," Caro said, grinning, "he wants me now. *Desperately.*"

"Because you slapped him?"

"I don't know if it was *because* I slapped him, but it certainly didn't hurt," Caro said, still grinning like a besotted fool.

Besotted . . .

"Oh, Caro," Anne said, "do you think you're besotted by him?"

Never mind outlawing blue-eyed men; they ought to be hanged like thieves for stealing a woman's future with a mere look.

"Anne, you're missing the point entirely. I'm quite certain, in fact I shall know in less than an hour, that *he* is besotted with *me*. Isn't it delicious?"

"Do you know, you sounded exactly like your mother just then," Anne said, getting out of bed and pulling a shawl around her shoulders.

"Did I really?" Caro said, springing up behind her and practically dancing over to the window. There was nothing to see out the window but the mews behind the house. By the expression on Caro's face, one would think she was surveying the splendor of Versailles. "How perfect."

"Why shall you know in less than an hour?" Anne asked, ringing for the maid to brush out her hair.

"Because," Caro said, still staring out the window, "I told

him that he must bring me a pair of pearl earrings if he wants . . . you know."

"You know . . . what?"

"Oh, *Anne*!" Caro said, turning to face Anne, her dark eyes lit like lanterns. "If he wants *me*. What else?"

Anne sighed. What else, indeed?

❧

ASHDON made his way from Westlin's town house on Upper Grosvenor Street to Dalby's house on Upper Brook Street by way of Grosvenor Square. He had hoped to avoid curious glances and malicious speculation that way; it proved a futile hope.

"Going back for more?" the Marquis of Dutton asked him after a quick bow of greeting.

Dutton was a bit younger, having come up to Eton as he and Calbourne were leaving it, their paths crossing but lightly in that final year. Ashdon did not know Lord Dutton beyond the gaming tables at White's or the dining tables of the ton. All to say, he had no reason or desire to talk with Lord Dutton about the events of last evening, no matter that Dutton had been a witness to it all.

The Marquis of Dutton appeared to be the sort of man who was insensitive to any desires but his own.

"I am out taking the air," Ashdon said. "Nothing more, Dutton."

Dutton fell into step beside him, without invitation.

"The air is so much more delightful on Upper Brook Street, is it not? I find myself drawn there. I should say you feel the same tug."

"You may say whatever you like, unfortunately," Ashdon said stiffly.

"Come, come," Dutton said. "We are men of a certain sophistication. Let us speak plainly."

"I was under the impression that I was speaking plainly, but let me be more so. I do not desire a companion, Lord Dutton."

"I could argue that," Dutton murmured.

"You seem determined to argue, no matter the subject."

"Do I? Perhaps it is merely that you are of an uncertain temper after last night's events."

"My temper is completely certain."

"Then perhaps it is I who suffer. Shall we put it to the test? Gentleman Jackson's?"

"Splendid. Two o'clock."

"Because you are presently engaged?" Dutton pressed.

Ashdon said nothing. He was enjoying the early spring air and the anticipation of smashing his fist into Dutton's rather pretty face at Gentleman Jackson's boxing establishment. He'd been on edge since Westlin's instruction that he ruin Caroline Trevelyan. A man didn't go around ruining girls lightly, no matter who her mother happened to be. And, her slap notwithstanding, he rather liked Lady Caroline. In fact, he suspected he liked her rather more because of that slap. There was something very appealing about a woman who could take care of herself.

"Did anyone ever tell you that you veer toward the dour?" Dutton said, cutting into his thoughts.

"It's been mentioned," Ashdon said. Considering that Westlin was his father, he didn't think it too unreasonable that he occasionally veered toward the dour. Given how his mother had spent the final years of her life, he thought the whole topic rather obvious. "Why are you pestering me, Dutton? We are not friends, and I don't know you well enough to call you an enemy. Unless you were hoping to change that?"

"Don't be absurd," Dutton said. "I don't pester my enemies."

"You are close to making a lie of that statement," Ashdon said with a half smile. Really, it was becoming absolutely necessary that he bury his fist in something. "Until two?"

"And until then you will be at Lady Dalby's, visiting her rambunctious daughter?"

"Lady Dalby's daughter does not concern you, nor does my schedule," Ashdon said, clutching his walking stick.

"And that answers all, doesn't it?" Dutton said, smiling slowly. "But if you see the lovely Mrs. Warren, please give her my regards. I will drop in on her later today."

"Best make it before two. You will hardly be in any condition to visit her after."

"Confident," Dutton proclaimed as they parted ways on the corner of Upper Brook Street and Park Street.

"Very," Ashdon said under his breath, leaving Dutton behind him.

It was just eleven when he knocked at Lady Dalby's door. Fredericks answered promptly, took his walking stick and hat, and announced him at the door to the yellow salon. The room was a study in elegant restraint. The walls were painted the color of the sun, the silk drapes and silk upholstery the exact same hue of vibrant yellow. Upon the mantel was a collection of Sevres porcelain in dark blue with a gold design. Lady Dalby wore white. She glistened like a teardrop in the sun.

"You are prompt," she said with a smile.

"And you are waiting," he replied. "What does it signify, Lady Dalby?"

"It signifies, Lord Ashdon, that much has changed since yesterday."

Sophia invited him to sit. Ashdon moved a shield-back chair from against the wall to sit near her as she perched on the sofa.

"You were expecting my daughter, I believe," she said. "My daughter is no longer available to you, Lord Ashdon."

"Excuse me, Lady Dalby, but I thought we had reached an agreement. Your daughter proclaimed an interest in becoming a courtesan. Was not my assignment to turn her from that course?"

"Lord Ashdon, do not mistake me for a fool," Sophia said softly, her manner as formal as a queen's. "Did you think I would not see what all saw last night? You are as debauched as the rumors of you indicate. That you want my daughter, that you want to lead her in the paths of debauchery, is without question. One has only to see you with her to know how tempted she is by you."

"Again, our agreement is plainly seen, Lady Dalby," Ashdon protested, ignoring the surge he felt to hear that Caroline was affected by him. "How else to teach her that the way of the courtesan is not to be *her* path unless I show her the dark side of such arrangements?"

"My lord," she said, "I am no fool. I have walked those dark paths. I know raw desire when it sits itself down in my salon."

"And you have labeled me such?"

"For myself? No. But for Caroline, I am very much afraid so, Lord Ashdon."

"I am much maligned, Lady Dalby."

"Are you?" she said with a smile. "And what do you have in your pocket, Lord Ashdon? Not a fine pair of pearl earrings?"

Obviously, Caroline Trevelyan had the discretion of a parrot. He did not answer Lady Dalby's question; whatever else he did, he would not be damned for a liar.

"Your silence speaks most clearly, Lord Ashdon," Sophia said. "I would offer you refreshment, but I think it would be wiser if you did not stay. I do not wish to appear rude, but I must protect my daughter. I'm certain you understand."

He most certainly did. He was being denied access to Caroline. How on earth was he going to satisfy his father's wish that he ruin the girl if he could not get near her?

❧

"This can't be right," Caro said from behind the closed doors of the white salon. "How can he be ruined by love if he can't get near me?"

Fredericks, his ear to the closed door that led to the hall, said quietly, "Trust your mother. She's a skilled woman, very wise in the way of things. All right, out you go now." And he cracked open the door and shoved her through it, straight into the hall so that she almost bumped into Lord Ashdon.

Ashdon looked exceptionally well, a bit flustered, but her mother could do that to most anyone. Caro gave Ashdon her best seductive expression and tried to remember what her mother had said for her to do. Oh, it seemed such a bother. Why could she just not marry the man? He'd been paid for, hadn't he?

"Oh, Lord Ashdon," she said in a rushed whisper. "Things have gotten in a twist, haven't they? Are you very put out?

Have you given up entirely? Say you have not. Say you still . . . oh, I am ashamed to say it." She had thrown in that last part. She supposed that her mother needn't know *everything*.

"What would you have of me, Lady Caroline?" he said. He seemed quite flustered and angry; it was quite delightful. "I am on the list of forbidden items, particularly where you are concerned. I am no longer welcome here."

"And I am forbidden to you, Lord Ashdon," she said. "I suppose that is the end of it."

"I suppose it is," he said, staring down at her. He had the most mournful blue eyes, soulful and seductive. How many women had he ruined with those eyes? Though, of course, it was not with his eyes that a man ruined a girl of good family. "It is for the best, I'll wager."

"Yes, you and your wagering. Such a reliable measure of everything," she said crisply. "I am so sorry to have wasted your morning, Lord Ashdon."

"Your anger would be better served directed at yourself, Lady Caroline. I am not the one who revealed all to her mother. A little discretion, particularly in a courtesan, would be well advised in future."

"Oh, *thank you*, Lord Ashdon," she snapped. "How kind of you to teach me the details of debauchery. Do you know, I think I shall thank my mother. I had almost forgotten how ill-tempered you are and how poorly we get on."

Ashdon took a step nearer, looming over her in a most predatory and masculine way. Her heart tripped and she held her breath involuntarily.

"I am only ill-tempered around you, Caro, and that is because I am ever thwarted."

"A fine excuse, to blame me for your bad temper. And stop using my given name. You are too intimate."

"No, Caro, that is the problem. Not intimate enough. Not nearly," he whispered before taking her chin in his gloved hand and kissing her softly, despite the harsh words they had shared.

A coil of longing wound down into her heart and twisted itself around her spine. She leaned into him, into the warmth and length of him, letting thought fall from her as his mouth caressed hers, moist and compelling. He was such a hard man, hard and sullen and angry, and his kiss was so soft and pleading, so gentle and coaxing. It was nothing at all as she had expected and she was quite undone by it. She placed her hands on his chest, a gentle touch to find him, to keep him under her hand in some small way, and was rewarded by the feeling of his quickened breath and thundering heart. He was not unmoved by her. There was something, some longing, some tenderness, somewhere.

She heard Fredericks moving behind the door to the white salon and, understanding coming slowly and dimly, pushed against Ashdon's fine coat and firm chest until the kiss was broken. As his lips left hers, he whispered, "Not enough."

And she lost all direction, all counsel, and threw herself against him, winding her arms around his neck to pull him down to her mouth. Not enough. Yes, he had said it. It was not nearly enough.

The second kiss took her beyond thought, beyond London, beyond reason. She was caught in passion and she wanted to stay caught. Freedom from this would be punishment.

It was Ashdon who unwound her arms from around his neck, who disengaged her body from his, who pulled his mouth from hers. And it was Ashdon who looked down at her with his soulful blue eyes and said, "I must have you, Caro. Tell me what I must do."

The wrong thing . . . he had said exactly the wrong thing.

The mist of passion fell from her like rain. She inhaled sharply, trying to find a breath in her that was not tinged with longing. She blinked, trying to remember what she was to say. Ashdon looked down at her, his hair tousled and glossy, his eyes riveting, his body . . . well, his body told the tale most well. The evidence of his passion was as clear as the spires of Westminster.

"I believe," she said, shocked to hear the cracked passion in her voice. She cleared her throat and tried again. "I believe I said a pair of pearl earrings would be most appreciated."

Something shuttered in Ashdon's eyes, but he nodded and pulled from his coat pocket a pair of exquisite pearl earrings. They were clearly of the finest quality, quite large and lustrous and of an impressive size.

"You are too thoughtful," she said, holding out her hand for the pearls. He dropped them into her hand as though they would burn him. "They are lovely. Thank you, Lord Ashdon."

"What next, Lady Caroline?" he said curtly. "I am barred from the house, and you, you are not to leave it, are you? How will you pursue your path if you cannot leave your family home?"

"I am young, Lord Ashdon," she said past the fist-sized lump in her throat, "but I am not a fool. Without the necessary funds, I cannot move out. Without the—"

"Necessary men," he interrupted in a hoarse voice, "you cannot acquire the necessary funds. I quite understand."

"I suspected you would," she said softly, staring at his mouth, feeling her heart race.

"What is it you require of me, Caro?" he said.

"A necklace to match the pearls," she said. "It would look most fine, do you not agree?"

"And what would I get for a string of pearls? A simple kiss seems hardly sufficient for so great a gift."

"Bring me the necklace and find out," she said, looking into his eyes.

"Not enough, Lady Caroline," he said. "I require something a bit more definite."

"More than a kiss," she promised.

"How much more?" he murmured, his eyes raking her.

Caroline licked her lips and said, "How many pearls in the strand? I will not cheat you, Lord Ashdon."

"Lady, that you will not," he growled, turning abruptly and walking out. The door slammed behind him, the house trembling in response.

Fredericks opened the door to the white salon and Sophia opened the door to the yellow salon. They stood looking at her expectantly as she stood in quivering isolation in the foyer.

Caroline nodded and fought to right her breathing before she spoke. "It went as you said, down to the last."

Sophia smiled and said, "Freddy, arrange for coffee, will you? We must plan the next assault."

⨳

HE'D been assaulted. There was no other word for it. Assaulted by her beauty, by her bold schemes, and by her mouth. God, that mouth. Ashdon was a half mile down Park Lane before he got hold of himself, and his passion, and his anger. As to that, he could not fix upon which was greater, his passion or his anger. He did not suppose it mattered which, as long as he could find a nice, long string of pearls and choke Caroline Trevelyan with them.

Returning home to face his father was out of the question in his present state. Given his state of mind, there was one place perfectly suited to his temper: Gentleman Jackson's. Pummeling something was the only solution to the problem of Caroline and even at that, he suspected it was but a temporary fix.

Thirteen

THE Marquis of Ruan stood in the corner of Gentleman Jackson's boxing establishment, his face more in shadow than in light, and watched with increasing interest the behavior of Lord Ashdon. Naturally, he had heard the rumors, he and everyone else in London. The difference was that he had heard them from the Earl of Westlin, Lord Ashdon's father, in a darkened corner at White's. It was not that he and Westlin were friends; he supposed that Westlin did not have many friends, his character and general temper being what it was, not that Ruan held that against Westlin since he was a man not given to idle and superficial friendships either. He liked his own company perfectly well and found that he did not tire of it, as he did with so many others. Solitude was a pleasure when one liked the company.

What had prompted Westlin to establish a confidence between them he could only guess at, and his first guess landed him, poetically, at the feet of Sophia, Countess of Dalby. He was one of the many who did not know her but knew of her. It had been twenty years or more since she had toppled London on its back, again, poetically, and still the town could not get enough of her. Truth or fiction, it did not seem to matter. She was one of those few who excited comment and speculation by merely passing through a room. Westlin was a prime example; from what Ruan had deduced, Westlin had not been in the same room with Lady Dalby for years, and yet he was still frothing over her.

He'd like to meet the woman who could do that to a man.

And from what Westlin had told him, it looked as though

the daughter possessed the same skill. One had only to study Lord Ashdon to see the proof of that. By all accounts, and Ruan was nothing if not thorough, Ashdon had been a completely normal man, given to normal impulses and giving into them in normal fashion, until he'd met Caroline Trevelyan.

He'd like to meet her, as well.

Watching Ashdon cheerfully pummeling the breadbasket of one of the club's sparring partners was a lesson in the violent emotions provoked by either Sophia or Caroline. Or perhaps both. He really must find a way to meet the ladies so as to make his own judgment. Westlin seemed highly suspect as a witness as his language was particularly volatile and vengeful.

Frustrated lust could do that to a man.

Still, lust notwithstanding, he and Westlin had come to terms, albeit strange ones. Westlin would sell him a piece of particularly nice land that Ruan's father had tried unsuccessfully to negotiate for for a full thirty years, if Ruan would keep him apprised of Ashdon's progress with Sophia's daughter. It seemed a simple enough arrangement, and certainly he was getting the most out of it. He had nothing to do but attend his regular functions and visit his normal haunts, but with a keener eye for what Lord Ashdon was about.

Westlin had explained it succinctly; Westlin could hardly keep tabs on Ashdon himself since it would be patently obvious to Ashdon that he was being watched and judged. Westlin could hardly buy surveillance on his son in his amorous pursuits as any man who could be bought to watch would hardly be welcomed into Gentleman Jackson's for a bit of sparing or Angelo's for a bit a fencing or White's for a bit of gambling. All in all, it was light duty to fulfill his father's dream.

What had surprised him, being as familiar with the rumors of Sophia and the Earl of Dalby and the Earl of Westlin as anyone else in London, was that Westlin seemed to want his son to succeed with Dalby's daughter.

But so few things were as they seemed and Ruan knew that better than anyone.

Ashdon landed a particularly solid blow and his sparring partner went down onto the mat. Whatever else could be said of Ashdon, he looked a man able to handle himself efficiently in a fistfight, though that skill would hardly help him in his tussles with Lady Caroline.

The Marquis of Dutton approached the ring and called to Lord Ashdon, "You anticipated our appointment by more than an hour, Lord Ashdon. Who am I to pummel now? You can hardly be at your best."

"I'll wager that less than my best will be good enough for you, Lord Dutton," Ashdon called back, brushing his dark hair out of his eyes with gloved hands and grinning like a fool to see Dutton climb into the ring to face him. "Five pounds says you are down in five minutes."

"You have a reputation for poor wagering, Ashdon," Dutton said, grinning in return. "Can you afford another loss added to your account?"

"Only if I double my bet," Ashdon said with a hoarse chuckle. "Ten pounds. Five minutes. Agreed?"

"Agreed," Dutton said cheerfully.

Ashdon landed the first blow, a solid hit to Dutton's well-sculpted jaw. Ashdon seemed to take particular satisfaction in it. What had occurred between these two? Was Dutton after the hand of Lady Caroline? He'd heard nothing of it.

"I suppose he's getting his back, after last night," Lord Henry Blakesley said pleasantly.

Ruan turned slightly, nodded a greeting, and asked, "Ashdon?"

"You haven't heard?" Blakesley said, his voice clipped with amused cynicism. "Lady Caroline, Lady Dalby's daughter, slapped him across the face last night in her mother's dining room."

Lord Ruan considered that for a moment and then said, "She must have been provoked."

Blakesley nodded and said, "I suppose it depends on whom you ask. The story as it is being reported is that Lady Caroline took it into her head to become a ladybird. Hard to see what could be said to her that would cause offense after that, if you take my meaning. I happen to have been present during the assault, mild as it was, and from what I could gather it looked as though Ashdon offered to be her protector and she refused him. Rigorously. You hadn't heard?"

No, he hadn't heard.

One could almost feel some sympathy for Ashdon.

⁂

"I don't feel a bit sorry for him," Caro said to Anne as they sat to tea in the white salon. "I practically threw myself at him so that all he had to do was *catch* me, and he fumbled even that."

"He didn't catch you?"

"Not in the way that he should have done," Caro said snippily.

Anne nodded and kept stirring her tea. She had spent most of the day in her room, contemplating the realities of either accepting or denying Lord Staverton's suit, if he made a suit, if she hadn't fumbled her own chance and not put out her hands to catch the willing Lord Staverton. If he was still willing.

Oh, this was a coil that had done nothing but give her a pounding head. She heard Caro talking, heard her words, but couldn't quite attend to exactly what it was she was saying. Something about Lord Ashdon, certainly. Ever since Caro met Lord Ashdon, her thoughts had been consumed by him. It was never to the good when a man consumed a girl that way.

What had consumed Anne's thoughts was how she would spend her future. And, to be fair, how Caro would spend *her* future. It was perfectly clear to her that both she and Caro would be best served in very reliable, very serviceable marriages. That was utterly in the realm of possibility and she intended to make every effort to achieve the possible, and she was going to make equal effort to see that Caro did the same.

A future as a courtesan was simply no future at all.

"What does your mother say?" Anne asked, courtesans and being consumed still invading her thoughts.

"Oh, she's as pleased as a cat," Caro said. "She feels the

whole thing is going beautifully, and I have to admit that she foresaw Ashdon's reaction down to the last snarl."

"But you are not to be a courtesan, are you, Caro? You are serious about marrying Lord Ashdon. Marrying anyone would be better than being a courtesan."

Anne had obviously revealed more than she intended because Caro's dark eyes filled with compassion. "This is about your mother, isn't it? How could I not have guessed that small truth when since our first day together we clacked along like two old draught horses that have walked the same field season upon season? Our mothers, our histories, are so alike."

"Alike?" Anne interrupted sharply. "They could not be less alike, Caro."

"I'm sorry, Anne. I didn't mean to upset you," Caro said, leaning forward to take her hand. Anne's hands were as cold as January, again revealing far more than she'd intended. "I can't help but think we are alike. Are we not?"

"Caro," Anne said softly, "your mother is unique, and because of her, your life has been equally unique, at least for the daughter of a courtesan."

Anne could see the questions in Caro's eyes, but Caro held her voice and silenced her questions. If Anne were going to tell this tale, and it looked as though she must, she would need to find her way carefully, cautiously, because it wound through a dark and tangled wood in her memory. She did not tread there willingly, but out of friendship. If Caro still had any lingering and clearly romanticized thoughts of pursuing a courtesan's path, she wanted to pull those thoughts from her, and if she had to revisit her childhood to do so, she would.

Anne stood up and walked to one of the front windows in the white salon, letting her gaze drift over the street, seeing nothing but her memories.

"My mother," Anne began, "ran off to be married, but she did not marry and that circumstance was both the beginning and the ending of all her plans. She could not go home. She could not make him marry her. She could not undo her ruination. All that was left for her to do was to find a way to survive. She found a way, perhaps the only way," Anne said softly.

"She sounds very brave," Caro said gently.

"Brave? I think she was desperate," Anne said. "She had one asset to her credit and that asset was beauty. Beauty alone is not enough, Caro. A woman cannot survive long on beauty; for one, beauty does not last, and for another, beauty wears thin without other qualities to magnify it. My mother had only beauty."

"Do you look like her?"

"Yes," Anne answered, turning to look at Caro in her sumptuous home wearing her fine clothes. "I have always thought so, but then, I do not know my father."

"Oh, Anne," Caro said softly. "Was he not the man your mother intended to marry?"

Anne turned back to the window. "No, Caro. I came along much later than that. My mother passed through many men's hands. Some of her liaisons lasted for as long as a year, but not often. She tumbled her way from man to man and as her beauty faded, so did the men. She rarely attracted men of title. She never could hold men of great wealth. She drifted, and I was forced to drift with her."

"Which is why you won't drift now," Caro said.

Anne turned again to face Caro, her dark eyes almost smiling, her expression compassionate. "Exactly. It does no good for a woman to rely on beauty, because beauty is fleeting. It is better for a woman to rely on intelligence and planning, as your mother does."

"You are saying that it was not for her beauty that men became besotted."

"I am saying that and more. Your mother is no longer a courtesan, Caro. She left that life as soon as she could. To walk into it would be the rashest folly. Promise me you will never make that choice."

"An easy promise to make," Caro said, standing and walking toward the window. "I have other plans now."

"Plans that include Lord Ashdon?"

"Precisely. You should have stayed last night instead of retreating to your room before the party was fully dead,

Speaking of that, what did you and Lord Dutton discuss last night? I never saw you after the two of you wandered into this very room."

"Never mind Lord Dutton. What happened after I left?"

She was *not* going to discuss Lord Dutton and what had happened in the white salon; if she thought about Lord Dutton and his wicked blue eyes too much she'd come too close to throwing all her fine advice about the perils of a courtesan's life right out this very window. Lord Dutton had that unfortunate effect on her.

"After I slapped Lord Ashdon, I had the most amazing epiphany, Anne. I don't want to be a courtesan anymore. All I want is to be Lord Ashdon's wife."

"I'm delighted, obviously. But, why the change of heart? Why marriage to the very man who was purchased for your use?"

"He was, wasn't he? I don't mind the sound of that as much as I did before," Caro said with a smile that was entirely wicked. "I wonder if I shall find cause to slap him once we're married. I do hope so."

❧

"SHE *slapped* him?" Westlin roared, his fair complexion going quickly ruddy.

The Marquis of Ruan nodded and took another mouthful of whiskey. It was never too early in the day to drink when one was keeping company with the Earl of Westlin. Westlin was the most predictably ill-tempered man he'd ever met.

"The girl wants to be a cyprian, and that ill-favored son of mine manages to provoke her to violence?"

"That's what they're saying," Ruan said evenly. "If it helps, according to Blakesley, Lady Caroline didn't look too terribly unhappy, even if she did slap him. I gather the general impression was that they were engaging in some sort of primitive foreplay."

"Primitive," Westlin grumbled, fumbling to light his pipe. "That fits."

"I thought you should know," Ruan said. "Just how far is this arrangement to go, Lord Westlin? I can't be skulking about after your son for the rest of the year. I have my own appointments to keep, after all."

"It won't take the rest of the year," Westlin said, scowling down at his pipe.

"Hardly comforting," Ruan said with a wry smile. "I'd like to set a time limit on this agreement of ours."

"I'm sure you would," Westlin said, looking up at him, his blue eyes cold under his bristling brows. Westlin's hair still carried the echo of his ginger-haired youth, but gray had softened the heat of his coloring. It was too bad the same couldn't have been said about his temper. Age hadn't done a thing for him there. "Give it until the end of the Season. I won't hold you to any longer than that. The property will be yours the first of July. Are we agreed?"

Three months spent trailing after Ashdon, who would in all likelihood be trailing after Lady Caroline, who would predictably be trailing after her mother, Lady Dalby. . . . Come to think of it, it wasn't a bad way to spend a few months. Finding out more about the famous Sophia, arranging an introduction, perhaps getting to know her intimately, well, the more he considered it, the more spending the next few months learning the shape of Ashdon's backside as he camped on the Dalby doorstep seemed like a fascinating way to spend the Season in Town.

"We're agreed," Ruan said, and he took a deep swallow of whiskey to seal the bargain.

❧

ASHDON and Dutton sat in companionable silence as they drank their whiskeys down in the pleasant and familiar atmosphere of White's. Dutton had taken a solid pummeling, delivered a respectable return, and had done so with good cheer. It was enough to be said of any man, and Ashdon, taking a careful breath against the bruise on his ribs, was considering Dutton in a more favorable light. A good fight could do that for a man.

Could the same be said of women? Caroline had certainly changed after slapping him, not that he wanted to invite that sort of behavior in a woman, no matter the result.

But, as hard as he looked at the thing, he couldn't ignore the fact that once the slap had been administered, she'd changed, gone a bit soft on him, if he could judge. And he could judge. He'd been judging females for more than a few years now, and he judged with some degree of confidence that, with the right handling, he could have Caro . . . for the price of a strand of pearls.

It was that last bit that galled.

She still wanted to be a courtesan, though the logic of that choice defied him. Then again, women weren't famous for being logical. She likely had some romanticized view of the whole thing, fed by her mother, and thought she could have the best of all worlds by being free to choose a man, or not, instead of being properly under the guidance and control of a man.

He was supposed to have been that man. He was supposed to have wooed her, won her, and discarded her, all for the public eye. All to the amusement of the ton, but most especially for the amusement of Westlin. It was to have been a morality play, acted out with the express purpose of punishing Sophia for her gall in publicly, and to the ton's vast amusement, discarding Westlin for Dalby twenty years ago.

Nothing, not from the very start, had gone as his father had planned. It was with some familial disloyalty that Ashdon could admit that nothing Westlin did with, for, and to Sophia seemed to go as planned. He had always blamed Sophia for that, as his father had done, but having met her, he was surprised to find that he could almost like her. And what he felt for Caroline went far beyond liking. Caroline Trevelyan, with her expressive and fiery eyes and flawless skin and delectable mouth, and, to be honest, her volatile temper, did something to him that he had not expected and did not welcome.

Ashdon had Westlin's plans before him and Caroline was to have been the means to a very deserving end. The trouble was that Caro was not going to sit quietly and be the means to anything. Caro was most definitely an end in and of herself. She would not be bound by expectation or necessity or any of the other things that bound women into society. Caro was a force, an erratic, tempestuous force.

Ashdon rather liked her for it.

"By the look on your face," Dutton drawled, "you're pondering the question of what to do with Lady Caroline."

Ashdon shifted in his chair and took another mouthful of whiskey. "I'm not accustomed to having my face read. Kindly desist."

Dutton grinned and shrugged lightly. "Your problem, if I may say so, is Lord Westlin. Left to your own path, you'd find yourself married to the girl and probably disgustingly content with the whole arrangement."

"Disgustingly content?"

"My dear Ashdon," Dutton said, lounging back in his upholstered chair, "women are to be enjoyed lightly, temperately, fleetingly. None of this hearts aflame nonsense."

"Hearts aflame?" Ashdon said, chuckling despite his best intentions. "Very poetical."

"Mock me, but you know I speak the truth. Given the slightest encouragement your heart would burst into fires of longing and devotion for Lady Caroline."

"Rubbish."

"As you wish," Dutton said calmly. "I propose an alliance, Ashdon. I find myself suddenly and unexpectedly interested in Mrs. Warren and I am quite certain that she is interested in me, though for entirely different reasons. I shall help you in your endeavors with Lady Caroline and you shall help me in my pursuit of Mrs. Warren. Agreed?"

"Interesting," Ashdon said, considering the Marquis of Dutton over the rim of his glass, "yet I can find no use for you, Dutton. My endeavor, as you put it, with Lady Caroline is going quite well. As to Mrs. Warren, I'm afraid that I don't know what you mean."

"You will not censure me for bluntness, Lord Ashdon?" Dutton said with a curt smile, waiting for Ashdon's nod that he continue. "I have recently discovered that Mrs. Warren is the daughter of a courtesan, which raises her immeasurably in my estimation. My interest in piqued. This lovely, self-possessed, modest woman; what has she seen? What does she know that other lovely, self-possessed, modest young women don't know? The possibilities delight me. I would know more."

"You could make things easier on yourself if you got yourself a courtesan of your own. Then all your questions would be satisfied."

"Yes, but how ordinary, Ashdon. How routine. I want to taste without paying. I want to experiment without cost. And I want to do it with Mrs. Warren."

"You expect me to procure her for you? I won't and I couldn't. You have an acquaintance with her. Make your own inroads."

"We are at a strange point, Ashdon," Dutton said over his drink. "The woman you want as a wife, wants to be a courtesan. The woman I want as a diversion, wants marriage. There must be some way we can help each other to the women we want, under the circumstances in which we want them."

Dutton, blast him, had a point, and he was quite right, it was a strange point.

"I don't trust you, Dutton," Ashdon said, studying the man across from him. Dutton was ruthless, that much was evident, but was he honorable? More, was he trustworthy?

"You think me ruthless," Lord Dutton said, his voice bland, almost bored. "I am. But I am not savage. Honor binds me as it does you. But in this battle between men and women, should not the men fight on the same side? I will not cross you. I have nothing to gain by it."

Possibly true, but a man's honor turned on the most fragile of points. Just look at Westlin for proof of that. His honor had been bruised by a courtesan's rejection, and twenty years later Ashdon was required to put honor to rights. Damned business, protecting one's honor.

"You know Lady Caroline as well as I," Ashdon said. "There is nothing you can do to aid me in . . . acquiring her."

"Acquisitions require blunt," Dutton said softly. "Do you have the means that Lady Caroline demands?"

That damned pearl necklace. Hell, no, he didn't have the

means. Ashdon stared at Dutton, not answering. Dutton spoke for him.

"What does she want?"

Ashdon swallowed and stared into his drink. He had nothing to lose and perhaps a pearl necklace to gain. He had to fulfill the terms of his father's honor. He had to meet Caroline's price if he wanted to see her again. He most certainly did want to see her again. As to Mrs. Warren, her reputation was safe, or as safe as it could be while living in Lady Dalby's house. As to that, had not Mrs. Warren made her own bed? He was not responsible to her, or for her. All his duty was to Westlin. And to taking Caro in his arms and under his mouth again. That was one duty he would fulfill gladly.

"A pearl necklace," Ashdon said, letting the die be cast. He would not rise or fall on Dutton's efforts, but a little help couldn't hurt.

Dutton nodded and took a deep breath. "She'd know a fake, certainly. With Sophia to guide her, they must be genuine."

It was with some pride that Ashdon realized he'd never even considered foisting fake pearls upon Caroline's delicate and deceitful throat. Was this not all of honor, after all?

"Certainly," Ashdon replied crisply.

"I want to help you, Ashdon, but I'm deuced if I can think where we can lay our hands upon a strand of pearls."

Ashdon knew the feeling. Pearls did not miraculously appear. His mother had had a lovely strand, but he was fairly certain Westlin had sold them years ago. Not only that, but from the look in Caro's dark eyes, he'd been certain she had a rather long strand of pearls in mind. Not that what she had in mind made a whit of difference to him; his only thought was to present her with the pearls, kiss every inch of her naked body, and leave her flat, her reputation in tatters around her ankles. Honor would have been served . . . and she'd be richer a strand of pearls.

Honor was a damned nuisance.

"You know," Dutton said slowly, staring at the candle on the table, his blue eyes illuminated like some devil dancing at Hell's gate, "I think I know how I can arrange for you to present Caro—"

"Her name is Lady Caroline, Dutton," Ashdon interrupted irritably. She was due the honor of her title, after all, no matter how her mother had acquired it. Damned insolence on Dutton's part and completely like him.

"Of course," Dutton said with a half grin, "but as I was saying, I think I know how we can find you a string of pearls for Lady Caroline's pretty neck."

Dutton paused, as if expecting an argument. Ashdon held his peace. Caro's neck was, in all truth, very pretty.

"I know someone who has a rather nice pearl necklace. If I can get the necklace for you to give to Lady Caroline, then I shall require from you a bit more than help in softening Mrs. Warren to my suit."

"I'm not going to abduct her for you," Ashdon said, "if that's what you're thinking."

"Don't be ridiculous, Ashdon," Dutton said. "I'm not as bad as all that. But it will be something more than a few kind words about me whispered into her pretty little ear."

"What, exactly?"

"I'm not exactly certain yet, but I am certain that you have need of a pearl necklace," Dutton said. "Are we agreed?"

He was making a deal with the devil, he was certain of that, but when honor and desire clashed within a man, what else was there but to make bargains with whomever would serve? Ashdon was wagering on his ability to get what he wanted while giving everyone else, his father included, what he wanted. All evidence to the contrary, Ashdon was a far better gambler than anyone gave him credit for.

"Agreed," he said, downing the rest of his whiskey in a swallow.

∞

"You agreed to do as I said," Sophia said to Caroline.

"I know I did, but we both know Lord Ashdon can't afford a single pearl, let alone a string of them. I shall never see him again," Caroline said. "It's simple logic, Mother. We have set a price and he cannot pay it."

"You sell him short, I think," Sophia said from her chair in the yellow salon.

"I'm simply being realistic."

"Ah, yes, your famous realism. It was that realism, that logic, that landed you here, wasn't it?"

There was nothing polite to say to that, so Caro said nothing. Sophia didn't seem to notice.

"If you had simply taken the husband I had bought for you, all of this could have been avoided."

"If you'll excuse me," Anne said, rising to her feet.

"No, Anne, stay," Sophia said, waving her back to her chair. "You don't need the level of instruction that Caro does—"

"Well, thank you, Mother," Caro said on a huff of indignation.

"But you could both do with a bit of sharpening," Sophia finished.

"I don't want to become sharp," Caro said. "It does not sound at all appealing."

"When dealing with men, it's best to be sharp," Sophia said. "And the fact that you have yet to realize that is precisely what I'm talking about. Now, both of you sit down and listen to me."

They sat, but Caro wasn't going to promise that she was going to listen.

Sophia held out her arm in an elegant arc and said, "You have noticed my sapphire ring before, haven't you?"

It was a difficult item not to notice as it was roughly the size of a pigeon's egg.

"Of course," Caro said.

"And just where do you think I got it?" Sophia asked.

"A gift from Father, I assumed."

"You assumed incorrectly," Sophia said. "I asked for it. To be precise, I made certain that the third Duke of Wilton understood that I would very much like a very large sapphire. The duke presented both himself and this ring within the week. I was given to understand that he sold his shares in a shipping company to provide me with this ring. I have never forgotten it or him, as was the point of the entire exercise, at least from his point of view."

"Mother! That's perfectly horrible!"

"Don't be ridiculous, Caro," Sophia said. "How else are you ever to get what you want unless you are willing to ask for it?"

"And," Anne said slowly, a light of understanding shining in her greenish eyes, "men accept the value you place upon yourself. It all starts with what you expect, doesn't it, Lady Dalby?"

"Precisely," Sophia said, smiling regally.

"But, Mother, I don't want to be a courtesan. I don't like this bargaining."

"I don't want you to be a courtesan either, darling, I never did, but I have come to believe that it would do you good to think like one."

"But to bargain as one?" Caro said. "It's horrible."

"Think of it as negotiating," Sophia said. "All interactions are negotiations in one form or another. You are simply negotiating for what you want. At this moment, you want Lord Ashdon."

"But shouldn't I already have Lord Ashdon?"

"Of course, but do you have him in the way that you want him?" Sophia said. "That makes all the difference, doesn't it?"

"It certainly does," Anne said firmly. "My mother was not as discerning nor as discriminating as yours, Caro. There is a difference, and the difference is felt completely by the woman."

"But what about the Duke of Wilton?" Caro said. "He sold his shares to buy jewelry for a woman. One can't help but feel sorry for him." It was fairly obvious to everyone in the room that she was not thinking of his grace, but no one was unkind enough to point out the obvious and embarrassing truth that she was feeling sorry for Ashdon.

"Caro, darling, if a man wants you, he's willing to do anything to have you. More than willing, he's eager to prove himself. Set him a task, an impossible task. When he meets it, he will love you for it because, in you, he has achieved more than he thought he could."

Silence blanketed the room in response to Sophia's words. Could it be so? If true, then Ashdon would want her more for having to struggle to attain her. He certainly had not wanted her when he had been bought for her. But to have to buy her for her to be valuable to him? That could not be right. That turned everything Caro knew of the world on its elbows.

"Lady Sophia?" Anne said, her greenish eyes gleaming. "I would like to change my mind about Lord Staverton, if it is not too late. If he is still interested, I would like very much to be his wife."

Caro turned in dumb amazement to look at Anne. What she saw on her face was pure resolve and something else entirely, something that looked almost like grim amusement.

"A very sharp decision," Sophia said with a nod and a wink. "I think your timing is perfect, Anne. Just perfect."

"Thank you, Lady Sophia," Anne said softly. "I only hope I can make him happy."

"Darling, he will be overjoyed. Any man would be to have you."

"Are you certain, Anne?" Caro asked.

Anne couldn't possibly want to marry Lord Staverton because she actually wanted him; it must be because Caro was getting married, she hoped, to Lord Ashdon. All this talk of marriage and how to manage men must have pushed her into a hasty decision. After all, Lord Staverton, however nice, was not a man to excite a woman's interest. That Caro was again thinking of Lord Ashdon when she was supposed to be thinking of Lord Staverton she ruthlessly ignored.

"Very certain, Caro," Anne said with a serene smile. "I cannot think of one reason why I should not welcome his suit, and I can think of many reasons why I would be a fool to reject him. It's not possible to be more certain than that."

"I should say not," Sophia said, leaning back against the silk embrace of the sofa.

"Mother," Caro said, "I think you have had very much to do with this decision of Anne's, and I don't think you are entirely free of bias. Lord Staverton is one of your oldest acquaintances, is he not? And you want him to have a wife, do you not? And Anne, because of being a companion to me, is not meeting the sort of men—"

"I am meeting exactly the sort of men who interest me," Anne said. "And being your companion is exactly why I am meeting them."

"Precisely," Sophia said. "Caro, you really must learn to look about you and see things for what they are. And speaking of meeting men, you two must leave this instant if Lord Ashdon is to have any hope of waylaying you."

"Pardon me?" Caro said, her mind still reeling with the combined assault of her mother and Anne.

Good, gentle Anne seemed to have grown a decidedly ruthless streak, doubtless as a result of spending time with Sophia and hearing her rather startling views about men. Caro was certain that her mother knew more than she did about practically everything and was equally certain that her mother didn't know what she was talking about.

It made for a rather exhausting day.

"Oh, Caro," Sophia said on an impatient sigh, "do try and keep up, will you? You have told Lord Ashdon, rightly, that he cannot see you until he produces a fine string of pearls. It will take him some time to find pearls. Most gentlemen, unless they have very generous mothers, cannot lay to hand fine jewelry of any sort. In short, Lord Ashdon is either going to be very busy trying to get his hands on a pearl necklace worthy of you, or he is rethinking the whole proposal. You, my darling, are going to remind him why finding pearls is necessary to his very life."

"To his very life? That's a bit dramatic, isn't it?" Caro said.

"It is, isn't it?" Sophia said, grinning. "Now, go and be dramatic, darling. Let Lord Ashdon find you. Encourage him in his hunger for you, a hunger which can only be fed by pearls."

"Come along, Caro," Anne said, rising to her feet. "Your mother is quite right. It is entirely the right move to remind Lord Ashdon of what he is missing."

Caro stood, but she had the distinct feeling that this time

it was Anne who, though she was talking about Lord Ashdon, was thinking of someone else entirely.

She really did need to learn how to keep up. Things, and people, were moving furiously.

Fourteen

It was exactly the wrong time of day for strolling about Hyde Park, but that is what Caro and Anne, with two footmen in attendance shadowing their steps, found themselves doing. They looked quite fine doing it. They were dressed beautifully and Caro's bonnet was particularly appealing, but they had no real destination and so their steps, as prettily as they were taken, faltered.

"I had no idea it was so difficult to walk when one has no destination in mind," Caro said softly to Anne. "I feel a bit like a bird on a string."

"We should have gone to Creed's for a bit of fragrance."

"Do you really think that Lord Ashdon is going to be loitering around a fragrance shop when he has pearls to buy?" Caro countered.

"Then we should go to a jeweler's."

"Too obvious," Caro whispered. "I don't think it works when the man *knows* you're checking up on him."

"I think you're right," Anne said softly. "Are you having fun?"

"Delicious fun," Caro whispered back, grinning like a girl. And it was fun, hunting the town for the man she had set her eye upon. Her mother might be a bit of a lunatic, but she certainly knew how to have a good time and how to instruct others to do the same. It was a lovely quality to have in a mother.

And then, just ahead, she could see the distinctive form of Lord Ashdon coming toward her driving a splendid gig, which he obviously could ill afford, the sun at his back and his brown curls lit to dark gold.

"There he is!" Caro whispered, linking her arm through Anne's as casually as possible. "Do you think he sees me . . . um, us?"

Anne laughed softly and said, "By the look on his face, I'm quite certain he does. 'Tis no wonder that man is an abysmal gambler, he wears every thought on his face."

"Ssshh!" Caro commanded as she checked her posture and lifted her bust to its best advantage.

"Nicely done, Caro," Anne whispered just before Lord Ashdon stopped his gig, descended, and made his bow.

"Lady Caroline, Mrs. Warren," Ashdon said, sending a tiny thrill into the pit of Caro's stomach at the mere sound of her name on his tongue. "You are not where I expected you."

"Lord Ashdon," they said in unison, and then Caro said, "You had expectations of me, Lord Ashdon? I had no idea."

Lord Ashdon stared at her, his expression solemn, his blue eyes shuttered. "You are wearing my pearls, Lady Caroline," he said simply, his voice a tune of longing.

"I am," she said softly in return, all thoughts of teasing him disappearing in the intensity of his gaze.

"They become you," he said.

"You are pleased. I am glad," she said.

Simple talk, nothing of wit or poetry, yet her heart drummed against her ribs and she felt herself falling into the blue enchantment of his eyes.

He smiled slowly and said, "I would see you draped in pearls, Lady Caroline, roped and tangled in pearls from your head to your knees."

Her heart stopped banging against her ribs to knock against her knees. Anne cleared her throat and moved off a few paces, the footmen following her beckoning gesture.

"Pearls," Ashdon continued. "My pearls wrapped around your naked body. Pearls sliding between your breasts, belted around your hips, cascading down the slope of your back."

"Lord Ashdon," she choked out, her heart hammering, "please. Stop."

"I have finally rendered you speechless?" Ashdon grinned gently and said softly, "I had not thought it possible, Caro, and all it took was a king's fortune in pearls."

"Pearls of the imagination," she said with a soft smile, teasing him.

"I have an active imagination, especially when I look at you."

"Yes, I should say so."

"Tell me, Caro, how long is your unbound hair? Will it cover the pearls of my imagination?"

"It covers my ears and would hide the pearls you gave me."

"But will it hide the pearls I will give you? Strand upon strand, reaching down to your—"

"Lord Ashdon!"

"Breasts?" he said, in spite of her warning. Anne was looking at a particularly ordinary patch of grass. The footmen were talking quietly between themselves and taking turns looking at the horizon.

"Lord Ashdon, *really*!" she said, crossing her arms over her breasts to smother their sudden tingling.

"I must know, Caro. I must know how long the strand must be. I would not have you wear pearls that are hidden in the dark masses of your curls."

"My hair is not curly," she said, instantly regretting how prim she sounded.

"Wavy, then? And to your . . . shoulders?"

"Is this any way to talk?"

Ashdon shrugged and grinned. "I'm having a good time. You?"

"I think you enjoy tormenting me."

"I think you're right," he said on a laugh. "Just answer my question. Let this one thing, the length of your hair, be something free of my imaginings. Please, Caro. Please."

His voice, so solemn, so sweet, so sensuous, ripped past all her moral training and the rules of etiquette to impale her on desire. The desire to please him. The desire to best him. The desire to drive him mad.

"Please?" she echoed. "I cannot refuse you when you are so polite, so earnest, Lord Ashdon." She leaned closer to him, caught the scent of him, felt her stomach drop another degree, and said as provocatively as she could, "My hair falls to my breasts, Lord Ashdon, where it curls most delicately. If you would give me pearls, which I surely hope you will, they must fall to here," and she drew a seductive line across the tips of her breasts with a fingertip.

She had the exquisite pleasure of hearing Lord Ashdon groan.

"Oh, look," Anne interrupted. "Is that not the Duke of Calbourne?"

It did look so, though why Calbourne should be walking about Hyde Park at this unfashionable time of day was beyond comprehension. Before she could gather her composure to greet the approaching Calbourne, Ashdon took her by the arm and said in an undertone, "And if I get you the pearls, what will you give me?"

"You will get to see me wear them."

"As I see you in my imagination?"

Naked? Hardly.

"As far as they fall, then yes," she said. He would never be able to afford a necklace of any length. Why, he would be doing well to afford her a pearl choker. She would be more than happy to show him her neck.

"As far as they fall," he murmured, his blue eyes gleaming like a cat's. "And will I get to touch you as far as they fall?"

A trickier proposition. She was not certain that she could trust Lord Ashdon to touch her neck without seducing her completely. In fact, she was completely certain that he would do just that, and that she would likely let him.

"Certainly," she said, putting her trust in Ashdon's poverty and abysmal skill at gambling.

"You are a sharp businesswoman, Lady Caroline," he said, stepping away from her and looking for all the world like a gentleman of the best of manners. Liar. "I shall endeavor to meet your price. Most heartily endeavor. How shall I find you?"

Oh, this was tricky. He must continue to think that her mother was against all contact, when of course the very reverse was true. Deceit was such a nuisance, requiring so much planning and remembering.

"Find Anne, Mrs. Warren, and she will find me," she said.

"Mrs. Warren? Yes, that will serve most well," he said. It sounded suspicious to her, but in what regard she could not determine.

"A fine gathering!" the Duke of Calbourne said as he joined them. "Is there an occasion or am I just lucky?"

"Just lucky," Ashdon said crisply.

"Lady Caroline," Calbourne said on a bow. "Mrs. Warren. A man is lucky to fall upon two such lovely companions in his wanderings."

"You wandered into Hyde Park?" Ashdon said. He was being somewhat rude and certainly abrupt. Caro could not think what was wrong with him, he'd been so pleasant just moments ago.

"Yes, I did," Calbourne said with a cheerful grin.

He was such a jovial man, was Calbourne. Caro had always liked that about him. Pity that Ashdon was so severe in his aspect, though, to be honest, she found Ashdon's severity rather beguiling. It made her want to make him laugh or make him angry or make him insane with desire, to just make him react, to break free of his solemn self-control in any way, for any cause. Well, no, truly, she wanted to be the cause. If she was going to lie to Ashdon, the least she must do was remain honest with herself.

"By way of White's?" Ashdon asked with a bit of a scowl. Really, this was rude even for Ashdon and completely out of bounds, to question a duke that way.

"Why, yes, actually I did stop in at White's for a bit. Seems I just missed you," Calbourne said, staring at Ashdon in a quite friendly manner considering the severity of Ashdon's tone. Sometimes, like now, Caro was not completely certain she wanted Ashdon for a husband; he could be quite grim when he felt like it, and he seemed to feel like it rather too often.

"Yes, it would seem," Ashdon said. "How fortunate that you found me."

"Yes, well," Caro said firmly, "you can have him, your

grace. Mrs. Warren and I simply must continue on or my mother will send the dogs out for us."

"You have dogs, Lady Caroline?" Ashdon said stiffly.

"Figure of speech, Lord Ashdon. Purely symbolic. No need to fear getting your fine breeches snagged on a dog's sharp tooth today."

"Looks to be your lucky day as well, Ashdon," Calbourne said softly, still grinning. "Lady Caroline, Mrs. Warren, good day to both."

"Oh, and Mrs. Warren?" Ashdon said. Anne turned to face him, her expression just shy of outright laughter. "Lord Dutton asked me to send his compliments. I believe he intends to call later today."

"Thank you, Lord Ashdon," Anne said. "You are most kind to relay a message that could surely have been brought to the house in the usual manner."

And with that, Anne walked on, forcing Caro to walk on with her, which is not to say she would have stayed. Lord Ashdon and his talk of pearls had played with her composure quite enough for one day. If he wanted to torment her further, he would just have to make an appointment.

It was with that thought that she put Lord Ashdon completely out of her thoughts for what had to have been a full two minutes.

∽

"You can't get her out of your thoughts, can you?" Calbourne said to Ashdon as they watched the women walk out of the park by way of Grosvenor Gate.

Ashdon thought about lying, but then decided that there was no point to it, not with Cal.

"No, I can't," he said. "Which works out very well, considering that it has become my duty to ruin her as thoroughly and quickly as possible."

"Westlin's idea?"

"Who else?"

"You are being unusually forthright, Ash. Things must be at a terrible state."

"I suppose that depends on how you define terrible," Ashdon said, staring after Caro until she was lost from view. "By Westlin's compass, I am right on target. By my own, well, I'm not certain that I have a compass where Caroline Trevelyan is concerned."

"You're in love with her." It was not a question.

"Don't be absurd; I hardly know her," Ashdon said sharply. "But I do know that she's not the person my father thinks her to be, certainly not the kind of girl one goes about ruining for sport."

"But this is about the mother, not the daughter, isn't it?"

Ashdon nodded. "As to that, Lady Dalby isn't quite what I expected either."

"I gather that is the usual impression of her," Cal said with a smile. "I've always found her to be both amusing and a bit frightening."

"Where her daughter is concerned, frightening."

"What are you going to do?"

"Ruin her," Ashdon said softly. "What else is there for me to do?"

"There are quicker ways to ruin a girl than a chance meeting in Hyde Park," Cal pointed out.

"Yes, there are," Ashdon agreed. "The wrinkle is that I must make her ruination to be completely of her own devising, a case of blood will tell, that sort of thing. My father is quite firm about it. This idea of hers to become a courtesan fits right in, naturally."

"Naturally," Calbourne said as they walked the horses through the park. The sun was low and the wind was picking up. Abysmal time of day to be strolling about, but when did women and logic ever pair up? "And the pearls? He's content to let you beggar the family to prove her bad blood?"

Ashdon looked at Calbourne askance. "You did hang about White's for a bit, didn't you? Run into Dutton at all?"

"Would you feel better if I said I beat it out of him?"

"Yes, actually, I would."

Calbourne grinned and said, "He told me about the pearls, but why didn't you come to me for them? You know I'd help you."

"Would you, Cal?" Ashdon said, stopping to stare at him. "Would you help me ruin a girl in the name of revenge?"

"It doesn't sit well, does it?" Cal said.

Ashdon shook his head and said crisply, "And I wouldn't have you share the experience. Stay clear, Cal. I'll work this out."

"With Dutton's help."

Ashdon shrugged. "If he can get me a strand of pearls, then yes."

"You don't worry about contaminating him?"

"Dutton? I don't think he can be contaminated. Besides, he has his own games to play with Anne Warren."

❧

"If he thinks he can play his silly games with *me*," Anne said in a furious undertone as they hurried toward home, "well, he is in for a jolt."

"Not Lord Ashdon," Caro said.

"Of course not. Lord Dutton," Anne snapped as they walked up the front steps.

"Lord Dutton? What sort of games is he playing with you?" Caro asked.

"The same sort of game that Lord Ashdon is playing with *you*," Anne said as the footman opened the door for them. "Only I am not a willing participant, and that makes all the difference."

"Oh," Caro said, completely lost.

She blamed Lord Ashdon. If she were not spending so much time thinking about him and about his wicked eyes and his devilish mouth and his lascivious imagination, she would have a thought to give to someone else. As things stood, she did not. Yet with the way he made her feel, she cared not. He was a wicked man to make her cast aside all thoughts of Anne and what she was going through with Lord Dutton, though what Anne could possibly be going through with Lord Dutton was a mystery.

Lord Dutton was no stranger to the Dalby town house, and he was certainly no stranger to Anne. Why, when Anne had first come to live with them, Caro had been almost certain that Dutton had entertained Anne's imagination quite a bit. But nothing had come of it and Anne had never said anything about an attraction to Lord Dutton, and that had been the end of something that had never really begun. All to the good, in her opinion, as Lord Dutton, for all his handsome looks and perhaps particularly because of them, was a bit of a scoundrel.

Caro was interrupted in her rambling musings by Fredericks, who said, "Lady Dalby would like you to join her for tea, Lady Caroline, Mrs. Warren."

"Wonderful," Caro said. "I'm chilled to the bone."

"She's not alone," Fredericks whispered as he opened the door to the yellow salon for them.

She most certainly was not. Lady Louisa Kirkland, her aunt and chaperone, Mary, Lady Jordan, and Lady Amelia Caversham, daughter of the Duke of Aldreth and Lady Louisa's cousin, all turned to look as Anne and Caro entered the room. It was quite close to being daunting.

Caro had never met Lady Amelia before, their social circles being wildly divergent, and she could not imagine what brought her here today. Or maybe she could imagine. London was a remarkably bad place to keep a secret. Suddenly, the pearl earrings dangling from her ears seemed to weigh a stone and she fought the urge to clap her hands over them in shame.

Sophia made the introductions, Anne and Caro sat upon the chairs that Fredericks provided for them, and there they sat, six women staring at each other in mute curiosity. Lady Amelia and Lady Louisa looked only slightly alike. They were both fair skinned, though Lady Louisa, with her curling red hair, was infinitely more so. Lady Amelia had lovely golden blond hair and sky blue eyes under dark blond brows. She was as beautiful as the rumors of her. Mary, Lady Jordan, sister to Louisa's deceased mother, who had wed the Marquis of Melverley, looked slightly foxed. There was nothing unusual in that, sad to say.

When the silence bordered on discomfort, Sophia, predictably, took charge.

"How fortunate, Caro, that you are wearing the pearl earrings from Lord Ashdon. Aren't they are as beautiful as I said they were, ladies?"

Caro, to her credit, lifted her chin and stared calmly at the ladies, who stared avidly back.

"We were, of course, talking of them, darling," Sophia said serenely, smiling approvingly at Caro. "It seems the whole town can talk of nothing else."

"How remarkable," Caro managed to say.

"Yes, but things are slow in Town now, the Season just barely begun," Sophia said. "What else to talk about but a broken engagement?"

Caro turned to stare at her mother, drinking in confidence from the amusement in her mother's black eyes.

"Is it true, oh, forgive me," Lady Amelia said haltingly, "I don't mean to imply otherwise, but it is just so remarkable that you refused Lord Ashdon's offer of marriage."

To the awkward silence *that* remark engendered, Lady Amelia stammered, "Oh, I'm so sorry! That did not come out right at all. What I mean to say is that, it is rather remarkable, isn't it? I mean, if Lord Ashdon had offered for me, I daresay I would have accepted him and gladly."

Caro decided in that instant that Lady Amelia Caversham was a complete hag and that if Ashdon ever looked at her, she'd flay them both.

"Don't be ridiculous, Lady Amelia," Sophia said soothingly. "Of course it's remarkable, I thought so myself, and I daresay that Lord Ashdon thought so most of all. He certainly had no anticipation that he was to be refused, but my daughter has her standards and Lord Ashdon, unfortunately, does not meet them."

Oh, well done, Mother!

"I believe we all have our standards, Lady Dalby," Lady Louisa said silkily. Lady Louisa, for all that her lineage was impeccable, was a bit of a tough. "It is just amazing to the point of being unbelievable that Lord Ashdon would fail to meet Lady Caroline's."

"Yes," Sophia said softly, her smile maternal, "we do have our various standards. Perhaps some could do with a bit of raising, but there you are."

Anne cleared her throat at that remark and looked down at her lap. Caro wasn't sure if Anne was trying not to laugh or not to vomit. It was into that congealed atmosphere that Fredericks opened the door and announced, "Lord Dutton is calling, Lady Dalby."

"Oh, how nice," Sophia said, taking in Lady Louisa's flushed cheeks. "Can he be convinced to wait? I am engaged at present."

"I believe he can wait, Lady Dalby, but he is calling upon Mrs. Warren," Fredericks said, staring at Anne.

The look that both Lady Louisa and Lady Amelia cast upon Anne was worth solid gold. Everyone and the chimney sweep knew that Louisa Kirkland was mad for Lord Dutton. It was equally well known that Lord Dutton was mad for his own amusement and little else. The daughter of a marquis hardly fit his bill of requirement.

All eyes in the room turned to Anne, who said casually, "Inform Lord Dutton that I am not at home, Fredericks."

"Yes, Mrs. Warren," Fredericks said with the trace of a smile as he backed out of the room.

It was absolutely delicious. Mrs. Warren, shunning Lord Dutton? How quickly would that bit of gossip travel through Town?

Louisa Kirkland looked ready to pop.

"More tea, Lady Louisa?" Sophia asked leaning forward. "You look as though you could use some refreshment."

"I'm fine," Louisa said crisply. "Thank you."

"I'm afraid we've kept you from an appointment, Mrs. Warren," Lady Amelia said, while casting nervous glances at her cousin.

"No, not at all," Anne said silkily. "Lord Dutton, if you'll excuse my saying so, can be a bit bold and rather a pest."

"A pest?" Lady Amelia squeaked.

"A charming pest," Anne said with a smile as she stirred her tea.

Really, Caro had never seen Anne behave so ruthlessly. It was completely delightful. After all, Amelia Caversham had never bothered to come to call before Lord Ashdon had made an appearance on her doorstep, and everyone knew that the only reason Louisa Kirkland suffered Sophia Dalby was for a chance at the Marquis of Dutton. It was all too, too obvious. It was only fair that an obvious revenge be enjoyed by the women of Upper Brook Street.

"I'm quite certain that Lord Dutton cannot enjoy being thought a pest," Lady Louisa said, her tone definitely clipped. "He clearly has no idea that his companionship is not welcome to you, Mrs. Warren."

"I find that difficult to fathom, Lady Louisa," Anne said softly as she stared Louisa Kirkland down, "as I have told him most directly that his attentions are not welcome, though I would certainly not imply that I have the right of refusal to the other women of this house. I speak only for myself."

"I find Lord Dutton a complete delight," Sophia said brightly. "Don't you, Lady Louisa?"

Louisa, caught out, said stiffly, "He seems a pleasant man."

"I've always enjoyed his company," Lady Amelia offered.

"His uncle was a macaroni," Mary, Lady Jordan, offered in a loose grumble. "Shares that trait with him, I do suspect."

Since everyone in the room had spoken to Lord Dutton's qualities, Caro felt the necessity of saying something of her own on the merits of the marquis.

"I always thought him a bit spoiled," she said, and when they all stared at her she added, "though it does not spoil his charm."

"Odd that you should mention being spoiled, Lady Caroline," Louisa said, sitting up as straight as her spine would stretch. "It was extremely generous of Lord Ashdon to give you those earrings, wasn't it? Especially as a marriage is not to take place. He *did* give them to you as an engagement gift, did he not?"

Caro answered as easily as if she had been telling the truth. The situation called for nothing less than hearty deceit.

"He did," she said.

"And he did not want them back when the arrangements were broken?" Louisa said.

"On the contrary," Caro said, making it up as she went, "he pressed these pearls into my hand and swore that, upon his very life, he would shower me with pearls until I changed my mind and accepted his offer. He was most ardent."

"And most convincing, I'll wager," Sophia said with a small smile.

Caro blushed uncontrollably, which she suspected added to the impression that Ashdon was wooing her enthusiastically. Would it were so. As the situation stood, he was merely bargaining for a mistress. What the dolt didn't seem to realize was that as a wife she would cost him far less than she was determined to extort as a courtesan.

That was the strategy as her mother had explained it, and it had made an odd sort of sense at the time, when she was not face-to-face with Ashdon, in point of fact. Facing him left her bereft of plans and of breath and left with nothing beyond an urgent desire to throw herself against his long, delectable body. Ardent, indeed. Ardent was the least of it.

"Upon his very life," Amelia whispered, her look gone dreamy.

"How dramatic," Louisa said cynically.

"Yes, wasn't it?" Caro said sweetly.

"By the sounds Lord Ashdon is making, I would wager that he and Lord Dutton are learning their lovemaking by the same book," Anne said.

Lady Louisa Kirkland dropped her spoon. It slipped onto her skirts and then tumbled to the floor where it gleamed like a weapon against the Turkey carpet, a traitor to her heart. It was in that moment that Caro felt complete sympathy for Louisa and forgave her all.

The same could not be said for Anne.

Fifteen

"Not at home?" Dutton said to Fredericks. "I bloody well know she *is* at home."

Fredericks, showing his American upbringing, shrugged. It was an entirely inappropriate response for a butler to make. Fredericks didn't appear to care.

"I'll wait," Dutton said stiffly.

He was not accustomed to being kept waiting. Nor was he in the habit of being refused an audience, and certainly not by the widowed daughter of a failed courtesan. Especially as he knew that Anne Warren had been doe-eyed around him for months. She wanted to see him; he *knew* that. This was some womanish punishment for kissing her, a kiss he knew she had enjoyed. He was not accustomed to having his kisses repudiated either. Anne Warren certainly had a lot to learn about how to treat a man, and he was becoming more and more determined to be the man to teach her.

"I'm afraid that's not possible, my lord," Fredericks said.

"Excuse me? Not possible?"

"That's right, my lord," Fredericks said in his particularly annoying American accent. One would think that after two decades in the country the man could learn to speak in a civilized fashion. "Perhaps another time."

He was being shown the door? Never, since he had come of age and become the darling of the ton, had Edward Preston, Marquis of Dutton, been shown anything less than enthusiastic hospitality. There was clearly some mistake afoot and he suspected it had Ashdon's name all over it.

He'd seen Ashdon and Calbourne in Hyde Park, seen them from a distance talking to Lady Caroline and Anne Warren, assumed that Ashdon was holding up his end of the bargain with Anne, and this was the result? Ashdon had mangled things badly, that was obvious. If this thing with Anne didn't sit up and bark, and quickly, Ashdon could forget getting the pearls he needed to coax Caroline Trevelyan into his bed.

How had such a simple exercise in seduction turned into such a tangle?

No woman could walk a straight line into a man's bed if her life depended upon it.

"Good day, my lord," Fredericks said, holding open the door. There was a footman on either side, flanking it. Fredericks, it seemed, was prepared for trouble. Ridiculous. Dutton had never in his life created a scene, and he wasn't going to create one over a very average, ginger-haired woman of uncertain reputation.

"I shall call at another, more convenient time," Dutton said as he walked out, his gold-handled stick clicking arrogantly on the floor.

"I'll tell Mrs. Warren to expect you, my lord," Fredericks said.

Damn if Dutton didn't hear a note of laughter in the man's voice. Impertinent, improbable American. Sophia ought to get herself a new butler.

❧

THE moment that Lady Dalby's butler closed the door after Lord Dutton, Louisa Kirkland made her excuses. The three women, with Lady Louisa in the lead, left the Dalby house as if they had wings. Whether they had found out what it was they had come to find was left to speculation. That they had found out more than they had intended was not.

Anne could have danced for joy. From the look on Caro's face, Caro was eager to dance right along with her.

"They'll be looking for Lord Dutton, of course," Sophia

said, looking out the front windows at the street. "If he's fortunate, they won't find him."

"Lord Dutton seems always to find fortune," Caro said.

"Yes," Anne said with a smile. "He does, doesn't he? One wonders how being denied what he wants will affect him."

Sophia burst out laughing and looking at Anne, said, "One wonders? Oh, come now, Anne. I don't believe any of us need wonder that. I'm quite certain, and so are you, that he is quite put out."

"One hopes," Anne said with a sly smile.

"What have we got against Lord Dutton all of a sudden?" Caro said.

"His good fortune, I should say," Sophia said, still gazing at Anne.

"And his never-ending expectation of it," Anne finished.

"Are you still interested in Lord Staverton?" Sophia asked, leaving the window to sit again on the sofa.

"Yes, more than ever," Anne said.

Sophia nodded. "You will not regret it. Now, off with both of you. We're to the Duke of Hyde's assemblie. Absolutely everyone will be there. Look your best. This will be a very interesting evening, I promise you."

The problem was, that sounded more like a prediction than a promise.

❧

"You'll be at Hyde's tonight, of course. It looks to be an interesting gathering," Sophia said to Lord Henry Blakesley in her white salon.

"Is that why you asked me to come? To make certain I would be at my father's entertainment tonight?"

It was just on seven and all the good little girls and boys were tucked safely away, preparing for another evening's round of fun. Sophia was not a good little girl, and she was wagering that Blakesley was not a good little boy. In fact, she was counting on it.

"I enjoy your company, Lord Henry. I would have more of it," she said, walking to the window and gazing out into the heavy twilight. It was a clear evening, the moon bright, a night for romance, if one believed that romance could be contained to a single kind of night. She knew otherwise.

"Really?" Blakesley said, his golden eyebrows rising just slightly. "The word was that Richborough was your companion of choice."

"I am allowed but one?" she said, laughing. "But you misunderstand me, Lord Henry. I am not asking for myself."

"Whom are you asking for, Lady Dalby?"

"Why, for you and no one else."

"You'll pardon me, but I've found that women don't think of others. They are simply too busy thinking of themselves."

"You are speaking from personal experience, surely. And of Lady Louisa Kirkland," she added softly.

"I speak only of myself, Lady Dalby," he answered just as softly, eyeing her like a particularly interesting snake. Wise Blakesley; he knew not to underestimate her. It was one of the reasons she liked him so well.

"A man of restraint," she murmured, letting her gaze travel the length of him. He was a tall man, lean and spare of frame. So many blond, blue-eyed men had a certain vacuous expression that displayed a sort of vapid hope that the world would treat them well; Blakesley had none of that look. He was cynical, sophisticated, and observant. And he was the son of a duke. Really, he could not have been more perfect. "I so like that in a man."

Blakesley bowed curtly in her direction and held his tongue. Yes, a man of rare restraint. He would serve very well.

"Will I see you at Hyde's?" she asked again.

Blakesley nodded, studying her through narrowed eyes.

"Do I frighten you, my lord?" she said on a trill of soft laughter.

"Let us say instead that I am wary, as any man should be when Lady Sophia looks too closely."

"A compliment," she said, walking toward him, her skirts rustling. "How lovely."

"Was it a compliment? I wasn't certain," he said, grinning slightly.

Sophia laughed. "Oh, I do like you, Lord Henry. I think we shall get on very well. Now, how best can we serve each other?"

"I can think of one way," he said, letting his gaze travel over her. She smiled and let him look his fill; looking cost her nothing, and she had found that it usually increased her negotiating power.

"And I can think of another way," she said, sitting down on a settee covered in white velvet and trimmed with pale blue braid.

"You and I are of an age, my lady," he said.

"Yet I have lived so much longer," she said.

"No, you only pretend you have."

"Pretend? You have not been listening carefully, Lord Henry. My reputation is built on solid foundations. Ask anyone, ask Richborough, if you doubt. Besides, this is still all of flattery. You and I both know who has engaged your interest. I love being flattered, but not when it is a blatant fiction."

"Lady Sophia, there is nothing fictional about my interest in you."

"Lord Henry, I applaud your chivalry. In the future, any rumors I hear of you being a cold man I will instantly decry. Now, shall we leave off flirtation and find in what way we may best serve each other?"

"I'm listening," he said, sitting on a chair opposite her.

"I'll be direct, shall I? The hour is late and we must still dress. My daughter has need of a strand of pearls."

Sophia paused. Blakesley crossed his legs and leaned back in his chair.

"I'm still listening," he said.

"A rather long strand. In fact, the longer and more luxurious, the better."

"There's nothing unusual in that, is there? Women usually want pearls, and the longer and more luxurious, the better. The question is why I should give Lady Caroline pearls."

"Because, Lord Henry, it will enrage Lady Louisa."

Blakesley uncrossed his legs and tipped the chair back so that it balanced on two legs and studied Sophia with cold and cynical eyes.

"Should I want to enrage Lady Louisa?"

"My dear Lord Henry," Sophia drawled, "if you have to ask, you truly are an innocent." She sighed and shifted her hips on the settee. "I suppose I should also mention that Lord Dutton might find it somewhat inconvenient if you were to give Caro pearls."

They stared at each other, the silence in the room full of weight and form, and then Blakesley said, "I'm still here, Lady Dalby."

Sophia smiled. Bless Fredericks for his weekly meetings with the other butlers in Town, otherwise, it might have taken her days instead of hours to find out that Dutton and Ashdon had worked out an arrangement.

"I knew you and I would get on famously, Lord Henry. Now, the most immediate question is, can you have a pearl necklace ready by the time of Hyde's assemblie?"

"Yes," he said.

"A long strand? Perhaps that lovely pearl necklace your mother used to wear?"

"And if I give your daughter my mother's necklace, what do I get in return?"

"Why, you'll get your necklace returned to you tomorrow, Lord Henry. This is no grab-and-run. This is for dramatic effect. You understand?"

Blakesley grinned and nodded. "I think so. I'll have the necklace, but I'll pick the time. Agreed?"

"Of course. You're a man of the world. I was certain you'd know how to best manage it."

"Flattery again, Lady Dalby," he said, shaking his head at her, smiling. "As fellow conspirators, I think honesty must rule between us."

"Then as fellow conspirators," she said, holding out her hand for him to take, "to a successful drama."

Blakesley kissed her hand lightly and said with a wry smile, "I suppose I must go home and rehearse my lines."

"Lord Henry, you will never convince me that you don't know your part by heart and haven't known it for a decade at least."

"Lady Dalby, you are entirely correct," he said, grinning.

Sixteen

ABSOLUTELY everyone was at the Duke of Hyde's magnificent house on Piccadilly, opposite Green Park. Everyone, that is, who was not at the Duke of Devonshire's just down the road. Those who traveled in Devonshire's circle, political and otherwise, did not travel in Hyde's. Sophia's choice had been made long ago. That the two houses were giving parties on the same night was in the same spirit of competition that had ruled them for decades.

Everyone enjoyed it completely. What else was London but a mass of alliances and changing loyalties? Tonight would only be more of the same. It was the predictability of viciousness and ruination, of engagements and liaisons, of gossip and firsthand accounts that made the London Season a season worth its ruinous price.

Ashdon, more aware than most of London's ruinous cost, was still gaming at White's when the assemblie at Hyde House formally began at nine. He had a pearl necklace to pay for, didn't he? He wasn't going to rely on Dutton, especially as he hadn't heard a thing from him since their bout at Jackson's. Talk was one thing, but a pearl necklace was quite another.

"How much are you down?" Viscount Tannington asked from behind him.

"I'm up more than fifty pounds, if you must know," Ashdon said.

"Saving for something specific?"

"If you have something to say, Tannington, just say it," Ashdon said, increasing his bet. "And don't stand behind me."

Tannington moved to Ashdon's right and said in an undertone, "The word is going around that Lady Caroline is in the market for a pearl necklace."

Ashdon felt his stomach clench and worked to keep his face neutral. "Isn't every woman?" Ashdon said lightly. His left hand was trembling; he fisted it and kept his eyes on the gaming table.

"I suppose so," Tannington said. "I suppose it's also true that whoever gives her pearls first will have her first favors. I thought you'd want to know."

"Why would you think that?"

Out of the corner of Ashdon's eye, he saw Tannington shrug. "Everyone knows you gave her pearl earrings. It doesn't seem fair for you to lose out on first favors because you can't raise the blunt for a necklace. Unless you didn't. Unless you got fair recompense on the earrings. Did you?"

Ashdon was out of his chair before Tannington could get out of the way, which was just perfect. Ashdon landed two solid blows to Tannington's gut before another member of White's pulled him off, a member who turned out to be Cal.

"Talk about her like that again," Ashdon growled in a fierce undertone, "and it's swords at dawn. You understand me?"

"Naturally," Tannington said stiffly.

"Good-bye, Tannington," Cal said, his hand heavy on Ashdon's shoulder.

"Until Hyde's," Tannington responded, and then he left the room, the sound of startled murmuring from the other members leaving with him.

"What now?" Cal said as Ashdon collected his winnings.

"Now I go to Hyde House. What else?"

"Without a necklace," Calbourne said.

"Unless Dutton has one on him, without a necklace," Ashdon said. "What else can I do?"

"I think the question is, what else can she do?"

Ashdon's gut tightened and he said, "I'm about to find out."

∽

THE crush was especially heavy at the entrance to the reception rooms of Hyde House, which of course was precisely the point. What other reason to have an assemblie than to see, be seen, and converse? The ground-floor rooms of Hyde House were ideally situated for the flow of foot traffic of the assemblie variety. One entered the double reception rooms fronting the house and proceeded to the right to the red reception room, then to the yellow drawing room, to the dressing room, the bedchamber, the closet, the antechamber, the music room, and back to the first reception room, done in an intriguing shade of blue. It was noisy, it was crowded, and it was great fun.

Sophia, Caro, and Anne were each wearing white muslin gowns with long enough trains to make negotiating the feet of the other guests a purely feminine challenge. Sophia was wearing her Westlin sapphires, a purely symbolic gesture, and wore a plume of blue feathers in her black hair to accentuate the point. Anne wore a pair of delicate garnet earrings and had arranged a petite strand of well-cut garnets in her dark red hair. The effect was striking. Caro, after much convincing, wore Ashdon's pearl earrings. Her throat was bare in anticipation of the gift of a pearl necklace. Other than her earrings, Caro's adornment was confined to a shell pink silk cord with hanging tassels that was fastened securely under her rather nice bosom. She looked innocent and virginal, which was completely intentional.

Sophia was anticipating a rather rousing evening.

"I don't see Lord Ashdon," Caro said from behind her fan.

"Darling, the point is that Lord Ashdon see *you*."

"And the difference is?" Caro said.

"Oh, Caro, you simply must learn how to play this game," Sophia said softly.

"There's Lord Staverton," Anne whispered. "Should we approach him?"

"No, darling," Sophia purred. "Let him come to us. It's so much sweeter that way, and he'll enjoy himself so much more if he can play the tiger to our gazelle."

"*Mother!*"

"It's a metaphor, darling, no need to be alarmed. And here he comes. Darling Staverton, he really is so good at this. You'll be blissfully happy, Anne, I promise you."

"Lady Dalby," Lord Staverton said with a crisp bow. He had quite a fine leg for a gentleman of his age. "Lady Caroline. Mrs. Warren," he said, his bow a tad deeper and his wandering eye wandering less than usual when facing Anne.

"Lord Staverton," Sophia said with a soft smile, "how well you look this evening. There is not a man here who is not envious of your well-turned leg."

"Nonsense," Staverton said, blushing like a girl.

Anne smiled to see him blush. It was most sweet of him to do so. He truly seemed a gentle man of good temper. And he was titled, let no one forget that.

"How is the evening thus far?" Sophia asked.

"Better since the arrival of the ladies of Dalby House," he answered. "You are looking rather lovely, Mrs. Warren, if I may say."

"Thank you, my lord," Anne said. At Sophia's delicate cough, she added, "And of course you may say. I welcome all your observations . . . and attention."

The result of that comment was that Lord Staverton blushed rather violently. It was completely charming. Whatever reservations Anne may have hidden away in the shadowed depths of her heart, though she was quite certain she had no shadows in her heart, vanished as she considered Lord Staverton's blush. This man, this gentle man, was her future. Lord Dutton was not going to be allowed to interfere with her future, just as he was not going to be permitted to interfere with her present. Lord Dutton could go drown himself in a vat of brandy at White's. And that was the last she was going to think of the devilish Lord Dutton.

"Dare I ask?" Staverton said. "May I enquire . . . is there any chance . . . ?"

"My darling Lord Staverton," Sophia interrupted, "you

are quite the most romantic man of my acquaintance. Since you are befuddled by hope, and Mrs. Warren is rather too reserved for such discourse, allow me to intervene. I have told Mrs. Warren of your regard, Stavey, and she returns it without hesitation. The wedding may take place at any date that best accommodates you. There. Have I acted out of turn? I do apologize, but one cannot watch two such dear, hesitant souls wander about without trying to guide and direct them. I hope I shall be forgiven for being forward?"

Lord Staverton, whose eyes were a very warm and cheery shade of brown, glowed. Anne could not help but glow at him in return. Her heart, far from feeling heavy at her decision, fairly soared above the room. Here was a good man, and she would make him a good wife. All other desires were like opium dreams, distorted and unhealthy and certainly unproductive.

Anne would always remember that she had begun her new life with Lord Staverton in Hyde House, in the red reception room.

Caro would always remember that Lord Henry Blakesley had ended her life as she knew it in the red reception room of Hyde House.

Caro never even saw him coming, which seemed symbolic somehow. As to that, Lord Henry Blakesley had never paid particular attention to her before, all his time being spent with Lady Louisa Kirkland, who was as mysteriously absent as Lord Henry Blakesley was disturbingly present. Yes, disturbingly. There was something distinctly odd about Lord Henry's manner; he was being entirely too attentive and standing entirely too close.

Caro, not without cause, suspected her mother had had a hand in this.

"Good evening, Lady Caroline," Lord Henry said, standing so that his foot was just touching her hem. It was flagrantly indelicate. She couldn't move an inch in the crush to disengage herself, and her mother and Anne were too busy fawning over Lord Staverton to even notice that Lord Henry was inching her into the adjoining yellow drawing room.

"Good evening, Lord Henry. Are Lady Louisa and Lady

Jordan with you this evening?" It was far from subtle, but then so was his foot, which had now crept into her skirts so that he was half buried in white muslin.

"No," he said with a smile. There was something almost sharkish in Lord Henry's smile. Funny, but she'd never noticed that about him before. "I'm here all alone tonight, acting as something of a host."

"Yes, and how is your father?"

"Hiding in the closet, last I looked," Blakesley said with a huge grin. He had quite nice teeth. She supposed that was common among sharks.

"He doesn't like these sorts of gatherings?" she said, trying to edge back a step and getting an elbow in the ribs for her efforts. It didn't seem fair that Blakesley was moving her fully into the yellow drawing room without any apparent difficulty, the sea opening before him, as it were. Caro lost sight of her mother and Anne in the next breath.

And caught sight of Louisa Kirkland and Amelia Caversham in the following breath. They were standing like two pale statues next to the fireplace in the drawing room, looking particularly stunning, unfortunately, as the room was decorated in a wash of pale yellow silk damask that suited them to perfection. Caro was equally certain that she had looked better in the more vibrant tones of the red reception room. Ah, well. Lord Henry didn't seem to mind.

"Of course not," Blakesley answered. "No man does, I should think. These affairs are for women, are they not?"

"Then why do men come?" she asked.

"Why, for the women," Blakesley answered on a short laugh.

"And a man will do anything in his quest for a woman?" she asked as Blakesley maneuvered her yet again to a spot opposite the fireplace and two pale statues, who were staring at her.

"Of course," he answered softly, his golden hair gleaming in the candlelight. Not only did the yellow silk compliment Louisa's and Amelia's looks, it did wonders for Blakesley's. She'd never before noticed how light a blue his eyes were, nor the rather fine quality of his complexion.

"So a man says," she answered, giving up all hopes of ever making her way back to the red reception room. The flow of traffic was forward, ever forward, and she was relentlessly being separated from her mother and Anne. It might not be a bad time to practice the game, as her mother so blatantly named it. Lord Henry seemed a willing candidate, and she certainly did not need to worry about offending him. Blakesley was rather known for being thick-skinned. "But when called to task? When called upon to deliver?"

"For God and country?" he said with a lopsided grin.

"Exactly. For God and country, yes, he will all and more. I have no doubt of it. But for a woman? What will a man truly do?"

"Lady Caroline, you intrigue me. You truly do," he said, eyeing her closely. She was not at all sure that she liked it. On the other hand, she was not at all sure that she didn't. "Shall we put it to the test?"

Which of course reminded her of what her mother had said earlier. "Tell me, Lord Henry, do men like to be put to the test?"

"I would say it depends on the test."

"Which is to say, it depends on the woman."

"If you say so," he said, staring into her eyes. He had the lightest blue eyes, like a clear winter sky.

"No, Lord Henry, that is entirely the point. I want *you* to say so."

"Yes," he whispered hoarsely, "it depends on the woman."

A shiver went down her spine. She was completely certain that shivering was an appropriate response to being pressed against a shark.

"Ask me, Caro," he whispered. "Test me."

"Test you to do what, my lord?" she whispered in return.

"What is it you want? What is it you would have?" Knowledge shone out of his blue eyes, and she did not like it. "Ask me, Caro. Let me prove myself upon your quest." Good God, her mother was *right*! "Say it," he urged.

She didn't know what possessed her. She didn't know where the words came from. She certainly didn't know why she was having this conversation with Lord Henry unless it was the power over him he seemed so willing to give her. Heady stuff, that.

"I want a pearl necklace," she whispered, staring into his eyes, uncertain what she would see there. She let the words hover in the air between, saw his eyes crinkle in satisfaction, heard him expel a breath she had not known he was holding. What Caro did not see in Blakesley's eyes was surprise. "Would you like to give me one?" she asked.

"I would very much like to give you one," he said, and he lifted his left hand, snapped his fingers, and a footman appeared from the far side of the large room carrying a small silver tray. The footman carried it high in his hand, above the heads of the crowded drawing room. It wasn't long before a path cleared for him. It wasn't long before the sounds of conversation stopped. But it was a very long time before the footman reached Lord Henry and lowered the silver tray and held out to the fourth son of the Duke of Hyde a long, coiled, pearl necklace. "Would you like this one?" Blakesley asked.

"It was just a game," Caro whispered, ducking her head against the roomful of stares.

"It is still a game, Caro," Blakesley whispered in return.

"I don't know how to play this game very well."

"Take the necklace," he urged softly, ignoring the entire room to look down at her with his very amused blue eyes. "It is your move, and it is the right one."

"Lord Henry, I don't think I should trust you to give me sound advice."

Blakesley laughed under his breath and said, "You are correct, but in this instance, you can trust me. Take the necklace, or better still, let me drape it upon you."

"I cannot!" she said, feeling her cheeks flush.

"Because of Ashdon? It is because of Lord Ashdon that you should take it."

Did the whole world know about her arrangement with Lord Ashdon?

"Why?" she said, staring at him, looking for deceit and seeing only amusement in his eyes.

"Wear my pearls and see what Ashdon will do next. That is how the game is played."

"A rather brutal game," she murmured.

Blakesley laughed as he lifted the pearl necklace from the tray and placed it carefully over her coiled hair and around her neck. "It is that, Caro. It is a very brutal game, but you want to win it, don't you?"

She most certainly did.

❧

"SHE most certainly did," Dutton snarled softly. "Anne Warren refused to see me. With that sort of help you'll never see a pearl necklace from me."

Ashdon and Calbourne, just arrived and still in the blue reception room, the first room on the assemblie circuit at Hyde House, had been accosted by Dutton the moment their feet had entered the house. It was a less than pleasant start to the evening.

"Do you *have* a pearl necklace for me?" Ashdon said softly as they moved through the crush of the blue reception room and into the equally great crush of the red. Ashdon did not see Caro, though Lady Dalby was talking with Mrs. Warren and Lord Staverton in intimate tones. Things did not seem to be going well there, not for Dutton at any rate; whatever it was that was being discussed, Lord Staverton looked delighted.

"As a point of fact, I do," Dutton bit out. "Not that I'm going to give it to you to throw away on Caroline Trevelyan. Not when things with Mrs. Warren are fouled beyond reckoning."

"You *have* a necklace? Pearls?" Ashdon said.

"Pearls, yes, down to her belly."

"Where did you get them?" Calbourne asked.

"Are you in this now, your grace?" Dutton said. "I wasn't aware we were forming a club."

"Where?" Ashdon said.

"If you must know," Dutton said, "I sold my thoroughbred, Highstep, to the Marquis of Melverley today. He paid me in pounds and pearls."

"No," Calbourne said in shock, "you didn't. Why would

you sell Highstep? He was the foundation of your racing stock."

Dutton shrugged. "I was thinking of selling Highstep anyway as I've had my eye on a foal out of Roxanne. This sudden need for pearls, Melverley's hunger for Highstep, well, the timing came together. It's too bad that you didn't hold up your end, Ashdon. These pearls are burning a hole in my pocket. Since Lady Caroline desires pearls, why shouldn't I be the one to give them to her?"

"We had an agreement," Ashdon spit out. "It was your idea to begin with."

"Yes, well, not all ideas bear fruit," Dutton said. "Mrs. Warren begins to pall for me. I don't know quite what I saw there. Now Lady Caroline, on the other hand, she's a lovely girl, so fresh, so innocent."

"Stay away from her," Ashdon breathed.

"If only you had a strand of pearls, you could hold me back with them. But, such a pity, you don't."

"I'll wager you for them," Ashdon said.

"Is that wise?" Dutton said. "I believe your whole trouble started with intemperate wagering. Besides, what could you possibly have that I would want?"

That was the problem. At the moment, precisely because of intemperate wagering, he had nothing. Given time, Ashdon could have won enough to buy Highstep and the pearls, but he did not have time and, worse, he did not have a string of pearls. And Dutton did. Worst of all, Dutton blamed him for the muddle with Mrs. Warren and would take his bite of revenge on Caro's unsuspecting skin.

"You know you don't want Caroline Trevelyan," Ashdon snarled. "Just hours ago you were hot for Anne Warren."

"I'm fickle," Dutton deadpanned. "Now, if you'll excuse me, I'm off to wrap these pearls around Caro's slender neck."

"If she'll have them," Ashdon said stiffly. Surely Caroline had *some* regard for him, some loyalty. She'd asked *him* for pearls, after all, not the whole of London.

"If? Ashdon, what you know of women would fill a

thimble," Dutton sneered as he moved through the crowd, obviously looking for Caro.

"You know, I think he might be right," Calbourne said.

"Thanks," Ash mumbled, pushing through the crowd behind Dutton, determined to find Caro, with or without pearls. He'd never trusted Dutton anyway; he'd be better served in gambling his way to the blunt for a nice pearl necklace. Why, if things continued as they had today, he'd have the necklace in a week. Watching Dutton's back, a week suddenly seemed a very long time.

"You do know," Cal said, shoving along behind him, nodding politely to the mamas on the wall, their unmarried chicks clustered close and smiling breathlessly in his direction, "that since she's made her decision to become a courtesan that any man who can meet her price will be the man who—"

"Yes, right," Ashdon interrupted. He didn't believe it, that was all. He didn't believe that Caro, no matter what she said, wanted to be a courtesan. Or rather, that she wanted to be a courtesan with anyone but him. There was something about the way she lit up when he looked at her, at how she melted into his kiss, that told another tale.

Of course, it was entirely possible that a skilled courtesan could make any man feel that he was *the* man. But it was also true that Caro was not a skilled courtesan. She was not a skilled anything, unless baiting him mercilessly was a skill.

"You want her, don't you?" Cal asked.

"That's rather obvious, isn't it?"

"Why do you want her?"

"Again," Ash bit out, "obvious."

Calbourne nodded and mumbled something into the folds of his pristine cravat.

"Speak up, Cal," Ash said. "Where *has* Dutton gone? Do you see him?"

"Just into the yellow drawing room, I believe. Actually, there's something of an uproar happening in there. Do you hear it?"

Cal, the tallest man in any gathering, always had the advantage of perspective.

"Yes, I believe so," Ashdon said. They'd lost sight of Dutton as he entered that room and now there was a bubble of noise drifting toward them. The combination of the two occurrences did not produce a feeling of contentment. Far from it.

"Ashdon," Calbourne said, "you are certain you want her? No matter the path, no matter the outcome?"

"'Tis not as serious as all that, Cal," Ashdon said. "I shan't need to slay any dragons for her, surely. She is a woman, a woman with a price."

His gut twisted a bit as he said it, but what of that?

"A woman with a price," Cal said softly, "and according to the gossip coming out of the yellow drawing room, a woman whose price has been met."

"Damn Dutton for his blasted interference!"

"No, Ash, not by Dutton," Cal said. "By Blakesley."

❧

"THIS can't be happening," Louisa Kirkland said, her chilled lips barely moving. "What has Blakesley got to do with her?"

"A pearl necklace to start," Lady Amelia Caversham whispered, staring at the spectacle of Caroline Trevelyan wearing Blakesley's gift of pearls. When Louisa stared in fury at her cousin, Amelia added, "Well, you can't have expected him to trail after you forever, Louisa, especially as you were chasing after Lord Dutton with his full knowledge. And speaking of Lord Dutton, here he comes . . . and there he goes."

Lord Dutton, looking rather more handsome than usual and certainly more determined, pushed his way through the increasingly crowded drawing room, for who could blame the entire assemblie for wanting to witness Lady Caroline's fall from grace with the most famous cynic among them, to join Blakesley and Caroline. Blakesley looked less than amused by the intervention of a third party. Caroline looked only slightly surprised and very much delighted.

It really was very hard to like a girl who attracted so much male attention.

"Let's get closer," Louisa hissed, dragging Amelia behind her through the throng.

"We don't seem to be alone in that wish," Amelia mumbled.

In truth, the entire room seemed to have shifted in the general direction of the far wall. It would have served Caroline Trevelyan right to look like a trapped hare faced with all that concentrated attention. Unfortunately, Caroline had the irritating quality of looking exotically beautiful no matter the occasion. Louisa had really never known a girl who was so difficult to warm to.

"What's he saying?" Louisa said, pushing past Lady Dalrymple, who stumbled against Lord Tayborn, who caught her clumsily. They were both past fifty. Lack of grace in movement was to be expected.

"I can't see them, let alone hear them."

"Oh, I can see them, just," Louisa said, sliding between the Lords Clybane and Darington. Lord Darington may have brushed his hand against her right hip, the lecherous fop.

It was when she was making sure that Lord Darington had his hands properly at his sides that Louisa heard Amelia gasp.

"What?"

"He's given her pearls!" Amelia said.

"I *know* that," Louisa said. "The whole room knows that."

"Not Blakesley," Amelia said, yanking on Louisa's hand so that she stumbled against a particularly knobby chair; Louisa felt her stocking rip. "Dutton!"

What?

Louisa used her very pretty fan to force her way through the crush and to almost the very feet of Lord Dutton, Lord Henry, and Lady Caroline. What she saw was beyond belief.

There Caroline stood, her black hair piled high and her white bodice cut low, with *two* strands of pearls around her throat. It didn't seem possible for things to get any worse.

Here were the two men she spent the most time with, one unwillingly, but still it was intolerable that Caroline should snag them both.

Louisa had a healthy interest in Lord Dutton; she could admit that. In fact, she wasn't the only woman in town to find the beautiful and elusive Lord Dutton fascinating. Which only made her friendship with Henry Blakesley more vital. Who else knew where Lord Dutton was likely to be? Who else could advise her? Who else could lift her flagging spirits when Lord Dutton ignored her very existence at yet another dinner or ball or assemblie? Why, none other than Lord Henry, ever faithful, ever reliable.

A reliable cad, that's what they both were, to run to Lady Caroline and pour pearls upon her, just because the silly chit had voiced an appreciation for pearls! And let none be fooled; there was no one in the room who was such an innocent as to believe that Lady Caroline would come out of this pearl arrangement with anything left to her but pearls. Her reputation was shattered. She'd never again be welcomed anywhere that anyone of taste and breeding would care to be welcomed.

Actually, it might be a good thing to let Caroline have her moment, as it was surely to be the last moment she ever had in Society.

Louisa had almost completely talked herself into a calm and rational deportment when she looked again at the pearls that Dutton had given Caroline. Rationality deserted her with a thud.

"Those are *my* pearls!" Louisa said. It was her misfortune that everyone in the room heard her. Including Lord Ashdon.

❧

"WHAT's she done now?" Ashdon said as he and Calbourne pushed their way into the drawing room.

"She's got herself two strands of pearls, that's what she's done," Cal said. "She's lovely, I'll admit, but are you certain you want a woman who attracts so much—"

"Competition?"

"I was going to say 'attention.' Though, now that you mention it, competition does seem right on the mark."

"I'm going to kill her," Ash said under his breath.

Cal nodded. "Understandable. But, given all the trouble she's caused you, I'd take my pleasure of her first. You might as well get your money's worth."

"I don't think she can give pleasure. All she can do is cause trouble. And give me a blistering headache."

"Yes, women are rather good at that. One wonders where they learn it. From what I can tell, they're nice enough as children. Must be something about the budding of breasts, must turn some nasty part of them on. Pity it can't be turned off."

"Cal," Ashdon said, "I appreciate that you've obviously put a lot of thought into the physiology of women, but I have more pressing concerns at the moment."

"Right," Cal said, nodding again. "Like how to get away with murder."

"Exactly," Ash said solemnly. "And how to lay my hands on a pearl necklace in the next ten seconds or so."

"I can help you there," Cal said. "I happen to have ignored just about everything you've said as it pertains to Lady Caroline. Everything except your determination to have her and your need for pearls to accomplish the deed. I have brought you pearls, Ash. Now, take them, and debauch the lady nicely."

Ashdon stared into Cal's eyes. "You don't want to be involved in this, Cal, you know you don't. I *will* debauch her, ruining her beyond all aid. How will you live with that?"

"Ash," Cal said softly, "how will you? This will eat at you every day until you are eaten through."

"I have no choice, Calbourne," Ashdon said stiffly.

"Of course you do. Take this girl, this girl you want so much, and marry her. It's what a man does when he wants a woman and the woman is suitable."

"Hardly suitable," Ashdon grumbled. "She accepts pearls like other women accept water."

"Then give her pearls, but make her yours. Ignore Westlin. Listen to your heart."

"I cannot ignore Westlin. I also cannot ignore her," Ashdon said. "These were your wife's pearls, were they not?"

"Given in good cause. Take them. I have no need of pearls this night, nor any other."

"I'll take them," Ashdon said, "because I must. The lady demands pearls. I demand the lady." Ashdon shrugged, his blue-eyed gaze as sharp as Venetian glass. "I will repay you."

"I know you will. Now, go and claim your prize before Dutton flies off with her."

Ashdon needed no encouragement. He slid through the drawing room as easily as a snake, the crowd making way for him almost magically. It was not magic. It was merely the ton letting the key player in this little drama attain his place upon the stage for the next scene. The scene in which Lord Ashdon presents the demanded pearls to the Lady Caroline, a lady who suddenly was awash in pearls.

That would change, immediately.

"Hello, Ashdon," Dutton said. "What brings you to this corner of the room?"

"Lady Caroline," Ashdon said in greeting, bowing stiffly in her direction. Caro curtseyed as much as her limited space would allow. Blakesley and Dutton had her hemmed about most tidily. That would change as well.

"Oh," Dutton said, "you must have pearls to join this party, Lord Ashdon. Have you any?"

"Pearls are the price, are they?" Ashdon said, staring at Caro. She had the good manners to blush. "How fortunate that I have come prepared. You wanted pearls, Lady Caroline?" he said, opening up his palm in front of her. "I have brought you pearls." The necklace lay in glimmering softness against his palm, overflowing it, spilling out in luminous globes of creamy white. They were extraordinary pearls, now that he looked at them.

"Thank you, Lord Ashdon," she said, her gaze locked onto his, her dark eyes unreadable and mysterious.

"Put them on," he commanded.

The room had stilled, watching this exchange play out. It was extraordinary, really, to see a lady of the realm sell herself in the public view. It was like watching a slave being tangled in chains, chains of pearls.

Caro took the pearls he held out to her and placed them over her head. They fell in a heavy line to her breasts, lost within the dark valley of her cleavage. Her head came up, her eyes smoldering and smoky, her gaze trapped in his. She remembered. He would see her, touch her, *have* her to the length of his pearls.

God bless Calbourne's wife for the length of her pearls.

"A most extravagant length," Blakesley said with a suppressed grin. "Mine can hardly compare."

"It is not the length, it is the quality," Dutton said. "One must never judge by size alone."

"Speaking from experience?" Ashdon said, his eyes firmly fastened on Caro. She looked a goddess, Venus, certainly. She would never pass for Athena. "You have my pearls," Ashdon said to Caro. "Take the others off."

"Why should she?" Blakesley said. "I anticipated you, Ashdon, certainly that must count. First come, first served."

Caro flushed again and looked down at her feet; she began to sidle away from them, skirting the back wall and making for the Hyde dressing room, the next room on the assemblie circuit. The crowds let her move, as long as they could move with her, which they did.

"You have no part in this, Blakesley," Ashdon said. "This arrangement was between Lady Caroline and myself, none other. You have stepped where you have no right."

"But wasn't the whole idea that my pearls bought me the right?" Blakesley said, one eyebrow raised quizzically.

"Exactly," Dutton said. "The price was pearls. I'll grant you that you met the price, but late. You are preceded, Ashdon. You must wait your turn."

"You are too crass, Dutton," Blakesley. "The lady will faint if you keep on."

The lady would run screaming from the room if they kept on. Why Ashdon wanted to protect her from that, he didn't know. Surely she had brought the whole thing down upon her own head. How else had Blakesley found out about the pearls if not from her lips?

"You must choose, Caro," Ashdon said. "You have set the price. You must choose the winner in this contest. Unless you prefer to entertain all three of us? At once?"

"Gad, Ashdon, but you're mean when you're crossed," Blakesley said. "Does competition so distress you? Must the field be cleared for you to win?"

Dutton laughed under his breath. It was then that Ashdon hit him in the breadbasket. He had to hit something, after all, and Dutton was such a convenient and worthy target.

Dutton bent over, Blakesley burst out laughing, Caro ran into the dressing room, and Calbourne said, "That's hardly like you, Ash."

Yes, well, very little was like him lately.

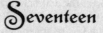

Seventeen

"THERE you are, Lord Westlin. I wondered where you were hiding," Sophia said with just the merest trace of a smile.

"Hiding?" he growled. "I was merely trying to avoid you."

"Is that so?" she said, letting her gaze travel from his grizzled head to his well-shod feet. "It's obvious that *one* part of you is very glad to see me again."

Westlin shifted his weight, trying to bury the bulge in his silk breeches. "You're a common wench, Sophia, no matter your title."

"And you're as randy as ever, and as ill-mannered, no matter your title."

"Bitch."

Sophia grinned and sighed, "Ah, it is as if twenty years have not passed, Westy. You make me feel young again. Thank you for that."

"Why is it that every conversation ends up being about you?"

"I don't know," she said liltingly. "It is strange how that happens. Perhaps because I am the most interesting person in any room? I do know that I have the best jewels. You do recognize them, of course."

Westlin turned a particularly unflattering shade of red, a color to be avoided at all costs with his ruddy complexion, and bit out, "I should. I almost beggared myself to buy them for you."

"Almost being the key point. One must learn not to make too much of things, Lord Westlin. You have an unfortunate habit for exaggeration. Why, just look at what you've done to your son. He was quite disposed to dislike me. A late gift from you, surely."

"And well deserved," he snarled, his erection tamed. For the moment. She knew exactly how to call it back and would, when it would cause Westlin the most discomfort. Some things in life were so charmingly predicable.

They stood in the doorway leading to the central stairs of Hyde House, away from the crush of people who were following the most social, most obvious route through the house. The blue and red reception rooms and the yellow drawing room could each be accessed by a cluster of small doors that led to the stairs. It was an easier, more private way to travel the circuit and had the advantage of avoiding the knot of people that had gathered like a stubborn cork in the bottleneck between the red reception room and the drawing room. Sophia knew exactly who the cork was and why. Now, all that was left was for Caroline to be Caroline; if she could do that, then Ashdon would behave predictably.

"Your daughter," Westlin continued, "runs true to her common blood, Sophia. She is at this moment draped in pearl necklaces from no less than three men."

"*Three* pearl necklaces," Sophia gushed. "Why, the most I ever managed was one pearl necklace. We both remember how that turned out, don't we?"

"You're *proud* of her?"

Really, it looked as though Westlin's eyes must soon jump off his face.

"For managing to acquire three pearl necklaces in a single night? I should only hope every mother can feel as I do at this moment. But tell me, they aren't inferior pearls, are they? Caroline is a girl, inexperienced, naïve, far too trusting, I should say. I would hate to have her cheated."

"Cheated! You can speak of that? To me?"

"Darling Westy," she said, lowering her voice to a seductive murmur. "Never tell me that you were cheated. We both know the truth of what passed between us, no matter what fiction you have invented to entertain Ashdon."

"I'll leave the past in the past, Sophia," Westlin said with a malicious smile. "What happens now is all that matters. You thought to arrange a marriage between my son and your daughter. It will not be. How could you think I would allow it? Ashdon will ruin her, but he will never marry her."

"And you know this how?" she said softly.

"You somehow think that a man who is eager to bed you will therefore be loyal to you, adopting your plans as his own. You are as naïve as you claim your daughter to be. A man wants a woman. So. What is that? It is nothing to want a woman. And it is nothing to have her. But there is nothing beyond the having."

"What coils you must invent to explain Dalby," she said.

"Dalby's choice of you was all of thwarting me. That rivalry was older than you by a decade. When you remember Dalby, Sophia, remember me. Without me, you could never have caught him."

"He was happily caught."

"As Richborough is caught?" he sneered.

"Ah, Richborough. Ever attentive. Ever ready to advise. How well he played his part," she said slowly, studying Westlin.

"The part I arranged for him."

"Oh, so it was you who invited Richborough to my bed? That, dear Westlin, is an invitation only I may render. Surely you, of all people, must remember that."

"You fell for a pretty face, Sophia," he sneered.

Really, when had Westlin developed the habit of sneering instead of simply speaking? It was a distinctly unpleasant mannerism. Someone should break him of it, and the sooner the better.

"And who does not?" she answered with a tiny shrug.

"He was in your bed not for your sake, but for mine."

"That sounds rather debauched, Westlin. You truly haven't changed, have you?" she said with a smug smile. "I shall never forget that night in July when you carried me down three flights of stairs so that we could entertain ourselves by the pearly light of a full moon by that very pretty pond on your property. You called me your wood nymph, and you, of course, were my satryr. What happy, happy times those were."

As she had expected, his breeches were close to bursting. It was too delightful.

"Ah, I see that you remember that night as vividly as I," she said, tapping him gently with her fan. "Tell me, is the pond still . . . full? Do the waters still rush wildly in turgid, frothing energy over that rather rocky and steeply pitched . . ."

She let her voice trail off as she stared at his erection, straining and pulsing now in her direction. "Oh, I see that they do," she said with a seductive smile. "How nice it is in these changing times that some things, the truly special things, stay the same."

"You shall not have him," Westlin gritted out. At least he was no longer sneering. "You shall not get your hands on Ashdon, but I will see your daughter ruined."

"As I was ruined? Come, come, Westlin," she purred. "Do I look ruined to you?"

"You look most desperately ruined," he said.

"What an ill-bred thing to say to a lady of the realm. Your manners, Westlin; you simply must get to Town more often. Such language, most ill-advised."

"Is that your attempt at a threat?"

"A threat?" she said on a chuckle. "How absurd. With what would I threaten you? Oh, how stupid of me," she said, her smile falling off her like a discarded mask. "Of course, your son. I could use Ashdon to wound you. But of course, I would not. Ashdon is a dear man, so earnest, so intense in a rather quiet sort of way."

"He *is* earnest, earnest in his obedience to me," Westlin said. "He will do as I instruct him."

"How fortunate that you have such a malleable, docile son. And he is how old now? Thirty? To ruin an innocent girl on your command, how proud you must be."

She had not thought it possible, but Westlin's eyes appeared to be turning red. Most remarkable. He certainly knew how to display a fine outrage. It was most considerate of him as she found provoking him endlessly entertaining.

But, as much fun as she was having, she simply must save something for another day. Revenge was a meal best enjoyed in small doses, if only so that the pleasure of it could be savored.

"Now, as charming as it always is to run into you, darling Westy, I must admire my daughter's triple strand of pearls. This is a moment that will be talked of for years. I don't want to miss a second of it. If you will excuse me," she said, not asking at all.

Sophia slipped into the yellow drawing room, a most admirable room to be sure; it was her favorite in the house and so lovely that Caro's moment should happen in it. Things could not be going better.

The room was an absolute crush of people, all gawking and squawking as if they had never seen a woman wear pearls before. Delicious. Things couldn't possibly be going better than if, well, than if she'd *planned* them. Sophia swallowed a smile. The crowd parted for her, as they must if they had any hope of seeing her reaction to Caro's fall from propriety. What look would do for that? Sympathy? Horror? Shock? Amusement?

That last had some appeal if only for being unique in situations such as these. She remembered quite clearly that when Lady Blanfig's only daughter was found with her bodice gaping in the yew maze of the third Duke of Northam's spectacular home, with Lord Pyworthy's right hand where it had no business being, well, Lady Blanfig had screamed so loudly and so long that she had been unable to utter another syllable for a fortnight. Sophia thought she must improve on that performance, she simply must. For one, she could not do without her voice for a fortnight. For another, screaming lacked a certain grace.

Pyworthy and the girl had been married for almost two years now, with two children to show for it. These things had a way of working themselves out.

Sophia smiled her way through the crowd, an expression of pleasant curiosity mixed with just a touch of parental concern painted on her features. She could just make out Caro, surrounded by Blakesley, Dutton, and Ashdon, all of them pressed almost into the far corner of the drawing room, like mice without a hole in sight. She was almost within speaking range when Richborough, of all people, stood in front of her, blocking her path. Really, it was most irritating. Richborough had played his part; it was time to exit the stage. Poor boy, he really didn't have much going for him beyond rather spectacular good looks and an old title. Fortunately for Richborough, that would be enough for him to exist nicely.

"Tannington has been following you all evening, Sophia," he said. At least fourteen people heard him. Richborough was so appalling indiscreet. She was so relieved to finally be finished with him.

"Has he really?" she said, looking around casually. "He has yet to catch me. I suppose I should slow down, shouldn't I? Though if he's not going to be quick off the mark, then . . ." She shrugged delicately. "Then again, the race doesn't always go to the swift, does it, Richborough?"

"What the devil does that mean?" he scowled. He did it very well, scowling, but he did it rather too often. Everything, in time, must pall, particularly a youngish man of no discretion.

"It means, darling, that I'm finished with you. You've run your race and you've done very well, but now," she said, patting his arm as she would that of the smallest of boys, "it's off with you."

"You," he stammered, scowling more deeply. He must think his scowls impressive. Some nurse had probably given him that mistaken idea. One must be so careful in hiring the right nurse with the exact right disposition. His nurse had clearly been too impressed with scowls. These childhood habits, once acquired, were so difficult to break. Why, just look at her darling Markham, the ninth Earl of Dalby; he had toyed with the notion of sucking his thumb. A good nurse and a dosing of vinegar had seen to that. Now Dalby had the loveliest mouth imaginable and quite the straightest teeth. "You," Richborough repeated. Oh, yes, she'd almost forgotten about Richborough.

"Yes? I?" she prompted. "I really must move on, darling. I see Caro, just there."

"You can't mean to end our *affaire*. Because of Tannington? Because he's trailing after you like some dog?"

"How charmingly put," she said sarcastically. "But no, not because of Tannington. Just because of you, darling. Simply you. You played your part brilliantly, if that's any consolation, which I'm sure it must be. You couldn't have managed Lord Westlin better if I'd given you a script."

Richborough blanched just slightly. It was an improvement over the scowl and she welcomed the change.

"What about Westlin?" he said. "If he told you anything—"

"But, darling, of course he told me absolutely everything. That's the way he does things. And of course, that's the way you do things as well. You see how well it worked out, how perfect a fit you were. Now, well done, and off you go."

"Sophia," he said, grabbing her arm as she walked past him.

"Let go of me, Richborough," she said softly and without any amusement. "Don't ever touch me again. And don't ever come to my home."

He dropped her arm as if scorched, which he most definitely had been, and she walked on, the scene of Caro and her three men awaiting her. Delicious. Sophia almost smiled in anticipation, but of course she did not; smiling in the face of Caro's *ruin* was not the appropriate response. Ruin, indeed. This night would be the making of her.

It was just then that Ashdon hit Dutton in the middle of his very nice waistcoat.

It was all Sophia could do to keep from laughing out loud.

Eighteen

CARO thought that, in the way of dreams and wishes, she ought to have been delighted. Three men, handsome and titled, were interested in her. Very interested to judge by the rain of pearls that was being showered upon her, arguing now as to who would have her, how, and in what order. Caro suppressed a shudder.

It was funny in a perfectly unamusing fashion how dreams could actually be frightening when they happened while awake. This was nothing, *nothing*, as she had imagined it. She had three pearl necklaces and three men and the whole world was watching to see how she would handle herself, as well as how she would handle the three men. She was absolutely in over her head.

She had no idea how her mother had managed it in her day.

If Caro had needed any further convincing that the life of a courtesan was not for her, and she did not, this moment, this ruinous moment, would have convinced her permanently. Just how did one go about choosing one man from among three? Because, no matter that Lord Henry Blakesley had given her pearls first, or that the Marquis of Dutton had given her pearls in the most seductive manner imaginable, it was Lord Ashdon, predictably tight-lipped and surly, whom she wanted.

Even if he did want her for a courtesan and not a wife.

Even if he had, obviously, told absolutely *everyone* that she was desirous of a lovely strand of pearls so that she had been besieged by absolutely hordes of men in the most fashionable assemblie of the year, and any hope she had of *ever* holding her face up in Town again was completely out of reach because of Lord Ashdon's rather big, though completely mesmerizing, mouth in telling what had obviously been a *private* communication to everyone he knew and a few he didn't.

What's more, she was almost certain that the pearls Ashdon had given her, in the most sullen way imaginable, weren't even his pearls to give. He didn't have any money. Who knew that better than she?

It was in the middle of these thoughts, as her tribe of three men argued and haggled right in front of her as if she were no more than a bit of lace to be fingered and bargained over, that Ashdon hit Dutton in the stomach so that Dutton lurched over, huffing, while Blakesley burst into impolite laughter.

While she was staring at the mess she had made in the drawing room of Hyde House, Ashdon grabbed her by the arm and pulled her into the large, rose-colored dressing room. They were not alone.

"Your grace," Ashdon said, bowing curtly, tugging her into a curtsey.

"Good evening, Lord Ashdon, Lady Caroline," the fourth Duke of Hyde said softly. "Bit of a row out there? Always happens at these affairs. I don't know why the duchess insists upon having it year after year. I suppose she must like rows."

Hyde was a soft-spoken man who had distinguished his name by performing well in the rebellion in the American colonies twenty-five years past. No one considered it his fault at all that the American colonies had been lost to Britain, least of all his wife, a native of the colony of Massachusetts. The Duchess of Hyde's father had made a fortune in shipping. The fourth Duke of Hyde knew what to do with a fortune. It had been an ideal match, particularly as Molly, the Duchess of Hyde, had been run out of Boston with the rest of those loyal to the crown.

Molly had given Hyde six sons in eight years, a respectable showing by Boston standards, she had declared, though the youngest had died before he left the nursery. William,

Marquis of Iveston, as Hyde's heir and one of the most eligible men in England, rarely ventured out during the Season for the very reason that he was one of the most eligible men in England. Iveston was his father's son in that respect. Lord Henry Blakesley, Hyde's fourth son, and part of the row that had happened in the yellow salon, clearly took after his mother, Molly, the Duchess of Hyde, and previously of Boston, Massachusetts, by all accounts a most raucous town.

Caro didn't think that Hyde knew that his son was involved in the disturbance, as was she, as was Ashdon. She didn't think it prudent of her to tell him. For once, it appeared as though she and Ashdon were in agreement.

"I'm sorry, your grace," Ashdon said. "I didn't mean to disturb your solitude. I only hoped to remove Lady Caroline from the—"

"Disturbance," Caroline supplied. What else to call it? A tussle for a future courtesan? No, that wouldn't do.

"Perfectly all right," Hyde said, dipping his head sorrowfully. "I suppose I must go out and mingle. Molly is certain to cause a row of her own if she finds me . . ."

Hiding was the word that sprang to mind, and which obviously could not be uttered.

"Taking a moment to gather your thoughts?" Caro offered.

Hyde's head lifted and he smiled rather brilliantly. "That's it, exactly. I shall tell her that, if forced. Enjoy the evening," he said with a lazy wave and made his way through the bedchamber, closing the dressing room door behind him.

They were alone, just. The sounds of the crowd, just beyond the dressing room door to the drawing room, were growing louder. Caro felt both exposed and hidden, like a hare holding still before the hounds, quaking and unmoving. If she just held still long enough, perhaps forever, the hounds would depart and things would return to the way they had been.

"Take off those damned pearls," Ashdon snarled softly.

Apparently things were not going to return to the way they had been. And perhaps that, she decided with a snarl of her own, was for the best.

"Will you kindly stop snarling commands at me? You cannot tell me what to do."

"Those pearls give me the right," he said, pulling her nearer to him. That wouldn't do at all; she was quite close enough to the snarling, wolfish face of Lord Ashdon and his impossibly blue eyes.

"Yes, about these pearls," she said, yanking her arm from his grasp and taking a step backward. Unfortunately, though the dressing room was large, it was still only a dressing room. They were uncomfortably closeted, wrapped up in silken damask within the greater boundaries of an assemblie in full force. It was only a matter of minutes before the tide of the crowd would force its way into the dressing room, and she had *so* much to say to Ashdon. "Where did you get them? You couldn't have purchased them, not honestly. You're completely without funds."

"But not without friends," he clipped out. "You enjoy saying that, don't you?"

"Saying what?"

"That I'm without funds, without blunt."

"Isn't it true?"

"There is much that is true that doesn't need endless repeating."

"Oh, endless repeating? Aren't you being a bit childish? I don't endlessly repeat—"

"You sold yourself for pearls, Caro," he whispered. "Sold for pearls. Pearls are the price and the price has been met."

"How vulgar you are!"

He shrugged. "I am merely stating the truth. Repeating the truth." He grinned. It was not a pleasant sight. "Now, as to our bargain. Take off Blakesley's pearls. Now."

"This was not part of our bargain," she said, ignoring the fact that her stomach lurched against her spine. Ashdon was rather good at getting stomachs to do unwelcome things, with a blow or without one.

"It is now," he said, and by his look, he was not going to tolerate argument.

Blast to what he would tolerate.

"I will not be ordered about. You have no right, Lord Ashdon. I am my own person and I—"

"You *will* be ordered about. I *have* the right, the pearls you took from me gave me every right I need. And you are not your own person anymore, Caro. You are mine."

Her stomach completely disappeared, dropping past her hips, her knees, and then she lost track of it. Her breath, caged and caught within her throat, was soon to follow.

"Take off Blakesley's pearls," he said softly, but there was nothing soft in his expression. He looked prepared to kill.

Without taking her eyes from him, she removed Blakesley's pearls. Ashdon held his hand out for them and, without a word, she placed them there. Her hand trembled. His did not. But his eyes burned blue and hot.

It was oddly erotic. She knew nothing about anything, but she knew that they were engaged in a very serious sensual duel and that, unless she fumbled badly, in obeying Ashdon's commands, she could get him to do almost anything. It was completely contrary to logic, of course, but it was suddenly as clear to her as if someone had shouted it into her face.

Perhaps she was her mother's daughter, after all.

Ashdon put the Blakesley pearls into his pocket and then said, "Now the Dutton pearls."

"But whose pearls am I wearing, Ash?" she said, her voice husky with tension as she lifted the Dutton pearls over her head. "These pearls you gave me, they cannot be truly yours. Do I not then belong to the owner of these pearls? Must I not, by the rules of the game, give myself to . . . the Duke of Calbourne?"

It was a guess, but, again, led by some strange instinct, she knew it was the right guess. And it was exactly the right thing to say.

She held out the Dutton pearls, tangling them in her fingers. Ashdon took a step nearer, his hand covering hers, peeling the pearls from her fingertips, his hand hot, hers chilled; erotic, there was no other word. Ashdon towered over her, his scent enveloping her, his eyes burning her.

"They are mine now," he said. "As you are mine."

His hand tangled in her hair at the nape, pulling her into him, holding her hip in one large hand as his mouth opened upon hers. He was hot, everywhere. Heat rolling off him, igniting her, pooling heat in her loins, gathering fire in her breasts, inflaming her heart.

As she flamed, she took him with her, setting fire to the ice that was Ashdon. Ashdon, who only burned when he burned in anger. Ashdon, who wanted nothing to do with her, yet couldn't leave her alone. Ashdon, who mocked her and scolded her when he wasn't pretending to ignore her, when he wasn't burning for her.

She could see that now, now that she was burning for him as he was burning for her. It was all so clear, the smoke of desire outlining everything in charcoal. He hated her because he wanted her. He hated that Sophia had bought him. He hated that she had rejected him to become anything other than his wife. There was no room for love when hate protected him so well.

But passion could turn hate to ash. Passion blazed and everything fell away, destroyed and then forgotten.

Passion, she thought, reaching for thought through the thrum of desire, the rhythm of need, trying to think when his mouth swept thought from her, passion . . . passion . . .

Ashdon's mouth trailed a moist path across her cheek and down her neck, his lips caressing her throat, kissing her, biting her gently. His teeth scraped pearls, moving them over her neck, causing the strand to slide between her breasts in sensuous curls. Her skin shivered and then flushed, her breath dragged in and gasped out, and she watched it all from passion's cage, a willing prisoner, an eager accomplice to passion's assault.

"Meet our bargain," he whispered against her skin, his hands poised under her breasts, her nipples tingling with the hope that he would touch her. He spoke in command, but it was a plea. He was desperate, scorched, and he begged to be burned even brighter. "Give me," he said, his voice cracked, "give me to the fall of the pearls. That much and no more. That was our bargain."

She did not know where the words came from, certainly not from her inexperienced heart. She knew next to nothing, nothing beyond what her mother had told her. Then again, that was more than most girls knew.

"You promise to take no more than the fall of your pearls?" she said on a gasp.

"I promise," he said, his hands sliding around to her back, pulling her to him, crushing her breasts against his chest. She groaned in need and he tipped her head back by pulling on her hair and kissed her deeply, groaning his own need into her mouth.

The sounds of the party were as nothing, the sound of the wind high in the trees, the sound of wheels clattering over the cobbles, the sound of the surf after a day at the shore. Nothing. Background. Purged of meaning eons ago. The only meaning left to the world was the passion and the need between them.

And the knowledge her mother had given her.

She turned her head slightly and broke the kiss, pushing him back with a gentle hand to his chest. He obeyed her wordless instruction. How had she known he would?

"You are many things, Ash," she said, shocked to hear the smoky longing in her voice, pleased at the flare of desire in Ashdon's eyes when he heard it, "but I never knew, until now, that you were a liar."

And with those words, passion broke into pieces.

"Is this a game to you, Caro?" he said hoarsely, his eyes glittering like sapphires.

She stepped back another step, her shoulders brushing against the silk-lined walls, the sounds from outside their sheltered box coming louder to her now as the spell they had made between them fell in wisps of anger and disillusionment to the floor at their feet.

"Isn't it?" she said softly, her chin up.

"And if a game, then you want to win it?"

"Of course. Don't you want to win? Hasn't this all been about what you shall do and what I shall do and who can come out the victor?"

Ashdon nodded and swallowed, crossing his arms over his chest, considering her.

"Then let us finish," he said slowly. "I have met your price, but you have yet to meet mine. Take down your bodice. I want to see what I've paid for."

"You don't mean," she said, startled, "but you can't mean *now!*"

"I do mean now," he said calmly.

"But we are hardly . . . alone. There are people all around us, ready to—"

"I do not care what they are ready to do, or what they will see. Being alone was never part of our negotiation. You should be more careful in the future. A successful courtesan lays out all the terms beforehand. Consider this a lesson you needed to learn. Someday, you might even thank me."

"You're a lout! A brutish, ill-mannered *monster,*" she shrieked softly. It was so difficult to be enraged when one had to keep one's voice down.

"So?" he said, sitting down on the single chair in the dressing room and crossing his legs at the ankles, his very posture screaming that he had not a care in the world and would not care if the whole world saw her with her breasts bobbing about in the open with nothing but a string of pearls to shield them. "I am a lout. Slip down your bodice."

"I won't!"

Ashdon raised an eyebrow. "Are you ashamed of your breasts?"

"I am not! My breasts are perfectly lovely."

Ashdon smiled and said, "I'll agree with you, or not, when I've seen them. I'll let you know my opinion."

"What? You can't mean to . . . grade my breasts?" she gasped, clutching her bodice to her.

"Why not? A courtesan must have the proper equipment. You want to earn the highest price, don't you?"

"Listen to me, you horrible man," she said between clenched teeth, "I . . . I've changed my mind about being a courtesan. This is all ridiculous and completely pointless."

"Not to me," he said evenly. "There is a debt to be paid, and you *will* pay it, Caro."

"I won't."

"You will, if I have to strip you naked to see it done," he said. One look at his set face and cold eyes and she believed him. "I have lost far too many wagers of late, as you are so fond of reminding me, to see this one lost for want of will on your part."

"You can't expect me to want to do this!" she said, crossing her arms over her breasts to stop their tingling. She was dismally afraid that some wicked part of her found this exciting.

This was no time to realize yet again that she was her mother's daughter in the most embarrassing of ways.

"Why not? You agreed to do it. No one forced you to make our bargain. Actually, in the efforts of honesty, you seemed eager enough just a few moments ago. Perhaps if I kissed you again? Fondled you? Perhaps then you could be led down the well-trod path of *wanting* to bare your breasts for me?"

"You are *horrible*, and wicked, and . . . *horrible!*" she choked out. Because, actually, there was some wicked truth to what he'd said. There was nothing for her but that she must hate him for it. "And what do you mean by 'well-trod path'? I can assure you that *I* have never done, have never even contemplated . . . that no one has ever—"

"Yes," he interrupted, showing every sign of colossal boredom, "I am quite sure that all this is new to you. Your innocence, one might even say your naïve behavior, assuredly speaks volumes on your behalf."

Caro reared back as if slapped. It was an insult and nothing less. Only Ashdon could make inexperience in debauchery sound like an insult.

She *would* be her mother's daughter, blast him. After all, they were to have been married, almost. In fact, she could have him for a husband at any time; one needed only to have him collected and deposited upon her doorstep, like a very bruised plum.

"Why thank you, Lord Ashdon," she said stiffly, "but I daresay *your* kisses wouldn't help at all." She had the exquisite joy of seeing him snap forward in his chair, his eyes gleaming like knives. "I'll certainly keep to our bargain," she continued. "How could I do otherwise?"

"This from the woman who broke the marriage contract arranged by her mother?" he said with a sly smile. "Now who is lying?"

"*That* was different."

"Yes, certainly. That would have required that you keep your clothes on until you were married. This is without doubt the better path."

"I choose my own path. That is the entire point."

"I was under the impression that the entire point was to get you bare-breasted, a feast for my eyes and hands and mouth. We can't seem to agree on anything, can we, Caro?"

Her nipples tingled in response to his words and to his gaze upon her, so stern and yet so sad. He was an odd man, this Lord Ashdon, odd in that he either seemed to be fighting some demon within himself or fighting her. She quite decided that she preferred not to share him with any demon. From now on, Ashdon would fight her, if she could manage it. She was quite certain she could.

She *was* her mother's daughter, and she was not going to let Ashdon forget it.

"I can think of one thing we'll agree on," she said.

"What's that?" he asked.

"In a few minutes, we're both going to agree that I have exceptionally lovely breasts."

She didn't have any idea at all of how to describe the look in his eyes, except to say that she liked it very much, even if it was a bit frightening. Still, although he looked rather fierce, it was a fierceness that made her smile deep inside. Very deep inside. It wouldn't do at all if Ashdon realized that she was winning.

What would her mother do in such a situation? She wouldn't act nervous or shy, and she wouldn't show any fear, that was certain. What was it about her mother that made men go limp and women try to emulate her, for she was copied, after a fashion. There was that time years ago when her mother had worn red and blue parrot feathers in her artfully arranged hair and for the next two months, every woman in town had worn parrot feathers. None of them, according to her father, had ever achieved Sophia's casual élan, but as her daughter, Caro fully expected to have a leg up in that regard. As to the parrot feathers, she remembered it so well because she had asked her mother about it when the price of parrot feathers had risen to unheard of heights, and she still remembered very clearly what her mother had said.

It must appear effortless.

Effortless. She had to loosen her bodice and display her breasts to a man, and it must appear effortless.

She could do that.

"The disturbance is rising on the other side of that door," Ashdon said. "If you still contend that you're going to actually honor our agreement, you'd best get on with it."

Caro cleared her throat softly and said, "Let them wait. I shall do this in my own time and in my own fashion."

Ashdon raised his eyebrows and held his tongue. It was a promising beginning. She didn't want Ashdon's voice in her ears, having his eyes upon her and his long legs stretched out toward her was quite enough. What she needed was to hear Sophia's voice in her head. What would her mother do? What would she say? After a lifetime of exposure, and after interrupting countless minor seductions between her mother and father, she had a solid notion.

Caro reached up with her left hand and slowly peeled off her elbow-length white glove. Ashdon watched her avidly, his clear blue eyes going smoky.

"I shall need to remove these, I'm afraid," she said softly, keeping her eyes on her arms. "I shall want my hands free when I untie my bodice and loosen it. Do you not agree, Lord Ashdon?"

"Uh, yes," he said. His voice sounded scratched and worn. She took that as a good sign.

She slowly slipped the other glove off and then slid both gloves through her hands, caressing them like a silky cat, before handing them to Lord Ashdon, saying, "Would you be so good as to hold these for me, Lord Ashdon?"

Ashdon leaned forward and took the gloves, laying them carefully over one of his knees. He never took his eyes from her and they glowed like blue embers. She took that as a good sign as well.

"I may have a bit of trouble with this cord," she said, fingering the long silk cord that was tied under her breasts and trailed down the front of her gown to her knees. "My maid had to tie it very tight. I might require your assistance, my lord, as the pearls you gave me tonight hang a bit lower than the cord. Do you mind?"

"No," he said. Actually, he didn't so much speak as growl. As Lord Ashdon was a bit given to growling, especially at her, she took that as a good sign as well. Things were going quite well, all in all. The fact that she could scarcely breathe was not going to be factored in.

He stood, filling the small room, the candles dancing at the movement, the moving shadows highlighting the arc of his brow, his fine cheekbones, his chiseled jaw. He was a tall man of well-turned leg and broad shoulders. He had a mouth not given to smiling and eyes that experienced joy too seldom. There was a sadness about him that intrigued her, for she could not name its source. Sorrow and sensuality tumbled within him, fighting for dominance. She was an ally of sensuality. Let sorrow retreat, abandoning the fight for him.

"They're lovely pearls, aren't they?" she asked, touching the strand at its lowest point. "I'm so glad you gave them to me."

He stood staring down at her, mute. She handed him the tasseled ends of her cording, which he took. It looked for all the world like she was his captive, led on a silken rope.

"Thank you, my lord," she breathed, avoiding his eyes. If she looked at him, she would remember who he was and who she was and that this was a game that she wanted to win, even if she had forgotten why. "This bodice tie is very weak. I shall have no trouble with it, but you, you must be very adept and very determined or the cording will defeat you. I should not want," she said on a broken sigh, "you to be defeated, my lord."

"I shall not be," he murmured, pulling her to him by the ends of the cording. "Not in this, Caro. Never in this."

She walked toward him with tiny steps, her head lowered, her gaze averted, but she did not stop walking. She came on. Her mother would have done no less.

When he had her close, when she was tucked under his chin and within the length of his arms, he stopped. She stopped.

His scent tantalized her. Ashdon had what she could only describe as a clean smell: clean linen, clean hair, clean skin. Like the top of a mountain, like winter on a lake, like a spring meadow. Like Ashdon. The world seemed full of scents, of perfumes and flowers and cloying, sweetly spiced odors, but Ashdon smelled clean, and because of him all other scents were the lie of clean. A mockery of Ashdon.

She loosened the tie of her bodice and let it gape open to reveal the top edge of her chemise. Her stays were small and did not cover her breasts. It was the French fashion, and everyone knew the French excelled at fashion. Besides, her mother had told her what to wear, from her skin to the pearls at her ears. Had she known this would happen? Had she somehow known that Ashdon would immediately demand his privilege bought with pearls? She had known about the challenge, it had been her idea, after all, but had Sophia known that Ashdon would be so angry and so impatient?

Of course she had known.

Perhaps it had not been Ashdon who had told Dutton and Blakesley of her pearl price. Perhaps that had been Sophia's doing as well. It was logical, or was it? She was not a courtesan. She was not going to be a courtesan. Her mother did not want her to be a courtesan and would never direct her down its path.

Then how did she find herself in the Duke of Hyde's dressing room with her bodice gaping and Lord Ashdon . . . bewitched?

Bewitched was such a short step from besotted.

Thank you, Mother.

Ashdon was staring down at her, his eyes burning with passion and need and perhaps just a bit of surprise. She gambled recklessly by looking at him, studying his face, watching the way his mouth opened to take in a heavy breath, to see the line of his dark beard trace his mouth, to note the sweep of his lashes as they reached for his brows and the smoky line of his dark lower lashes.

His eyes smoldered.

She smoldered.

The strand of pearls rolled against her skin, gathering between her breasts, falling out of sight into the hem of her chemise. Ashdon had his hands around her ribs, his thumbs pressed just under her breasts, the cording tangled in his hands and falling over her wrists.

She couldn't breathe. Her heart hammered under her ribs and she knew he had to feel its wild beating.

Someone hammered at the door to the dressing room from the drawing room. Ashdon pulled her into the shelter of his arms and turned her so that his back was to the door, shielding her.

"This is madness, Caro," he growled. "Tighten your laces. Cover yourself. I won't see you ruined this way."

"I won't have my honor questioned, my lord," she said softly. "Let the world call me ruined. You and I shall know that I was paying a debt of honor."

"Honor be damned! I won't have you ruined for some stupid game, started for what reason I can't even remember now."

"Can't you, Ash?" she said, tipping her head up to look at his chin. He had a dark beard. She liked that. "You gave me pearls. I give you all that falls within their scope. Don't you want to touch me? Don't you want to see if my breasts are as lovely as I claim?"

He swore something, she couldn't tell what, and then his mouth was on hers and his fingers were in her chemise, pulling it gently down, his fingertip grazing a swollen nipple.

She arched into his hand with a moan of longing and aching and confusion. Could anything feel like this? Could hands on skin do this?

Her bodice collapsed against the cording around her ribs, Ashdon's hands on her breasts, hard and hot, gentle, relentless. His kiss delved deep and long, and she opened her mouth to consume him. The pearls twisted against her breasts; he fisted his hands in the white length of them and pushed her from him, her mouth still seeking his, open and wet, starving for the taste of him.

He stared at her, his eyes a blaze of blue, his breath coming in pants that sounded loud and harsh in the stillness of the silk-lined room. He held her, controlled her, by the pearls, twisted tight now around her neck, his clenched hand a mass of veins and muscle. He looked hungry, hungry and wild, beyond speech, almost beyond thought.

It was the same for her. She was beyond everything but the need for Ashdon.

"Don't resist," she urged in a hoarse whisper. "Take what you have won."

"What are you?" he breathed. "To say such things, to want—"

"A woman," she breathed, interrupting him. "Nothing more. Just a woman. Tell me it is not a woman you want."

He shook his head like a man coming out of a nightmare on a cloud-thick night, lost and seeking, afraid. "You don't even know what you're saying. You don't even know what you're offering."

"Then show me," she said, staring into his eyes, wanting him, wanting him to want her.

The door to the dressing room thundered in its frame, the sounds of the assemblie rising to a roar of curiosity and frustration. Ash pulled her to him roughly, the pearls his chain, and kissed her hard, fast, and then released her and the pearls.

"Cover yourself," he barked.

She tried. She did, but her hands were clumsy with passion, trembling with what they'd done and what she'd wanted him to do. He was right; she wasn't at all certain she knew what it was she wanted, but she knew she wanted it from him.

Ash stood barring the door as she fumbled with her bodice. Her chemise was twisted, her lips felt swollen, and her hair felt tumbled. She was certain she looked as if she had been, tumbled, that is.

The door flew inward with a bang, the crush in the drawing room surging behind it. Caro jerked her head upward, her hands to her floppy bodice while Ashdon stood directly in front of her, a shield from curious eyes. At the front of the group stood Lord Henry Blakesley, fourth son of the Duke of Hyde. He wore an amused expression, as was his habit. At his side stood Sophia, whose expression fluctuated between amazement and approval.

"How lovely," Sophia said. "I see the wedding is back on."

Nineteen

"SOPHIA, I must protest," Henry Blakesley said from the small confines of the closet. "I gave Caroline pearls as well as Ashdon. I don't see why he should be entitled to marry your pretty daughter just because he locked her in a dressing room. Give me five minutes locked with her in this closet and then let Caroline choose between us."

They had, by force of nature, the nature in this case being the absolute crush of humanity and the flash fire of gossip, been practically pushed from the dressing room through the gold bedroom, a highlight of these assemblies as the bedposts *were* covered in gold, and into a room which was not officially on the circuit. The closet had nothing to recommend it. It was even painted a completely lackluster white. Still, it did afford what little privacy they were going to find tonight and Sophia was adamant that Caro not leave Hyde House with matters unresolved.

Which meant, of course, that Caro must be married forthwith, the matter decided immediately.

That Ashdon had competition for the delectably tousled Caro seemed to annoy him unreasonably.

Blakesley couldn't remember ever having been so entertained at one of these affairs.

"I don't think the pearls are the deciding factor here, Blakesley. You do remember the pearls I gave her just moments after your grand gesture," Dutton said. "I'm still being considered, isn't that so, Caroline?"

When Dutton had forced his way into the closet, Blakesley had thought Ashdon just might hit him again. It was only for lack of space that he didn't. Give Ashdon room to swing and he'd wager on a different outcome.

"Don't pretend you give a damn about her," Ashdon snarled at Dutton. "Six hours ago you were hot for Anne Warren."

"Lord Ashdon! Such language!" Sophia said, one corner of her mouth tipped up in a wry smile. "Please remember that my daughter is a lady and an innocent." And when the pause lengthened to the breaking point, Sophia added, "Isn't she?"

"Of course!" Ashdon said.

"Of course," Sophia said, nodding sweetly.

No one asked Caroline, as it would have been awkward and no one wanted to make her feel any more awkward than she already must feel. It was perfectly obvious to anyone with a working knowledge of a ladies' bodice, and all here must admit to at least that, that Caro's bodice had been trifled with. And if the bodice, then Caro. Marriage was the order of the day in times such as these.

Blakesley thanked God that he had never personally experienced times such as these, no matter what he said to annoy Ashdon. Though, in all truth, it was more that Sophia had implied that his involvement would help her daughter that he tarried, baiting Ashdon. That, and Lousia Kirkland knew exactly what was going on in this closet, as did the whole house, and he found a peculiar joy in baiting her as well.

Blakesley was equally aware that Sophia had implied that as well. A clever woman, was Sophia Dalby. He must take care never to fall into the center of any web she spun.

"I don't suppose *my* opinion matters," Caroline said calmly, or at least calmly considering that she was destined to be the scandalous example mothers frightened their marriageable daughters with for the next ten years, conservatively.

"Of course it does, darling," Sophia trilled as she took Caroline's gloves from Ashdon's clenched fist and handed them casually to her daughter. Blakesley swallowed a laugh and ended up with an explosive cough.

"Pardon me," he said to the room at large. Ashdon frowned at him. It wasn't a punch in the gut, but it was something.

"Now, which of these fine gentlemen would you like for a husband, Caro?" Sophia said. "You may choose freely as they have each freely compromised you, a lovely girl of good home without a blemish to your reputation, until, that is, they gave you, in the full view of all Society, a rather inappropriate, too personal, and far too expensive gift of pearls. Isn't that right, Lord Henry? Lord Dutton? And, of course, not to be forgotten, Lord Ashdon."

Blakesley reconsidered the whole thing. He *had* been punched in the gut, but not by Ashdon. Damn Sophia for her cleverness. He had been *pushed* into this by the promise of a small revenge against Louisa Kirkland. It was a fine revenge if he ended up married to Caroline Trevelyan!

"I beg your pardon, Lady Dalby," Dutton said stiffly, "but it was not I who had your beautiful daughter trapped in that dressing room."

"And wasn't it kind of Lord Ashdon," Sophia countered politely, "to remove Caroline from such a squalid scene? I cannot thank you enough for that, Lord Ashdon. My poor girl, abused in front of absolutely everyone in such fashion . . . if I'd only been in the room, I might have been able to prevent it. But," she sighed, "as I was not, I am so fortunate that Lord Ashdon took, dare I say it, a father's role in attempting to protect my innocent daughter. She *is* innocent, isn't she, Ashdon?" Sophia prompted.

"Of course!" Ashdon bit out. "But I am hardly a father to her."

He sounded rather insulted. Sophia looked entirely too pleased. Blakesley decided, for the moment, to hold his tongue and see exactly how Sophia led this merry chase to the altar.

"Naturally not," Sophia said. "Merely a turn of phrase and entirely complimentary to you, Lord Ashdon. You did, in fact, present my daughter with a rather spectacular, by all accounts, strand of excessively long pearls, quite in the company of these two gentlemen. Are those your pearls which she is now wearing?"

"They most certainly are," Ashdon said.

He said it with some, oh, what to call it? Pride of possession? Ownership? Blakesley crossed his arms and leaned against the door to the antechamber. Caroline was almost certainly blushing. How very interesting. What *had* happened in that little room?

"And the other pearls? Don't tell me you've lost them, Caro."

"I certainly did not," Caroline said, fussing with her bodice tie. How *very* interesting.

"Then where are they?" Sophia pressed.

At this question, Caroline most definitely did blush, and now it was Ashdon's turn to cough. Sophia merely raised her ebony eyebrows and waited.

"Lord Ashdon has them," Caroline finally said, mumbled actually.

"Really?" Sophia said, looking with keen interest at Lord Ashdon. "Did you give them to him or did he take them off you?"

"*Mother!*" Caro hissed, pulling on her long evening gloves furiously. "Really!"

"It is a good question, Caro, kindly answer it," Sophia said.

"I will answer it, Lady Dalby," Ashdon said. "Lady Caroline gave me the pearls because I demanded that she do so."

"I see," Sophia said softly. "And did you also demand that she keep the pearls you gave her?"

"In a manner of speaking, I did," Ashdon replied.

Any fool could see where this was going and not a one of them was a fool.

"And she still wears them, I see," Sophia said with a soft gleam in her eyes. "Caro, since you refused the pearls of Lord Dutton and Lord Henry, in a manner of speaking," she added with a wry smile for Ashdon, "it seems you have made your choice. It is my pleasure, Lord Ashdon, to welcome you into the family. You will, of course, return the pearls in your . . . pocket?" At Ashdon's nod, she continued, "To these gentlemen. Their offers were rejected. It is only proper that their goods are returned to them, perhaps to be put to more fruitful use later in the Season."

What? Not bloody likely. Blakesley took his pearls and shoved them deeply into his pocket. Dutton, he was astonished to note, did not. Dutton, who might have been a fool after all, smiled at his pearls, at Sophia, and at Ashdon of all people, before slowly pressing his pearls into his pocket. He was still smiling when he bowed his departure, but not before kissing Caroline's hand and murmuring something against her glove.

Ashdon looked ready to sock him again. Damned nuisance that there wasn't enough room in the closet for that sort of thing. He was going to speak to his father about that, perhaps get some carpenters in to smash out a wall or some such. There was entirely too much fun being missed merely for lack of space.

And with that thought, Blakesley made his departure. He did not kiss Lady Caroline's hand. He did, however, kiss Lady Dalby's.

"WHAT a lovely young man. I do wonder whom he shall find now that Caroline is removed from consideration," Sophia said as Blakesley left the closet on the heels of Lord Dutton. They had both exited through the antechamber, which led to the music room, the last room on the assemblie circuit. It was the route they would all follow at their own exit out of Hyde House. Ashdon was hardly looking forward to it.

His father was going to kill him.

Ashdon found, after a rather cursory consideration, that he didn't much care. His thoughts were all of Caro, her flushed skin, the pearls tangled around her nipples . . .

Calbourne's pearls. He was going to have to repay that debt immediately, if not sooner, because he knew without doubt that he'd never return the pearls to Cal. They were Caro's pearls now.

"Just where did you get those pearls, Lord Ashdon?" Sophia said, as if she could read his mind. According to his father, she almost could.

"Does it matter now?" Caro said before he could answer.

"It's rather impolite to question the source of gifts, isn't it, Lady Dalby?" he said.

Sophia smiled at his rebuke and said, "Already working as a pair, are you? I would so love to know what happened in that dressing room. Something scandalous, obviously, but perhaps something also quite . . . delicious."

Caro turned her back on her mother at that and began fussing again with her bodice tie. She couldn't seem to get it exactly as she wanted it. On that, he quite agreed with her; he wanted that damnable tie destroyed so that he could have his hands on her bosoms again, and this time without a riot taking place on the other side of the door.

This did no good. Thinking of Caro, of *that*, only distracted him.

"How charming," Sophia said lightly, letting her gaze run over him; Ash resisted the urge to fold his hands over his groin. "I see you are all eagerness for the wedding. How fortunate that all the legal business is behind us, all that nasty wrangling, now we can devote ourselves to the joys of ceremony."

"What do you mean by *nasty wrangling*?" Caro said, turning back around to face them. Her bodice appeared completely intact and unfussed with, the pearls dipping down into her cleavage where they were lost to shadow. This time he gave into the urge and let one of his hands hover casually over his groin.

Sophia laughed lightly behind her hands, giggled really. When he turned to scowl at Sophia, she *winked* at him. No wonder his father hated her so; she was quite willing to drive a man to murder.

"Only the most normal of meanings, darling," Sophia said to Caro, completely ignoring Ashdon as suddenly as she had made him the center of her jest. Impossible woman. "I've arranged a very nice settlement upon you, one which will insure that you will never want for anything. No matter what your husband gets into."

"*Gets into?*" Caro said.

"Now, darling, it is simply the most disagreeable habit to repeat what everyone says. You mustn't fall into bad habits just because you've chosen to marry a man with . . . oh, well, I suppose that was impolite as well, but now that we're family, I suppose we may speak freely."

It was hardly as if she was asking his permission now, was it?

"You and I both know," Sophia continued before anyone could interrupt her, "that Lord Ashdon has a history of intemperate gambling, surely not uncommon, but usually not so . . . oh, what is the word I'm searching for . . . not so reliably dismal. I merely want to protect you and your future children against his—"

"Dismal record?" Ashdon supplied bitingly.

"How nicely put, Lord Ashdon," Sophia said. "So helpful of you, really, and so refreshingly honest."

"Thank you," Ash said, bowing curtly and extremely sarcastically.

"If you didn't like his dismal record, why did you put him forth as a husband for me?" Caro said. She was as direct and almost as rude as her mother. Ash could see that it was a perfectly acceptable defense against Sophia's normal discourse. One could not fight fire with a feather, after all.

"Why did I buy him for you, do you mean?" Sophia said gaily.

"All right, Mother," Caro said crisply, "that is exactly what I mean."

"Well, obviously, and I mean no disregard for *you*, Lord Ashdon, simply because I *could*. There is a certain joy to be had in doing whatever one wants, particularly at my age." At Caro's furious look, Sophia said, "But more to the point, because I thought you two would get on very well together, which of course you do, and, with the matter of your security settled beforehand, I thought you'd make a good match between you. Was I wrong?"

"You were not wrong," Ashdon said before Caro could get a word out. He didn't quite trust Caro not to throw the whole marriage idea away just to spite her mother, and, though he knew without a shadow of a doubt that his father might well cut him off without a shilling, he wasn't entirely confident that his father had much more than a shilling to punish him with anyway.

"Aside from being consistently referred to much in the manner as a cut of beef one is purchasing, I have always been agreeable to the match made between Caroline and myself. I trust you will support me in that statement, Lady Dalby?"

"Certainly," Sophia said serenely.

"And now that I have become acquainted with Caroline—"

"Such understatement," Sophia cut in. "It is perfectly within the truth to say you two are *well* acquainted now."

"Which is surely to our mutual gain," Ashdon said, taking Caro's hand in his and pulling her gently to his side. "I have formed an attachment to your daughter, quite a firm one, and I *will* marry her."

"You sound quite set upon her," Sophia said, smiling at him.

"I am," he said. "No other woman will do for me. It must be Caro."

"Well then," Sophia said, shifting her gaze to Caro, her expression enigmatic, "if it must be Caro, then Caro it shall be."

Twenty

THERE was nothing for it; they had to leave the closet and face the crowd that thronged within the colossal magnificence of Hyde House. Sophia appeared undaunted by the prospect, Ashdon resolved, and Caro, well, the best description might have been overwhelmed.

She was to marry Ashdon after all. Not because he had been bought for her, at least not *only* because he had been bought for her, but because he had no wish to marry elsewhere.

He wanted her. He wanted her enough to defy his father, for she well knew that the Earl of Westlin had nothing but rancor for Sophia and her children. Simply being Sophia's child was enough to make an enemy of him, though now that Westlin was the father of her husband certainly they must find a way to happily coexist. Or at least peacefully coexist. Or at the very least behave in a civil manner to one another in public.

Caro only hoped they wouldn't have to begin right now, being civil, that is. She would much rather wait until she and Ash were safely married and Lord Westlin could do nothing to change that fact. At this moment, with the veil of ruination and scandal her most prominent accoutrement, she was less than confident about almost anything.

Though Ash, his hand firmly on the small of her back as they slipped without overdue fanfare along the edge of the antechamber until they reached the music room, made her feel confident about almost everything.

She was quite aware that her thoughts were illogical and ridiculous. She was also quite certain she'd never had an illogical and certainly not a ridiculous thought in her entire life, but that was the effect Ashdon had on her. She was simply muddleheaded and what was worse, she didn't care.

He liked her. He was, dare she say it, bewitched by her, or at least by her breasts. She supposed he had seen more than one pair of breasts since his wet nurse and that he knew what enchanted him or not. She enchanted him. She was positive of it.

Obviously, the thing to do was to get bare-breasted again, and as soon as possible. It was not beyond logic that his father might still yet convince Ash to do his worst, that is, to abandon her in some fashion as to ruin her completely. Her mother had warned her about that, knowing Lord Westlin as she did. Intimately, that was the gossip. She had no reason to doubt it. So, while she was feeling simultaneously without confidence and glowing with confidence, she had to get Ashdon back to her breasts.

It had been . . . amazing. She still felt jumbled, her knees like water and her breath uneven. She rather liked the sensation, just as she rather liked the sensation of Ash's hands on her, and his mouth . . . oh, yes, her bodice had to disappear at the first opportunity.

Caro watched the way he looked at her, and at the pearls as they dangled between her breasts, sliding this way and that as she moved; it was this very look that gave her what little confidence she had. She was confident of one thing and it might well prove to be the *only* thing of any import. Ashdon liked very much, very much indeed, the way she looked wearing his pearls.

She didn't even need to be her mother's daughter to know that.

With that confidence and her little plan of removing her bodice foremost in her thoughts, Caro walked into the music room, the final room of the Hyde House assemblie, with Ashdon at her back and his pearls between her breasts. She held her head up and was certain she wasn't blushing.

Well, almost certain.

"Darling, that blush quite becomes you," her mother said softly, just as she was about to greet their hostess, Molly, Duchess of Hyde, "and Ashdon is positively *besotted*. Whatever it is you are doing, he appears to enjoy it immensely. What else should a woman do but keep doing it?" And with a laugh and a squeeze on the hand, Sophia gaily greeted Molly, as if she had not a care in the world.

"Your grace," Sophia said serenely, "what a lovely gathering. I am so delighted to have been, once again, included."

"Included?" Molly said. "Without you, the guests would fall asleep where they stand. One can only admire gold leaf so many times before even gold becomes tiresome. Now, tell me, Sophia, what divine devilishness have you concocted this year?"

"What have you heard?" Sophia said with a half smile.

"Only what half of London has heard by now," Molly said with an answering smile. Molly had hair the color of a newly minted sovereign, entirely natural, eyes of gunmetal gray, and a smile that burst forth with endearing frequency. It was her smile, by all reports, that had gathered Hyde to her heart. Anyone who argued that her father's fortune had secured Hyde had never met Molly and been captured by her exuberant joy.

"And that is?" Sophia said as the two of them made their way, completely unimpeded for the crowd parted for them as though for Moses with his staff, to a relatively quiet corner of the lavish music room.

"That your daughter plunged into the life of a courtesan with all the grace of a swan taking to the sky, with three pearl necklaces, each worth a rather large fortune, draped around her neck. I'm almost certain I saw a play to this effect when I first arrived in London," Molly said, her brow furrowing in thought. "Of course, my son was never in any play I ever saw, and he *was* in this one."

"You know how these things twist in the telling, your grace."

"Oh, you misunderstand me, Sophia. If Henry wants the companionship of a woman, that is entirely his choice. I only hoped he would have the civility not to choose the daughter of a friend."

Sophia laughed with such obvious delight that Molly had no choice but to laugh with her.

"He did not. He has civility and more to recommend him," Sophia said. "In fact, he gave Caro the pearls to please me."

"To please *you*? Sophia, you have, by any measure, the most devious mind I have ever witnessed. You are"—Molly paused—"a complete delight."

"Thank you, your grace," Sophia said, dipping her head in acknowledgment.

"Now, I trust you have been complimented enough for one night? Tell me everything."

Which, of course, Sophia did not. She was not the sort of woman to tell anyone *everything*, but she did tell Molly enough to keep her satisfied and to give her a better than general understanding of events.

"Westlin may well have a fatal seizure of some sort," Molly said musingly when the bulk of the tale was told. "It would hardly surprise me."

"Well, it would surprise me," Sophia said, "and it would ruin everything. How can a revenge be enjoyed when the object dies prematurely? It misses the point entirely."

"He does deserve it, doesn't he?" Molly said softly. "He was rather an oaf with you."

"Hardly anything as serious as an oaf," Sophia said. "Rather say a clumsy puppy with far more yip and bite."

Molly studied Sophia shrewdly. "You've traveled rather far in your revenge upon him for merely a yippish pup."

"It was a pleasant journey," Sophia said mildly, "and Caro will be well served with Ashdon."

"Oh, yes, that's a match nicely made. They should get on well together. If Westlin can be made to heel."

"Molly," Sophia whispered, "you and I both know that *all* men can be made to heel. It is so very convenient that they come equipped with a lovely little leash and are so very eager to be led about by it."

Molly chuckled riotously and said, "What is it about these English girls? They seem to never have quite got the grasp of things, if you understand me."

"Molly, you are as English as any of them."

"In politics, yes, but there must be something about the air in the colonies, something a bit . . . savage perhaps that aids a girl born in America to see things, and of course I mean men, in the proper light."

"It has been an advantage."

"One that you've passed to Caro?"

"One hopes. But I can see you've done Lord Henry the same service. He is remarkably astute for a man."

"Yes, I almost could pity the girl he will eventually marry."

"Oh, I shouldn't worry about her," Sophia said with a soft smile, observing the room. "She'll find her way."

Perfumed and powdered, bored and spiteful, that was London. She had done very well here. She did not regret a moment of it, at least not out loud. She most certainly did not regret Dalby and the children he had given her. Markham and Caro were the future, and she had invested heavily in the future.

Sophia was well accustomed to seeing a good return on her investments.

"It is still rumored that you are the impoverished daughter of a French aristocrat," Molly said.

"How charming."

"Very. Naturally, I said nothing to correct the impression."

Sophia looked down at Molly, who was fetchingly petite, and said, "You need not keep my secrets, Molly. Westlin surely has not."

"Yes, but Westlin resents you so violently and so obviously that no one would think to believe him."

"Forgive me," Sophia said, "but I also find that equally charming. It is so refreshing to think of the Earl of Westlin being discounted, his opinions and pronouncements subject to obscurity. How completely delicious."

"It is, isn't it?" Molly said, smiling. "But, with Caro to marry the lovely Lord Ashdon, can the truth be ratified? If I tell it, it will be believed and it could cause Caro some trouble with Ashdon, not to mention your son, Lord Dalby. The ninth Earl of Dalby will be needing a wife before too long, and an heir."

"I think," Sophia said, watching Caro with Ashdon from across the room, Ashdon ever at her side, Caro deliciously flushed, "that Caro can manage Lord Ashdon. In fact, I think she'd rather enjoy it."

Molly laughed. "She's your daughter, then."

"Oh, yes," Sophia said, smiling as she watched Caro. "She's most definitely my daughter."

"Then you shan't mind if tales of your origins become more than rumor and fantasy?" Molly said. "I would not want to speak amiss, Sophia. We colonials must unite before the London throng."

"Molly, you have never needed my permission. You are a duchess, after all, and as for being a colonial, wasn't a war fought over just this point? You are English to the bone, which was the start and finish of the whole bloody war and all that hysteria over inequitable taxation."

"And you, Sophia?" Molly said softly. "What will be said of your bones?"

"Only good things, I trust," Sophia answered. "Say what you will, Molly. My dear Dalby is buried these seven years, my children well planted in English soil and blooming effortlessly . . . I do believe even the truth cannot harm them now."

"My dear Sophia," Molly said with a skeptical grin, "no woman is best served by truth. Let truth dwell elsewhere, I say."

"I would never presume to argue with you," Sophia said, arguing, "but in this case, I do believe that Caro, and Ashdon, would be well served by truth. Let us see where it takes them, shall we?"

"You have some plan, some devious twist, not that I can see it, but I know that look by now, Sophia, and if you want the truth out"—Molly shrugged delicately—"I am more than pleased to do my part. It looked to have been an excessively dull Season. Now, it looks to be rather more interesting."

"That I can promise you, your grace. It will be very interesting," Sophia said.

"And not just because of Lady Caroline and Lord Ashdon,"

Molly said with a discreet motion of her hand. "The Viscounts Tannington and Richborough are having some sort of heated exchange behind the harp. I do hope they don't damage it; it has just been restrung. I wonder what it is they're arguing about?"

"I wonder, indeed," Sophia said with a small smile of satisfaction.

Molly saw her smile and understood its implications immediately. "You've done something. Something to . . . Richborough?"

"Darling Molly," Sophia said softly, "am I to be held to accounts for the misbehavior of every man in London?"

"My dear Sophia," Molly rejoined, "is that a declaration of intent?"

To that, Sophia only smiled more fully.

❧

THE Marquis of Ruan, unwilling coconspirator of Lord Westlin, having heard quite enough of the conversation between Tannington and Richborough to understand its gist, that of who had greater claim to the charms of Sophia, turned his full attention back to the lady in question. She was smiling like a cat over a bowl of clotted cream. He had a strong inclination to smile with her.

Which was the entire problem of Sophia; she made a man want to do all the things she wanted him to do. Dangerous skill, that. A man must be wary around a woman like that. Wary . . . and yet, still intrigued.

She was an intriguing woman, and her allure went far beyond her appearance, radiant though it was. She was tall and slender with skin the color of cream and as smoothly flawless. The arch of her black brows and the high bridge of her narrow nose, her full red mouth and delicate little chin, all bespoke a lineage in the aristocracy. She had a decidedly French look, though that may have been more in the cut of her white muslin gown than in her curling black hair and sparking black eyes.

But it was the look in those dark eyes that made her more than a beauty. Sophia looked as though she held the secrets of the ages in those eyes and found the world's secrets vastly amusing.

Intriguing.

He simply must have a closer look.

Ruan slid through the crowd in the music room, a colossal knot of people who he expected were gathered more for the benefit of observing Lady Dalby and her attractive daughter, Lady Caroline, than for the magnificence of the stunning new aqua wallpaper and gilded harp in the Hyde House music room. He suspected that Lady Dalby was quite accustomed to attracting a knot of people around her. He also suspected that she rather liked it.

Lord Ruan stopped before the Duchess of Hyde and the Countess of Dalby and executed a curt bow of greeting. It was only proper to greet his hostess, after all, and then Molly could provide an introduction to Sophia. Neat and simple.

And so it happened, exactly as he'd planned it, as far as the introductions anyway. Beyond that simple beginning, things spun rapidly in unexpected directions.

"We have never met, Lord Ruan, and yet I feel I know you," Sophia said after he had complimented the Duchess of Hyde on the beauty of her new wallpaper and Molly had responded in kind by complimenting him on the fineness of his matched grays, purchased the previous week. Just as he was drawing breath to respond to Lady Dalby's remark with some innocuous comment that at some point, all members of the ton must know each other, she continued. "It is surely because you have been following me, close and yet so shy? Awaiting a moment, the perfect moment, for an introduction? You must learn to be more forward, Lord Ruan. A man of your years and distinction simply must learn not to skulk about in corners, all eyes and no tongue."

He was struck speechless. Molly's discreet cough, only just covering a rather girlish giggle, readjusted all his expectations. Sophia was clearly a woman who demanded that all expectation be adjusted upon meeting her.

"I ask your pardon, Lady Dalby," he said. "Now that I know your preferences, I shall be all tongue."

Molly gasped so loudly that she choked. Sophia neither gasped nor choked. Sophia Dalby raised her chin and looked him over. He let her look; in fact, he rather enjoyed it. He let the silence, a silence in which they studied each other blatantly, grow until Molly Hyde grew a bit pink about the throat, and then he said, "And now it is you, Lady Dalby, who is all eyes and no tongue."

"And is that your preference, Lord Ruan?" Sophia asked politely.

"Lady Dalby, do you seek to know my preferences? I am flattered."

"Lord Ruan, you are easily flattered."

"Lady Dalby, with a woman who is all tongue, I am easily won."

He feared Molly Hyde was close to fainting. Sophia was not.

"But, Lord Ruan," she said with a cold smile and slow shake of her head, "I am not. If you will excuse me?" she asked of the duchess and of him. He could do nothing but bow in acquiescence. "Will your eyes follow me, Lord Ruan?" she whispered as she passed him.

Sophia walked exactly four steps away from him before she turned her head and gazed at him from over her bare white shoulder, a few artful black curls skimming her back. His eyes had followed her—how could they not? Their eyes met. She smiled, and then she turned and walked away. His eyes followed her until she was lost in the crowd.

Intriguing.

Twenty-one

INTRIGUING man, that Lord Ruan, though rather forward for her tastes. Sophia had absolutely no time for intrigues; she had to get Caro married to Ashdon at the first opportunity. Tomorrow would suit her very well and, by the look on Ashdon's dear face, as soon as possible would suit him very well indeed. *Well done, Caro.*

She also had to arrange for the banns to be read for Staverton and Anne Warren. Everything there must proceed with propriety and precision; Anne deserved nothing less, as this marriage would move her into the peerage. No shadow would be allowed to blight it.

Sophia was also perfectly aware that Lord Westlin would do everything he could to ruin both marriages. Tiresome, but there it was. He was the most tenaciously ill-tempered man, always pushing about, determined to make a fuss about the most inconsequential things. Like the marriage of his heir to the only daughter of his first mistress. Really. Sophia smiled. Was that anything to make a fuss about?

&

EVERYONE was making such a *fuss*. Caro didn't enjoy it the least bit. Just because she had been given pearls by three gentlemen; it wasn't as if she had *asked* for the pearls. That had to count for something. Judging by the look on Ashdon's face as he nodded in curt civility to Lord Drayton about something to do with horses, Ashdon didn't act as if he thought it counted for much. He acted, now that her bodice was firmly in place and had been so for almost a quarter of an hour, as if *she* were somehow to blame for the pearls, the bodice, and even the betrothal.

It occurred to her, a bit late she had to admit, that Ashdon just might be as famously ill-tempered as his father. That wouldn't do at all. She was *not* going to live her life being snapped at and blamed for rain when he wanted sun, or whatever it was that made Ashdon so snappish.

She was well aware, experience being a wonderful teacher, that Ashdon could be kept docile, one might even say *malleable*, when her clothing was in a certain state of relaxation. But she couldn't spend her whole life walking about without her bodice tied. Even if it did feel rather wonderful when he touched her ... *there*, she must maintain some standards, and walking around bare-breasted was going to be one of them. Or not walking around bare-breasted. Whichever. The whole subject made her wooly-headed.

Lord Drayton had just finished speaking, his voice rambling off gradually as was his habit, and she was certain Ashdon was going to reply with an equally long-winded reply about bloodlines or some essentially boring rejoinder, when she hissed quietly at Ashdon's shoulder, which was all she could reach without him bending down to her, which of course he would not do, being the ill-tempered oaf that he was, "I did not *ask* for those pearls, you know."

"Excuse us, Lord Drayton," Ashdon said politely, his hand very firm on her elbow, possibly so that she couldn't poke him in the stomach with it, as he led her toward the doorway of the music room. She'd considered it. "You certainly *did* ask for the pearls you're wearing," he breathed, smiling at Lady Hartington, who grinned back at him. Lady Hartington was at least seventy and so her grin looked rather more like a leer.

"I only asked for these because you seemed so determined to *buy* me with something!" she snarled softly, smiling frigidly at Louisa Kirkland, who had almost magically appeared in the doorway to the blue reception room. Louisa had clearly gone the wrong way on the assemblie circuit. How gauche.

"As a courtesan, these sorts of gifts are both expected and required," Ashdon ground out, smiling rather too brightly at Lady Louisa. Louisa smiled brightly in response.

Wasn't it just lovely that Ashdon saved all his good cheer and civility for Louisa Kirkland?

"You know, Lord Ashdon," she said with brittle sweetness, "while I'm well aware that you're an ill-tempered *lout*, I did think you possessed some small intelligence. I'm so sorry to be proven wrong on that account. I can't think what sort of children we shall produce between us. In fact, if not for the fact that *you've ruined me completely*," she said, keeping her very false smile perfectly in place on her very stiff face, "I would refuse to marry you and take up the life you seem determined to foist upon me."

He appeared almost speechless. It didn't last long. Pity.

"Foist upon you?" he growled, nodding savagely at Louisa Kirkland as he not very politely dragged her into the blue reception room. Louisa Kirkland blanched and nearly tripped in getting out of Ashdon's path. That bit was rather nice. "*You* are the one who refused me! You are the one who declared it was her life's goal to become the plaything of any man with the price to play. You are the one who demanded the damned pearls in the first place."

"You know perfectly well that the pearls were just a . . . test," she said, pulling her arm free and ignoring the stares they were drawing. Guests were entering and leaving the house by the main doors in the blue reception room. Actually, they were rather more entering than leaving. She supposed she and Ashdon were drawing a crowd. She supposed she should care. She didn't. "Or you'd know perfectly well if you had any sense at all."

"If I had any sense at all," he growled rather too loudly considering that at least two dozen people were staring at them avidly, "I wouldn't have beggared myself in trying to avoid meeting you. I wouldn't have taken a strand of priceless pearls from Cal. I wouldn't have defied my father, and I wouldn't have dragged you into Hyde's dressing room to do this!"

He kissed her then. He pulled her to him by her arms,

leaving bruises she was certain, and kissed her hard on the mouth. It did all the things to her that his kisses always did. Weak, breathless, wobbly, and warm in places she hadn't known existed until Ashdon had started kissing her.

When he released her, he whispered harshly, "I'm going to marry you, Caro. It's going to ruin me, but I'm going to marry you."

"That's all you ever had to do, Ash," she sighed, still trying to clear her vision from that kiss. "Can't you see that marrying me is more fiscally responsible than paying for me?"

He didn't answer. He dragged her out into the London night, without even stopping long enough for her to retrieve her wrap. She didn't bother to make a fuss; Caro was too busy thinking that going about bare-breasted definitely had its advantages.

∽

NATURALLY, Westlin made a fuss when he heard about it. It was to be expected. In fact, the entire assemblie waited for it as confidently as one awaits the dawn.

He did it quietly, that much can be said for him, but perhaps it might have been that no one was paying particular attention to Lord Westlin. The whole of the assemblie was discussing, politely, greedily, and speculatively, the obvious evidence that Caroline Trevelyan had grown quite completely into her mother's daughter.

Naturally, comparisons were made to the night that Sophia had inspired both Westlin and Dalby to come to blows over her. Those who remembered that evening almost twenty years earlier were practically pummeled for their recollections. No one asked Westlin, for obvious reasons.

Sophia, also for obvious reasons, felt it impolitic and impolite to speak to anything that had or had not occurred twenty years previous. She said quite openly that she had no wish to upstage her daughter's rather stellar success on the marriage mart, stating without hesitation that she was certain, and was equally certain it was obvious to all, that Lady Caroline and Lord Ashdon had a markedly tempestuous and therefore passionate regard for one another and that she could speak from experience that marriages built on such foundations bore rather delicious fruit.

Delicious, that was the word she used and she used it somewhat frequently.

Ruan was becoming rather too keenly aware that he noticed too much about Sophia Dalby. He was also aware that he was intrigued by her use of the word *delicious*.

What *had* happened twenty years ago to earn Sophia both Westlin's enmity and Dalby's title?

∽

"PURE folly," Staverton grumbled to Anne, his future viscountess. "Westlin has a talent for trouble and he practices it diligently."

"You don't think he can stop their marriage, do you, Lord Staverton?" Anne asked softly. They had made their way slowly through Hyde House, trailing well behind Caro and Lord Ashdon, paused in the now infamous rose dressing room, and were now in the music room. Anne had a colossal headache. She wanted to go home, have a drink of chocolate, and then strangle Caro. In exactly that order.

What had Caro been thinking to have three men toss pearl necklaces at her, and at the most-talked-of event of their social year! It was exactly the sort of adventure that ruined a girl and made marriage, respectable marriage, an impossibility. Small chance now of Lord Westlin approving the match, and what heir would risk disobeying his father? Oh, Lord Ashdon was well away now and Caro without a hope of happiness.

"I think he'll try," Lord Staverton said grimly, "and poor luck for Caroline if he does. Westlin keeps a tight fist around Ashdon's throat, always has done, and Ashdon has been taught well to heel to Westlin's voice."

Anne's heart sank to her feet. "But why does he hate Lady Dalby so? This is all of her, isn't it? Do *you* know what happened twenty years past, Lord Staverton?"

Lord Staverton blinked rapidly and cleared his throat

noisily. "I do, but it's not a tale for mixed company, Mrs. Warren. That's all I'll say on the matter. Except to add that Lord Westlin is behaving like a complete idiot, as usual."

"Isn't it comforting when people react just as you expect them to?" Lord Dutton said, entering their conversation unannounced and uninvited. Unwelcome as well, as long as Anne was compiling a list of offenses.

"If they react well, then yes," she answered, before turning to Lord Staverton and smiling up at his uneven eyes. They were *nice* eyes with a thoughtful and considerate gaze, very much unlike Lord Dutton's sharp blue gaze.

"I had no idea you were an admirer of Lady Caroline's," Lord Staverton said to Dutton. "I suppose you're put out that she returned your necklace?"

"Do I look put out, Lord Staverton?" Dutton said softly, before turning to look down at Anne.

Anne turned her eyes away to admire the truly magnificent crystal chandelier hanging from the ceiling of the Hydes' music room. It glimmered like ice, rather like Lord Dutton's clear blue eyes.

Anne hated ice.

"I have found," Lord Dutton continued, "that one woman, however beautiful, however skilled, is very much like another. Don't you agree?"

"I certainly do not," Staverton huffed, casting a crooked glance over to Anne. Anne returned his look with a smile and a subtle shrug of her shoulders. "And I find your conversation in this company entirely ill-conceived."

"Oh, I think Mrs. Warren, a woman who certainly possesses her own skills of less than mysterious origins, will not disagree with me. Perhaps she would even add that, from her perspective, one man is very like another."

Staverton banged his gold-handled cane on the floorboards, causing at least twenty people to hush their conversations and look their way. This was exactly the sort of attention Anne abhorred and, once again, it was Dutton who was to blame. Perhaps Caro was more of an innocent in the evening's adventures than she had supposed. It was Lord

Dutton, after all, who'd been directly responsible for both of their misadventures at Hyde House. The man seemed to crave unwelcome attention.

"I won't have it!" Staverton blustered. "You, sir, will not speak so in front of a respectable woman, the woman to be my wife."

"It's quite all right, Lord Staverton," Anne said softly, laying a hand upon his arm. "I have learned through unfortunate experience that Lord Dutton is wanting in self-control and the most basic aspects of deportment. He cannot seem to help himself, and so he requires that we show him every courtesy and every indulgence."

"Married?" Dutton said, staring at her. "You are to be married?"

"Yes," Anne said softly, quietly enjoying the look of stunned disbelief on Dutton's face, the shock that rolled beneath his striking blue eyes.

"As of when?"

"As of tonight, sir, though it is hardly your concern," Staverton said.

Dutton seemed to collect himself, drawing his shoulders back and his head up. "You have no need for this, then," he said, reaching into his pocket and holding out a long strand of pearls toward her. They gleamed in the candlelight, soft and white.

"What is this, tossing about pearl necklaces to every woman?" Staverton said. "Some sort of wager posted at White's, is that it?"

"No," Dutton said stiffly, staring at Anne, his eyes the blue of a winter sea. "No wager."

"It had best be some damned wager or I'll—" Staverton said.

"It is no wager," Anne said, cutting Staverton off before he found himself maimed or killed in a duel, "but merely a jest. A jest that Lord Dutton began yesterday in Lady Dalby's salon. It is a jest that has gone on too long, has it not, Lord Dutton?"

"Yes," Dutton said softly. Then with a smile he said, "I beg your forgiveness, Lord Staverton, Mrs. Warren. My timing is off. The jest fell flat. I wish you all happiness." And with that, he bowed and left them, the pearls dangling loosely from his fist.

"Poor Dutton," Sophia said, coming up to them from somewhere behind the harp. "It is a rare night when a man cannot *give* pearls away."

"Poor Dutton, indeed," Staverton said. "The man has the most unpleasant way with a jest. 'Tis a wonder anyone speaks to him."

"Yes, 'tis a wonder," Sophia said, looking coolly at Anne. "What is your opinion, Anne, on Dutton's social success, for it is inarguable that he is a desired guest at any event."

Anne swallowed the lump in her throat, pushing it down past her heart and into oblivion, and answered, "Simply put, Lady Dalby, he is both titled and eligible. 'Tis all that is required of a man, is it not?"

Sophia laughed lightly and said, "It is certainly all that *I* require of a man. But if that is what is required of a man, what is then required of a woman? Best you should answer that, Lord Staverton."

"Damned silly jests, Sophia," he grumbled. "I don't know what's gotten into everyone tonight."

"It must be that rash of pearl necklaces making their way around the room," Sophia said with a smile. "How can a woman not become muddled under such conditions? But tell us, Lord Staverton, play out this jest, the last of the night. What is it that a man requires?"

"Oh," he said reluctantly, "perhaps a docile disposition."

Sophia laughed and patted Lord Staverton on the arm. "Are you certain, Stavey? That lets me out entirely, for no one has ever deemed me docile."

"Perhaps accommodating is a better word," he said. "What I mean to say is that, well, a man likes for a woman to be, well . . . pleasant."

Sophia raised a black eyebrow and simply smiled at him. "Then you have made a lovely choice in Anne, for she is the most pleasant woman of my acquaintance, though I must warn you, she is hardly docile."

Anne stood quietly, content to let Sophia and Lord

Staverton tease each other, as was their custom. They were old friends and their relationship was entirely comfortable. She looked, she dared guess, supremely docile at the moment.

"I disagree with you on that, Sophia," Lord Staverton said, "for one only has to gaze upon Mrs. Warren's lovely face to see the sweet docility and effortless charm of her person."

It was a lovely, sweet compliment and Anne smiled in the glow of it.

Until Sophia said, "You should ask Lord Dutton if he finds lovely Anne docile. I fear he has provoked her ire with some misbehavior on his part."

Anne looked at Sophia in shock. What was this? Sophia was going to spoil things with Staverton by throwing Dutton and his unwelcome attention into the mix? And how had Sophia guessed at Dutton's kiss? She had certainly said nothing of it.

"What's this, Mrs. Warren?" Staverton asked, his hand protectively on the small of her back. "Has he insulted you?"

"No," Anne said. "Not exactly."

"I'm almost certain that Lord Dutton would say he has flattered her," Sophia said, looking compassionately at Anne. Anne had a sudden and violent urge to kill Sophia. It was very unlike her. "But we all know how odd his perspective is on things."

"He made advances," Lord Staverton said solemnly. One could almost see him mentally picking through his pistols for the duel he would fight in Anne's honor.

"He made mistakes," Anne said softly. She wished ardently for Caro to still be at Hyde House. Caro was such an effective lightning rod for scandal.

What an ugly thought. She quite shocked herself.

"How kindly you put it, dear Anne," Sophia said. "Of course, a woman alone in the world . . . we grow accustomed to these sorts of . . . adventures, don't we, Anne?"

"Do you mean to say that he . . . he has been pursuing her?" Staverton said.

"And really," Sophia said conspiratorially, "who can

blame poor Dutton? Anne is a beautiful widow with neither chick nor child. I don't know if he had marriage in mind; did he mention marriage to you, Anne? But an eligible man about town and a likely widow . . . well, isn't there a play to that effect? In any regard, who can blame him?"

Sophia ended with a bright and brilliant smile. Anne was not smiling and certainly not brightly.

"I can blame him and do blame him," Staverton said.

"As well you should," Sophia consoled. "As the man whom Anne has agreed to marry, you have every right. You have many options, certainly, but were I you, Stavey, I would marry Anne without delay. That will stop the poor fellow cold and squash any rumors that may be clawing their way to life. Marry Anne and you save her from his misguided attempts at what he may consider flattery. Did you feel flattered by Lord Dutton's attention, Anne?" Sophia asked sweetly.

It was now Anne who was mentally sorting through an array of pistols.

"No," she said stiffly. "I did not."

"Of course you did not," Sophia affirmed. "Which only illustrates how very misguided poor Dutton is, Stavey. He cannot detect an interested widow from a disinterested one. Yes, the thing for you to do is to marry Anne on the spot, as it were. You simply must do it, if only to save Dutton from himself."

And in that instant, Anne knew that it was not Dutton Sophia was trying to save from himself. It was Anne whom she was trying to save, from Lord Dutton.

❧

"THOSE pearls were my grandmother's, saved for me," Louisa Kirkland said. "They weren't to be sold or bartered or whatever else to Lord Dutton so that he could pass them off to Caroline Trevelyan. I don't know what my father was thinking."

"I wonder why he did it," Amelia Caversham said softly, watching Lord Dutton as he left his conversation with Lord Staverton and Mrs. Warren and made his way to the Duke of Calbourne on the far side of the blue reception room. Amelia had never been to a gathering before in which so many people refused to leave. It was certain to go down as the most entertaining event of the social year.

"I should think that was obvious," Louisa said stiffly.

Amelia smiled and looked askance at her cousin. Louisa had always been headstrong, but she had acquired her uncertain temper at the exact moment she had acquired a fascination with the devilish Lord Dutton. There was more than one woman in London with the same malady and, as far as Amelia could tell, there was no cure for it. She thanked God almost nightly that she was immune to the considerable charm of Lord Dutton. Of course, her immunity could have sprung almost directly from her constant observance of Louisa struggling under the cloud of his inattention. It was a most potent immunization.

"What is obvious, at least to me," Amelia said, "is that Lord Dutton, until tonight, has paid no more attention to Lady Caroline than he has to"—she had been on the cusp of saying *you*, but didn't. Poor Louisa was in enough of a snit as it was—"anyone else. I think he had someone or something else in mind when he presented those pearls to her."

"*My* pearls," Louisa said.

"Not any longer, they're not," Amelia said. When Louisa opened her mouth to argue, Amelia hurriedly said, "Don't you wonder, Louisa, why Lord Dutton, who has never before looked at Caroline Trevelyan except to say hello and good-bye to her, would suddenly present her with a pearl necklace? In fact, don't you find it odd that three gentlemen in one evening would do so?"

"She probably asked for a pearl necklace, that's all," Louisa snapped. "There's no mystery here, Amelia. She had the cheek to ask for pearls and pearls were showered upon her. Not unlike her mother, is she? I heard something similar happened to Lady Dalby, though with sapphires. Like mother, like daughter."

"Do you mean to say," Amelia said softly, watching Lady Dalby laugh with Mrs. Warren and Lord Staverton, rumored to have sealed their engagement this very night, "that all a woman has to do is to ask for what she wants? And then, she gets it?"

Louisa turned her bright, red head to stare at Amelia. Amelia stared right back at her. Was it truly as simple as that?

⤸

"It's as simple as that, Lord Westlin," Lord Ruan said. "Lord Ashdon said he'd marry her. He has ruined her, after all. What would you have of him?"

"I'd have revenge of him, that's what," Westlin said.

"That's between the two of you, of course," Ruan said mildly. "I can only tell you what he said his intentions are. By all appearances, he would seem as good as his word."

"Are you implying that he's not as good as his word?"

"I'm implying nothing. I'm only keeping you informed as to your son's actions, per our agreement. Now," Ruan said, ignoring the bad taste in his mouth, "I believe I've met my portion of our agreement. I shall expect the title to the property to be delivered to my home by tomorrow noon, if that's convenient."

He didn't care a blister if it was convenient; Ruan was overeager to end his association with the Earl of Westlin. The more time he spent with Westlin, the more impressed he was that Sophia had been able to manage his company at all, and the less impressed he was with Westlin that he'd mismanaged an affair with certainly the most fascinating woman he'd yet to meet. Small wonder that alliance had ended with an explosion that was still rocking London Society. It was obvious to him, and therefore must be more than obvious to Sophia, that Westlin would like nothing better than to use his son to deliver some blow of vengeance to Sophia's daughter.

Certainly ruining her should have been enough for any normal lunatic, but one couldn't discount raving lunacy when dealing with Lord Westlin.

"Lord Westlin?" Ruan prompted.

They stood in a corner of the blue reception room, surrounded by knots of people all speculating avidly about

Lady Dalby, Lady Caroline, Lord Ashdon, Lord Dutton, and Lord Henry Blakesley; by virtue of the fact that he was talking with Lord Westlin, Ruan rather assumed that they were speculating about him as well. He didn't care for it in the least.

"Yes, I suppose you're right," Westlin grumbled. "Though I'd have preferred it if you'd kept on until the end of the Season."

"Yes, well, fate rarely takes one's preferences into account."

"Tomorrow at noon is not convenient for me," Westlin said. Ruan supposed it was not, as Westlin might well be at his son's wedding tomorrow at noon. "Come round Friday, if you would. I'll have the papers ready."

"Friday it is," Ruan said, taking a step away from Westlin, and all the speculation, he hoped. He had not missed the fact that Lady Dalby had cast more than one cool glance in his direction in the last few minutes.

"I have to admit to being impressed, Lord Ruan," Westlin said before he could take a second step.

"Oh?" Ruan said.

"Yes," Westlin said with a humorless smile. "I almost expected you to ask me what everyone else is eager to know. You must have determined that my plans for my son involve Sophia Dalby and her black-haired daughter, as you are involved, however peripherally."

"Actually, Lord Westlin," Ruan said pleasantly, "I prefer living life on the periphery and will allow that a man's affairs are strictly his own concern. Good evening, sir," he said with a crisp half bow, leaving Westlin in his corner, boxed in, as it were.

Of course, he wanted to know what bloody cord bound Sophia to Westlin, but he wasn't going to listen to Westlin's version of events. Ruan much preferred the view from the periphery as well, as it gave one a clear and unimpeded look at things.

Ruan made it a point to walk past Sophia and Lord Staverton on his way out. Sophia made it a point to ignore him completely. Ruan smiled as he donned his hat; only a woman very aware of a man took the trouble to ignore him completely.

Now, perhaps there was something he could do to save Sophia from Lord Westlin. To be honest, she didn't look the sort of woman who required saving. Then again, he suspected he'd have a good time trying.

Twenty-two

"HELP. Save me," Caro said as she straightened the seam on her right glove.

Ash looked at Caro from his side of the Westlin town coach and scowled at her. She found it rather attractive, strangely enough. That was the whole problem with Ashdon, she found almost everything he did strangely attractive. One might almost say *compelling*. It was getting to be rather ridiculous.

"Someone," she said in a monotone, "save me."

"Whom are you talking to?" Ashdon asked.

"To no one, really," she said. "I just want to be able to say honestly that I called for help, though no help was forthcoming. These are just the sorts of questions one is asked after an abduction. I have to be able to hold my head up and look my children in the eyes when this tale is repeated. God forbid I should have to admit to my future daughter that I went willingly with the man who defiled me and ruined my good name."

"And I am that man?"

"Who else?"

"I am also the father of this future daughter?"

Caro raised her eyebrows and lifted her hands in a gesture that clearly said *who else?*

"Is no one going to ask for my version of events?" Ash said, the barest smile hovering over his mouth.

"I certainly hope not."

"No, they never do in these sorts of situations, do they?" Ashdon said calmly. "One always assumes the worst of a fellow while believing the absolute best of the woman."

"Are you implying that it is you who have been abducted?"

"Are you implying that I have not?" he countered. She could just make out his features in the darkened interior and he looked to be . . . but it could not be . . . was he *smiling*?

"I'm afraid I must be the one to inform you, Lord Ashdon, that it is always, and I mean *always*, the woman who is the injured and innocent party in these affairs."

"Innocent, of that there is no doubt," he said, crossing his arms over his chest and slouching down so that his legs were almost entangled with hers. Completely inappropriate, obviously. She felt her heart skip three beats. "You are such an innocent that it seems not to have occurred to you that you are completely ruined."

"Not occurred to me? I am completely aware that I am completely ruined. Believe me, Lord Ashdon, a girl does not leave the schoolroom until she knows in every particular the various and devious ways a man may ruin a girl of good name."

"You seem remarkably calm about it."

"Do I?" she said. "Another result of my education, I daresay."

"Perhaps you had better call for help again," he said softly.

"Why?"

"Because I have just decided that I am going to kiss you."

Her heart gave up skipping and ran so fast she could not be bothered to try and count the beats, and then it slammed into her hips where it lay, shattered and prostrate.

"You are remarkably calm about it," she managed to whisper.

"I should hope so," he said softly. "I own the goods, after all."

Her heart leapt to life. "I should say not."

"Those pearls, Caro," he breathed, "those pearls draped around your throat, give me every right to you."

"Easily repaired, sir," she said, lifting the pearls from her breasts to lift them over her head.

"Don't!" he said sharply, and she obeyed. It was most humiliating. "Never take them off. Never, unless I take them off you myself."

"Like a badge of ownership?" she said sharply. "I hardly think so!"

"Exactly like a badge of ownership," he said. "I bought you, Caro, and, if you behave yourself, I may even marry you."

"You *may* marry me!" she barked out. "I am *ruined*, Lord Ashdon. You bloody well *will* marry me!"

"As I said, you are surely an innocent to be so calm about the fact that I hold your life, in the most symbolic sense, in my hands. Which reminds me, I would like to hold your breasts in my hands again. Kindly lower your bodice."

"I will *not*!" she said, her heart hammering wildly. He was not going to marry her? "And what do you mean you may even marry me? You made your intentions plain at Hyde House, both symbolically and verbally."

"For your mother's benefit, yes," Ashdon said. "Do not tell me, Caro, that you are ignorant of the enmity between my father and your mother. What else has all this," and he spread open his hands to encompass the coach, the two of them, the whole of London, "been about if not them?"

Oh, God.

"But you said you would marry me," she said, sounding pitiful and knowing it, but unable to stop herself. She was rather disgusted with herself for not being able to stop herself where Lord Ashdon was concerned. "You told my mother."

"And I told my father, by way of the gossip that is surely running through Hyde House since our departure. I'm sure he's quite annoyed."

"Isn't your father always quite annoyed about something or other?" she asked, feeling as if the pearls were burning circles into her skin, but unable to defy Ashdon and remove them. She was a silly fig of a girl, quite as innocent and ignorant as he claimed.

"I think this will mark him rather more than usual," Ashdon said. "Are you going to lower your bodice or not?"

He was back onto that again?

"No, I am not," she said, resisting the urge to clamp her hands over her breasts in outrage. She was not going to give in to outrage. She was going to proceed logically and rationally. Sense would rule the day, as it must in a civilized world. It was so unfortunate that Ashdon didn't appear civilized at the moment, a definite flaw in her hastily devised plan to distract him. "Are you saying that you spoke of marrying me merely to annoy your father?"

"Must we talk of my father *now*? I would rather speak about your bodice and those pearls, sinking just out of sight into the deep shadow of your cleavage. You were quite right, by the way; you have the loveliest breasts. I would so enjoy seeing them again. Kissing them. Holding them in my hands."

Her heart quivered like a captured bird, which did her no good at all.

What would her mother do?

Inspiration.

"How charmingly put," she said. "Very well. I will lower my bodice, but only if we continue our conversation about your father and our marriage."

"You're negotiating with me?" Ashdon said with a wry grin. At least she hoped it was a wry grin; in this light, he could well have been leering at her and she would be the last to know the difference.

"If you must call it that," she said.

"How charming. And here I thought all our negotiations were past, the pearls bearing the proof of that."

"I'm beginning to hate these pearls," she said. "I'm almost sorry I ever asked for them."

"I'm not," he said, and this time there was no doubt. He was leering. She could hear it in his voice. Blasted sot.

"You're not foxed, are you?" she said. If intoxicated, that would explain much and ease her fears.

"Because I said I liked your breasts?" he said.

"Of course not!" she said sharply. Really. How insulting. "Because you are not acting like yourself, Lord Ashdon."

"Am I not? You know me well, then?"

True enough. She hardly knew him at all, but what she

knew, she found either irritating in the extreme or compelling in the extreme. Some days one wished for a simple mediocrity, a comfortable complaisance. Particularly on days like today. Particularly with Lord Ashdon.

And if wishes were horses, beggars would ride.

"I thought I knew you," she said, trying for pity, a sort of innocence that would arouse his chivalric training.

"Take down your bodice and get to know me better," he said.

So much for chivalric training.

"Talk to me about your father and my mother and I'll loosen the tie," she said.

"You are a determined negotiator."

"I am a determined virgin."

Ashdon laughed and shook his head at her. "It hasn't occurred to you that I could slip my hands inside your gown without any assistance from you? You are already ruined, no matter what we do or do not do."

"I believe at this point, Lord Ashdon, *everything* has occurred to me, including the fact that you are baiting me just to get me to refuse you."

"You *are* refusing me. Your bodice is still up."

"I meant about marrying you," she said.

Ashdon sighed and leaned back against the squabs. "You can refuse me, you know. You have a brilliant start into the courtesan's life."

"You'd rather I be a courtesan than your wife?"

"Isn't that what you wanted for yourself when this marriage was first broached by your mother?"

It was the perfect opportunity to tell him the truth, though telling the truth to a man was always a risk as their emotions ran a strange course. But as risks went, she had little to lose at this point.

"Lord Ashdon," she said softly, one might even have said *meltingly*, "I have hoped for marriage all my life, as I expect most women do. I wanted to be pursued. I wanted to be admired. I never wanted to have a man, mired in debt, to be procured for me. And then," she said over his rising anger, a force she could feel in the close confines of the darkened carriage, "I met you."

Caro loosened the tie to her bodice and eased it open, letting the sheer white muslin tumble down to fall against the swells of her breasts, let it be remembered, her *lovely* breasts. Ashdon's anger melted into desire. She could feel that, too.

"How could I ever be a courtesan?" she continued. "Yours are the only hands I want to touch me. Yours, the only mouth. Yours, the only breath I want mingled with my own. I am ruined, Lord Ashdon, for any other man. I am ruined, and you are the man who has ruined me. Will you not take the spoils of your conquest?"

He did.

Ashdon wrapped his arms around her and pulled her onto his lap, his mouth taking hers in gentle plunder. She sighed into him, into the heat of him, into his scent and into his embrace. She wrapped herself around him, her arms around the starched linen at his throat, her tongue around his, her slippered feet around the bulge of his calves, and dove into his kiss without a thought of surfacing. Let passion take them both. He had said it: she was ruined. There was no going back, only forward, into marriage if she could make him bend against her will.

He would bend. He would bend against desire and then she would have him.

Ashdon's hands went to her bodice and she moaned in supplication, urging him onward, past the pearls and everything they stood for, to her flesh. To desire.

Her bodice gaped, a flimsy barrier, and then his hand was on her breast, his thumb rubbing her nipple, her body fired by streams of passion. Thought fled. Sensation ruled.

She was lost. All that was left was for Ash to find her.

His mouth trailed along her cheek, to her ear; she shivered. Away from her ear and down the line of her throat; she moaned. His hand cupped her breast, his thumb flicking hard against her nipple; she groaned and her hips twitched against the hard ridge of his erection. He groaned. It was a minor victory in this war of desire, but she took it, enjoyed it.

"You would not have a gambler," he breathed against the rise of her breast as his hand pulled her bodice down and down until she felt the full impact of the chill night air on her skin, the full impact of his hand upon her skin . . . the full impact of Ash. "No gambler," he mouthed, "yet you gamble for stakes higher than I ever have. You've gambled your life, Caro. You've gambled it all. On me."

"Have I lost, Ash?" she whispered, her mouth against his neck, feeling the pulse of his life and his passion beneath her lips, driving what was left of caution out of her very bones. "Have I lost everything?"

He kissed her in answer, his hand plunging down further into her bodice until she heard the rip of fabric and knew she was completely bare-breasted before him, just like in the dressing room. Nothing like in the dressing room. This was raw passion in the dark. There was no pounding against the door, no threat of interruption, no possibility of censure.

She spun downward into passion, seated firmly on Ash's lap. She fell out of her life and into his. She was caught by his hand and by his mouth, teased and tasted, consumed and consuming.

His hand pressed between her legs and she pressed them closed against him. She wanted his touch, ached for him, but as instinctual as it was to want him, it was equally instinctual to deny him. Not that. Not yet. Certainly not now.

"Open for me," he breathed against her mouth.

She could not speak for want of air. She shook her head instead. *No.*

"Open, Caro."

"Have I lost everything?" she repeated, her voice breathy and high-pitched. She sounded afraid.

She was.

"I've lost everything," he said hoarsely. "Why not you?"

In the next instant she was no longer afraid. She was furious.

"You've lost nothing, you great oaf, nothing you did not toss away with both hands."

She pushed him, pushed against his shoulders with her

hands. He did not move an inch. He was stone, and just as sensible.

"I am not tossing you away, Caro," he said roughly. "I am keeping you."

She ignored the tremor that ran through her. She was going to ignore everything from now on that did not serve her well, and she had decided, somewhat belatedly, that Lord Ashdon did not serve her best interests. And to top it off, he truly was as ill-tempered, and ill-mannered, as his father. Her mother had been quite wrong about that when she had assured her that Ashdon only required careful managing. Wild boars could not be managed.

"I am not going to be *kept* by you, Lord Ashdon," she said. "Since I am not going to be your wife, which is entirely your choice, then I am not going to be your ladybird, which is entirely *my* choice."

For answer, he dropped his head and suckled her breast.

She grabbed the hair on the top of his scalp and pulled his mouth off of her.

He cursed in response.

She smiled in response.

He grabbed her wrists, but she slipped off his lap and landed on the floor of the carriage, her wrists still caged in his hands.

That part could have gone better.

"Let *go*!" she snapped, tugging on her wrists.

"I don't know," he said slowly. "I think I rather like you at my feet, bare-breasted, manacled."

For answer, she bit him on the knee.

He cursed even more roundly, adding in a few words she hadn't heard before. He didn't let go of her hands, and so she bit him again. Harder.

He let her go. She hurriedly planted herself on the squabs opposite him and, thinking it over rather quickly, let her bodice continue to gape around her rib cage, leaving her completely and scandalously exposed. She thought that last bit was something her mother might have done. Besides, he'd seen, touched, and tasted it all now anyway.

"Blast it, Caro! What the devil are you biting me for?"

She held out one arm in stiff command, directed right at his chest, but not actually touching him. She might be naïve, but she was not stupid.

"We are going to talk, Ash, and you are not going to kiss your way out of it!"

He studied her, studied her breasts, actually. She resisted the urge to cross her arms over them. She also resisted the urge to throw herself into his arms, but there was no reason for him to know anything about that.

"You know you'd rather my kisses than any conversation we could find between us," he said in a hushed voice.

"If you try to kiss me, I'll bite your lip," she said coldly.

"Quite the little biter, aren't you?" he said. "Definite possibilities there, if you learn some self-control."

"I hardly think you are the person to lecture anyone on self-control!"

"At least I have all my clothes on," he said, his voice smiling.

"Exactly my point. I am not the one who has done this . . . this . . . to me. *You* did it."

"And rather proud of it, actually." He was definitely grinning now. Stupid sot.

"It's nothing to be proud of, but we're not going to talk about that, and we're not going to kiss, and you're not to *touch* me until we get a few things settled between us before this coach arrives at Upper Brook Street."

"You know, Caro, you really must learn not to assume so much."

"What the devil does that mean?"

"Simply, what makes you so certain that my coach is taking you home?"

Her stomach sank to somewhere near her knees, but she wasn't going to let him know that either. He already thought her laughably innocent and unsophisticated. She was more than tired of that presumption. Being a virgin did not equal being gullible.

At least, she didn't think it did.

"Don't be ridiculous," she said on a huff of disbelief. "Of course you're taking me home. Where else would a—"

"A man who has paid for an up-and-coming courtesan go? Not to his home, certainly."

"I wasn't aware you had a home in town," she said scathingly. "Not a home of your own at any rate."

"Of course you weren't aware of it. I keep it for nights such as this. And women such as you."

"You mean women you've publicly pledged to marry?" she said chillingly. She was more than tired of his continual references to her brief and, yes, idiotic, plan to become a courtesan. "How delightful, Ashdon. You've bought me a house in Town. Or are we renting?"

"I thought it was *you* I was renting," he said calmly.

How could he remain so calm? Weren't her lovely breasts staring him, in a manner of speaking, in the face? Perhaps it was too dark for him to be fully devastated by the sight of her breasts as he had been in the Hyde House dressing room. Oh, for the illumination of even a single candle to help her along with the impossible Lord Ashdon.

"No matter where we are going, Lord Ashdon," she said, "we are going to get a few things settled before we get there."

"If we are going to talk, perhaps you should readjust your bodice. You look positively Amazonian sitting there, your dress collapsed around your waist."

A positive sign, surely. He was distracted by her breasts. Of course, she was distracted by her breasts, exposed to his gaze as they were, his body just a foot from hers, her nipples throbbing and erect . . . but distractions were not going to stop her now. She was going to marry Ashdon, and he was going to cooperate about it.

"Oh? I hadn't noticed," she said, running the pearls through her fingers. He moaned softly, the sound coming from deep in his chest. Finally, she had Ashdon where she wanted him. About time, too.

"Stop touching those pearls, Caro, or you won't be a virgin long," he growled.

"Since we're to be married soon, I won't be a virgin long no matter what."

"Is that an offer?"

"Absolutely not. I was merely pointing out the obvious."

But she let the pearls drop to lie coldly against her breasts. Now that Ashdon was on his side of the coach and she on hers, she was becoming rather chilled. Best to get this negotiation done with quickly. She could hardly imagine a worse fate than a chest cough on her wedding night.

"Now then, Lord Ashdon, you have quite ruined me, in all ways, for any other man," she said calmly. "You have declared your intention to marry me. Will you not marry me after all?"

"There is more to this than you imagine, Caro," he said, dipping his head down, hiding the gleam of his blue eyes from her.

"I don't think so, Ash," she said. "I know there is some revenge between our parents meddling in our actions. I know that you might feel, however wrongly, that you should like your own revenge upon me. For wanting to be a courtesan. For not wanting to be your wife. But I have explained that, haven't I? I wanted to be wanted. Don't you want me, Ash?"

"It's more complicated—"

"Just answer me," she interrupted. "One question at a time. Do you want me?"

"I want you," he said, his voice like a wolf's growl. "Don't pretend you don't know that, Caro, not when you sit there like the most jaded seductress, mocking me, enticing me."

"I sit here, dear Ash, with my breasts bared, because I know no such thing. I am well in over my head. I am using every card in my possession. Were I confident of anything, I would not sit here as I am."

"Then cover yourself, Caro. God knows I can't take much more."

She couldn't either. The desire to throw herself in the way of his hands was almost more than she could bear. Caro pulled up her sagging bodice and retied the string. But for the tear in the side seam, she looked almost presentable and she could enter the house without shame.

Unless, of course, one discounted the shameful fact that she arrived at home from within the dark and private and completely unchaperoned confines of Lord Ashdon's coach. That bit would be somewhat difficult to downplay. All the more reason for her to marry Lord Ashdon at the earliest opportunity. Tomorrow ought to do nicely.

"I am covered, Lord Ashdon," she said. "You can look now."

"Caro, whatever made you think I had stopped looking?" he said. "I have looked and will look again, whenever the opportunity presents itself. And if it does not conveniently present itself, I will make my own opportunity. You were quite right about your breasts. They are lovely. Do your other parts compare as favorably?"

"Lord Ashdon! This is hardly an appropriate conversation for us to be engaging in!"

"You would prefer not to engage in conversation but in some other activity? I daresay I agree with that."

"That is not at *all* what I am proposing," she said stiffly. "You have the most determined talent for avoiding the point, which is," she said quickly, when he took a breath to interrupt her, "that you have proposed marriage and I have accepted. When is the blessed event to occur? Given your preoccupation with my . . . parts, I would say that tomorrow would suit us both."

A well of silence enveloped his side of the coach, like a tangible pall of misery. He was the most *emotional* man, first determined lust and then, quick as rising sparks, dejected gloom. It was going to take a very considerable amount of effort to stay abreast of his moods.

"You have an objection to tomorrow?" she said. "I know it will take a special license, but I believe my mother has—"

At that, he interrupted her by laughing. To say that Lord Ashdon suffered from an extremity of mood shifts was putting it delicately.

"Is something amusing?" she said.

"You are," he said. "You are supremely amusing, Caro, the more so because you are so blind to it."

"If this is an attempt at flattery, it is a failed attempt."

"I do apologize," he said, sounding anything but apologetic. She couldn't help but return to her original supposition that Lord Ashdon was completely foxed.

"I do accept," she said, sounding anything but accepting. "Now, shall we plan the wedding?"

Ashdon once again pushed his morose silence all over her wedding plans.

"Is there something you wish to say, Lord Ashdon? I would prefer it to this deafening silence," she said.

"I'm taking you home, Caro," he said softly.

"I was never in any doubt of that."

"I'm taking you home and I shall do what I can to redeem your reputation, little enough as it may be, and I shall not see you again."

This after she had let him see her bare breasts? He *was* foxed. And she was ruined, beyond repair or redemption.

"I'm sorry, but that will not do," she said calmly, ignoring the pounding of her heart and the shortness of her breath. "I have been ruined, by you, Ash, and you shall make it right."

"I'm trying to make it right, Caro," he said under his breath.

"Marrying me will suffice."

Again, his silence spoke for him. It was with the utmost irritation that she realized she was beginning to be able to read his silences.

"You are not going to marry me," she said slowly. "You believe marrying me would serve me more ill than ruining me."

"I do," he said. "I don't want to hurt you, Caro. I don't believe I ever did."

"How reassuring," she said stiffly, sniffing against the cold night air. It was *not* emotion that made her sniff and wipe discreetly at her eyes. All wild emotion resided within Lord Ashdon's twisted heart, not her own. "If I may be so bold, why did you give me these pearls, Lord Ashdon? Why did you make a mockery of my good name in the Duke of Hyde's dressing room? Why did you kiss me? Why did you . . . touch me?" she said, wiping the single rebellious line of tears running out of her right eye with brutal ruthlessness. No tears. Not now. Not ever. Not over this . . . miscalculation. "You have ruined me, Lord Ashdon. Was it not done willfully?"

"You said you wanted to be a courtesan. You said you did not want to be my wife," he said softly.

That again. She was not going to be distracted by that, not when it had taken place as long ago as yesterday. Not when everything had changed since then. Everything, it seemed, except Lord Ashdon.

"I have reversed both positions, Lord Ashdon. Did you fail to notice?"

"Some positions may not be so easily reversed."

"Yet your heart is surely not to be counted among the constant and irreversible."

"My heart has no part in this."

Caroline snorted indelicately, crossing her arms over herself like a welcoming vice. "I quite agree. Your heart, surely, is to be discounted among all such conversations and considerations, Lord Ashdon. Your heart, if it beats at all, beats a false tempo."

"Do not do this, Caro. Do not tear your heart up over this."

"Do not worry about *my* heart, Lord Ashdon. It is well beyond your reach."

"I will make it right. I swear it, Caro. I will right this wrong upon your name."

"And how will you do that, Lord Ashdon? Will you take back your kisses? Your promises? Your pearls, at least those are easily returned."

She lifted the pearls over her head, and he barked at her, "Leave them! The pearls are yours, no matter what else. Wear them. I would that you would wear them every day of your life."

"Which I'm certain you pray will be short indeed."

"You want me to suffer," he said.

"Yes," she said, sniffing back her pointless tears, "I want you to suffer miserably. Can you do that, Lord Ashdon, or will you renege on that as well?"

He was silent, his favorite response.

It occurred to her, in that stilted silence, that she was mishandling him completely. Her mother would never engage in such dreary tactics. Her mother would entice and charm and cajole and, more importantly, her mother would get her way. Caro used Ashdon's silence to rethink everything, trying to see the world and the men who galloped across it, from behind her mother's eyes.

It was a remarkably insightful view.

The most important fact facing her was that she must get her way in this. Ashdon must marry her. She was ruined, yes, but she would only be completely ruined if Ashdon slipped the net. Married, the whole pearl escapade became an amusing story, the sort of story that enhanced a woman's reputation instead of destroying it. With the proper handling, obviously. Caro had no doubt that her mother could manage the story. What was essential now was for her to manage Ashdon. He simply must be managed into marriage.

"You have me at my worst," she said. "I apologize, Lord Ashdon, for my temper. Of course I will keep your pearls, as a remembrance of you. Each time I wear them and they fall upon my breasts, I will remember you . . . and your hands."

Ashdon shifted his weight on the squabs and grumbled something. She took it for a good sign.

"I hope that when you see me wearing them about Town, you will remember as well, the fit of your hands . . . there, and the way I responded to you." She paused and sighed seductively. When she heard him take a rattled breath, she added, "And, obviously, I will keep them because I have earned them."

She could almost make out the coarse word he used, but not quite. Well, onward and upward. She would do better.

"You have told me, reminded me, really, of my first impulse to follow the courtesan's path. I had thought to do so. Until I saw you. Until I met you. Seeing you, feeling as I do about you, about your tumbled hair and piercing eyes . . . did you know what I first thought about your eyes, Ash? I thought that they would pierce me through, and my next thought, I blush to admit, was how some other part of you would pierce me. And of how much I wanted that."

"Stop, Caro," he growled. "Stop it."

"I don't want to stop," she whispered, slowly taking off her right glove, sliding it down her arm, tugging it from each finger. "I want you to know everything, now, as we part. You must have noticed I have an addiction to honesty, Ash. I don't want to be turned from it, especially not now when everything is lost to me. When you are lost to me."

"I'm trying to do what's right," he said, his voice gone hoarse as he stared at her gloveless hand. Remarkable how seductive and erotic a simple woman's arm could look, bare and white in the darkness.

"I know you are," she breathed. "But I wonder if you understand where you've left me. How can I be a courtesan now, Ash, when you are the only man I want to touch me?"

"It will pass," he gritted out. Did he say, *God help me*? She wasn't certain. She'd like to think so.

"It may," she sighed. "But what a pity that would be. I like this, Ash. That is my guilty secret. I like what I feel for you, the heat, the hammering, the blind dizziness that assaults me when you look at me, when you touch me. I don't think I can find this with any other man. Or am I wrong? How many men will it take to drive the imprint of your touch from me? How many beds? How many arms? How many mouths pressed against my skin will drive the memory of your kiss from my heart?"

"God, Caro! Stop this!"

Ashdon grabbed her by the arms and shook her twice. His touch was a scald against her bare arm that they both felt. He jerked back against the squabs like a wild thing bayed by hunting dogs.

"I can't stop," she said, leaning forward to lay a hand against his cheek, well aware that her bodice dipped and the weight of her breasts spilled forward. "I wanted to be wanted. I told you that. It is nothing but the stark truth. But shall I tell you another truth, Ash? I wanted *you* to want me. You."

"I do want you," he murmured.

His eyes were glittering and his cheek was hot, his beard rough beneath her fingertips. He was breathing though his mouth, his breath moist and hot on the inside of her wrist. She shivered with longing and let him feel it.

"I believe you," she said softly, letting her breath wash over his face. "Your desire is more gift to me than these pearls could ever be."

She leaned forward and kissed his cheek, her lips pressing against the sharp bite of his beard. A parting kiss, not unlike the simple kiss of a friend. And nothing like it at all.

"I want you, Ash," she whispered against his face. "I want you right now. What sort of courtesan can I be when the only man I want between my legs"—she moved her mouth to lightly touch his lips—"is you?"

Twenty-three

THEY were married at eleven the next morning. It was simple, really. Her mother had acquired a special license on the same day she had acquired Lord Ashdon's debts. Lord Westlin was invited, naturally, and, naturally, did not choose to attend.

Ashdon did not seem particularly concerned. In point of fact, Ashdon did not seem particularly anything. One would think a man crossing into marriage would display some emotion, but Ashdon displayed only resolve. Caro did not think resolve qualified as a particularly flattering wedding day aspect, but Caro was, ironically, resolved to ignore everything about Lord Ashdon's aspect and be happy. She had won the man she'd targeted, her mother's rather violent description for a courtship, and she was going to rejoice in it and in him.

Just because it had been a rather unusual courtship was no reason not to enjoy herself now. She had the husband she had sought. He had come into the marriage willingly, one might even say *eagerly* after the episode in the coach. And everything, now that it was all concluded, was going to be wonderful. Things would settle down. Lord Ashdon would stop displaying his resolve, and she would stop having to display her breasts to get him to do the most mundane of things. Like marry her. Like want her. Like . . . love her.

For a very logical girl, it was more than disturbing to realize that, while she had the husband she'd aimed for, she wasn't at all certain she had the husband she'd planned for.

It seemed to her that she'd been rather more logical before she'd set eyes on Lord Ashdon. He had a way of muddling every thought just by looking at her. A skill of that sort could lead to a most disturbing state of affairs in a marriage, unless it was his thoughts being muddled by merely looking at her. That would have been quite nice. But, looking at him across the table at the lovely wedding breakfast her mother had arranged, he did not look at all muddled. He looked, she couldn't help repeating, *resolved*.

"A lovely wedding," her mother said from the head of the table in the capacious dining room. "Quite the loveliest of the Season, I daresay."

Anne and the Duke of Calbourne made murmuring noises. Ashdon did not make noises of any sort. He probably couldn't think what precise noise would sound *resolved*.

"Have you made plans, Lord Ashdon, as to where you and Caro will spend the next month or two?"

"I have not, Lady Dalby," Ashdon said. He seemed to be moving from resolved to grim. Lovely.

"Might I suggest France? Absolutely *everyone* is there now since the treaty has been signed. If you have any desire to see France, now is the time. I daresay that this peace will not last, as no peace between France and England ever shall last. Still, France has the most delightful fashions and quite the best gardens."

"It's a cynical position you take regarding politics, Lady Dalby," Ashdon said, "particularly as it is strongly rumored that *you* are French."

"I?" Sophia said with a smile. "I am not French. And as to politics, how can one not be cynical about politics?"

"I did not know you had an interest in politics, Lady Dalby," Ashdon said. "It is perhaps the one thing not whispered about you."

"Really? How very odd," she said softly. "Yet, one of the pleasures of family, darling Ashdon, is that we should have no secrets between us."

"Should I excuse myself?" Calbourne said, pushing back his chair.

"Not at all necessary, your grace," Sophia said. "I just don't understand where these silly rumors are born and why they never die. I am not French. I have never claimed to be French, though I should not mind being French."

"Then you are . . . ?" Ashdon prompted.

"Why, English. What else?" Sophia asked with a grin. "Isn't it obvious?"

No one answered her, but it was quite obvious to everyone that there was nothing at all obvious about Sophia Dalby, unless it was her charm and appeal. Sophia and Caroline were as unlike as any mother and daughter could ever be and as soon as Ashdon realized that she was nothing but a pair of breasts, which surely even he must eventually tire of, the marriage would be over, or as over as marriages in the ton ever were. He would live his life. She would live hers. They would toil out two or three children between them and then see each other occasionally at parties.

Ashdon had likely reasoned that out already, which would explain both his resolve and his descent into grim. She could quite feel herself following him.

"Where would you like to go, Caro?" her mother asked.

"Oh, I suppose France would be amusing," she said, staring down at her napkin.

"I do believe my daughter is suffering from bridal nerves," Sophia said lightly. "You will be considerate of that, won't you, Ashdon?"

For answer, Ashdon merely stared at her, grimly.

"I think, Lady Dalby, that Ash is suffering a bout of nerves himself," Calbourne said in an attempt to cover the awkward silence. "It is not only brides who feel the jangle of nerves upon the event of marriage."

"Were you a nervous groom, your grace?" Anne asked softly.

"I was convinced I had lost three teeth, they were chattering so violently," Calbourne said.

"And you were an eager groom?" Sophia asked.

"I'll go so far as to say I was willing," Calbourne said. "I don't know that I had the intelligence to be eager. I was but twenty and there was little in my thoughts but gambling, hunting, and—"

"Certainly women," Sophia interrupted, laughing. "I've

yet to meet a man of twenty whose thoughts were not preoccupied with women."

"Preoccupied, yes," Calbourne acknowledged, "but a tangle of fear and longing that only confused me."

"How honestly you put it," Anne said. "May I congratulate you, your grace? Most men would not admit to confusion and never to fear."

"Do not put too much upon it," Calbourne said. "I can admit it now because it is long ago and I am well past it. Women no longer frighten me," he said with a wry grin.

"How fortunate for women," Sophia said with an answering grin, before turning her attention to Anne to ask, "And was your husband a nervous groom, Mrs. Warren?"

"I think he was," Anne said with a smile of remembrance. "I didn't know it at the time, of course. He seemed to me all that was strong and true and brave."

"Which is precisely how a bride should see her husband," Sophia said.

At which point all eyes turned to look at Caro. Even the footmen standing against the walls were looking at her.

Resolve, resolve, resolve.

Unfortunately, she could not find resolve. All she could find was fear, longing, and a large dose of anger. Let Ashdon be Resolve. She would be Anger, though perhaps more refined. Let it be called Outrage.

"Once more I find myself stepping out of tune," Caro said, looking at her mother with a sarcastic smile frozen on her face. "I am clearly the most unlikely of brides . . . with the most unlikely of husbands."

Ashdon jerked his head up from his contemplation of his beefsteak and stared at her. He did not look resolved. She considered it a vast improvement.

"If I am not mistaken," Calbourne said politely, "that is the entire point. Most husbands on their wedding day feel completely unlikely, though most brides are not able to see it. You are very astute, Lady Caroline."

"I daresay, your grace, that I should not be praised for what even a blind beggar could discern," Caro said. "Lord

Ashdon has been artfully maneuvered into this marriage and, far from seeing him as strong, brave, and true, a more honest description of him would be cornered, caught, and, because he is a gentleman, *resolved*. Do I do you an injustice, Lord Ashdon?" she asked sweetly.

"You do yourself an injustice, Caro," Ashdon said, staring forcefully into her eyes. "All women set their traps, indeed they are taught to do so from the nursery, but when a man is cornered, as you put it, he is the one who decides whether or not he will be caught. And since we are sharing secrets with what Lady Dalby has so graciously deemed family, I will share this: there is not a man married who does know that it was *he* who was the hunter, he who set the trap, he who cornered, and he who caught the woman he had set his eye upon."

Sophia clapped lightly and said, covering Caro's stunned silence, "Well said, Lord Ashdon. Charmingly put."

"You will agree to what I've said, Lady Sophia?" Ashdon said.

"I would be a fool argue it," Sophia said serenely.

Yes, well, Caro would most definitely argue it, fool or not.

"I do apologize for this," she said, turning her gaze to Anne, Calbourne, and her mother, "but I'm certain I'm not revealing anything you don't know, however vulgar it is to speak of it."

"It is best to avoid vulgarity whenever possible, Caro," her mother said. "Perhaps we should leave you to discuss this privately. Shall we take coffee in the yellow salon?"

And before Caro could take another breath, Anne, Calbourne, and her mother were out of the dining room, closing the door behind them.

"I suppose you're going to chastise me for vulgarity as well," Caro said to Ashdon once they were alone.

"Not at all," Ash said, looking pointedly at the footmen until they blushed and left the dining room as well. "Say what you wish. I have no desire to be heavy-handed with my wife."

"You have no desire to be *anything* with your wife," she said. "You didn't even want a wife!"

"Don't be absurd, Caro," he said, cutting into his beef-steak. "It was my duty to take a wife."

"That is not the same as *wanting* a wife."

Ashdon looked up at her, his blue eyes piercing into hers. She was getting rather sick of that as well. Ash could go about with his *piercing* eyes elsewhere, where he could bliss-fully pierce some other woman with them.

Which only showed how outraged she was since she would happily kill any woman who was pierced, blissfully or otherwise, by Ashdon's eyes . . . or any other part of his anatomy.

"You know very well I wanted you," he said.

"And I know very well what you wanted me *for,*" she said, pushing her chair back and standing up. She felt the over-whelming urge to pace and she saw no reason not to give in to her urges.

"I should think you would," he said, leaning back in his chair, tipping the front legs off the floor, "as you worked diligently and most provocatively to bring me to that state of desire."

"So you admit I trapped you."

"I admit nothing of the sort. Do you think yours are the only kisses I have enjoyed? The only breasts I have fondled? The only nipples I have—"

"Yes, yes, I take your point," she said, feeling a blush ris-ing from her nipples, one pair out of thousands he had ap-parently tasted, the brute.

"I don't think you do, Caro," he said, breaking off a bit of muffin to pop into his mouth. That he could sit quietly and calmly eating while she was trembling in fear and longing and confusion, like any normal bridegroom, made her want to poke him in the eye with something sharp.

Honestly, she had never had a violent thought in her life until she had met Ashdon. He was a *horrible*, degrading influ-ence on her. She wouldn't be past her rights to kill him for it.

"Oh?" she said sharply. "Wasn't your point that you've seen thousands upon thousands of breasts and chose mine from among the throng because it was *time* for you to marry?"

"Well, they *are* lovely breasts," he said with a smile. "Quite as advertised."

He had the nerve to *laugh* at her? Caro looked around for something sharp, something that would look like a plausible accident. The candlesticks on the dining table might do the job. She could say he had an attack of some sort, fell forward, and impaled himself on the silver. It was *such* a pleasing image.

"*So* glad that you found them satisfactory, Lord Ashdon," she said. "I don't know what I would have done had you found my breasts less than pleasing to your jaded eyes."

"Oh, I'm not as jaded as all that," he said, popping another bit of muffin into his mouth. Hadn't there been a general back fifty years or so ago who had choked and died on a muffin? Certainly it was possible for it to happen again, perhaps with a bit of help?

"Another muffin, Lord Ashdon?" she asked. "I'm sure cook has more."

Ashdon brushed off his hands and pushed his chair back from the table. "No, thank you."

"Not at all," she said. Well, if not muffins, then she was back to considering the silver candlesticks.

"We were discussing my jaded eyes and your lovely breasts," he said, laying his napkin on the table.

"If we were discussing anything as vulgar as that," she said, "it was only because I was making the point that you only married me because you felt compelled to."

"And weren't we discussing that most men feel compelled to marry, in one form or another?"

"It's hardly flattering," she said, walking toward one of the three windows along the back of the house.

"It's very flattering, Caro," he said, coming up behind her, his breath fanning her hair. "A man must marry, but it does not follow that he must marry anyone."

"We both know why you married me," she said, misting the glass with her breath. She simultaneously wanted to throw herself out the window, throw Ashdon out the window, and tumble with Ashdon to the carpeted floor in an ecstasy of bare breasts and hot kisses.

She was a tattered mess of a girl.

"Caro, I tried to tell you this last night, before you attacked me with your breasts," he said, laying his hands on her waist, preventing her from spinning out of his reach so that she could hit him with a candlestick. "I tried very hard, one could almost say desperately, to avoid marrying you."

"I'm so glad you made it a point to inform me of that," she said, trying, one could almost say desperately, to step down hard on his instep. He was wearing boots. She was wearing slippers. It was a failed attempt, but she felt better for trying.

"Caro, listen to me," he said, his voice harsh and low in her ear. His breath on her skin made every nerve shiver in what could only be called delight. Unfortunately. She ignored his breath and the unfair things it did to her. "You know what enmity exists between my father and your mother."

"It's all on his side," she said, interrupting what she felt certain was going to be a lecture on every detail of why he hadn't wanted to marry her. "My mother never even thinks of Lord Westlin, and she certainly never speaks of him."

"Is that so?" Ashdon said softly. "I wonder if that's true?"

"Of course it's true!"

"Yes, well," he said, crossing his arms about her so that his hands cupped her breasts. She expelled her breath sharply and tried to twist free, but that only resulted in her nipples rubbing against the hard heels of his hands. A jolt of fire rippled through her breasts, sending a bolt down to her loins.

She twisted again, as innocently as possible.

"As I was saying," Ashdon said, rubbing his palms over the crests of her breasts. And she wasn't even twisting, the cheat. "I don't think you understand just how determined Westlin is to get revenge upon Sophia. He has made it his life's work, in a sense, and he has trained me to be his . . . tool."

"How nice for both of you," she said, throwing her weight

against his hands in what should have been a convincing attempt at escape. That her breasts were pressed more deeply into his palms was merely a happy coincidence.

"No, Caro," he said, holding her tightly against him, his breath suddenly harsh and labored. "It wasn't nice at all."

She held her breath against the pain she heard in his voice, all games of seduction and broken bodice ties and even silver candlesticks flushed from her thoughts in a torrent. She was certain of one thing: she did not want to hear one more word about his father.

"Did you never wonder why I gamble?" he asked.

"I assumed it was because you enjoy gambling, bad as you are at it," she said.

She'd meant to sound saucy and bold, but her voice came out thready and frightened. Ridiculous. Everyone gambled. It was the way of things. There was nothing mysterious about it.

"I'm not bad at it," he said, still holding her close to him. They did not move; she scarce dared to breath. Ashdon had some weight upon him, clearly put there by his father, and he was attempting to dislodge it onto her. Unfair! Yet, did not married couples share their burdens? She supposed so, but not before they'd shared their hearts.

There it was. Caro tried not to flinch before the stark pain of the thought. Ashdon had not given her his heart and perhaps more dismally, he had not asked for her to share her heart with him. Was this marriage, so new, truly just a bargain made and kept? Was she to be nothing more than a would-be courtesan who had snared a husband by seduction?

Yesterday, the thought had been seductively amusing.

Today, she was not amused.

"You seem very bad at it," she said.

"Yes, don't I?" he said. "It was Westlin's idea, you see. He instructed me to gamble and, whenever possible, to lose."

Ashdon laid his chin softly on the top of her hair and continued, holding her very fast, but not allowing her to turn and look at him. She knew without question that his avoidance of her scrutiny was entirely intentional.

"That seems rather stupid," she said. "Who makes a plan to lose money?"

"My father," Ashdon said simply. "He didn't want me to lose a lot of money, only enough to attract your mother's attention. He believes, you see, that Lady Dalby is quite ruthless, particularly where men are concerned, and most particularly where Westlin is concerned. You can see how my being his heir would make me irresistible to her, or so he claimed. As it turns out, he was right. Sophia bought me, as you well know, by paying off my debts."

"She was just trying to help me find a husband," Caro said. "It had nothing to do with Westlin."

"Didn't it?" Ashdon said, kissing the top of her hair in an almost parental fashion. Things were just going from bad to worse. "I lost rather more than Westlin had instructed, which he was furious about, by the way, but I wanted to put myself beyond Sophia's interest, the debt so high that no one would willingly pay it off. She paid it off, Caro."

The flush of desire faded from her eyes as they stood so, staring out at the mews and the treetops beyond the first-rate homes of Mayfair. Below them, she could hear the muted voices of men, stableboys and grooms, perhaps a footman or two hunkered down on their haunches, gambling when they should have been working.

She had gambled, had she not? She had gambled on Ash, and she wasn't certain anymore what winning was supposed to look like. He was her husband. Was that enough? What did she want in a husband? She didn't know anymore, all she still knew, even now, was that she wanted Ash.

Was that very wise of her?

Probably not.

"She paid it," Caro said quietly. "She bought a husband for me, but before he married me, he ruined me. Was that part of the plan?" She had to be quiet now, quiet and careful, because everything was falling apart, breaking into fragments, and if she were not very careful she would break into fragments, too.

"I married you, Caro," he said, turning her in his arms to

face him. She looked into his eyes because she had to. She had to see what was there, wondering if she would recognize deceit or devotion or anything at all. "I married you, and you'll be the Countess of Westlin. That was never in his plans."

"Then what was the plan? How does going into debt, attracting my mother's attention, function as a revenge?"

He said nothing and the silence pummeled her. Logic. Reason. She'd always been the most reasonable, the most sensible of girls. She knew what the revenge was supposed to have been. It was so obvious. Everything wasn't falling apart, it was falling together, the picture of events finally clear.

What a fool she had made of herself.

"How you must have laughed," she said, staring down at his polished boots. She never wanted to look in his eyes again. A strange marriage that was going to make. "Of course now that I understand things, I can see how determinedly you were trying to avoid me while you put yourself in my mother's path. So difficult, wasn't it, to get her alone, to make an impression on her, whilst her ignorant and ridiculously unsophisticated daughter was throwing herself at you. Did my mother know?" Caro chuckled flatly. "Of course she knew. Lovely men come to her house to see her; they do not come to see her innocent daughter. No man ever wants Caroline. How absurd to even contemplate it."

Ash grabbed her by the arms and pulled her to him. As if that mattered now. "I wanted you, Caro. I wanted you so much that I married you to have you."

"Yes, well," she said lightly, ignoring the wash of tears that blurred her vision, "that might simply be a new version of the plan. There must be hundreds of ways to punish my mother for what happened twenty years ago through her gullible daughter. You and Lord Westlin will have such fun working them out together, a true father and son bond the likes of which has never before been seen. What a pair you'll make, Lord Westlin striding about London's drawing rooms snarling insults about Lady Dalby while Lord Ashdon keeps Lady Dalby's daughter well out of Town so that he may pile all sorts of abuses upon her in his father's name. What delicious fun."

"It will not be that way," he said through clenched teeth. Rot his teeth. She wanted to pull them out, one by one.

"Told your father that, have you?" she said, yanking free of his grasp and striding to the dining room door that led to the yellow salon. It was rather difficult to stride in her narrow gown, but she did what she could. Ash caught up with her in two strides and stood in front of her. He was obviously intelligent enough to know that to touch her now would be extremely unwise. "What happened, Ash? Did my mother ignore you? Did she fail to fall to your rather too obvious charms, forcing you to make do with her second-rate daughter? I don't think I shall be much of a revenge for you, I'm afraid. As unnoticeable as I am, certainly a revenge with me at its heart would be equally unnoticeable."

"You have it wrong," he said in a growl of temper. "You have everything wrong."

"I don't think so," she said, facing him with her chin up, her tears gone. "Shall I review the lesson as I've learned it? Your father is angry with my mother and has been angry for twenty years, which certainly must exhaust him, but being a stalwart and resourceful sort, he arranged for you to share the burden of revenge with him. You were to be his tool, as you put it, and as his tool, you were sent to . . . oh, how to put it delicately? There is no delicate way, is there, Ashdon? You were sent, by way of debt, to be my mother's plaything. A male courtesan, as it were. She was to buy you, and she did, but the problem was that she did not buy you for herself, but for her unappealing daughter. How else to find a man for poor Caro unless to buy her one? Certainly my mother has no need to buy herself a man when they throw themselves at her twice a day in the worst of weather and six times a day in the best."

"Caro, that's—"

"No! You started this. You will allow me to play it out," she said coldly. "I am a part of this farce, certainly I should be given the opportunity to say my lines without interruption." Ashdon held his tongue, his expression once again grim. She could well understand that particular expression now. "What I don't fully understand is how becoming my mother's bed thing would have paid the debt of revenge Westlin so earnestly seeks. I don't understand that bit, Ash. I don't understand anything, do I?"

Ashdon continued to hold his tongue. It might well be a new habit of his. She rather thought he needed one, and this one would suit her on most occasions. The hard reality was that, no matter how it had started, it had ended in marriage. They were hooked, and there was no unhooking them.

Life had never looked so long nor, she dared say it, grim.

"Do you know, Ashdon? Will you tell me? I am as you found me, revoltingly innocent. Were you to insult her in some fashion?" He stared at her, silently. It was growing more than slightly irritating. Habits should not be practiced to the exclusion of all else. It made one a rather dull companion. "How does one go about insulting a woman?" she said, the sounds of light male laughter mingling with female conversation coming to her from beyond the door to the yellow salon. Calbourne seemed to be enjoying himself. "Particularly as that woman is beautiful, don't you find my mother beautiful, Ashdon? But of course you do. All men find my mother irresistible."

"Caro, it is you who are irresistible."

"Yes," she said flatly. "Naturally. But you *do* find her beautiful, don't you? Charming? Amusing? Seductive?"

"No, I do not," he said in typical fashion, that is to say *grimly*.

"Don't be tedious. Of course you do," she said, suddenly sick of the whole conversation. Did it matter what Westlin had hoped for with Sophia? How could it matter now? She was married to Ashdon and her mother had not taken Ashdon for a diversion, no matter how Westlin had arranged things.

Caro was suddenly caught out of her thoughts and into Ashdon's arms. His mouth was upon hers before she had a chance to insist that he stop. And she would have insisted, she was quite certain of that. His kiss was blistering, angry, and invasive, as if he meant to stop her from speaking ever again, as if he meant to drive all thoughts and all objections and all conjectures from her mind and heart, as if he meant to possess her utterly.

Which, of course, he already did. They were married, weren't they? They were married, and there was nothing to be done about it.

As Ashdon's hands ran up her ribs to her breasts, and as her nipples ached deliciously in response, and as she moaned when the blunted thrust of his desire met the soft ache of her own desire, she thought that perhaps there was one thing to be done about it. They could and perhaps *should* consummate their marriage.

Immediately, if not sooner.

Ashdon, it became obvious, had the same idea.

He pulled back to look into her eyes, his mouth just an inch above her own.

"You said you wanted me," he whispered. "I won't ask if you still do. I don't dare. But know that I want you. And I mean to have you."

She would never know if he had been offering her a moment to refuse, to turn the situation along a different course, because before she quite knew what she was doing, her hands were on the back on his neck, tangled in his hair, and she was pulling his mouth down to hers again. He complied, quite willingly it seemed.

And that was the very last coherent thought she had for quite some time.

Ash leaned back against the closed door to the yellow salon, taking her with him, sheltered in his arms, devoured by his kiss. He kissed her hungrily, deeply, as if searching for something he had just discovered was lost to him, something precious, something rare. She responded with her own hunger, her own need, finding the answer to her hunger in his mouth.

It was savage. It was wonderful.

He lifted her skirts, inching them up in his hand, crushing them in his fist, running his fingertips over the length of her stocking, past her knee, to the trembling flesh of her thigh. She burned. She shivered.

He did not care. He did not stop.

That was wonderful, too.

Dimly, she could hear the voices in the room beyond; the deep modulated tones of Calbourne, the sharp lilt of Sophia, the quiet good humor of Anne. Dimly, she was shocked. They were just beyond the door. A footmen could enter the room at any time from the two other doors to the dining room. Two doors! It was scandalous, unsafe, unsound to tumble against the walls and furniture with Ash. Anyone might interrupt them.

No one could interrupt them. Not at this. Not anymore.

His hand was on her thigh, his mouth on her throat, moving down in gentle bites and nibbles to her chest, to the lift of her bosom, to her nipple. He bit her through the muslin and she jerked against him, moaning.

"Sshhhh," he breathed, lifting his head to bury his mouth along the nape of her neck, biting her, kissing her, his tongue trailing a line along her neck to her throat to the tip of her chin.

Lifting her up, he turned her so that she was pressed against the bumps and ridges of the paneled door, as he was pressed against her. One arm wrapped around her waist while the other slid its way up her thigh to the swollen, aching juncture that throbbed for him. He touched her, a single feathered touch, and she banged her heels against the door and groaned.

"Sshhhh," he whispered as he slid his finger into her effortlessly. She was wet. He liked that. She could tell.

Her narrow skirt and chemise were bunched around her hips as he held her up, her head just above his own. She ran her hands into his hair and down to his shoulders and back, caressing him, learning his shape, the feel of him, the clean scent of him. She was poised above him, open and wide and helpless.

His hand moved down to his hips and when he was finished there, he cupped her, fondling, caressing. And then he pierced her.

She felt a pop, and then a burning sensation, and then all she felt was Ash. She groaned and bit her lip. He withdrew and then plunged in again, hard. Her head banged against the door. She wrapped her legs around his waist, her arms about his neck, and gave herself into his care.

He did not disappoint. He drove into her again and again, murmuring her name, kissing her mouth, her throat, her shoulder. He pulled off the fichu that had decorated her gown so that he could taste her flesh. He moaned and drove hard into her. She was pinned against the door, helpless to avoid his driving need, feeling the build of tension, the answering need to thrust toward him, the hunger in her very blood for his touch, his mouth.

His hand slipped down between them, fondling her on that tiny bud of sensation, and when the tide took her and threw her down, when she grimaced and grunted her way to the place where Ashdon took her, it was his voice that guided her back.

Panting, her head tilted back against the door with a gentle bump. Exhausted and just a bit frightened, her legs wilted from around his back and collapsed against the door. He lifted her, freeing her, and set her on her feet, her skirts falling back to the floor as they had been just moments before. Except for her missing fichu and the wild manner of her breathing, she was certain she looked exactly as she had just minutes before.

Except, of course, that she could not stand and fell in a graceless lump at Ashdon's feet. Ashdon, the lout, grinned down at her while he fastened his breeches.

"I'm flattered," he said, reaching out a hand to her.

"Don't be," she said, taking his hand as he helped her to her feet. "I didn't eat enough breakfast, that's all. If you are going to prop me up against a door anytime you choose, particularly in the middle of meals, then you must be prepared for the unavoidable consequences."

"Such as you falling at my feet?" he said politely. "I rather like those consequences, Caro."

"You would," she snapped, checking her hair for damage. It felt extremely damaged.

"Have I abused you greatly?" he said softly, looking not at all repentant. "I do apologize. I shall try not to make it a habit to take you against every door in every house we inhabit. But I shall not be rash enough to make any promises to that effect. You, my dear wife, are irresistible."

It suddenly didn't matter quite so much what her hair looked like.

"Do you really think so?" she asked, hating the needy sound of the question but helpless to stop herself.

"Hasn't it just been demonstrated?" he responded. "I certainly did not expect to deflower my wife in the dining room merely an hour after the wedding."

"Perhaps you lack discretion and self-control."

"I've never lacked for them before."

Caro raised an eyebrow and pierced him with her gaze. Yes, pierced. It seemed appropriate.

"I've explained to you about the gambling," he said, fussing with his cravat, which had looked perfectly acceptable until he had started fussing with it.

"Perhaps you should explain it again."

Caro sat down at the dining room table, as did Ashdon. They acted as if nothing had happened, though she was sore between her legs and missing her fichu and Ashdon's cravat was a mess.

"Now that I have you irrevocably, perhaps I shall," he said.

Irrevocably. It sounded high-handed and completely barbaric. She rather liked it.

"I'll go over it rather quickly, shall I?" he said. "As we have agreed that I'm lacking in self-control and discretion where you are concerned, I find myself looking at the other doors and even the windows of this room speculatively. I don't know how much longer I can keep myself in check. Perhaps you could drape a napkin over your very charming décolleté?"

"I will do no such thing," she said stiffly, feeling herself blush under his gaze. Charming décolleté, indeed.

"I discover you are a wife who enjoys the scent of risk. How delightful."

"And I discover you are a husband given over to distraction."

"Only with you, Caro. You are a profound distraction."

Caro could feel herself smile. The only thing that made it tolerable was that Ashdon was grinning right back at her. It was rather charming of him.

"If you would proceed, Lord Ashdon," she said. "I have other things with which to occupy my day."

"Of course. There are so many windows and doors in this house, after all," he said, winking at her. *Really!* "Now then, briskly, Westlin and Sophia are enemies, whether your mother will admit it to you or not. There was some disturbance in their relationship some twenty years ago or thereabouts, and Westlin has made it his life's purpose to achieve a revenge upon her, the variety of little importance. Nor the cost, I might as well mention."

He said it so swiftly, so casually, but his eyes told the truth. His eyes, as usual, were sheathed in melancholy. The cost. What had been the cost of Westlin's revenge? Certainly Ashdon had paid. What had he said? He'd been fashioned as a tool for his father's revenge against her mother. Twenty years in the making, Ashdon had been but ten when his forging into a weapon for his father's hand had begun.

No, the cost had not been counted.

"He sounds a fool," Caro said crisply. "One should always count the cost. Or as my mother puts it, one must set the price as the very first condition of any action. A trifle mercenary, perhaps, but nonetheless true."

Ashdon smiled and shook his head in amusement. "I was taught to hate her, you know, and kept a careful distance from her. She was like a pox, Westlin said, and must be avoided until he judged me ready to withstand her."

Caro's heart melted and sank into her hips. This was what she feared. This was what she'd always feared. No man would want her when he could have her mother. She did not blame her mother. She never had. Sophia was legendary and deservedly so. What was left to Caro but to have a husband bought for her? And here he stood. Before marrying Lord

Dalby, men had paid to have Sophia. For Sophia's daughter, a man had to be paid to take her.

There was nothing charming about her at all. She scanned the table looking for a likely napkin for her completely pathetic décolleté.

"Of course," Ashdon continued, crossing his legs, "Westlin was completely wrong, as I've discovered."

"Oh?" she said distractedly, casually scanning the floor for her fichu.

"Sophia is unique," he said, watching her as she avoided his gaze. "I rather like her, but you are the woman I could not withstand, Caro."

Her gaze jerked up to him, her fichu and her décolleté forgotten. He was doing it again, piercing her with his blue eyes.

"I beg your pardon?"

"As well you should," he said. "I was twenty years in being prepared to manage Sophia, but none at all in preparing against you. I rather think twenty years would hardly begin to be enough. I am looking forward to putting it to the test. Twenty years from now, let us see if I can resist lifting your skirts and taking you in our dining room. Shall we wager on it?"

Her breath was trapped in her throat, her heart trapped in her lungs, but her smile, her smile broke free and completely took over her face.

"I do think you should give off wagering, Ash," she said. "You have no talent for it. And I should hate to be the one to ruin you."

"Darling Caro," he said, rising to his feet, displaying his arousal most spectacularly, "you have already ruined me. The whole town is talking of nothing else. You must do *something* to restore my good name."

"I can't think what," she said, watching him as he walked around the table toward her. Her stomach was fluttering and her breasts tingling and he hadn't even touched her, well, unless one discounted the piercing quality of his eyes. She didn't. With Lord Ashdon, nothing could be discounted.

"Then let me show you," he said, taking her by the hand like the most gallant of gentlemen and leading her to the dining room door that led to the white salon.

This time, he removed his coat and cravat. This time, her slippers fell off.

She could only imagine what would happen the next time. She laughed just thinking of it.

Twenty-four

THE Duke of Calbourne, Lady Dalby, and Mrs. Warren sat in the white salon listening to the sounds of rhythmic bumping and moaning coming from just beyond the door to the dining room. The exact same sounds had been heard while they were in the yellow salon just a half hour before. They had, for the sake of civility and good breeding, changed rooms. They, for the sake of delighted curiosity, did not change rooms now.

"Lord Ashdon seems to have lost all control," Sophia said, smiling as she took a sip of coffee. "How completely delicious."

"Delicious, Lady Dalby?" Calbourne asked, fidgeting with the hem of his coat. He looked quite red about the ears, poor darling.

"But of course, your grace. Certainly no average girl could reduce her husband of an hour to such a state of . . . desperation. I hesitate to admit it, but I think my daughter has quite surpassed me, not that I'm not delighted, of course. One does like to see one's children do well in the world, do they not, your grace?"

"My son is not yet eight, Lady Dalby," Calbourne said with an uncomfortable smile.

"Yes, but one can never begin planning too early for one's child," Sophia said. "More coffee, Mrs. Warren?"

"No," Anne said, squirming in her chair, "thank you. I did think I might go up and refresh myself." Anne was halfway out of her chair by the time she had finished speaking.

"Nonsense," Sophia said. "You look beautifully refreshed right now, doesn't she, your grace?"

"Uh, yes," he said, casting his glance about the room disjointedly as the sounds of banging on the other side of the door rapidly increased in tempo. "Beautifully. Refreshed. Beautifully."

Anne sank back down upon the chair with a sigh.

"You are aware, of course," Sophia said, "that you cannot desert Caro now. There must be reliable witnesses, and I'm afraid I don't qualify. There are certain people of an unhappy and suspicious frame of mind who might believe that I invented this entire morning."

"I will never breathe a word," Calbourne said stiffly.

"Oh, come now, your grace," Sophia said. "That defeats the purpose entirely. I *want* you to breathe more than a word. I want you to repeat every detail. The clock declares it to be just past one. You will both agree that Caro and her darling Ashdon have been making merry in the dining room for just over an hour? Details are so important in these cases. They simply make all the difference between an interesting deception and the startling truth."

Something fell in the dining room and they all stopped to listen. It sounded rather large. Perhaps the sideboard?

My darling Caro, what have you done to the poor man?

"One twenty-two," she said, looking at the very pretty clock on the mantel. "I wonder how much longer he can keep it up?" At Anne's gasp of shock, Sophia said, "Merely a manner of speaking, Anne. You cannot think I meant it literally."

But, of course, they did. And of course, she had.

If there was any way to begin a marriage, this was definitely it. Poor, dreary Westlin would be spinning in his grave, though, unfortunately, he was not in his grave yet.

Well, the day was young.

❧

THE day was still young when Lord Westlin found his way into White's looking for his son. It was less than pleasant to find that a bet had been placed regarding the exact hour of his death upon learning that Lord Ashdon, his heir, had married Lady Caroline Trevelyan. The odds were that he would die at exactly 6:15 that evening.

The Earl of Westlin, swearing violently, left the club. As soon as he was out of earshot, the betting continued more vigorously than before, with the favored time now shifting to four as it was now three and no one who had seen his face could believe he would last more than an hour in that condition.

It was in that state that he arrived at Lady Dalby's town house.

Fredericks opened the door and said, "Lord Westlin. How interesting to see you again. Come to celebrate the nuptials?"

"You are not called upon to make remarks to guests, you ignorant American," Westlin said, clutching his cane like a club.

"I know I'm not called upon," Fredericks said, "but I make a special effort, for those I have special memories of."

That they remembered each other from earlier days was memorable to them both, for differing reasons, naturally.

"Announce me," Westlin commanded.

"Certainly," Freddy responded. "If you'll wait here?" He pointed to an exact spot on the floor as if he expected Westlin to sit and stay, rather like a large, unwelcome dog. It need not be stated that the comparisons were obvious.

Westlin was shown into a room done all in white in which Sophia stood to greet him, similarly dressed in white with a large pale green shawl draped across her back. She wore jade earrings that dangled down to caress her throat in the most seductive manner imaginable. The white salon. He'd heard of it, as had everyone else in London, but only he knew the significance of the room. The blanc de Chine cup held pride of place, as well it should.

"Ah, Westlin," she said, "you finally made it, though I'm sorry to say the wedding was hours ago. It was a delightful affair. I'm so distraught you missed it."

"Show me the license," he demanded, his hand out.

"You mistrust me?" she said with a raised brow. "When have I ever lied to you, Westy?"

"You're lying to me now, pretending that I was invited to this horror when you *know* that, had I come, I would have put a stop to it."

"I know no such thing. I did send a messenger round with an invitation. I would certainly want my daughter's marriage to begin on the proper footing, wouldn't I?"

"I don't think you care where her feet fall as long as they're planted on a mattress!"

"Really, Lord Westlin," she said in mock severity, arranging the fringe on her shawl in obvious boredom, "I must ask you to restrain yourself. Such vulgarity. And we are family now, aren't we? We must strive for civility, no matter our past differences. One must do one's best by one's children."

"They're really married, then?"

"They really are," she answered with a smug smile.

"But not yet consummated."

"Most assuredly consummated," she said. "There are witnesses."

"What the devil do you mean there are witnesses!" Westlin roared. "How can there be witnesses?"

"My dear Westlin," she said softly, "they were married barely an hour when he"—she shrugged delicately—"I suppose one might say he *had at her*, which you will surely believe as you had that very same tendency. Do you remember our carriage ride through Hyde Park? I lost everything but my earrings."

"Blast it, Sophia! I will not believe it! He cannot have done—"

"But I assure you, Westy, he has done. The Duke of Calbourne was sitting exactly where you are now when, well, the sounds coming from the dining room could only have one meaning. He is your son, after all."

"I will not have your child be the Countess Westlin," he snarled, tightening his grip on his cane.

"I would love to hear what you plan to do to stop it," she said serenely, leaning back against the sofa, studying him. "Particularly as my daughter could well deliver your son's heir in precisely nine months."

"He'll put her aside," he growled.

Sophia laughed in delight. "I hardly think so. She has him quite in the palm of her hand. I daresay I have never seen a man so well managed. It's quite delicious to see. I do hope you'll stay so that you may see it for yourself."

"Ashdon is here?"

"Not at the moment, though it took a full hour of false starts before he was finally able to make his departure. He almost couldn't bear to leave her," Sophia said. "It was rather precious."

Revolting was more like it, but that was neither here nor there. He knew Sophia, and he knew that their dance of revenge went beyond this moment of triumph she was clearly enjoying.

"What do you want?"

"I beg your pardon?"

"What do you want? What will it take to make this marriage disappear?"

"You never cease to intrigue me, Lord Westlin, which surely stands in your favor," she said slowly. "And do sit, Westy. My neck is growing stiff." He remained standing out of pure stubbornness. "Sit, Lord Westlin," she commanded sternly. He sat. "There," she cooed, "that's so much better, isn't it? Now we can converse properly and in complete civility."

"You managed it very well, didn't you?" he said in a low tone.

"I like to think so," she said.

"You've had your revenge, then, Sophia," he said. "I concede the point. Now, let's get this undone. You can't want your daughter in my family any more than I want her there."

"But of course I do, darling. I want her there completely. She's marvelous for Ashdon, that poor child you have mishandled for far too many years, and she'll be marvelous for you as well. You shan't be able to manage her, Westlin. She will be quite too much for you. So unlike your dear, sweet, docile wife. You mishandled her as well, which was truly awful of you."

"This has nothing to do with her," Westlin said.

"Darling," Sophia said, "this has everything to do with her. Did you not realize that? You can't have thought I'd have spent so much time and effort on a discarded lover? Goodness knows, I have more than enough of those and we get on quite well. You, on the other hand, used me to inflict a blow upon your wife. That was very wrong of you and quite unforgivable."

Unfortunately, he knew exactly what she was talking about. He could admit now, barely, that it had been a poorly conceived idea. Certainly it had not had the result he had intended. Where Sophia was concerned, *nothing* turned out as planned. He was more than tired of that particular trait of hers.

There was a soft knock on the door to the white salon and then Fredericks stuck his head in.

"Lord Staverton is here, Lady Dalby."

"For Mrs. Warren?"

"No, for you. He's just come from White's."

"Show him in, Freddy."

"I have no interest in discussing this publicly," Westlin said, standing.

"Do sit down, Westy. You must learn not to pop about so," Sophia said. "Lord Staverton will not stay long. You would create more gossip if you ran out now. After all, most of London shall soon know our children were married this morning. We must put a good face on it; call it parental duty if you must. Always lovely to see you, Lord Staverton," she said, rising to give him her hand. "And how are things at White's?"

Lord Staverton halted upon seeing Lord Westlin, but shrugged slightly, nodded a greeting, and then proceeded to ignore him. Most people had found it to be the best way of dealing with Lord Westlin and his uncertain temper.

Staverton cast an uncertain glance at Westlin and said, "You're certain you wish to discuss this now, Sophia?"

"Why, naturally," Sophia said regally, sitting down upon the silk cushion. "Lord Westlin is family now, after all. We certainly need keep no secrets from *him*, no matter how much he might prefer it."

"What the devil do you mean by that?" Westlin snarled.

"Now, really, Lord Westlin," Sophia said glibly, "you must learn to keep your temper on some sort of rein, no matter how loosely held. You are becoming quite the social outcast, which I'm certain must hurt Caroline in some way, and so therefore I cannot allow you to continue on as you have done. 'Tis a new day, darling," she said with a calculating smile, "and you must adjust to it. Or die trying."

"A poor attempt at a threat, Sophia," he said.

"Darling, if ever I threaten you, you shall most assuredly be in no doubt of it," she said softly. She watched Westlin suppress a shiver with complete delight. "It was merely an observation, and a suggestion, that was all. We simply must do something about your rather laggard sense of humor. All the fun seems to have gone right out of you. I do remember you as laughing on occasion," she said, and then, putting a hand to her chin said, "or was that Lord Atwick? I was forever getting the two of you confused when I first came down to London, wasn't I? Tell me, Westlin, was it you who laughed when I had myself delivered in place of the brandy or was that Atwick?"

"It was Asterley," Staverton said.

"Oh, yes," she said dreamily. "Asterley had the most engaging laugh, as well as his other engaging qualities."

"Good lord," Westlin muttered. "Must you parade your list of customers before us all?"

"Why, of course I must, as it is so very entertaining to provoke you. Why should I stop?"

"For the sake of your daughter's propriety for one!"

"Oh, but I never talk about these things in front of my children. One must keep up appearances, after all, but *we* know the truth of things, of how things were before this new, conservative age descended upon us like, well, to be blunt, like a blade. I blame the furor in France, I truly do. Things were so much more pleasant before revolution became the order of the day, although the new fashions are quite enjoyable. I never did care for the tightness of those old-fashioned stays."

"The proof of your upbringing," Westlin said, snarling

yet again. The man had almost no other way of communicating, obviously. How terribly tedious.

"Are we onto that again?" Sophia said. "I happen to have enjoyed my upbringing, Lord Westlin. I rather think you could have done with some of the same. I think it would have done wonders for your temperament, at the very least."

"I hardly care what your opinion is of the matter. Of any matter, as far as that goes."

"Yes, well, more proof, I'm afraid, of my point," she said. "But come, come, we are boring Lord Staverton to tears, though he is too much the gentleman to admit it. What is the word at White's, darling? I am all aquiver."

"The Duke of Hyde grumbled a bit, claiming that he suspected you had played a part in the events of last night, but he will honor the wager," Staverton said. "His man will be around tomorrow with the blunt."

"It is so pleasant to wager against a man who has the funds to pay his accounts," Sophia said, eyeing Westlin. "And Viscount Tannington?"

"He's coming over himself," Staverton said. "I do hope you know that he took this bet merely for the opportunity to meet you."

"Yes, and isn't that charming of him? I do so enjoy eagerness, especially when it combines with money."

"What bet are you talking about?" Westlin snapped.

"Why, the bet I had Lord Staverton make that Caroline and Ashdon would marry by six o'clock today," she said, smiling pleasantly.

"I beg your pardon?" Caroline said from the door to the white salon. Freddy stood behind her with an apologetic look on his face, as if that helped.

"Darling, come in. Have you met Lord Ashdon's father?"

Caroline, her dark blue eyes stormy, made her curtsey, said the appropriate greetings in the appropriate tone of voice, took a graceful seat on the sofa next to Sophia, and then said stiffly, "You made a wager, Mother? About me? *At White's?*"

"Won the wager, to be more precise," Sophia said. "These

distinctions are so important, as your husband knows perhaps better than all of us."

"We were not discussing Ashdon. We were discussing your bet," Caro said.

"You see how good she shall be for you, Westlin," Sophia said. "You shall not run riot over her."

Caroline gave a cursory glance to Lord Westlin before turning back to her mother. "I do not care for having my name on White's betting book, Mother. It is not at all the thing I aspire to."

"But, darling, your name was already there. Why not make a profit on the ignorance of others?"

"What do you mean?" Caro asked. "Why should my name appear as a bet?"

"Because you're *her* daughter, you ignorant girl," Westlin snapped.

Caro turned to consider him for several long moments, so long, in fact, that the Earl of Westlin turned a bit red about the ears.

"I would so like to have a pleasant relationship with you, Lord Westlin," Caro said eventually, "as you are my husband's father, but do not mistake me for a girl who requires your approval. My husband is fairly bewitched by me and that is quite all I require."

"Impudent girl!" he sputtered.

"Yes," said Sophia with a grin, "and isn't it delightful? There is nothing better for a girl than to be impudent. I do fear that this modern education of women quite drives all impudence out of them. I don't know what England will come to without a good supply of impudent women."

"As if you care about England's future!" Westlin argued.

"But of course I care," Sophia said softly, her eyes gleaming. "I care very much. In fact, I give it quite a lot of thought."

"And I am giving quite a lot of thought," Caro interrupted, "to exactly why my name should appear at White's and what you did about it, Mother, and what I shall do about it now. As impudent as I may be, it does not seem at all the thing."

"But of course it is the thing, darling, because you shall make it so. I daresay that in a year, eligible girls will be desperate to have their names appear on White's betting book. It shall become the new fashion, a mark of excellence."

"I don't think being the subject of a public wager shall ever be fashionable," Caro said.

"Listen to your mother on this," Lord Staverton said from his slouch on the side chair. "I've never known Sophia to be wrong about things of this sort."

"You mean the tawdry sort, obviously," Westlin said. "That my son's wife should be the subject of bets . . . revolting."

"Come now, Westlin," Sophia said smoothly, "do not pretend that you are a stranger to White's betting book. Your name has appeared there more than once."

"But not my wife's!"

"Perhaps because people forgot she was alive?" Sophia said brightly. "But of course, I never forgot her, poor dear."

"We were speaking of your daughter," Westlin said, "not my wife."

"Yes," Caro said, "and the nature of that bet. What was it?"

"I can't think that it matters now," Sophia said evasively, arranging the fringe on her shawl so that it draped more elegantly over her white arms.

"It matters to me," Caro said, staring at Sophia.

"Yes, well, I don't suppose it could do any harm to tell you, particularly as I've made quite a lot of money as a result," Sophia said.

"And that's all that matters?" Caro said stiffly. "Making a profit?"

"Darling, let me assure you, it is far more enjoyable than suffering a loss."

"There are more things to be lost than money," Caro said, her voice tight with emotion.

Sophia looked into her daughter's eyes and smiled lightly. "Of course there are, Caro, but why lose money when the opportunity to make it presents itself?"

"And I was that opportunity?"

"In a manner of speaking," Sophia said. "The way I understand it, the Earl of Westlin and his brother, Baron Sedgwick, became engaged in a rather vigorous discussion at White's that, as these sorts of discussions inevitably do, ended up as a bet on White's book. The argument and subsequent bet being that Sedgwick, a delightful man, you'll so enjoy him, Caro, bet Westlin that Lord Ashdon would be courting you by the end of the Season. Lord Westlin obviously bet that his son, the charming Lord Ashdon, would *not* court you. But, of course, Lord Ashdon not only courted you, he married you, and swiftly. And there you have it. The bet was made. I bet against Lord Westlin and I have won." *As usual.* Sophia didn't say it aloud, but those in the room heard it as clearly as if she had.

Of course, she *had* stumbled into ruination, been enticed to it by Ash, actually, which had been the cause of her swift marriage, but if Lord Westlin didn't know about her being ruined, she wasn't going to be the one to enlighten him.

"That was the bet?" Caro asked suspiciously. "The bet was about me? About Lord Ashdon and *me*?"

"Why, of course, darling. What else?"

They all looked at Caro expectantly, even Lord Staverton with his wandering eye seemed to have focused on her more intently that she would have thought physically possible.

"I, well," Caro said, fidgeting with her fresh fichu; she never had found the other one that Ashdon had so purposefully disposed of in the dining room. "I was under the impression that things were rather more about you and Ashdon."

"Things? What things are you referring to, Caro?"

"Just . . . things."

"I can't imagine what you mean," Sophia said with a laugh. "Here you are, in the flush of impudent youth and flagrant beauty. I can't think how Ashdon resisted you for as long as he did."

"Three days?" Caro said sarcastically.

"Darling, I am quite certain he was besotted after three

hours. He just didn't realize it. Men are rather slow about these things," Sophia said, winking at her daughter. "They often require much patience and careful handling. An important point to remember as you begin your life together."

"Women's rubbish," Westlin said in a low snarl. "If you are going to lie to your daughter, at least do it well. Tell her the rest, Sophia, or I will."

"Can't you keep things civil, Westlin?" Staverton said, getting up from his chair and moving to one of the street-facing windows. "Let things settle. They are as they are."

Caro could feel her stomach dive into her hips before bouncing back to lodge under her heart. She was, however, fairly certain that she was maintaining a poised and politely bland expression, which was all that mattered.

"She looks like she's about to cast up her accounts," Westlin said.

"Don't be absurd," Sophia said. "My daughter would never fall to such behavior, especially not in front of her husband's father."

Which of course, straightened both her spine and her resolve.

"I feel perfectly fine," Caro said sweetly. "Thank you for your concern, Lord Westlin. In this instance, it is completely misplaced."

Sophia smiled in approval and nodded serenely. Whatever had occurred, Lord Westlin was *not* to see any weakness in her; that Caro understood very well.

"Of course, if there is something I should know, I should be more than eager to know it," Caro said. "Mother? Is there more?"

"Nothing of particular interest," Sophia said. When Lord Westlin began to grumble, Sophia continued, "Only that I wagered you would marry Lord Ashdon by six o'clock today. I made a tidy sum on that, as well. Well done, Caro."

Oh, Lord. She and her mother both knew how *that* had been managed. It had been her mother's idea, after all, the entire pearl price, which would naturally result in the pearl seduction, which would even more naturally result in either ruination or marriage, and in her particular situation, both.

She had been used. By her mother. For profit. Perhaps even for revenge.

Had Ashdon been right about her mother? Had this all been about wielding some blow against Westlin and nothing at all to do with her happiness?

No, not even Sophia could be so coldly calculating.

Though it was her mother who had convinced her that a pearl seduction was the only way to reliably achieve the elusive and completely contrary Lord Ashdon. It had seemed a logical plan at the time, particularly for a girl who had limited options. All right. She had had *no* options, or none that she could see, anyway.

Had she been managed from the start?

It *had* been her mother's idea to marry Lord Ashdon initially, hadn't it? Somehow, it had become *her* idea, or she had been persuaded to think it was her idea.

How very convenient that Sophia's only daughter was married to Lord Westlin's only son. What a very tidy revenge, and for profit, too. Her mother, she well knew, never discounted the possibility of profit.

Caro was developing a very healthy headache.

"And well done to Ashdon," Staverton said from his window post, the late afternoon sun slanting across his features. "He wagered against the Marquis of Dutton that he'd wed you and bed you before four o'clock today. He was collecting from Dutton as I left White's. A tidy sum, too."

She was on her feet and at the door of the white salon before she knew it. She had to get out of this room before she did cast up her accounts, all over Lord Westlin's feet. Not that he didn't deserve it for having such a horrid son.

"What a clever man," Sophia said smoothly, "to be paid twice for the same act. Perhaps he is better at money than he first appeared. How fortunate for Caroline."

Caroline turned to face her mother, her eyes wide with shock.

How fortunate for Caroline. Oh, yes, how very fortunate. He'd done it for money. He'd done it *all* for money. He was more of a courtesan than she could ever have dreamed of being.

The door opened behind her and she slipped back an unsteady step into the opening, slipped back and felt Ashdon's hand on her back, steadying her. She knew his touch; even through her clothes, she knew his touch and yearned for it.

She'd like to kill him for that.

"Hello, my irresistible wife," he murmured against her hair.

His scent tantalized her, bracing and enticing. She could hate him for that as well. What wiles *hadn't* he used to make a pound off her too-willing flesh?

She stepped sharply away from his touch and faced him. He looked the complete innocent, the scoundrel.

"I'm surprised you don't jingle when you walk," she said.

"I beg your pardon?" Ash asked, still playing the innocent, loving husband.

"I said," she snapped, slamming the door to the white salon closed, "that I'm surprised you don't jingle when you walk. From all the money you've made at my expense. From all the bargains and wagers you've made with me at their heart. From all the times and ways you've sold yourself, and me, for money."

Ashdon actually had the *cheek* to look grim. The man had no shame, certainly no morals, and it was highly questionable whether he would continue on with all the parts he'd been born with.

"I think you should know now, Caro, that I shan't discuss financial matters with you. That is not the way our marriage shall be arranged."

"Fine!" she said, staring him down. If he thought he could frighten her with a grim and forbidding look, well, he didn't know her at all, did he? "You may or may not discuss what you wish. You will understand, of course, that while you are making pronouncements about how our marriage shall be arranged, I shall be making funeral arrangements. For you. Freddy? A candlestick, if you please?"

Without any hesitation and certainly no reluctance, Freddy handed her a nicely solid silver candelabra. It would work beautifully as a weapon, and Freddy would never testify against her. Of that, she was certain.

"What the devil do you think you're doing?" Ash said. His tone was harsh and condemning. She could hardly have cared less.

"If you will just stand still for a moment, I am going to hit you soundly on the head. Preferably the face. I should so like to disfigure you. Permanently. It will be a closed casket, of course."

"Caro—"

"My name is Caroline," she interrupted. "You may call me Lady Caroline, if you must call me anything at all."

"Caro," he said sternly, eyeing the candlestick, which she had raised over her head and which was growing somewhat heavy, "put that down. We must talk a few things through."

"Oh. Now you're willing to talk? Well, there is nothing to talk about, is there? It was all a lie. Everything. From the very start." She was starting to cry. It was most embarrassing. Of all things, she did not want Ashdon to see her cry. "Everything was for the money. It was never about me at all. You probably hate the very sight of me. No wonder you hurried through our . . . well, what to call it? Not our wedding night. It isn't even night yet. You just wanted to get it over with, didn't you? I suppose I should be grateful you didn't fling my skirts up over my head so that you could forget who—"

"Caro!" he roared. She dropped the candlestick. It made a dent in the floor and rolled dully to a stop at Freddy's feet. "Enough!"

"Yes, enough," she said stiffly, sniffing back her tears. "Fully enough. Freddy? The door."

Freddy complied and opened the door. Ashdon grabbed her in his arms as she tried to pass him, crushed her to him, and kissed her savagely. She was on the edge of losing herself in his kiss, which was completely usual. She was completely disgusted with herself for her girlish weakness where Lord Ashdon was concerned. It was time for a completely different sort of action altogether.

She kneed him in the groin.

It was rather more than satisfying to see him drop to one knee and turn white about the gills.

Apparently, she had struck him rather hard for even Freddy groaned. She was sorry for that, but she couldn't see how it could have been helped.

Caro ran out of the house and down the steps with no thought as to where she would go, but certain that she had to go . . . away. Away from Ashdon. Away from the cruel truth of her marriage. He didn't love her; he didn't even particularly want her. He had needed money and so he had agreed to marry her, and then made a bet that he *would* marry her. How had her mother put it? Paid twice for the same act? And just when had he made that bet, anyway? That bit of missing information loomed quite large.

If she could stop crying long enough she would kill him.

She ran down Upper Brook Street to Park Lane and began walking briskly, certainly nothing to draw attention to herself, unless one discounted the fact that she had no hat, no spencer, and was wearing the wrong shoes for walking. She was forced to discount all three items and pretend that she was out for a healthy stretch of the leg. It was a bit of a struggle to maintain a good pretense when she was crying like a child, but she was fortunate in that no one was out. No one she knew anyway.

The sun was sinking behind the trees of Hyde Park, the birds were chirping gaily in their final moments before seeking their nests, the breeze was fresh and cool, and she couldn't stop crying.

It had all gone badly awry. She had a husband and, as much as she wanted to, she probably shouldn't kill him. Murder was rather frowned upon, no matter how stellar the provocation. Ashdon would live on, but she could not live with him.

She just couldn't, not now that she knew he had never felt the slightest breath of interest in her beyond the money he could make because of her. He had flirted and flattered her, just like the finest courtesan the town had ever seen, and now he had her. Or she had him. Whichever. But they didn't want each other, not really. He wanted the soothing jingle of coin and she wanted . . . she wanted . . .

Ashdon.

Caro sniffed and cursed herself for not having a handkerchief to hand. She pulled off her fichu because, honestly, she looked shabby enough without proper shoes and no coat, what was to be gained by wearing a proper fichu to cover her décolleté? There was no one who cared what her décolleté looked like in any regard. Their marriage was a pretense, and therefore the pretense of Ashdon falling to bits over her fine and lovely bosom was superfluous now. She carefully arranged her delicate fichu in her hands and then blew her nose on it.

It was at that most inopportune moment that she heard the sound of running footsteps behind her. She turned slightly, wadding the fichu in her hand, and beheld Ashdon running toward her.

He did not look grim. Neither did he look resolved. In point of fact, he looked furious.

Without meaning to do so, but with no inclination to stop, Caro began running away from him. Indeed, it was the only logical response, wasn't it? She certainly would not be foolish enough to run *toward* a furious husband who had just been severely kneed by his wife. Even if he had deserved it. Even if it didn't look to have incapacitated him for long.

Life was so consistently unfair, no matter how logical one was about it. She was beginning to wonder if being logical wasn't a highly overrated attribute. Being logical certainly hadn't helped her much that she could see.

It was becoming increasingly obvious that she was going to lose her race against Ashdon down Park Lane. If life had been fair, she would have been able to outrun him, or at least to have kept her advantage of a head start. Or at the very least been wearing something a bit more solid on her feet than fragile silk shoes.

Whatever her disadvantages in a footrace against her husband, she was not going to stop running. Let him drag her to the ground, if he dared. Let him haul her off into the depths of Hyde Park, slung over his shoulder like a captive. Let him tear the very clothes from her body . . . yes, well, and that was the whole trouble, thinking like that.

She was prevented from finding out if Ashdon would catch her and what he would do with her when he caught her by the timely intervention of a passing landau.

A shadowed face presented itself at the window, the landau slowed, the door opened, a large hand with delicate tattoos encircling the wrist reached out to her, and she was, with great finesse, hauled inside. Her last thought as she was being lifted into the dark confines of the mysterious landau was that Ashdon would be furious to have lost the chance to throttle her. It was for this reason that she entered the landau grinning.

Twenty-five

A dark and chiseled face, almond-shaped black eyes, and a red fox fur hat appeared from out of the gloom.

"Oh, hello, Uncle John," she said as she straightened her skirts on the carriage squabs. "Back from France so soon?"

"Should I kill him?" her uncle said in answer to her rather tame greeting.

"Please don't," she said, trying to catch her breath from that awful run. "I think it would be more fun if *I* killed him."

Uncle John smiled in his fashion, which is to say that he made a gesture with his mouth that was slightly above a grimace. His shining black eyes did the actual smiling.

"Agreed. Who is he?"

"Oh," she said on an exasperated sigh, "he's just my husband."

The conversation was entirely in French, of course, as Uncle John, Sophia's brother, was more comfortably fluent in French rather than English, though his English was flawless. Once she had admitted that the man pursuing her was her husband, Uncle John had tapped the roof of the landau and it had stopped. She had seen the fury on Ash's face; she knew full well that he was still running to catch her.

"I wish you would drive on," she said. "I have no wish to be battered by my husband."

"He would hit you?" When she merely shrugged her answer, he said, "Did you hit him first?"

"In a manner of speaking. But it was entirely deserved!"

John grunted and dropped his gaze, which she understood full well was his way of laughing uproariously.

"This is Lord Ashdon, Westlin's heir?" John asked.

She could definitely hear the sound of Ashdon's feet on the stones. His feet sounded furious.

"Yes," she said, her gaze jerking from the open window to John's face. "But how did you know? We've only been married this day."

John nodded and looked out the window expectantly. It was quite clear he was waiting for Ashdon. Why was it that men always grouped together in situations such as this? One would almost think that Uncle John thought she *should* get thrashed by her husband on the mere technicality that she had struck him first, though not without immense provocation. Let no one forget that striking detail.

Men were so illogical about these things, particularly when it concerned *that* part of their bodies. Ridiculous, really. Of course, her mother had told her that this would be the result if she ever chose to use that particular brand of dissuasion.

It had been worth it.

Her mother had told her that, too.

"It makes a nice revenge," John said softly, staring at her.

Oh, that. Revenge again. She couldn't escape it, no matter how hard she ran. Her indignation tumbled down and lost all its heat, leaving her with nothing but sadness and the painful emptiness of lost hope.

"Is it all of revenge?" she whispered.

"Let's find out," John said in an undertone, his words almost swallowed by a quick banging against the landau door just before it was thrown open to reveal Ashdon's enraged face and heaving chest.

Even enraged, his face did such lovely things to her heart. Completely unfair, of course, but there she was, shackled to a husband who could melt her with a look and he only interested in her for the money.

"You have my wife in your possession," Ashdon growled, staring at the stranger who had lifted Caro into his landau. "Release her."

The man, dark haired and of sternly arranged features, answered Ashdon in a language unknown to him. Caro jerked her gaze to the man, obviously startled. What was equally startling was that Caro spoke to the stranger in what Ash could only surmise was the same language.

Ashdon lunged into the landau and grabbed the stranger by the knot in his cravat. "Who are you to my wife?" The man did not so much as flinch. Ashdon snagged Caro's hand and pulled her so that her hip rested against his; if he had to throw her from the landau, so be it. He might actually enjoy it.

The stranger spoke again, and this time Caro responded in French.

"Don't be ridiculous, Ashdon," she snipped, trying to pull her hand from his, unsuccessfully. "This is Uncle John, my mother's brother. He's just back from France."

As if coming from France explained anything at all.

"Sophia's brother," Ashdon said, looking for a resemblance and seeing it, though dimly. The same dark hair and eyes, the same self-possessed gaze, the same superior smirk; yes, all that, but little else. This man was dark of skin while Sophia's complexion was fresh cream. This man's features were sharp and hard while Sophia's were the fine angles and curves of the oldest French nobility. "He speaks French, but not English? Yet they're brother and sister?"

Uncle John answered in French. "We have not seen each other often over the years."

There were a thousand questions Ashdon could have asked, but he thought the simplest would serve him best. "Why?"

John shifted his gaze to Caro, who returned John's look expectantly. "Because of one war or another," John answered, which raised rather more questions than it answered. "You have a dispute with your wife," John said calmly. "Finish it. In English. I will not intrude."

"I will do what I wish with my wife," Ashdon said, staring hard at Caro's unusual uncle, "in any language I wish. But not in front of you."

"I am her uncle. Until the dispute is settled," he said, shrugging one shoulder slightly, "she will remain in my protection."

"She needs no protection beyond that which I can give her," Ash said in soft menace.

"Well spoken," John said.

"Yes, well, I can bloody well protect myself," Caro said, sounding oddly annoyed.

Women were such fools about these things, thinking that they could do as they wished without counting the cost of their actions or their words. It would be his task to teach her otherwise. He was looking forward to it.

"Uncle John? Will you take me back to Dalby House, please?"

"I think Lord Ashdon is not ready to return to your mother's house," John said, still speaking in French.

And then he spoke again in that strange language that Ash couldn't name. Whatever it was he said, Caro turned a bit red on the chest, in the exact location that should have been covered by a fichu. The woman needed to learn to keep better account of her fichus. He wasn't going to allow her to parade her bosom all over London.

"What the devil language is that, Caro? You speak it as well, don't you?"

"Of course I do," she said as the landau lurched forward at John's tap. "I've been speaking it since I was a baby."

"And?"

"And it's"—she smoothed her muslin skirts, refusing to face him—"it's Iroquois, if you must know. My mother and Uncle John are half Iroquois."

Twenty-six

IT was at that precise moment that Ash stopped speaking French. He bloody well didn't care if Uncle John was offended or not.

"When were you going to tell me?" he asked Caro.

"I don't know that I was ever going to tell you. I can't see what business it is of yours."

"You can't? My being your husband means nothing?"

"I don't know who your grandparents are."

"Really? I find that odd since everyone knows my ancestry back to the twelfth century."

"How delightful for you," Caro said primly, staring out the window. "Where are we going, Uncle John?" she asked sulkily. "If not Dalby House, then where?" That she asked it in French Ash took to be a sign of civility since she could have chosen to speak in Iroquois. It was a small courtesy, but he appreciated the effort it took given their present state of disquiet.

"I'm taking you into Hyde Park. The dispute will be settled there."

"I don't see why," Caro said stiffly. "Or how."

"You will," John answered her, looking at Ashdon as he spoke. It was not a particularly cheerful look.

"I'd like you to explain things to me," Ash said to Caro, in English.

"I don't care what you'd like at the moment," she said, staring out the window at the growing twilight. "There are many things I'd like that I can't have. I don't see why you should get what you want when I can't ever seem to have the things that I want."

Caro's voice sounded thick and full, full of tears, most likely. He understood that he was at fault somehow, but for the life of him, he couldn't riddle out what he'd done wrong. He'd finally turned his finances around and actually made some money for a change, and the very woman who scolded him with every other breath of being a hopeless gambler was angry now that he was finally winning.

If that wasn't just like a woman.

"If it's not too inconvenient," Ash said, addressing Uncle John in French, "I'd be very interested to hear the details of my wife's ancestry from a reliable source. I'd also like an explanation as to why we're in the wildest section of the park."

"Hyde Park," John said quietly. "Isn't that where duels are fought?"

"In the past, yes," Ash said.

"There is your answer," John said. "There is a dispute. It must be settled. Caroline's father is dead. As her mother's brother, it is my duty to make certain you are the man for her. The right man."

Ashdon felt his hair bristle on his scalp. "I am her husband by law."

"By English law. But I am not English, and it is my law that will decide."

Caro stirred at his side and leaned forward on the seat. "I said you didn't have to kill him, Uncle John."

Ash looked askance at Caro and said, "Your wifely devotion knows no bounds, does it? I suppose I should be flattered."

"You should be," she said. "I told John quite clearly that I would kill you myself."

"The Iroquois in you, no doubt."

"I certainly hope so," she snapped. "If you're so interested in my ancestry, let me enlighten you. My grandmother was English and my grandfather a Mohawk of the Iroquois Nation. They had two children, John and Sophia. There. Satisfied? Oh, and let me add since you are so particular about bloodlines, that my mother is a cousin to Georgiana, Duchess of Devonshire. Is that rarefied enough for you?"

"Blast it, Caro, that wasn't at all what I meant!"

"Of course not," she said sarcastically. "By the way, Uncle John, how was France?"

"Full of Englishmen," John said.

"You rounded up my brother without too much trouble?" she asked.

"Trouble is entertaining in the right circumstances," John answered. "He's home, as is Josiah Blakesley."

Ash didn't need any explanation to understand the gist of the situation; having been up at school and chafing to be free of it in his own day, he deduced that Markham, the ninth Earl of Dalby, and the youngest Blakesley had run off for France a few hours after the Treaty of Amiens had been signed. Uncle John, as the oldest male relative in Sophia's household, had been called upon to bring him to heel. Though called upon from where? Surely Sophia's brother did not reside in England. It wasn't possible that he should have been kept a secret for so many years if he had. Ash didn't quite have the energy to focus on his newly realized uncle by marriage, not when he had a bristling wife seated next to him.

The landau slowed to a stop. The only sounds surrounding them were the call of night birds and the soft lap of the Serpentine. They were not far from the palatial houses of Mayfair in miles, but in the soft dark of deepening twilight, it felt almost as if they were on another continent. Or perhaps it was the savage look in John's black eyes that gave Ash that impression.

From far off, through the wood, came the sound of footfalls landing lightly on soft spring grass. John motioned for him to get out of the carriage, which he did, instructing Caro to remain within. Ash did not want her out here. Something was amiss. She must have felt the same for she obeyed him, and they both knew how unlikely that was. Yet the very air was pregnant with hostile expectation. And suddenly from out of the darkness came the shapes of three men running. They ran lightly, effortlessly, and nearly silently.

In a heartbeat, they were upon him. They gathered in silence around John and as a body, they turned to him, studying him. John spoke softly to them in Iroquois. Caro cried out, "No! Don't!"

John barked a command at Caro and she stilled instantly. Ashdon tensed, sensing what was coming. A man did not attend Eton without learning what was surely coming.

"You must prove yourself, Lord Ashdon," John said slowly, and then he pulled a long, curved knife from out of his boot.

Twenty-seven

"Do I at least get a knife?" Ash asked, taking off his coat and waistcoat. His white linen shirt glowed softly in the darkness. He was, as far as it was possible to be, a perfect target.

"If you want a knife," John said softly, "come and get mine. If you can."

Ash grunted and nodded, untying his cravat and pulling it from his neck. It fell in a long tangle of white to lie atop his coat. The linen of his shirt gaped open to reveal a tautly muscled chest. Fat lot of good muscles would do against a blade.

Caro felt the muscles in her stomach clench in protest, but she didn't quite know what to do about it. When she'd protested, John had reminded her, starkly, that she was a daughter of the Wolf Clan, granddaughter of a Mohawk sachem, and to remember what was expected of her. Which was true, of course, and which she did, but which didn't help Ash much. And she wanted to help Ash. She just didn't know how; she wasn't even sure why. That bet still chewed at her. When had he made the bet? When he was arguing that he still wasn't going to marry her?

"Ash?" she called out. "You don't have to do this."

"Really?" Ash said calmly. "I'd like to know how you think I should avoid it."

"Relinquish her," John answered. "I test your worth, that is all. Relinquish her and you may walk away."

"Never," Ash said softly.

"Then you will be cut. Many times," John said. "I will make you bleed for her."

"Go to hell," Ash answered, facing John.

John had also removed his coat and waistcoat. They stood facing each other, their features cut by the dim lamplight from the landau. The driver sat upon the box, facing the darkness, his shoulders hunched up to his ears. He had driven John before, that was obvious.

"Is it to be between us, or will your sons also try for a piece of me?" Ash asked, his blue eyes gleaming like new steel in the night.

"They may partake of whatever is left of you," John answered. "It is their right."

"If they earn it," Ash said, lunging at John.

Caro held her breath high in her throat, held herself motionless as Ash leapt through the air, his elbow aimed at Uncle John's throat. John turned at the last moment, deflecting the worst of the blow, and slashed out with his knife, slicing through Ashdon's shirt, slicing into the flesh along his left side. Ashdon twisted against the blow, keeping the blade along the ridged protection of his ribs. As he twisted, he wrapped his arms around John's neck from behind, pulling his head back, exposing John's throat. It was a killing position, except for the fact that John had the tip of his knife pressed to Ashdon's belly. One move and either could have killed the other; Ashdon by breaking John's neck and John by gutting Ashdon like a deer.

They froze, each breathing heavily, softly, patiently.

"What do you want, Caro?" John asked, staring at her from the darkness. "Say the word and I will rid you of him."

Ashdon looked at her from behind Uncle John, his arms bulging with twisted muscle as he held John in a viselike grip. Ash stared. He did not speak. He did not plead or cajole or demand. He only stared in that solemn, penetrating way of his, mute, as always.

Words would have helped. Words would have been nice. But it suddenly struck her that Ash might not know the words to use to ask for what he wanted. Perhaps he'd never been taught those words. Perhaps no one had ever told him that he could ask for what he wanted, and perhaps no one had ever cared if he got what he wanted or not.

She cared.

"I want him," she said softly, walking toward them. "I've wanted him from the first look, pathetic as that sounds. Do I want him now that he's bled to have me?"

She stood in front of them, searching Ash's face for . . . something. Why had he made her dance such a dance to have him? Why had he fought to keep her now? She could make no sense of it.

"Caro?" John asked, prompting her.

"I want him more than ever," she said softly.

Their gazes held, locked upon each other, swimming in depths of emotion and secrets that pressed against her heart. But that was all she could read. He would not let her dive deeper. With a cough, he lowered his gaze, releasing her.

"You're a bloodthirsty bit of baggage," Ashdon lightly said as he released his hold on John.

"Best you remember it," she said, turning from him, her legs wobbly. "Are the boys to have at him as well? I would so love to get home and change into a proper pair of shoes."

The boys stepped forward out of the darkness of the wood and into the feeble light of the carriage lamps. They were, by some standards, on some continents, still boys. But not by any standards they recognized.

They were George, John the Younger, and Matthew, and they were her cousins. They were mostly older than she, but not by much, and they were much more like their father than Sophia was like her brother. Or at least it seemed so to her. She often wondered if her mother would agree with that assessment. She did not know them well, they did live on another, distant continent, after all, but they were her cousins, and as her cousins she felt completely within her right to torment and tease them as she did her brother, also a John, but called Markham since infancy, even though he was legally Dalby now as the ninth earl.

"Take off your shoes, Caro, and I will let you walk in his blood," George said. Ashdon turned to face this new challenge, but Caro kept walking toward the landau. George was always saying things of that sort. He had a rather tortured sense of humor.

"I am not going to walk around Hyde Park in my stockings, George," she said. "It is quite bad enough that I am without a proper coat."

"And a fichu. Try to keep them attached, will you?" Ashdon said. "I would hate to have to thrash everyone in town who has seen your fetching décolleté. As these are your cousins, I will allow some laxity."

"How generous of you," she said. "Now, shall we get in and get on? You are bleeding and might need a stitch or two."

"Worried about me?" Ash asked.

"Only that you'll bleed on my dress. I rather like this dress," she said loftily. "I do suppose a proper introduction is in order." She stopped at the door to the landau. Her cousins trailed her like hounds, Uncle John at the rear. She would not be surprised if they had some final blow against Ashdon in mind; it would not be unlike them. "Lord Ashdon, my cousins: George, John the Younger, which has been shortened to Young for the sake of simplicity, and Matthew. Cousins, my husband, Lord Ashdon."

It was then that they did indeed thrash Ashdon. She supposed it was a point of honor for them, but whatever the cause, Ashdon gave as good as he got. At least there were no knives involved.

It was a quick scuffle, a few punches thrown, a few caught. They all kept their feet, which was the important thing in a fight. It was also important, perhaps of equal importance, that a woman watching men fight not react in any way that would cause a man embarrassment. They were rather particular about that, she had learned, and so Caro watched Ashdon get a bit pummeled and do some pummeling in return, which would surely result in some rather nasty bruising, but little else. She held her tongue, her posture, and her composure. All in all, she was more than a little proud of her performance.

"All finished, then?" she said when the four men stood heaving in breath after breath, staring at each other in what she could only call amiable hostility. Men were so odd, so often, yet so charming in their oddity. Quite irresistible, really. The way Ash looked just now, his shirt torn, his hair mussed, his muscles taut and glistening with sweat . . . Caro's own breath started to heave just looking at him. "I'm certain Mother must be twitching with worry over my having been gone so long. And without the proper shoes."

"She'll be twitching with something," Uncle John said with a wry twist of his lip.

"Just out of curiosity," Ash said, picking his cravat up from the ground and throwing it over his shoulder, "I understand the knife bit, just, but why the rest of you?"

"Two weeks ago, right before we left for France, none of us had heard of you," George answered. "Now you're married to Caro. You must have done something to have met and married that fast. Figured we owed you for that something."

"Yes, well," Ash said, throwing his waistcoat and coat over his left arm, "it was something, but perhaps not what you imagine."

"Like what?" Matthew asked. Matthew was the youngest, a full year younger than Caro, but not so much a boy that he couldn't imagine quite a bit. She didn't like this conversation at all.

"I am not at liberty to say," Ashdon said stiffly, offering Caro his arm.

"Then let Caro tell it," Matthew said, stepping forward. Good lord, but he looked to have grown an inch in the past two weeks. His shirtsleeves didn't quite cover his wrists, and she was certain that he'd been properly attired when he'd set out for France.

"What are you wearing, Matthew? That can't be the right shirt," Caro said.

"It's the one you gave me," Matthew said, "but that's not what I'm waiting for you to say."

"So sorry," she said, climbing into the landau with Ashdon's assistance. He was still bleeding. She was not going to say a word about it. She had her pride, too, and she was not going to be one of those women who fussed about every little thing. "That's all I'm going to say."

The cousins stared at her as she arranged her filthy skirts; really, she hadn't dressed at all properly for a jaunt through the woods and fields of Hyde Park. Her shoes were going to have to be tossed out and she had always rather favored these shoes. Except for getting married, it had been a dismal sort of day. Being stared at by her cousins wasn't helping. Now that she thought about it, they had the same sort of focused and intense stare that Ashdon was so fond of displaying. It was altogether unnerving and completely irritating. When her Uncle John joined in with his killing stare, she quite gave it up.

"Oh, all right!" she said. "The short version is that I made a bargain of sorts with Lord Ashdon and the result was that"—she coughed and looked out the landau window, which was ridiculous as there was absolutely nothing to see at this time of evening—"was that . . ."

It might have helped if just one of them had said something, some small thing to ease her into it. But they didn't. They all sat, all five of them, as if they could not deduce what it was she was trying to say. Blast men for their blindness in the most obvious of situations.

"Well, to hear Lord Ashdon tell it," she snapped, out of patience with the lot of them, "I attacked him with my breasts. Absurd, naturally, but there you are."

To which they all shifted their stares to Ashdon. Upon which Ashdon nodded fractionally. And after which they all, every one of them, stared at her breasts.

Not at all what she had intended, but that was just the sort of day it was.

Twenty-eight

THEY arrived back at Dalby House without further conversation. Of course, that was likely because her breasts had captured what little attention a man had to begin with. Honestly. Uncle John seemed to find the whole thing far more amusing than it actually was, which is to say, it was not amusing in the least. Nevertheless, he kept nodding his dark head and grunting. Almost prostrate with laughter, he was.

Caro was never so glad to get out of a carriage in her life, and considering the past few days, that was saying quite a lot.

Ashdon followed her up the few steps to the front door and whispered as Freddy opened the door, "*Now* will you wear a fichu?"

Odious wretch.

Sophia came into the foyer as they entered and, upon seeing Ashdon in his dirt-smeared, bloodstained state, said sweetly, "Oh, I see you've met my brother."

"Yes," Ashdon said, handing his coat to Freddy while he buttoned his waistcoat, "always nice to meet the in-laws."

"Isn't it though?" Sophia said as Lord Westlin came into the foyer behind her, followed by Lord Staverton. Was there anyone who *wasn't* going to come out of the white salon?

In point of fact, Markham came down the hall from the dining room, where she was quite certain the sideboard had yet to be repaired from the day's earlier adventure. Her wedding day was now made complete.

Filth and inappropriate attire notwithstanding, Caro threw herself into Markham's arms and lost herself there. It had been months since they'd seen each other and, as troublesome as he could often be, she adored him. She had known since the age of two that he returned the emotion entirely. As well he should. She was a wonderful sister to him.

"You set them on me, didn't you?" Markham said into her hair. "I ought to thrash you, but you look like you've been thrashed already today."

"I don't wish to discuss it," she said into his cravat. "And if I did wish to discuss it, I would say that you entirely deserved to be set upon as you should have been applying yourself at Oxford and not on the streets of Paris."

"First one, then the other," Markham said, pulling her back from him and searching the throng behind them. "No need to ask which one is Lord Ashdon. He looks even more thrashed than you. Uncle John's work?"

"And the boys. He doesn't appear to mind, though, so I shan't mind either."

"Clever girl."

"I like to think so."

"And all this other I've been hearing about since I've been hauled back to hearth and home? Where is the logic in that, Caro? It doesn't sound at all like you, and that's just from what I could get out of Anne. Anne wouldn't mouth a word against you and Mother wouldn't speak of it at all, which only put me on the scent rather more vigorously, wouldn't it?"

"Freddy, I suppose," she said, sighing and straightening her hair.

"Naturally. But what's to be done now? He's married you, so that's settled, but is he worthy of you?"

"Is anyone?" she said sarcastically.

"Probably not," he said with a grin.

"You are such a brother," she said, turning to look back into the heart of the foyer. Ashdon appeared rather more damaged in the light of a dozen candles, and more grim. Again. Where was the man who had teased her about her fichu?

Lord Westlin had taken one look at the assemblie in the foyer and retreated back into the white salon. Unsociable sot. It certainly wasn't going to be pleasant having to deal with Lord Westlin on a regular basis; it was a good thing she was as levelheaded and unflappable as she was or things might come to a nasty head.

Uncle John and his sons did not look more civilized in the white candlelight. John's features were hard and chiseled, his skin dark, his hair actually a dark brown where Sophia's was black, but his was straight as a stick. He had a look to him that spoke of wildness and wilderness.

George, his eldest son, had John's nose and mouth and brow, but softened. His black hair was waved, as hers was, and he had a long dimple in his left cheek that did nothing to detract from his raw masculinity.

John the Younger was the tallest and leanest of them all, his skin the fairest, his dark brown hair lit with faint gold lights. Young had the thick brows and long nose the boys all shared and looked, oddly enough, more like Markham than any of them, including her.

Matthew, still growing vigorously, had pale blue eyes. They were his grandmother's eyes and he was the only one of all of them to get them. Paired with his olive skin and black hair, he was a boy growing rapidly into a strikingly handsome man.

Though at the moment they were all somewhat tumbled as a result of their tussle with Ashdon and because they had run in that peculiar long lope of theirs behind the landau on the way to Hyde Park. Markham, however, looked resplendent in his fawn breeches and dark blue coat. The coat was exquisitely cut and fit Markham to perfection.

"Did you get that coat in Paris?" she asked.

"I did," he said proudly. "Won it in a game of whist, had to have it altered a bit, but isn't it a fine bit of cloth?"

"Gambling," she said on a huff of angry air. "Is there any reason to gamble for a coat when you have the funds to buy a perfectly lovely coat yourself? One that would be made to fit?"

"Of course there's a reason," he said, his dark eyes shining. "I always have a reason for what I do. It's fun, that's why. You must learn to find the fun in things, Caro."

"Oh, must I? It's a bit late for me now, isn't it?"

"Because of Ashdon?" Markham said, looking down the

hall at his new brother by marriage. "Isn't he any fun at all?"

"I wouldn't exactly call him fun." Though being thrown onto the sideboard like a trifle and being sampled for his pleasure had been . . . memorable. She could feel her nipples harden and her breasts grow heavy just thinking of it. Caro took few steps away from the dining room door, forcing Markham to keep step with her.

"Like his father, then? All growl and spittle?"

Caro reared her head back and pushed against his arm. "He is *not* like his father! That is not at all what I said."

"No?" Markham said innocently. "What did you say, then? You don't mean that you actually *like* him, do you, Caro? That could prove rather awkward, having a *tendre* for one's husband. I know Mother did it, but she makes her own fashion, doesn't she? I'm not at all certain you can pull it off."

"Did I *say* I felt anything for Ashdon?"

"No," he said softly, wrapping an arm about her waist, "but some things are so obvious they don't need to be said."

Oh, dear. This was bad, very bad. A sophisticated woman of her stature did *not* go about with her most vulnerable and private emotions on her face, or anywhere else for that matter. It simply wasn't done.

"You make the most unwelcome comments, Mark. Did you know that?"

"Of course. It's a good thing that I'm so handsome or no one would forgive me anything. But I am handsome, particularly in my new coat, and therefore I am forgiven everything. Mother has even given over being angry about my jaunt to Paris. I think the coat turned her head," Markham whispered conspiratorially.

She barely heard him. Ashdon, rather the worse for wear, turned to stare at her from down the wide hallway that separated them. He was still bleeding, his shirt sporting a damp, red patch. He had a bruise coming up on his left eye and his knuckles were scraped raw. He looked absolutely horrible, and never more wonderful.

"Has Mother planned on dinner for all of us?" she asked,

staring at Ash, filling her eyes with the sight of him. He looked uncommonly rugged, and her heart was doing strange things in her chest.

"Yes, including Lord Westlin, if he'll stay. She's more than a little determined to bring him into the family fold, which I suppose is appropriate now that he's family. I don't know that I like having him about, given their history. You have no idea what it's like to have a mother who, well . . . who . . ."

"Oh, don't I?" she said, watching as Ashdon took his coat from Freddy and slipped it on, covering the bloody patch on his shirt, as well as covering the line of his shoulders and chest and arms.

"It's different for a man, a son," Markham said, flicking a piece of lint off his sleeve.

"Different does not mean worse. Believe me," she said. "So, I suppose I shall need to change for dinner. And Ashdon can't go into a meal looking as he does." Even though he looked slightly more irresistible than usual. "Could he borrow something of yours, Mark? You're of a size."

Markham sighed heavily. "I suppose I must. Where are you staying, by the by? Not here."

"It hasn't been decided yet," she said, moving down the hallway toward Ashdon, drawn almost magnetically, as it were. Her heart was doing very strange things as she studied the open line of his linen shirt and the taut flesh revealed in the gap. Very strange things, indeed. "We really haven't had the time to discuss it."

"Really? You've had all day."

"Yes, well," she said, fussing with her sleeve. "It's been a busy day. Naturally."

"Naturally," Markham said, looking down at her altogether too curiously. Anyone would think he was trying to read her thoughts. It was a good thing he couldn't because her thoughts were all of Ashdon and the broken sideboard in the dining room. "I couldn't help notice that the sideboard has lost a leg, torn clean off by the look of it. Two footmen were hauling it out of the room just as you arrived home. What happened to it?"

Caro sniffed regally and said, "Something landed on it rather awkwardly, I was told."

"What sort of something?" Markham said.

The answer came to her instantly. She really did think that she was making vast strides in becoming sophisticated as measured by the ease with which she could tell a profitable lie.

"One of the cats. That fat tiger cat that's always in the kitchen. Horrid thing was after the ham."

Markham's dark eyebrows lifted. "He must be fat if he can break a solid mahogany leg."

"He's not fat!" Caro said. "He just . . . landed awkwardly."

"So you've said," Markham answered, studying her rather more closely than she liked.

"Then I presume there's nothing more to say on the matter," she said. "I must dress for dinner, Markham. Would you care to meet Ashdon now or after he's wearing your clothes?"

"Since you put it that way, I should think now would be best."

"Then behave yourself, Mark. Don't make a fuss. He's only my husband."

"Only your husband," Markham said. "Yes, that has a calming effect."

Sophia was talking to Ash as they approached. "We simply must convince your father to stay to dine with us. A simple family affair, obviously, with the most simple of foods. It would appear most peculiar if he did *not* stay, don't you agree, Lord Ashdon? You'll talk to him, of course."

"Of course," Ash answered, looking not at all agreeable to the idea. In fact, he looked a trifle pale.

"Mother, I simply must get Ashdon up to my room. He's had a rigorous afternoon and requires attention. Oh, and this is my brother, the Earl of Dalby. Markham, my husband, Lord Ashdon. There, now that's done, we'll just disappear upstairs for a moment or two. I really should look at Ashdon's wound. You do know that Uncle John attacked him without cause, don't you?"

"Nonsense, Caro. John never attacks anyone without cause. It's something of a point of honor for him," Sophia said. "I'm quite certain Lord Ashdon provoked him outrageously."

"If I did, I fail to see how," Ashdon said grimly. Darling Ashdon, always going grim when crossed. It was slightly adorable.

"You were chasing after my niece," John said. "What could I do but thrash you for it?"

Ashdon's eyes widened. "You speak English? When you said you did not?"

"It is not necessary for everyone to know everything," John said, his dark eyes twinkling.

"How utterly true," Sophia said with a sly smile. "But Caro, were you truly running down Park Lane? And was Lord Ashdon truly chasing you?"

Caro could only nod. She couldn't believe she'd done it now, of course. It was highly illogical to run from one's husband, particularly down a public street. Particularly as he could run faster than she could. A complete waste of time, really.

"How delicious," Sophia said, grinning, "and how clever of you, darling."

"Clever?" she said.

She had just deduced that it had been a colossal mistake in judgment. Her mother was always saying something to confuse her knowledge of things. Thinking logically was so very complicated when her mother was around, constantly offering advice and comment on the most mundane of subjects. Like running down the street away from an enraged husband.

"How clever of you to understand that there is simply nothing a man enjoys more than chasing after things, especially a woman. Isn't that so, Lord Ashdon?"

"I've never run down a woman in my life," Ash said stiffly.

"But now you have, and wasn't it fun?" Sophia said with a smile.

Ash allowed a crooked smile to escape him as he said, "Tolerably."

Caro almost fell out of her shoes.

"Excuse us," Ash said, taking her arm in his hand. "My wife is exhausted from her exertions. We'll just go upstairs for a bit." And he led her, quite authoritatively, from the foyer to the stair hall.

She shivered at his touch. It was his first touch since she'd kneed him, which had resulted in him chasing her. Which had then resulted in his being knifed by her uncle and beaten by her cousins. Quite a memorable wedding day, even without the sideboard.

"And now I have you," Ash said softly as he tugged her up the switchback stairs. Her stomach clenched in a not altogether unpleasant sensation.

He might try to punish her for that well-placed knee in his groin.

She just might let him. She might even let him chase her again since he seemed to enjoy it so much.

"I don't know what you think you're going to do with me," she said. "As you said, it has been a day of exertions. You look quite the worse for it."

"Oh, do I?" he said calmly. They'd reached the top of the stairs. "Which is your room?"

"You need Markham's room. That's where his clothes are, and you need a change of linen, at the very least."

"I need something, but it's not linen," he said.

She knew very well what he was referring to; she'd been married for most of the day, after all.

"I can't think what you mean," she said loftily. "You look a perfect disaster. Surely we must see to your wound."

"Exactly what I had in mind," he said, pushing open doors rather more violently than was absolutely necessary. She found it thrilling, actually. This violent, demanding Ashdon was completely irresistible. Of course, the quiet, grim Ashdon had been equally irresistible. It was a good thing she was so accommodating in her tastes, at least as far as Ash was concerned. "First things first," he said. "And first wounds first."

Oh, my. Her stomach tumbled into her shoes, snagging her feet and making her trip.

Ash pulled harder on her hand, tugging her along. "Now, now, you must keep your feet. At least for now."

That sounded ominous, deliciously so.

It was with sudden clarity that she knew why her mother said "delicious" so often and for what cause.

Caro couldn't have agreed more.

"You don't think that we're going to . . . to . . . well, to do *that*, do you?" she said in the most outraged tone she could produce, which wasn't much since she was rather hoping he had exactly that in mind.

Ashdon had pulled her to the top of the stairs and was pushing open doors now, without even knocking, rude as that was. The first door he tried was, unfortunately, the door to Anne's room. And Anne was sitting by the single window in her room, crying silently. At Ashdon's rude entry, Anne spun to face them and stood, all in one motion. She did it gracefully, her skirts twisting prettily around her legs and her cheeks turning a very lovely shade of pink. Ashdon stopped in his tracks, bowed, and said, "Excuse us, Mrs. Warren. Are you quite all right? Is there anything we can do to help?"

As much as Caro loved Anne, it was all rather anticlimatic and much more civilized than she had been led to expect. Gone were her hopes of having her skirts tossed up and a seam or two ripped.

Ah, well.

"No, I'm sorry," Anne said, moving toward the door. "I'm certain you want to be alone."

"Don't be silly, Anne. This is your room," Caro said. "Ash can just wait to thrash me until we fix things with you. Now, why are you crying?"

"Lord Ashdon! You're bleeding!" Anne said, a hand going to her mouth in shock.

"Nothing but a scratch," Caro said briskly, pushing past Ash, who looked at her with his eyebrows raised in amusement. "He assures me it's nothing and I quite believe him. He couldn't possibly be so vigorous if he were bleeding to death. Now, what on earth can have you so unhappy? It's not Lord Staverton, is it? He hasn't cried off, has he?"

"No," Anne said, sinking back down on her chair. "Not yet."

"Not yet? Why would he ever? He's besotted, Anne, completely besotted."

"Oh," Anne said softly, "these things can change."

They'd better not. She'd worked very hard to bring Lord Ashdon under her very pretty heel and he was going to stay there for life, blissfully besotted with her. There simply was no other course open to him. She only hoped Ash was intelligent enough to know that.

"Change?" Caro said, looking suspiciously at Ashdon, who was looking not at her, but at Anne. "I don't see why."

"Let me assure you, Mrs. Warren, that I can think of nothing my father could say that would turn Lord Staverton's affections from you. He is firmly fixed. So firmly, that I think even Westlin can see the futility of any argument he could make," Ash said, standing over Anne in gentlemanly concern.

"Why on earth would Lord Westlin seek to turn Lord Staverton from Anne?" Caro said. "What business is it of his?"

To which Anne only looked at her with sorrow-filled eyes. To which Ash answered, "Because Westlin believes Mrs. Warren is his by-blow."

To which Caro collapsed in a heap of dirty muslin and torn stockings upon a very conveniently placed daybed. "Oh, dear."

Twenty-nine

"Oʜ, dear," Sophia said in an undertone. "He actually said that? Lord Ashdon said that he'd been attacked by Caro's breasts?"

"He did," John answered solemnly, his eyes betraying his amusement.

"How intriguing," Sophia said with a soft smile, "and how clever of her. I wish I'd thought of that."

John grunted his reply, which Sophia understood to mean that she'd thought of enough on her own to mourn the loss of a single ploy, which of course was ridiculous as a woman could never have too many strategies, a concept she communicated to her brother by a single raised shoulder and a double eyebrow raise.

She knew he understood her answer very well. For all that they'd seen little of each other over the years, they had the benefit of a common past, an unusual past that formed a very firm foundation for their present relationship. There was no one she trusted more. Not that she trusted him completely.

"Where did you find Mark and the Blakesley boy?" she asked.

"In the usual place," he said. Which meant a place of drinking, gaming, and whoring. Not unusual in a man of his age, but hardly exemplary.

"You think he could use a change of scene?" she asked.

"And a change of purpose," John added.

Sophia cast her gaze over her nephews as they stood in solemn repose on the edges of the yellow salon. They were young men, but men of composure and poise, men to whom self-control was a necessity and not an idealized concept. She understood her nephews from bone to skin, and because she did, she also understood that her son was already walking a different path. It was not a path she would willingly choose for him.

John Markham Stuart Grey Trevelyan, the ninth Earl of Dalby, named for her brother, stood talking to George, laughing about something that George only smiled at. Mark looked a bit soft. A bit indulged. A bit . . . debauched. George, on the other hand, looked ruthlessly self-sufficient. It was not a comparison she enjoyed making.

Really, what choice was there? He would learn more that would serve him well in the dark forests of New York than in his rooms at Oxford, or in the gaming hells of London.

"Take him," she said, staring at her son, letting him go. When he returned, he would not be as he was now. She said a silent good-bye to the boy she had known and loved. "It must seem his idea."

John merely nodded.

"For how long?" she asked, turning her head to look at John.

"Two years," he said.

Her heart clenched at the words, but her eyes did not show her anguish. Such were the skills that Markham needed to learn, skills that only living among the Wolf Clan could teach him. He had gone before to live with the Wolf Clan, both he and Caro had gone, but they had been children then. Her darling Dalby had died and after a half year of mourning, she had taken them to her brother. They had performed the Mohawk grief rituals, rites that healed her more than any English observances could, and then she had left them to John and his wife. They had learned much, but they had been the lessons of childhood, a year within the Iroquois Nation that had shaped them into a slightly more pragmatic version of what they were: children of the English aristocracy. Now Markham would learn the lessons of a Mohawk warrior.

He would not return the same. Which was exactly the idea.

"When will you leave?" she asked.

"I'm not certain. It would be best if he decided."

"Yes, that's true," she said softly. "Caro will miss him."

"When she has a new husband to entertain her?" John said.

Sophia smiled. "That's true as well. If Ashdon is up to the mark, she shouldn't notice that Mark is missing until he's a month gone. I rather think Ashdon is up to the mark, at least to judge by my sideboard."

John grunted twice and lowered his gaze, his version of raucous laughter.

"It is a good beginning," he said, "though she doubts him. It is why I challenged him. Let him prove himself for her. He did, but still the shadow of doubt is in her eyes. Why?"

"Because of Westlin."

"And because of you."

"I suppose so."

"Was it for revenge, Sophia? Did you pair them and make a fine revenge upon your old enemy, bringing your seed into his house?" John asked.

"It is a fine revenge, isn't it?" Sophia said. "And I so enjoy that Westlin thinks of it that way, but I wouldn't use Caro to punish Westlin. You know that."

"Then why doesn't she know it?" John said.

"I think," Sophia said softly, "because I am Sophia and she is Sophia's daughter."

John nodded and lowered his head. As always, they understood each other very well.

❧

CARO clearly did not understand anything about anything, which was becoming annoyingly routine. She could only hope that it wasn't also becoming obvious.

"I beg your pardon?" she said, staring up at her husband as he stood in front of Anne.

"Mrs. Warren," Ash said, "Lord Westlin could say nothing that would dissuade Lord Staverton from his alliance with you. Lord Staverton has known my father longer than any of us and he therefore knows how to stand firm against Westlin's—"

"Fits?" Caro supplied.

"Arguments," Ash said.

She thought *fits* was more to the point, but if Ash wanted to call Westlin's fits arguments, she supposed he could do so. He obviously and understandably didn't want to think ill of his father. He must be positively exhausted in trying to think well of him.

"You should also know that my father, not without cause, thinks that everyone of a certain age who possesses ginger hair is his get. You should not put too much upon it, Mrs. Warren."

"You are too kind to say it, Lord Ashdon, but Lord Westlin would only suppose ginger-haired children to be his get if he knew he'd had a prior relationship with their mothers," Anne said, rising to her feet. "And so it is with me. I regret it, though I can't undo it. I realize that this is an extremely awkward turn of events, and I will promise you that I will not continue my friendship with your wife."

"Mrs. Warren," Ash said, taking her hand in his and bowing over it, "not a one of us chooses our fathers, our mothers, or our siblings. If we do share the same father, can we not console each other over our mutual and miserable fate? I, for one, would enjoy having a sibling and I could not wish for one more lovely and kind than you."

Upon which, he kissed Anne on the hand.

Anne's eyes filled with tears and she shook her head to clear them. It was futile. And as to that, Caro's eyes were swimming as well as she considered her husband. That was truly the kindest, most gallant display she'd ever witnessed.

She loved him quite unreservedly, which was ridiculous, since he'd never done a single thing to earn her love and quite a few things to earn her anger. Logical and true, yes, but obviously meaningless. She loved him anyway. In point of fact, she seemed to love him more with each passing moment and what had he done but throw her against a wall, toss her upon a sideboard, drape her in pearls he couldn't afford, chase her down Park Lane, and look entirely too fondly at Anne?

Her stomach rolled and twisted and delicious bubbles of delight burst up into her throat. She felt an idiotic smile spread itself all over her face and tears dampening the corners of her eyes. She even found herself forgetting about the bet.

Logic had seriously failed her.

"Use logic, man," Westlin said to Lord Staverton. "You can't want to marry her. She's the daugher of a common whore, and my bastard on top of it. Think of your family name."

"She's a lovely woman, a respectable widow," Staverton said stubbornly. One thing that could be said for Lord Staverton was that he made the most loyal friend. He was immovable once his affections were fixed and he was not too quick to fix them, which only meant, of course, that his alliances were considered by all to be based on near infallible judgment and shrewd perception. By all, with the exception of Lord Westlin.

"And were you thinking of your family name when you tumbled with a common whore?" Sophia said, entering their conversation without invitation and without remorse. "Not that I agree with you, Westlin, about Anne's mother. She was quite lovely in her day and much sought after. As you perhaps know better than any of us."

"A man plays, a woman pays," Westlin said stiffly.

"Yes, such a common and distasteful expression," Sophia said. "I quite remember when you first quoted it to me. I did not find it at all amusing, but of course, in my case, 'tis the man who pays, and the woman who plays, isn't it? Quite satisfying."

"We were not speaking of you," Westlin said, bristling. Well, he often bristled. Sophia barely bothered to notice anymore.

"Weren't we? How odd," she said, smiling at Lord Staverton, who looked more than relieved to have been spelled in his confrontation with Lord Westlin. Another common occurrence for those who were forced to speak with Lord Westlin.

Westlin hadn't always been this way, of course. He'd once

been quite handsome, very wealthy, and occasionally devastating in his charm. All long ago now, so long ago in fact that few people remembered the old, young Westlin. But she did. And she knew that she had been the chief cause of his present ill temper, a foul mood that had lasted a full two decades. She was rather proud of that, particularly as he quite deserved it. She was only sorry that Ashdon had been made to bear the brunt of Westlin's temper. She'd had to rescue the dear boy and by what better means than Caro's unflagging will and wit? They were, without doubt, perfectly paired.

"But if we aren't to speak of me," she said, sitting down gracefully, one might even have said *languidly*, on the yellow silk sofa, "then I must insist we speak of Ashdon and Caroline before we go into dinner."

"I am not staying for dinner. It's enough that I'm in the same room with those . . . those . . ." he said, gesturing not at all discreetly in the direction of her brother and his sons.

"Relatives?" she cheerfully supplied. "But we are all related now, darling. Let's learn to enjoy it, shall we?"

"You enjoy it, that's plain," Westlin said. "What a devious revenge, to have my grandchildren, the heirs to the earldom, be part savage."

"One hopes the greater part," Sophia said in liquid tones, which she knew would annoy him . . . well, savagely.

"Give over," Staverton said. "You've been on this for years, Westlin, and what's it got you? Indigestion and bile and little else."

"You've always been enamored of that in her," Westlin said to Staverton.

"And you haven't?" Staverton countered.

Really, she hadn't heard Staverton speak so much in years. Having Westlin attack his choice in a bride must have stirred up something rather violent in him. How delicious for Anne.

"Come, come," she said with a smile, "as much as I enjoy having men fight over me, I must in this case insist that we stay on topic, and the topic is Ash and Caro. Agreed? Now," she said, without waiting for anyone's agreement since it was always such a waste of time, "I propose the most miniscule of truces between us, Westlin, for the sake of our children and our future grandchildren, the little savages." She paused to smile, enjoying the blaze of disgust that flickered in Westlin's dark blue eyes. He really was the most entertaining victim. It was most obliging of him. "This is what I want to do; I want you to give the happy couple that lovely house you have rented out on Curzon Street. They should do nicely there, such a pretty location."

"I will not!" Westlin responded, predictably. "As you say, it's rented out."

"And you need the money from that rental, poor darling," she supplied. "I wouldn't dream of depriving you of income, Lord Westlin, particularly as I know how desperately you need every shilling. I presume you aren't aware of it, but I have acquired not a few of your debts. I will call your debt to me canceled if the happy couple may take possession of the Curzon Street house. I shall want the papers drawn up to my satisfaction, naturally."

"Which means?" he snarled. Again, most predictable of him.

"In Caro's name, of course," she said sweetly, "and fruit of her loins, to put it poetically."

"How much? How much in debt to you am I?"

"Darling, does it matter? More than you can afford, obviously. What's that old saying? If you have to ask, you can't afford it? Give them the house, Westy, so much simpler, really."

He grunted and crossed his arms over his chest. She took it that he agreed. What choice did he have, poor darling?

"You haven't asked what I will give the bride and groom, so I shall tell you. You remember the pearls, don't you?" Westlin started and uncrossed his arms. Of course he remembered. The pearls were what had started the whole thing, that and the blanc de Chine cup. "I'm going to give Ashdon his mother's pearls, that lovely strand you gave to me all those years ago. You really shouldn't have, Westy, especially as they were your wife's pearls, from her side of the family, and not really yours to give. From Charles II, weren't they? Treasured by her family and her most valued possession? Really not the sort of thing one gives away."

"You understand nothing of English law," he said. "Those pearls were mine. Everything of hers was mine the moment I married her."

"I understand everything about English law, darling, I just don't happen to like most of what I know. In any regard, Ashdon shall have the pearls. They belong to him, and I daresay he has a new appreciation for the value of a fine pearl necklace, don't you?"

"Your girl's going to be draped in pearls, Sophia," Staverton said, "what with the Cavendish pearls of Ashdon's mother and the strand he's got off of the Duke of Calbourne. I suppose he could return those, if he chose."

"I should be very much surprised if Lord Ashdon did not require Caro to be drizzled in pearls morning, noon, and night," Sophia said. "He has the funds to pay for Calbourne's pearls, now that he's won his wager. Oh, yes, and speaking of wagers, I have a gift for you, Lord Westlin, in a gesture of peacemaking between our separate houses now joined."

"What?"

"Because your poor wife is dead and because her pearls are back where they belong, I have decided to forgive you for that farce of a meeting you arranged between us all. It is quite one thing to have a discreet affair and another altogether to force your faithful wife and the mother of your heir into a face-to-face confrontation with your current mistress. That I was wearing her pearls was simply beyond the pale, wouldn't you agree?"

Sophia's voice was cold as she remembered that day. The hurt in the Countess of Westlin's gentle blue eyes had haunted her for a year. She had broken it off with Westlin that night, an act he had not even begun to forgive and, because he could not look too closely at his own culpability, had blamed an old rival, her darling Dalby. And then there was the matter of the blanc de Chine cup.

"It was between us," Westlin said.

"I assume you mean between you and your sweet wife. I couldn't agree more, though I think you had the advantage of her in both will and force. What you should never have done was drag me into it. But once I was in, darling, what could I do but play to win?" Sophia smiled coldly.

"I tried to make it up to you," Westlin said.

Staverton mumbled some excuse and joined Markham in conversation across the room. They were starting to draw looks from the other side of the salon. She really did not want Markham to know what had happened all those years ago as it had absolutely nothing to do with him, but might put him off Caro's new husband. Things could get so complicated when past grievances bled into present associations. She couldn't think of a war that hadn't been begun on just such a footing, and while it was mildly entertaining to watch England and France engage in war after war, it was not conducive to family harmony to have the same thing going on.

"Yes," she said, "but not very well. By then, of course, I was experienced enough to understand that you had no skill for this sort of thing, Westy. A clear case of the flesh being willing, but the spirit . . ." She shrugged. "You never should have approached me as you did. My darling Dalby dead not a year and you having gifts delivered to my home. My reputation as a distraught widow of a distinguished man was almost shattered. How did you think it would help your cause to treat me like the most trifling lightskirt?"

"That cup is worth over one thousand pounds!" Westlin shouted.

All in the room turned to look at him. Sophia smiled and shrugged a single shoulder. They all, as a body, turned away. Clearly, Westlin was overmatched, and they knew it to a man. It had always been so, only now she was old enough to know it. And revel in it.

"Yes, darling," she soothed, "but I am worth so much more. It was very crass of you not to realize it. The Countess of Dalby does not accept stray gifts from unwelcome men."

"I did not think I should have been unwelcome," Westlin said stiffly.

"But you quickly learned otherwise, didn't you? How clever you are. How easily taught," she said silkily. "Now here is the thing, Westlin. You may have the cup back. It has quite served its purpose and I daresay I've quite outgrown my delight in it. Take it. Sell it if you wish. I'm quite certain I don't want my daughter to be saddled with the debts to your estate that will certainly be revealed upon your death. What an unhappy day that would be."

They both knew she was not referring to his death, merely to the dismal likelihood of debt. It was common knowledge that he'd run through his wife's money in the first five years. Westlin, like most of his sort, lacked self-discipline. Sophia's gaze slid over to Markham; he was listening intently to something George was saying, John putting in a word now and then. It shouldn't be long now, perhaps even by dessert. She would save her son from Westlin's fate, no matter the cost.

"You always were the most damned prickly woman, taking offense at the unlikest of things," he said in a soft growl.

"Are you certain of that, Lord Westlin? I was under the impression that you were simply the most dull of gentlemen, unable to see an insult unless it was directed at him exclusively. Ah, well, I suppose we must agree to disagree. And now, I think dinner must be served. You are staying."

It was not a question. There was no confusion as to that.

"I'll just go see what's keeping Caro, shall I? Poor Ashdon must be tended by now, don't you think?"

She wasn't asking, and she didn't wait for a reply. Nodding to John to carry the duties of host in her absence, she left the yellow salon and made her silent way up the stairs to Caro's room, only she didn't get as far as Caro's room as Lord Staverton, as well as Caro and Ash and Anne, were all clustered in apparent confusion in Anne's room. Oh, dear. Could they not even dress without supervision?

"I don't care a whit what anyone says," Staverton was saying to Anne's back. "I shall marry you and no one else. Westlin can go to the devil."

"Didn't I tell you, Anne?" Caro said from her spot on the small recamier, her torn and muddy shoes hanging over the edge. "Any man would be a fool to give you up."

"Darling," Sophia said to her daughter as she entered the

room, "go and change for dinner. And see to this poor, be-draggled husband of yours. Surely Mark must have something that will suit him. We dine in minutes and I would so hate to keep Lord Westlin waiting on this, our first of what I am certain will be many cozy family dinners."

That got everyone's attention.

It was with some apparent relief that Ashdon left the room, dragging Caro by the hand behind him. She didn't look at all put out by it. How well that was working out. Staverton left with a final, lovesick look at Anne. She could hardly have been more pleased. When she and Anne were alone, Sophia sat on the recamier and patted the silk cushion, motioning for Anne to sit beside her. Anne did so, though not especially eagerly.

"You are upset about Lord Westlin," Sophia said bluntly. "You think he is your father, and I will admit, he well could be. And you think that he will ruin your chances with Staverton and, even more to the point, your life among the ton as Staverton's wife. Have I got it right?"

"Exactly right," Anne said, dry-eyed. She was a practical woman, who had been, in the kindest of terms, practically brought up. She had seen life's worst and chosen to reach for life's best. Sophia sympathized completely.

"Anne, your fears are based on fact. I will not deny it. But you do not have possession of all the facts, and I do, or at least more than you do. Westlin spread his seed upon every possible, that is to say, every available field."

"And my mother was available."

"That she was," Sophia acknowledged, "as were a great many other women, from the highest ranks to the lowest. You may not know it, but Westlin was rather the thing in his day, and many women, I'm certain he would say *most* women, were more than willing to give him a go. You are not the only redhead in England, you know."

"But I am the only one whose mother was a courtesan."

"Ridiculous. I can think of three off the top of my head, but of course, I am including actresses. In any regard, what you do not know is that I am most directly responsible for Lord Westlin's tearing about through town in some typically

misguided effort to prove some obscure point about his masculinity or irresistiblility or some such other stupid nonsense
that gets into a man's head and blinds him to all reason."

Anne was staring at her with her mouth open.

"Yes, well," Sophia continued, "because I feel responsible, I feel responsible for *you*, the possible fruit of his deliri-
ous overindulgence. I will not see you cast down or cast out.
You *will* have your lovely marriage to Lord Staverton and
you *will* be accepted into the ton, if that is your wish. For
myself, I think the thrills are highly overrated. Now, the
only thing left is to ask you if you have confidence in my
ability to see it through."

Of course, there was only one answer to that and they
both knew it. Sophia dared to say that everyone in London
knew it.

Anne threw her arms around Sophia's neck and whispered, "Thank you. You are the most wonderful, the most
amazing woman."

It was a sure bet that everyone in London knew that as
well.

❧

THE moment they were in Markham's rather Spartan room,
Caro turned to Ash and said, "I shan't be put off a moment
longer, Ash. Did you marry me for love or for money? Was it
only to win the bet that you seduced me in Hyde's dressing
room and made a ruined woman of me?"

"I think everyone knows by now that it was *you* who ruined me with those vicious breasts of yours, popping out at
all times and places, grabbing a man and not letting him
loose," Ash said, practically ignoring her as he lifted his
torn shirt over his head and gave her an unobstructed view
of his naked torso.

It was the first time she had seen his naked anything. She
was enjoying the view immensely.

"I should hate to rummage through your brother's
things," he said, unbuttoning his trousers casually. "Would
you find something for me?"

"Call for his valet. He knows where things are. I certainly

don't," Caro said, mesmerized by the sight of Ashdon's heavily veined hands moving about his narrow hips.

"Oh, I'm not going to call for his valet, Caro. I don't want him to see what I'm going to do to you."

Her stomach dropped three inches, exactly.

"I shan't let you do anything to me," she said icily, watching as he grew stiff under the loose gap in his trousers. "Besides, you've changed the subject again, which you always do."

"I have not," he said, checking his wound. It had scabbed over, messily, and was almost completely closed. "You seem to think that I go about popping women's breasts out of their bodices, or worse, let myself be purchased with a marriage license and bit of blunt. I can assure you that this is my first marriage and I entered into it willingly. Now, lift your skirts like a good girl. I am going to thrash you with my nice, long stick."

"Ash!" she gasped. "There is no call to be vulgar!"

Her stomach dropped another three quarters of an inch. Exactly.

"Was I being vulgar?" he asked, lifting his gaze from his wound to pierce her with his blazing blue eyes. "I thought I was merely being obvious. I suppose you would prefer it if I lifted your skirts, but I am wounded you know, and on your behalf. I thought you might"—he shrugged, the muscles in his shoulders bunching and rolling deliciously—"like to help."

"I'll do no such thing. And especially as I am not at all convinced that you wanted to marry me for myself."

Ash paused and looked at her, really looked at her. She tried very hard to let him see what she had hidden from view all her life. It was not always easy being Sophia's daughter. In fact, it was never easy.

"I did want to marry you," he said softly. His hair was tousled and falling into his eyes. She tried very hard not to let it distract her. This was very important, and she was very tired of having the same argument with him again and again, the same fear chasing her.

"You didn't act like it," she said in an undertone.

"I suppose that's because I didn't want to want to," he said.

"Because of my mother."

"Partly. But mostly because of my father."

She sat on the edge of a large upholstered chair, kicking off her battered shoes and tucking her dirty stockinged feet under her skirts. Ash moved forward slowly until he stood in front of her, his blue eyes mournful. He grabbed a footstool and sat down at her feet.

"He wasn't a kind man," Ash said, staring at the hem of her skirts. "To my mother. To me. I've told you that he made me his tool, his method of revenge on your mother for rejecting him."

"She rejected him?"

"Oh, he didn't tell me, but one hears things. Get some of the old ones at White's drunk and you hear all sorts of stories," he said, reaching out and under her hem, finding her left foot and pulling it out. "I heard the stories about the Indian bit; didn't know what to do with that bit of doggerel." Her foot rested in the palm of his hand. Her stockings were filthy. She was mortified.

"You heard about my mother," she said.

"You don't have to be at White's to hear about your mother," he said, smiling.

Caro didn't smile back. She felt queasy, her stomach in rebellion from being yanked about so often. Always Sophia, never Caroline. Her mother had grown children and she was still the most talked about, the most desirable woman in London.

"I suppose not," she said softly, keeping her eyes down. She had a smear of dirt on her skirt exactly two inches long. That seemed important, somehow.

"My mother," Ash said. "I think she loved him once. I don't know why, but sometimes she'd speak as if she did or had or remembered something about him no one else saw. He drove it out of her. By meanness, by coldness, by isolation. He left her alone too much and wouldn't let her come to Town, except once. Once she came to Town, and it broke her completely. I don't know what happened, what he did, but she was never the same."

Whatever it was, it had probably involved Sophia. Why else the war between them all these years?

"That's when he began talking to me," Ash said. "About her. Always about her."

No need to ask who *her* was. Ash was caressing her foot, his index finger tracing the arch, the ankle, the instep. She tried not to shiver and failed.

"He's a hard man," Ash said. "Driven in his need for revenge. It seemed noble to me as a boy, but now I'd call it an obsession. Once I met Sophia, I understood."

Caro pulled her foot out of his hand and tucked it back under the shelter of her skirts.

Ash looked at her and she steeled herself against the anguish in his blue eyes. She'd done quite enough damage to herself because of those blue eyes.

"You may not realize it, having been with her all your life, but she's an unusual woman."

"You don't say?" Caro said coldly.

"She's strong," Ash said, reaching out to trace her two-inch smear of dirt.

It just so happened that the stain was directly over her curled knee. It also just so happened that no matter how put off she was by Ashdon's words, she had yet to be put off by his touch. It was crushingly illogical. It was a good thing she had given up on logic. Raw emotion was going to be her guiding force now.

It was also, by pure coincidence, a good thing she found his touch emotionally pleasurable or she would have kicked him in the face.

"It's what so infuriates my father, I think," Ash said. "I wasn't worried, not for her. It was when I met you that I started to worry."

"I beg your pardon?" Caro said, shifting her weight, moving the dirt smear. It was now positioned over her upper thigh. Fancy that.

"I didn't think you were like her," he said. "I mean, why

should I? She's the one everyone talks of and she's the one who arranged for your marriage without consulting you. I thought that you were just another proper girl who had been subjected to a proper education and would submit properly to the proper husband. And then I met you," he said, looking up at her. "And then I knew."

"Knew what?" she whispered. He sounded . . . almost besotted.

"That I had to protect you from him, from Westlin, what else? I couldn't ruin you, which was his plan from start to finish, and I couldn't marry you, couldn't bring you into my life and into his. He hates Sophia. He wants to destroy you just to punish her."

"Destroyed? I hardly think so," she said, leaning her head back against the chair.

"Yes, I came to that conclusion as well," he said, letting his other hand slip under her tattered hem and slide along her foot to her ankle to her calf. "You're just like her, just as strong, just as compelling."

"You certainly didn't seem very happy about it," she said, pretending to ignore the fact that both of his hands were under her skirt and that he was slipping her garters down her legs. Her stockings soon followed. She was past caring if her feet were clean.

"Because I wasn't," he said bluntly. Her eyes, which had been drooping, snapped open. "I saw what he did to my mother, what he tried to do to Sophia. I'm his son, trained to be his heir in all things. His tool, Caro," he whispered hoarsely. "Do you think I wanted that for you?"

Caro's head lifted from the cushion and she studied Ash's face in the candlelight.

"You were afraid that you would bully me as he bullied your mother? You were afraid of what you would do to me? Afraid of what you would become?"

"Yes," he said, lowering his head, avoiding her eyes. "I want to protect you from that. From me."

Her heart broke into a thousand points of pain. He'd been trying to protect her. He'd run from her, pushed against her, avoided her, pointlessly, because he was afraid he'd hurt her.

"You would never do that to me," she whispered, inching forward on the chair and wrapping her arms around him. He was hot to the touch, smooth and firm.

"I appreciate your confidence," he said, kissing her neck, tugging at her bodice.

"But that's not what's important, is it?" she asked. "It was something else that convinced you."

"It was you who convinced me," he said, lifting her skirts to her hips, wrapping her legs around his hips. "It was you."

"What did I do?" she said, kissing his shoulder, the line of bone, the soft skin of his throat. "I'll do it again."

"I like the sound of that," he whispered as he kissed her. She opened her mouth beneath his, swallowing his passion and his need for her, devouring him, savoring him. He was delicious.

"Tell me. What did I do?" she said, pulling her mouth from his. He was not going to get out of declaring himself that easily. Not again.

"It's who you are," he said, his mouth nuzzling the swell of her breasts. She was never going to wear a fichu again. "You fought me at every turn, demanding your due, fighting for what you wanted. If I tried to do to you what Westlin did to my mother, you'd kill me for it."

"I'm not at all clear on what Westlin did to your mother, but I can state truthfully that I have a list of things which I will kill for," she said with a crooked smile, a tear fighting for release from her right eye.

She was not going to ruin this moment with tears. She was going to revel in it, remembering it for all her life. Remembering every shadow of emotion that flitted across Ash's lovely face. Remembering the exact moment when Ash declared his overwhelming, undying, illogical love for her.

He loved her. *Her.* Not Sophia's daughter. Not the means of a little revenge. Not a way to fill his purse.

"You have a list?" he asked.

"I'm very organized and highly logical. I'm surprised you haven't noticed."

"I've been too busy noticing other things."

He'd got her bodice loose, not such a feat considering the general condition of her dress. His teeth brushed against a nipple and she gasped softly. Very softly. She had not forgotten that Anne was in the very next room, most likely talking to either her mother or Lord Staverton. Possibly both.

"You're completely besotted, aren't you?" she said.

"Completely," he said, ripping her skirt with both hands so that she lay naked to the waist.

"You can't live without me, can you?"

"Can't and won't," he said, thumbing the core of her desire and making her groan and arch under his hand.

"You do know that I'm still angry that you wagered on me. Very presumptuous. Highly irregular," she said, pressing against his hand, clenching her teeth against her moans.

"I made five thousand pounds, Caro. Aren't you happy that I finally won?"

"Five," she gasped as his finger entered her, stroking, "thousand? Are you still in debt?"

"Only by eight hundred pounds," he said, licking his way across her breasts, his finger plunging into her, his thumb doing wicked circles within her folds.

"Eight hundred," she gasped, her head thrown back against the upholstery. "That's a lot of money. How will you earn it? You've married as many women as you're allowed."

"True," he said, "and also true that I married the only woman that I want."

"But when did you make the bet, Ash? After the pearls or before? Did you make a bet that you could and would ruin me?"

"Cal made the bet. After the pearls. After the carriage and the vicious and premeditated attack of your breasts on my resolve. When I knew I couldn't live without you. That's when," he whispered.

And with that, he plunged into her, holding her legs around his waist as she balanced on the edge of the chair. It was molten, a fire of longing met and married. He held her against him, pressing her to the edge of reason and then pushing her over into the abyss of passion. She fell freely. She had already decided that reason was vastly overrated.

"Are we ever going to make love in a bed, Lord Ashdon?" she said, panting against his neck, feeling the damp curls of hair on his nape, breathing in the scent of him.

"Eventually."

"Am I ever going to be able to toss off a really good scream? I feel quite certain I could deliver a good one if there weren't so many witnesses always about."

"Definitely."

"And are you ever going to be able to make a wager that will match that eight-hundred-pound debt?"

"I could," he said, ripping through the rest of her dress so that she lay naked amid the ruins of her gown on her brother's bedroom chair, "make a wager that you will deliver a child nine months from now."

"To the day, Lord Ashdon?" she said, sprawled before him.

"To the hour, Lady Wife."

She pulled him to her by the growing-before-her-very-eyes sign of his affection and regard. Some things were just too obvious to be argued against.

"Ashdon? Make the bet."

Epilogue

DINNER had been a late affair, due completely to the fact that Caro and Ash simply could not resist having at each other on any available surface. Charming, to be sure, but one did like to eat at regular intervals. It would all be so much easier when they were ensconsed in number nineteen Curzon Street. They could ruin their own furniture to their heart's content.

What had happened to Markham's bedroom chair was simply beyond repair.

Sophia, sitting in the white salon and sipping a solitary cup of tea, smiled in satisfaction. Things were going quite well there, as she had known they would. Caroline quite had the gentleman in the palm of her hand, and there was no better nor happier place for dear Ashdon to be. Such a lovely boy. He had turned out quite well considering the depth and vigor of Westlin's rather annoying influence.

Markham had, as predicted, announced his determination to go to America with John and the boys at the first opportunity. First opportunities could be arranged or disarranged with comforting precision. She hadn't quite decided when his first opportunity should arise.

Sophia, to meet his expectations of her on the occasion of his declarataion, had protested and expressed the sorts of doubts that were common to mothers. In the face of her objections, he had been more determined than ever to go. Naturally. She hadn't yet decided if they should leave before the Season was over or not. She wasn't at all sure what John's reaction would be to having his sons in town for a London Season. And she wasn't at all sure she cared what John's reaction would be. It might, after all, do his sons some good to meet and mingle with the aristocracy of England.

It might do England some good as well.

So many things to be considered, and she had the luxury of time to consider them. The house was quiet. Mark, John, and the boys were riding in Hyde Park; Caro and Ash had departed for Chaldon Hall, the impressive home of the second Earl of Westlin begun during Elizabeth's reign and quite nicely maintained and improved upon since, but also and not less important, the favored residence of Westlin. She anticipated that Westlin would be remaining in Town for the near future. How delicious. Caro and Ash would have such fun ruining *his* furniture for a change.

Caro married to a man she adored and with a home of her own on Curzon Street to be decorated to her tastes, Markham out of the trouble simmering in Paris and soon off to New York to learn that there were more reliable ways of measuring a man than by the stiffness of his cravat or his capacity for brandy, Anne and Staverton to be married in a few short weeks . . . life was going to be singularly lacking in adventure or even entertainment.

She could acquire a man, but it was a rare man who could entertain, let alone provide any sort of adventure.

She was becoming rather jaded, and she wasn't sure she liked it.

Freddy brought in a pot of chocolate as she sat contemplating the quiet order of her imminently boring life.

"You'll change this room? No more need for white now, is there?" Freddy asked as he set the chocolate pot down on a butler's tray near the fire. She liked tea well enough, but there was nothing like a nice dose of chocolate on a drizzly late afternoon.

Westlin had taken his precious blanc de Chine cup home with him last night. The entire point of the white salon had been removed with the cup.

"Yes, I was thinking rose damask for the walls, in honor of Caro's spectacular victory in the Hyde House rose damask dressing room. Such a night should be celebrated and memorialized, don't you think?"

"Rose? That's a sort of pink?"

"Between pink and red," Sophia said, inviting Freddy to sit. They were alone on this floor of the house at this particular hour of the afternoon and as no one would witness the familiarity they enjoyed, no harm could be done to either of their reputations. "I could reupholster. I saw a lovely blush silk damask last week."

"What else? Without the white cup . . ." Freddy shrugged.

"I could buy a collection of French porcelain," she suggested. "French porcelain goes well with rose."

"You could buy? Why should you buy?"

Sophia smiled. "It is more fun when someone else does the buying."

"Well, figure out what you'd like, so's you're prepared when asked."

"You have a lot of confidence in me, Freddy."

"Just experience, Countess. Oh, there's the door. Excuse me, back to butlering."

A minute or two passed before Freddy opened the door and, without asking if she was *in* or not, ushered in, of all people, Lady Louisa Kirkland. For once, she was without her cousin, Lady Amelia Caversham, and her chaperone, Lady Jordan. That spoke volumes. Sophia couldn't help but be the slightest bit intrigued.

"Lady Louisa Kirkland to see you, Lady Dalby," Freddy announced, winking gleefully.

The old sot. He probably thought he was doing her a favor by keeping her busy with a spoiled and sullen young woman who was reliably shy on the proper manner of conversing with a woman of her stature and experience, most particularly her experience.

Sophia could feel herself rising to the occasion almost immediately, her spine stiffening, her chin lifting, and her sense of adventure waking up. Freddy, on his better days and her worse ones, knew her better than she knew herself. Thankfully, she very seldom had worse days.

Sophia rose to her feet to greet her young guest, her recent conversation with Anne perhaps making her too aware of Louisa's vibrant ginger hair, and then motioned Louisa into a seat.

It was to the girl's credit that she came straight to the point.

"Lady Dalby, thank you for seeing me."

"Not at all. Can I offer you a cup of chocolate?"

"Yes, thank you."

Upon which Freddy made a quiet exit to give the ladies privacy while he waited for a footman to fetch another cup. With the room to themselves, Louisa wasted no time. Sophia found herself more intrigued by the moment.

"I find myself in a bit of a dilemma, Lady Dalby. I don't quite know how to go about . . . fixing it."

Sophia merely raised her eyebrows in pleasant curiosity and kept stirring her chocolate.

"I," Louisa said, a faint blush staining her cheeks. She was a stunningly beautiful woman, which was likely the chief source of her troubles. Beautiful women were wont to stumble about, expecting their beauty to save them from all sorts of misadventures. Unfortunately, the opposite was more likely to be true, though certain misadventures could have rather pleasant results, at least to judge by her decidedly vast experience. "I . . . am certain that I don't have to tell *you* about . . . well, about my pearls. About the entire pearl evening that took place at Hyde House two nights ago."

"No," Sophia said in quiet amusement. Really, the girl was most entertaining, "you don't have to tell *me*."

"I don't know how it happened exactly, that is, I don't know all the details," she said, gaining speed and confidence as she progressed. Charming, really. The one thing that could be reliably said about Louisa Kirkland was that she consistently displayed a certain boldness of character. It was the one character trait Sophia admired above all others. Definitely in the girl's favor. "But I was given a rather lovely strand of pearls by my grandmother, and somehow Lord Dutton got them from my father, Lord Melverley, and attempted to give them to your daughter."

"Well, my dear, Caro doesn't have your pearls. Why come to me?"

Which of course was a complete lie. Sophia knew *exactly* why this exotically beautiful and confused young woman had come to her. That she was a woman who had lost her pearls? Sophia could not possibly have been more sympathetic.

"I would like, that is, I noticed, we *all* noticed, how well things have gone for Lady Caroline and I was wondering . . . I was thinking that you might . . . be . . . able . . ."

The poor dear was stuttering to a complete halt. As much fun as it was to watch her stumble about, Sophia drew the line at outright cruelty. She was periously close to the line now and cruelty, unless absolutely necessary, was not a character trait she enjoyed. At least not too excessively.

"You would like your pearls back, wouldn't you?" Sophia said, setting down her cup.

"Yes," Louisa said stoutly. "I want my pearls back."

"Then, darling, we shall simply have to get them for you."

Turn the page for a preview of
the next historical romance from Claudia Dain

The Courtesan's Secret

Now available from Berkley Sensation!

London 1802

"THERE are certain circumstances upon which it is absolutely essential to seek out a courtesan," Louisa Kirkland snapped.

"If you're expecting an argument from me . . ." the Marquis of Hawksworth drawled, and gave a halfhearted shrug.

"Oh, shut it, Hawksworth," Louisa said. "Why should I expect something as energetic as an argument from *you*, of all people?"

It was entirely within her rights to talk to a marquis in such an abrupt manner, or at least this particular marquis. Hawksworth was not only her cousin, but he was an unrepentantly lazy boy of twenty who ought to have better things to do than lie around all day dozing on a sofa.

Which is exactly where she had found him when she had insisted he accompany her to Sophia Dalby's town house. Not that she would permit him to enter with her. No, that would not do at all. No, Hawksworth had to remain outside, engaging in whatever activity best suited him, likely a nap, while she went inside to face Lady Dalby in what was certain to be a most uncomfortable conversation.

But then, most conversations with Sophia Dalby were uncomfortable. She was entirely certain that it came from Sophia having been a noted courtesan in her day, though it was equally possible that Sophia had always been a woman other women found uncomfortable.

"And what am I to do whilst you're with the delightful Lady Dalby?" Hawksworth asked, neatly proving her point. Louisa had yet to meet a man who did not find Sophia Dalby delightful. It was most annoying.

"Isn't there someone you might call upon? Someone in the vicinity who would admit you?" Louisa said, straightening a seam on her glove as she prepared to approach Sophia's door on Upper Brook Street. It was a very nice address, the houses quite respectable, and Dalby House was a literal stone's throw from Hyde Park. Of course, Sophia had married into her fine address, but didn't most women? It had been a neat bit of work, and if Sophia could manage that, she could certainly manage the little thing that Louisa needed of her. "Doesn't Mr. Prestwick live on this street? Go and call upon him."

"And his lovely sister," Hawksworth said with all the laziness he could muster, which was considerable as he had such practice at it. "I could do with another look at her."

If there was one woman Louisa disliked, a ridiculous notion as she found it necessary to dislike quite a few women, most particularly Anne Warren, it was Miss Penelope Prestwick. Miss Prestwick was that impossible combination of sweetness and seduction that Louisa found intolerable and men found compelling. That the Prestwick viscountcy had more money than was entirely in good taste only made her more irritating, obviously.

"Of course you could," Louisa said. "I'm quite certain you are not the first man to get a good look at Miss Prestwick. I should be careful around her, Hawksworth. She wouldn't mind being a duchess one day and you would so nicely fill the bill."

"Thank you," Hawksworth drawled politely, missing the point entirely. "Shall we say half past? Or shall you require more time with Lady Dalby?"

"I shall be brief. I would advise you to be the same."

"Half past, then," he said agreeably. Hawksworth, for all that could be said against him, had a most even and agreeable disposition. It was his finest trait. It may also have been his only trait.

Louisa wasted no time in watching Hawksworth amble down Upper Brook Street toward the Viscount Prestwick's town house. She had other matters entirely occupying her thoughts.

Louisa was admitted, looked over not at all discreetly by Fredericks, the Dalby House butler, and a most inappropriate butler he was, and ushered into Sophia's famous white salon. Everything connected to Sophia was famous in one fashion or another, and Louisa did not waste time in ferreting out the particulars as to the source of fame for the white salon. It was a salon, like any other, except that it had the obvious distinction of being swathed in various shades of impossible to maintain white.

It looked immaculate, of course.

Sophia rose to her feet, greetings were exchanged, and Louisa, without shame and certainly no hesitation, proceeded to the point of her visit.

"Lady Dalby, thank you for seeing me."

"Not at all. Can I offer you a cup of chocolate?"

"Yes, thank you," Louisa answered.

She didn't particularly care for a cup of chocolate, but it served its purpose in getting Fredericks out of the room to send someone for another cup. In the silence and quiet of their momentary solitude, Louisa studied Sophia briefly.

She knew her, of course. They were not strangers to each other, though they were hardly friends. Louisa had studied Sophia as much as anyone else in London had done, which is to say, minutely. Yes, she was beautiful, darkly aristocratic, flawlessly seductive, relentlessly charming. But what woman could not claim the same list, with some little bit of effort?

Which was the entire point, really. Sophia, as far as Louisa could discern, accomplished her list of credits entirely without effort.

"I find myself in a bit of a dilemma, Lady Dalby. I don't quite know how to go about . . . fixing it," Louisa said.

Sophia merely raised her eyebrows in pleasant curiosity and kept stirring her chocolate.

"I," Louisa said, a faint blush heating her cheeks. Blast having red hair and the complexion that went with it. Every emotion showed on her skin. It was beyond embarrassing. "I . . . am certain that I don't have to tell *you* about . . . well, about my pearls. About the entire pearl evening that took place at Hyde House two nights ago."

"No," Sophia said in obvious amusement, "you don't have to tell *me*."

Obviously not, as Sophia, somehow, had orchestrated the entire shameless event. Shameless, yes, but so very to the point. Caroline, Sophia's daughter, had in a single evening, acquired three very likely men: the Lords Dutton, Blakesley, and Ashdon. Each man had presented her with a pearl necklace, and each man had sought her favors, shamelessly and ruinously. The obvious problem being that Caroline had not been ruined in any meaningful sense of the word. No, Caroline had made her choice, the handsome though somber Lord Ashdon, and she had been married to him the very next morning. It was perfectly obvious to Louisa that Caroline had married the man she'd wanted and that she'd arranged things perfectly to get him.

It was even more obvious that Caroline Trevelyan, at the innocent age of seventeen, could have arranged no such thing. Her mother, the ex-courtesan, had been behind it all.

If it could be done for Caroline, Louisa saw no reason why it could not be done for her. Unless, of course, Sophia did not care to help her get what she wanted. Sophia, rather too intelligent for comfort, likely suspected that Louisa did not hold her in the highest regard. Or she hadn't. Until now.

"I don't know how it happened exactly," Louisa said, plunging forward and ignoring the clever glint in Sophia's dark eyes, "that is, I don't know all the details. But I was given a rather lovely strand of pearls by my grandmother, and somehow Lord Dutton got them from my father, Lord Melverley, and attempted to give them to your daughter."

"Well, my dear," Sophia said, taking a small sip of her drink, "Caro doesn't have your pearls. Why come to me?"

It was perfectly obvious to Louisa that Sophia knew *exactly* why she had come to her, but that, being Sophia, she wanted Louisa to crawl over broken glass and beg for her aid.

Fine. She could do that.

"I would like, that is, I noticed, we *all* noticed, how well things have gone for Lady Caroline and I was wondering . . . I was thinking that you might . . . be . . . able . . ."

It was far easier to contemplate crawling over broken

glass than to actually do it. This begging for help business was decidedly difficult. She was completely certain she did not like it one bit. Even Lord Dutton's dashingly beautiful face grew a bit dim in the light of the amusement in Sophia's eyes.

"You would like your pearls back, wouldn't you?" Sophia said, setting down her cup on a very elegant Directoire table.

"Yes," Louisa said, holding Sophia's dark gaze. "I want my pearls back."

"Then, darling, we shall simply have to get them for you."

&

IT was as Lord Henry Blakesley was leaving the Prestwick town house that he bumped into the Marquis of Hawksworth about to go in. Where Hawksworth was, Louisa was not far distant. Where Louisa was, Dutton was almost certainly to be.

Louisa made rather a point of that.

"All alone today, Hawksworth?" Blakesley asked. "Dutton left Town, has he?"

Hawksworth smiled slightly. "Certainly you'd know that as soon as I."

A point, and well taken. Louisa not only made use of her cousin to escort her around Town, she made equal if less comfortable use of him. He did not particularly like being used as a sort of tame hound to sniff out the elusive Marquis of Dutton, but that was how Louisa chose to use him.

Blakesley knew precisely how that sounded and he didn't care for it in the least. Unfortunately, he did nothing about it. He didn't care to think too deeply about why.

"You're calling upon Mr. Prestwick?" Blakesley asked, changing the subject.

"Or Miss Prestwick," Hawksworth said casually. Hawksworth did most things casually; he was becoming almost famous for it. "They are a pleasant family, are they not?"

"Most pleasant," Blakesley said. "Mr. Prestwick is just within. I believe you were at school together?"

"Yes, and he spoke so often and so well of his sister."

Blakesley smiled. "She is eager to wed, so I'm told."

"Aren't they all?" Hawksworth said with a pleasant smile. "She is in season, I should think, her age and circumstances being at that precise point."

"You are not afraid of getting caught in the matrimonial net?"

"There is a season for everything, Lord Henry," Hawksworth said languidly. "It is a waste of energy to fight against the seasons. They change most regularly, no matter our preferences."

"And you will ride the change, enjoying all of spring's abundant pleasures?" Blakesley offered.

"Precisely."

"You are of a mind to marry Miss Prestwick?"

"I do not know Miss Prestwick," Hawksworth said pleasantly. "It is not the season for me to wed, and so I may dally where the mood takes me. Miss Prestwick might be pleasant enough to dally with in this off season for me, in all propriety, of course. I find myself here; there is no reason why I should not avail myself of blessed proximity."

"Of course not," Blakesley said, more amused by Louisa's cousin than he had ever been before. For such a young man, he was either more naïve than his peers or more sophisticated. It was so very difficult to decide which. "You have left your cousin somewhere safe, I trust? Or did you come to Upper Brook Street on your own?"

Blakesley knew Louisa's habits well enough to know that she had dragged her cousin here and then shucked him off like so much mud on her shoe. Hawksworth was of a disposition to allow it. Blakesley was not.

Hawksworth smiled in lazy good humor. "She is calling upon Lady Dalby. She made it very clear that she did not want my company when she did so. Perhaps she will welcome your company more than mine. It is hardly possible that she would welcome you less."

Or was it? Gone to see Sophia Dalby? Blakesley did not like the sound of that. Sophia Dalby had a way of managing things, a way of manipulating events and people until things were all muddled into a pattern that no one could have fore-seen and few would welcome.

Except, he suspected, Sophia herself.

What was Louisa doing tangling herself up in Sophia's skirts?

"I think I shall call upon Lady Dalby. Care to join me, Lord Hawksworth?" Blakesley asked. "I can promise you that Sophia is more entertaining than Penelope Prestwick could dream of being."

Hawksworth smiled languidly and shrugged slightly. "I am at your disposal, Lord Henry. It is to Dalby House for the both of us. I do not care to think what Louisa will do when she sees us."

"It will be entertaining, at the very least," Blakesley said with a slanted smile. "What more can be asked of an after-noon call upon a countess?"

Claudia Dain is an award-winning author and a two-time RITA finalist. She lives in the Southeast and is at work on Sophia's next attempt at matchmaking. Visit her website www.claudiadain.com.